SALINE DISTRICT LIBRARY

P9-CRD-097

Mystery Ben
Benrey, Ron, 1941-
Humble pie : a novel

Humble Pie

Humble Pie

A Novel

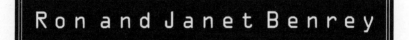

Ron and Janet Benrey

BROADMAN
&HOLMAN
PUBLISHERS

NASHVILLE, TENNESSEE

SALINE DISTRICT LIBRARY
555 N. Maple Road
Saline, MI 48176

© 2004 by Ron and Janet Benrey
All rights reserved
Printed in the United States of America

0-8054-3067-9

Published by Broadman & Holman Publishers,
Nashville, Tennessee

Dewey Decimal Classification: 813
Subject Heading: FICTION

Unless otherwise stated, all Scripture citation is from the NIV,
the Holy Bible, New International Version, copyright © 1973,
1978, 1984 by International Bible Society. Also used is the
King James Version of the Holy Bible.

1 2 3 4 5 6 7 8 09 08 07 06 05 04

This book is for:

Andrew, Angela, and Jeffrey
(our favorite mysteries)

and

Ann and Doug Brown, Cathy Nagy-Kendig, and
Mike Kendig
(our favorite neighbors)

Wisdom says:

To fear the LORD is to hate evil;
I hate pride and arrogance, evil behavior
and perverse speech.
—Proverbs 8:13 (NIV)

```
┌──────────────────────────────────────────┐
│ ╔══════════════════════════════════════╗  │
│          Prologue                        │
│ ╚══════════════════════════════════════╝  │
└──────────────────────────────────────────┘
```

THE FIFTY OR SO PEDESTRIANS who walked past Bombay Spices & Rices
between ten and eleven that rainy Saturday morning all failed to take
notice of the vehicle that was poised to murder Dennis Grant. This surprised the police, because Hampton Lane—a narrow street in Ryde,
Maryland, that dates back to late eighteenth century—was designated
"No Parking" along its entire five-block length. Surely some passerby
must have seen a car or truck idling in Schooner Alley, which was directly across from Ryde's lone Indian grocery shop.

   In fact, the police could locate only three witnesses to help them
identify the hit-and-run vehicle that had accelerated to nearly fifty miles
per hour before it struck Dennis Grant. One clearly remembered seeing
"a big, dark-colored SUV zoom down the street and knock Dennis off
his bicycle." The second vaguely recalled "a large black sedan" seen out
of the corner of his eye. And the third—well, she didn't actually see the
accident, but she did hear "the deep roar of a powerful engine, followed
by a loud thud."

The detective in charge of the investigation tried every memory aid in her detecting toolbox, but none of the three could dredge up specific details to support a positive identification. As the first—and best—witness explained, "It was pouring and I was clomping along Hampton Lane at full speed—head down—trying to avoid all the puddles in the old, uneven sidewalk."

The vehicle in question was easy to describe: a full-sized Ford pickup, shiny black, with a fiberglass truck cap over its bed and a hefty steel-brush guard bolted to its massive front bumper. Anyone who had bothered a second glance would have seen that its front license plate had been carefully obscured by mud and that its driver was all but hiding from view. He or she—it was impossible to tell which—had on a Baltimore Orioles baseball cap and was fully screened by the current issue of *The Ryde Reporter* held open across the steering wheel.

The driver, occasionally peering from behind the newspaper, had observed each soggy pedestrian on Hampton Lane with a twinge of concern. There was great risk involved in running down a bicyclist on a public street. With luck, there would be fewer witnesses when the time came to act.

Speaking of time . . .

The driver glanced first at the dashboard clock and then at the man and woman arguing inside the small Indian grocery shop. "It's almost ten-thirty, boys and girls—that's enough fighting for one day." The driver's murmur trailed into a sigh. Everything about Dennis Grant became complicated—even killing the man.

That's probably how Dennis made it to the ripe old age of forty-two. The thousand other people who had good reasons to kill him simply gave up.

The driver laughed out loud at the thought. Dennis Grant was a pompous fool who preened and postured and chose to behave like minor royalty merely because he wrote the chairman's speeches. When Dennis worked at Hardesty Software Corporation, no one could stand him—no one, that is, except Mitch Hardesty. And so, for nearly two

years—until he left to take another job—the productive occupants
of Hardesty's executive suite had had to put up with Dennis's self-
important lectures about ecology, and why Indian cuisine was more
environmentally friendly than American food, and how driving a car on
short trips around Ryde was a crime against nature, and why every able-
bodied employee should pedal to and from work on a bicycle, just as he
did.

Well, Dennis Grant had delivered his last lecture.

The driver had followed Dennis to Hampton Lane from his home
in Algonquin House, a plush condominium tower that overlooked the
Magothy River. That chore had been unexpectedly easy because Dennis
wore a bright orange rain suit that was visible a hundred yards away,
even during a deluge. The driver stopped halfway down the block until
Dennis had chained his fancy mountain bicycle to a parking meter in
front of Bombay Spices & Rices, and then backed the big pickup truck
into Schooner Alley. It was an ideal vantage point; Schooner Alley was
almost directly opposite the small shop. The driver could see almost
everything that Dennis Grant did inside.

Twice before, on two Saturday afternoon reconnaissance trips,
Dennis had led the driver to Hampton Lane. On both occasions he
had spent no more than fifteen minutes replenishing his supply of
pungent ingredients for the strange curries and vindaloos and *biryanies*
that he proudly brought to the office in an original Charlie Brown
lunchbox.

But today something unexpected had happened. A woman in a
well-worn Burberry raincoat, carrying a large umbrella in her left hand
and a yellow plastic file envelope in her right, strode down the street
and into Bombay Spices & Rices.

The driver recognized the woman immediately: Pippa Hunnechurch,
an executive recruiter who had worked briefly for Hardesty Software
Corporation.

What had she done for the company?

The driver remembered. It was a small assignment. She had found a new writer for the Internal Communications staff. No big deal—but her presence in the executive suite had been annoying. All that never-say-die British enthusiasm wore on the nerves, not to mention her overblown camaraderie with the administrative staff. So what if she had once been a secretary herself? These days she was rubbing shoulders with corporate executives. And the consulting bill she submitted was for lots more than any secretary at Hardesty earned.

Did she also like Indian food?

Why not? Pippa Hunnechurch had made no secret of the fact she was from England. The English seem to love Indian food. Perhaps she was stocking up on spices and rices too.

A thin layer of condensation had formed on the inside of the truck's windshield. The driver directed the air conditioner through the defroster vents and soon had a clear view through the shop's plate-glass front window.

The driver had no difficulty spotting Dennis and Pippa inside the store. They were standing near the solitary check-out counter, his head shaking, her hands gesturing forcefully. Were they conversing or fighting? It was impossible to tell from across the street, although the driver could see that Dennis was now holding the bright yellow file envelope.

Pippa gave something to Dennis. What could it be?

The driver stopped musing about the envelope when Pippa abruptly turned her back on Dennis.

Whoo-ee! Someone said something wrong. Was it he or she?

Pippa stormed out of the grocery shop and trod through three large puddles.

There goes a really mad headhunter.

Dennis emerged into Hampton Lane a few seconds later, carrying his usual parcel of food, looking exceedingly pleased with himself. He tucked the yellow file envelope inside his rain suit.

He seems on top of the world. He has gotten something he wants!

The driver thought about the yellow file envelope again. *Speeches!* Of course! Pippa Hunnechurch would have samples of his speeches. That's why Dennis Grant looks so happy—she gave him some of the speeches he'd been searching for.

Did she have THE speech to give him? Did she know what it contained? Had she also become a threat?

The driver muttered a curse. A minor typographical accident had created a major crisis—a silly error that Dennis had described as a "dropped widow." No one—not even Dennis—had understood its significance back then.

Oh, but you understand now, Dennis. You've figured out nearly everything.

The driver watched the speechwriter unlock his bicycle. *Why did you have to be such a prodder and poker? Why couldn't you leave well enough alone?*

The driver answered the question aloud in a determined voice. "Because Dennis Grant is an arrogant jerk who thinks he has a chance to become a bigger hero. He has become a liability you can't afford to leave alive."

The driver peered left and right as Dennis mounted his bicycle. Pippa Hunnechurch was nearly a block away, splashing her way toward Ryde High Street. There were two other pedestrians in sight, neither of them paying attention to Dennis.

So long, Mr. Grant. The world will be a better place without you.

The driver put the truck in gear, waited for Dennis to begin pedaling along Hampton Lane, and then floored the accelerator.

Chapter One

THE WOMAN LOOKED AS GENTLE AS A LAMB when I saw her standing in the doorway to our reception room. She even resembled a lamb, with a young roundish face, close-cropped curly black hair, and enormous dark brown eyes that darted hither and yon. She seemed wary about entering the world headquarters of Philippa Hunnechurch & Associates; I found myself chuckling at her apparent lack of self-confidence. Many novice businesspeople don't know what to expect when they deal with an executive recruiter for the first time. They approach even small, two-person head-hunting firms like ours with a certain hesitation—until they're sure we're harmless.

"Come on in!" I said, cheerfully. "You're right on time for the seminar."

Her response was a grunt—a low-pitched growl, really—that should have warned me this particular businesswoman, with the aggressive temperament of a hungry great white shark, was anything but a novice and was using those lamblike eyes to plan a fast getaway.

Lamentably, my guard was down because I had seen the woman many times before. She worked in our building and kept a schedule similar to mine. I made it a point to arrive in the lobby at eight-thirty on weekday mornings—and so most days did she. She would trot off to one of the office suites on the first floor, while I took the elevator to the fourth floor. Her first name was Kelly; I learned her last name weeks later. For now I shall call her Kelly the Shark.

Kelly the Shark's gaze fixed on me; she began to move forward. Determined as I was to be a cheerful hostess, I suppressed my curiosity about the thick envelope she was carrying and wholly ignored the determined expression that had taken over her quiet countenance. Instead, I assumed that she was eager to attend the hour-long presentation on executive recruiting we had scheduled on that Friday afternoon in early June. True, Kelly looked scarcely older than a college kid, but Ryde, Maryland, was fast becoming a hotbed of advanced technology, and many fast-track executives in town were mere months past earning their Ph.D.s and MBAs.

In any case, I urged a copy of our brand-new brochure into her hand. "Hot off the press. It will tell you all about us."

The Shark folded it in half and tucked it in her purse. "Thank you, I'll read it later."

Thus encouraged, I shooed her into our spanking-new conference room; she went willingly, holding her blasted envelope tight against her chest. There were five other people inside—chatting with one another, drinking tea, and nibbling on scones. Kelly scanned the room like a radar antenna but said nothing. I assumed that she was shy in unfamiliar social settings, so I offered her a warm smile and said, "We've nodded to each other on many mornings, but we've never been formally introduced. My name is Pippa Hunnechurch."

"Pippa?" she said, suspiciously, "I thought your name was *Philippa?* Your recruiting firm is named Philippa Hunnechurch & Associates."

Still picturing Kelly the Shark as a potential client, I ignored the startlingly unpleasant edge in her voice and cranked my smile up a full notch to melt.

"My friends call me Pippa," I said, "because my full name seems to go on forever: Philippa Elizabeth Katherine Hunnechurch. I am a Brit by birth, a resident of Ryde by choice, and a headhunter by occupation. I am thirty-eight by the inexorable march of time and recently remarried after eight years of widowhood."

Kelly stared at me as if I had lost my mind. I suddenly realized that I was spouting the litany of facts I use to explain my background to those people who care about me. Mercifully, I stopped myself before I reached what my new husband, James, had dubbed "our last-name compromise." I answer to Pippa Huston in Atlanta, where James hails from, and to Pippa Hunnechurch in Maryland. James had shrewdly observed three facts: "First, it makes no sense at all to confuse your clients by changing the name of your consulting firm. Second, tacking Huston to the end of your supersized string of names will make your handle too long to fit on a business card. And third, the initials on your luggage work fine with either Huston or Hunnechurch."

I raised my hands and made the T, time out, sign that American football referees use during those head-knocking exhibitions that James chooses to watch on Sunday afternoon. "What I *meant* to say," I said, "is that Pippa is the traditional English nickname for Philippa."

The Shark grunted again, then added begrudgingly, "My name is Kelly," she gestured with her thick envelope. "Why did you bring me into a roomful of people?"

Ooops!

"I seem to have made a mistake," I said. "I thought you were here for our seminar." I pointed at the screen hanging in the front of the room. The projected image was a title slide that read: "How to Work Successfully with an Executive Recruiter."

"I don't care beans about head-hunting," she said. "I want to talk to you—in private. I won't need but a minute."

"Pippa doesn't have a minute right now," said a voice behind me. "Our seminar is about to begin."

The voice belonged to Gloria Spitz, my small firm's one and only "associate."

Kelly glared at Gloria—a reaction I wrongly attributed to jealousy. Gloria is twenty-five, tall, blonde, and a knockout. She looked even more stunning that day because she had recently returned from her annual two-week training stint with the Maryland Army National Guard and was still glowing from all the exercise involved in climbing over obstacles, firing machine guns, and practicing hand-to-hand combat.

Kelly, alas, had no idea that Gloria was a weekend warrior or that she moonlighted on occasion for Collier Investigations, a private detective agency in Baltimore, or that she had been trained in crowd-control techniques. And so Kelly made the mistake of ignoring Gloria's blunt directive.

"We can do this the easy way," Kelly said to me, "or we can do it the hard . . ."

Kelly didn't get the chance to finish. Gloria grasped Kelly the Shark's elbow and spun her around toward the assortment of goodies we had laid out on top of our new buffet.

"Pour a cup of tea and relax," Gloria said, firmly. "Try a fairy cake. I baked them myself."

The Shark broke loose from Gloria's grip, pivoted to face me once more, and hissed: "I'm not hungry." But she didn't make the mistake of challenging Gloria again.

"What do you think she wants?" Gloria whispered to me as we walked to the front of the room.

"I've no idea," I whispered back. "If she's a salesperson, her approach needs lots of work."

Gloria rapped on the conference table. The merry chitchatting in the room faded away.

"Good afternoon, everyone," I said. "It is my pleasure to welcome you to our offices. Please find a place at the table, and we'll begin."

Perhaps it sounds silly, but I was inordinately proud of our new conference room. Four weeks earlier it had been our file and storage room—a grimy repository of office supplies, canisters of tea, cartons of copy paper, and many hundreds of candidate files stuffed with résumés, interview notes, and sundry related documents. As you might expect, executive recruiting generates mountains of paper. But you may not realize that a headhunter never willingly purges her files because information gathered today may be priceless years from now. One never knows how fast a rejected candidate will climb the ladder to success or if a contact made in passing will be vital in a future search.

Despite our small size as an enterprise, Hunnechurch & Associates was fast running out of storage space in our three-room office suite, which consisted of the reception room (it also doubled as Gloria's office), an inner office for me, and what our lease euphemistically labeled an all-purpose utility room. We crammed our candidate files into a bank of four lateral file cabinets in our storage room, and we had three more overflow file cabinets in our reception room.

The builder who had restored the five-story, eighteenth-century leather warehouse on the northernmost end of Ryde High Street—not the most convenient location in Ryde—had assumed his tenants would be newly created small businesses that would graduate to larger offices elsewhere. In fact, the historic redbrick building had become a much-loved home for a diverse collection of CPAs, lawyers, management consultants, public relations agencies, specialist dentists, and one headhunting firm. We all faced the challenge of operating ongoing businesses in relatively small suites that had been sized to keep rents affordable.

James came up with a brilliant solution to our rapidly multiplying files. "Do like the big companies do. Scan your documents onto CD-ROMs and throw away the paper copies."

"Abandon my paper documents?"

"Every last sheet. When you need to read an old résumé, pop the appropriate CD-ROM into your computer." He added, almost as an afterthought, "While you're at it, why don't you turn your ugly storage room into a proper conference room."

"A conference room!" I cooed. "I've always wanted my own conference room."

We went to work. I rented a self-feeding document scanner and hired a part-time assistant to feed our collection of old correspondence and miscellaneous paperwork into the wondrous machine. It had taken less than six weeks to transform every scrap of paper in seven large filing cabinets into a single drawer full of indexed and organized CD-ROMs.

James, Gloria, and I repainted the utility room one weekend. We purchased new carpeting, a rectangular conference table made of cherry wood, a matching buffet, eight comfortable swivel chairs, and a pull-down screen hanging from the ceiling.

"Why do we need a screen?" I'd asked James.

"For client presentations, of course. I'll lend you one of my electronic projectors. You can connect it to your laptop computer and dazzle your clientele with PowerPoint slides."

I should have married a computer whiz years earlier!

The first presentation I created was "How to Work Successfully with an Executive Recruiter."

My five guests had chosen seats at the conference table. Kelly the Shark, though, grabbed one of the extra chairs along the side wall—the better to glare at me, I supposed.

I took my position next to the screen and nodded toward Gloria, who was operating the laptop computer. She touched the space bar, advancing the next slide: "Our Agenda for Today."

James is a comfortable public speaker; I am not. He has tried to convince me that it's wholly unnecessary to be nervous when talking about something you know well. Nonetheless, as I surveyed those five agreeable faces, I felt my knees begin to tap together in a staccato rhythm. I offer my unplanned-for bout of stage fright as an excuse for the two mistakes I made in quick succession.

Gloria and I had decided not to waste time with introductions—our guests had had ample time to meet one another over tea and scones. Forgetting our plan, I began. "You all know me. Why don't we take a few moments to introduce ourselves."

That was the first mistake.

My second was to point to Kelly the Shark. "Why don't we start with you?"

She stood up sneering, "There's no need for me to introduce myself, Mrs. Hunnechurch," she said. "I hate to ruin your little get-together, but I have *real* work left to do this afternoon."

She strode to the front of the room and shoved the thick envelope into my hands.

"I am an attorney," she said. "The envelope I just gave you contains a legal document that commences a lawsuit against Hunnechurch & Associates. The plaintiff in the action is Hardesty Software Corporation. You are advised to discuss these papers with your lawyer—without delay." She took a deep breath and finished up with a chilling declaration: *"You have been served!"*

Before I could respond, she pulled a small digital camera out of her pocket and pointed it at me. I was still blinking from the flash when I heard our front door shut behind her. I eventually received a copy of the inane picture she had taken of me—my eyes glowing red from the flash, a bewildered stare on my face, the thick envelope in my right hand.

I remember feeling stunned—and at a complete loss for words—as I looked out on the incredulous faces of the five potential clients who had watched Kelly the Shark announce that one of the most respected companies in town had taken steps to haul me into court.

Chapter Two

I SLAMMED MY LONG-SUFFERING FRONT DOOR with enough force to make the pine-board flooring in the foyer quiver, then threw the envelope full of legal papers the length of our hallway. "I've had a truly rotten afternoon, James," I bellowed. "Hardesty Software is a brood of vipers! And I'm ready to flog that silly twit of a woman!"

Much to my amazement, I heard David Friendly's voice boom from the depths of our kitchen: "Our pastor recently defined 'a brood of vipers' in a sermon," he said, in a mock English accent, "but I am unclear as to the precise nature of a 'silly twit.'"

James's voice spoke an answer in an exaggerated Southern drawl: "Why, sir, *ah* believe that a silly twit is a cross between a nitwit and a country bumpkin—with a spoonful of nincompoop thrown in for good measure."

Joyce Friendly's voice added: "I wonder what 'silly twit of a woman' Pippa has in mind? I hope she's not mad at me."

I dashed into the kitchen to find three amused faces grinning at me. An instant later I remembered that I had invited David and Joyce

Friendly for dinner that evening. James had agreed to prepare his spectacular Down-South Shish Kabob.

Blimey! They must think I'm thick as a brick!

I now felt like a complete prat—on top of my distress that Hardesty Software was taking me to court and my anger that Kelly the Shark had wrecked my seminar.

After Kelly had fled our offices, I tried to restart my presentation—to no avail. Two of our five guests abruptly remembered "other commitments," and the remaining three simply left without explanation. Who could blame them? The last thing a company needs is a legally challenged headhunter.

I'd made it through the rest of the afternoon by concentrating on one comforting notion: *James would know what to do next.* He was an experienced corporate consultant who often worked with attorneys. He would interpret the legal papers; he would guide me through the crisis.

I'd raced home anticipating a quiet heart-to-heart chat with my husband. Instead, I found myself the hostess at a miniature dinner party that could easily stretch late into the night.

Don't rain on James's shish kabob, I told myself. *Put the lawsuit out of your mind until later.*

"A thousand apologies," I said. "My afternoon got the best of me."

"The best cure for a rotten day is lots of hugs," James said.

I threw open my arms. "Pile them on!"

James obliged—then Joyce, then David, then James once again.

Joyce and David Friendly were my age—and among my closest chums in Ryde. David was the business writer for *The Ryde Reporter,* our local two-issue-a-week newspaper. Four years earlier he had authored the first story ever written about Hunnechurch & Associates. Our personalities meshed when he interviewed me; we became great lunchtime buddies, often breaking bread together, frequently sharing "intelligence" about Ryde's business community.

Joyce is an operating room nurse at Ryde General Hospital. Our friendship had developed slowly and steadily. We spent many a "girl's night out" together and knew we could trust each other with our innermost thoughts.

Joyce poked her head around James's arm and said to me, "How about a hot *cuppa*? We just made a fresh pot."

"Tea would be lovely. I will relax on my comfy sofa while James incinerates supper."

"You can't go into the living room, my love," James murmured in my ear. "Not yet."

I pulled away from his arms. "*Why* can't I go into my living room?"

"I have a surprise for you."

"Ah." I exercised every fiber of my willpower to keep a frown off my face.

The "surprises for Pippa" began soon after we returned from our honeymoon. Hardly a day went by without James bringing home an exotic new toy—complete with a dubious justification of why it made perfect sense for us to acquire that particular item:

A blue Volkswagen Beetle convertible for me, complete with leather upholstery ("much more elegant than the antique Miata roadster you used to drive").

An enormous Range Rover, in British racing green, for him ("we often travel together and need a larger, more substantial vehicle than a Beetle—so why not a well-regarded British classic?").

A fancy wireless telephone system with its own message center ("we both have important jobs; people need to be able to reach us").

A massive gas grill that filled a quarter of the diminutive garden behind our house ("if we're going to cook at home, let's do it right!").

A home exercise machine, tucked into the corner of our dining room, that resembled a forest of springs, pulleys, and cables ("neither of us has time to go to a gym regularly; this machine will keep us fit and trim").

A computer with enough power to control the International Space Station ("information technology changes every day; we have to keep pace").

I gritted my teeth and dearly hoped that James's latest gadget was small enough to store on a top shelf. The two new cars out front—James's many surprises inside—and all the appliances, crockery, linens, and knickknacks we had received as wedding presents threatened to overwhelm our little house.

I had purchased 735 Magothy Street before I ventured out on my own as a headhunter. It was a narrow, two-story row house, built in 1867, that was listed in the Ryde Historical Society registry of historic homes. The woodwork, the plastering, and the pine-board flooring were all original.

My love for Hunnechurch Manor knew no bounds, but I did recognize its limitations. In common with many mid-nineteenth-century houses, the rooms were few and small: a living room, dining room, and kitchen on the ground floor, two small bedrooms and a bathroom upstairs. Our three closets were tiny, and to make matters worse, one of our bedrooms was chockablock with miscellaneous Edwardian furniture that Mum had shipped to me from England three years ago, not realizing how petite a house I owned.

Hunnechurch Manor was bursting at the proverbial seams. . . .

A joyful shout from David interrupted my ruminations about floor space: "Way to go, Pippa! When did you start consulting for Blanchette & Ross?"

Oh dear! I had forgotten about the thick envelope I'd flung down the hallway. David must have retrieved it and read the return address in the upper left-hand corner.

"This is obviously a big, fat recruiting contract." David weighed the thick envelope in his hand. "My congratulations, *Ms.* Hunnechurch." He smiled at me slyly. "Is there anything you want to share with this hardworking business reporter? I would dearly like to know what kind of new personnel Blanchette & Ross is adding."

I shrugged—too flabbergasted to do anything else.

"Can't tell me, *huh?* Well, I would expect them to swear you to secrecy. Blanchette & Ross is a *powerhouse* law firm. Kyle Blanchette used to be a lawyer in the Justice Department, and Ken Ross made his bones as a tough prosecutor in Baltimore." David issued a sinister chuckle. "They're probably outstanding clients, but I'd sure hate to be staring at that pair of wolves across a courtroom."

"Same here!" James chimed in. "I've heard that Blanchette & Ross never take a case unless they're absolutely positive they can win."

I might have begun to blubber if Joyce Friendly hadn't arrived at that moment with a mug of tea. "David, stop bugging our hostess," she said. "Pippa doesn't want to talk about her clients at dinner on Friday night."

The tea was steaming hot Darjeeling—my favorite—but it didn't warm the chill I felt in my bones. *Hardesty Software had thrown me to legal wolves!*

My mind filled with images of stern-faced judges, mustachioed bailiffs, bleak stone prisons, and ferocious attorneys tearing me to tatters. The pictures popping into my head came from the Charles Dickens novels I'd read as a child; but then I'd never been sued before, so I didn't know what could, or would, happen in a real American court.

The next two hours sped by in a blur; I only remember scattered snippets:

James prancing around our garden—assembling two-foot-long skewers of lamb, vegetables, and secret barbecue sauces. He is inordinately proud of Down-South Shish Kabob, a concoction he developed during many years of trial and error.

David tossing the salad—while attempting a mid-Eastern belly dance to the accompaniment of "Dixie," as hummed by Joyce and James.

The sound of frying mosquitoes—as our new bug zapper, another recent surprise for me, buzzed and sputtered merrily in the center of the garden.

I empathized with every doomed insect. Would the Blanchette & Ross powerhouse zap my little recruiting firm?

Even though I mostly picked at my food, James's Down-South Shish Kabob was a great success. James, David, and Joyce consumed seven skewers of the stuff. My appetite improved a whit when James served another of his culinary inventions, pecan pie cheesecake, for dessert. I ate two big pieces and thoroughly enjoyed every bite.

━━━━━━━

"Do I really have to shut my eyes?" I asked, although I had already decided to play along with their scheme. How could I refuse? James and David acted as excited as little boys in a toy shop.

I closed my eyes. James propelled me into the kitchen and on through to the living room.

"Open your eyes *now!*"

I did—and saw a plasma panel TV, almost five-feet wide, hanging on the wall opposite my favorite overstuffed sofa.

"A new telly?" I asked hesitantly.

"A *complete* home theater system," James proclaimed. "There's the TV tuner, audio decoder, cassette player, VCR, and combined CD and DVD player." He pointed at a wooden cube, about two feet high, that sat on the floor below the plasma panel. The front bristled with flaps, slots, control knobs, and levers.

The plasma panel looked like a miniature storm door bolted to my wall; it would take a lot of getting used to. And I would probably need a week of training to learn how to turn the blasted thing on.

I ignored my desire to scream at James and asked civilly, "What have you done with our old telly?"

"I stowed it in the closet under the stairs." Then he added cavalierly: "I'll have the carcass trucked away next week."

"That *carcass* has *decades* of life left," I protested, remembering how I had struggled to pay for the set three years before.

"In that case we'll donate it to the church thrift shop."

I noticed that something else was missing too. "Where are our rabbit ears?"

"In the trash can. We have our own little satellite dish now. I'm amazed you didn't spot it when we were in the garden."

This I had to see.

I trotted to the kitchen and out the back door. There it was: a gray "saucer," the size of a plastic trash can lid, mounted level with the edge of the roof, pointing to the southern sky. I chided myself for not looking up during dinner.

"I ordered the full satellite programming package," James said when I returned to the living room. "Besides regular TV, we can even watch European channels. This evening, for example, we're going to view a fabled English social event."

"*What* English social event?"

Joyce began to giggle and gave the joke away.

"We're going to see our *wedding* on the telly?"

"Exactly!" James held up a shimmering DVD. "I had our wedding photos put on a disk, just like a movie. That's the *real* surprise. We can make as many copies as we want and send one to everyone we know."

"Do we really want to bore our friends and relatives with our wedding snaps?"

"There's *nothing* boring about our wedding," James loaded the DVD into the player.

David had been waiting for this moment. He sat down on the sofa, flourished an oversized remote control, and pushed a button. The remote made a *chirping* sound. In quick succession . . .

- the plasma panel lit up.

- billowing American and British flags filled the screen.

- a baritone English voice intoned: "Welcome to the wedding of Philippa Elizabeth Katherine Hunnechurch to James Lamar Huston."

- the strains of Elgar's "Pomp and Circumstance No. 1," better known to Americans as "Land of Hope and Glory," filled the room.

We might have been standing inside an orchestra pit. I spun around, looking for the source of the all-encompassing music.

James anticipated my question: "Our new home theater system has *seven* speakers that generate true surround sound."

"Don't you think the music is a bit loud?" I half shouted.

David worked the remote again, producing several *chirps* that made the volume too soft, too loud, then finally just right. Winston answered the final *chirp* with a loud *squawk*.

Winston is a *budgie*—a parakeet, if you prefer—who once lived in my kitchen but was displaced to a corner of the living room when James surprised me with a vast, new refrigerator ("it really is more efficient to buy in volume; for that we need capacious cold storage"). Winston is a loyal bird, easily recognizable by his light blue feathers, bright yellow beak, and no-nonsense disposition. I glanced at Winston's cage. He stood tall on his perch, his feathers ruffled, looking ready for a fight.

I began to snicker.

"What's so funny," James asked.

"Our home theater system speaks budgie language. I think it just said something disreputable to Winston."

"Please save the bad jokes until after the presentation," he said as he sat down with great dignity next to David. Fortunately, neither of them saw Joyce clamp her hand over her mouth.

I must admit that our "wedding movie" was tolerably short and remarkably entertaining. A talented graphics person had choreographed several dozen of our photographs to familiar English tunes, creating the illusion of motion by panning and zooming the images. I also acknowledge that our photos were spectacular on that humongous plasma display and that James looked dishier on the screen than any of today's crop of male cinema stars.

I, too, had "cleaned up nicely" for the wedding. My typical English mug looked presentable on the screen: prominent cheekbones, longish nose, pale blue eyes that some people describe as gray, and—my best feature—a peaches-and-cream complexion. I went to a chichi stylist in Chichester three days before the ceremony. He looked, and pondered, and deliberated—and finally decided to leave my naturally dishwater blonde hair in the simple, mid-length style that I wear every day.

James and I had exchanged vows on the last Saturday in April, at All Souls Church in Chichester, England. After the mid-morning ceremony, we hosted our wedding breakfast at the Ship Hotel on North Street. Despite its misleading name, a "wedding breakfast" is really a luncheon.

Why Chichester? Because I grew up in that small city in West Sussex, near the south coast of England.

Why All Souls? Because the church's Vicar, Stuart Hunnechurch-Parker, is married to my sister Chloe.

Why the Ship Hotel? Because the Ship is a charming, eighteenth-century townhouse that was transformed into an elegant hotel. It seemed the perfect place to entertain after our nuptials.

The Ship also served as James's digs during our stay in Chichester. James and I—both American citizens—were required to spend fifteen days residence in Chichester before we could apply for a "common license" to marry in a Church of England edifice. I bunked with Stuart, Chloe, and Mum in All Soul's parsonage.

Our mandated sojourn in Chichester gave us ample time to tour southern England and gave James ample opportunity to play with our new digital camera—another of my prewedding surprises ("we'll save a fortune on film and processing"). We returned to America with several gigabytes of sightseeing photographs stored in James's laptop computer; James's graphics guru transformed the lot into a clever rapid-fire montage at the end of the DVD.

I found myself entranced by the kaleidoscope of images until the screen filled with medieval torture implements that had been on display in a beautifully simulated dungeon at the West Sussex Museum. My mind instantly assembled a chain of connections: dungeon—prison—court—judge—lawsuits—lawyers—*Blanchette & Ross*.

I felt my face go white, and I dropped the half-full mug of tea I was holding.

My first inclination was to pretend I'd had a simple accident, but the suspicious stare on James's face convinced me to fess up: "I can't hold it in anymore," I howled; "I'm being sued by Hardesty Software. That thick envelope is full of legal papers with my name on them."

───────────

We went back to the kitchen. Joyce and I stood sipping coffee while the boys sat at the dinette table reading—and rereading—Hardesty's allegations against Hunnechurch & Associates.

"Who is Dennis Grant?" James finally asked.

"A speechwriter. I placed him at Militet Aviation earlier this year."

David looked up from the papers. "This complaint asserts that you unethically recruited Dennis because you wanted to punish Hardesty for terminating their relationship with you."

"Poppycock!"

"Can you be more specific?" James said.

"With pleasure!" I lubricated my voice with a hearty gulp of coffee and told my side of the story.

Back in early February I'd been summoned to the offices of Ben McDonald, Hardesty Software's vice president of human resources. I went eagerly. Hardesty was a rising star in software development; they sold complex software applications to every branch of the federal government. I coveted them as a client.

Ben told me that Hardesty was "experimenting" with the use of executive recruiters and gave me a trial assignment: find a marketing writer.

As part of my initial research into the requirements of the job, I spoke to several members of Hardesty's communication staff—including Dennis Grant, who wrote speeches for Mitch Hardesty, the company's founder and chairman.

I quickly identified a perfect candidate, an experienced technical writer named Sonia Frasier who had spent five years with a technology-based advertising agency in Baltimore. She was promptly hired by Hardesty.

Believing that I had passed the company's test with flying colors, I asked for a follow-up assignment. Ben explained—unhappily, I recall—that Mitch Hardesty had personally made the decision to give all future assignments to Nailor & McHale, one of America's largest recruiting firms.

Certainly I was disappointed, but why would I harbor ill feelings against Hardesty? Over the years I've lost many competitive skirmishes to Nailor & McHale. They are excellent headhunters and tough rivals.

A week or so later—it was the end of February, I believe—Dennis Grant came to my office, résumé in hand. He told me that he deserved to earn more money and that he viewed his tenure at Hardesty as a stepping-stone to a better job with a major corporation.

As it happens, Militet was looking for a speechwriter.

"And the rest is history," David said.

"Indeed! Militet hired Dennis in record time. It seemed a match made in heaven."

"Except for your alleged ethical breach," James began ominously.

"My ethics are impeccable."

"The complaint asserts that you met Dennis Grant as part of a consulting engagement at Hardesty."

"True!"

"It goes on to say that you subsequently sought Dennis out—that you actively recruited him away from Hardesty Software."

"False!"

James didn't skip a beat. ". . . in violation of your fiduciary responsibility to protect the trade secrets you learned during your assignment."

"I can't begin to imagine what that legal gobbledygook means."

David took over: "Hardesty claims that Dennis Grant was a valuable corporate resource, a kind of trade secret. When they introduced him to you, they didn't expect you lure him away with a better job offer."

"I didn't lure him away from Hardesty, David. He showed up at my front door."

David riffled through the stack of papers. "I quote from page four of the complaint: 'Mr. Grant was surreptitiously approached by Ms. Hunnechurch on three separate occasions and advised that his career would suffer if he remained at Hardesty. Because of her reputation as a competent recruiter, Mr. Grant eventually came to believe Ms. Hunnechurch's assertions. Ms. Hunnechurch further told Mr. Grant that she had already prepared a résumé on his behalf and had *marketed* him to a large corporation in the area. These actions represent egregious *consultant malpractice* on the part of Hunnechurch & Associates, Executive Recruiters.'"

"What does 'egregious' mean?" Joyce asked.

"Flagrant and outrageous," David said, with a shake of his head.

"Every last word is nonsense," I said, my voice growing louder than I had meant it to. "It's a pity that both of you seem not to believe me."

James stood up and took my hand. "Please don't kill the messengers. Naturally, we believe you. The trouble is . . ."

"*What* is the trouble?"

"Mitch Hardesty has a great reputation as an executive. Moreover, a law firm of Blanchette & Ross's stature doesn't invent accusations like this. We have to assume that they carefully questioned Dennis Grant, then used his statement to prepare the complaint."

"But why would Dennis lie about me?"

James folded me in his arms.

"We'll find out," he said. "I know a good lawyer in town too."

I snuggled against his chest. "I feel better already."

I really did feel better—until I saw David out of the corner of my eye. *Why,* I wondered, *had a frown abruptly appeared on his face?* I made the mistake of asking.

David gave me a pained smile. "I just thought of something. It's a good bet that Hardesty issued a news release this afternoon announcing the lawsuit against you. Don't be surprised if you find your name in the *Baltimore Sun*'s business section on Sunday."

This time I gave in to the urge. I blubbered away.

Chapter Three

DURING MY FIVE YEARS as a headhunter, I had recruited dozens of attorneys. I evaluated their résumés, gave advice on what to wear and how to behave at interviews, and often snickered along with them at the latest lawyer jokes they told. I'd grown used to thinking of lawyers as *my candidates*; whenever we met, I was the person in charge of the situation. The legal complaint that Kelly the Shark stuffed into my hand neatly turned the tables on me. I now needed the help of a good lawyer to extract me from a thoroughly unpleasant situation. All at once I'd gone from a giver of professional advice to a wholly out-of-control seeker.

I offer this to explain why I felt curiously fragile at ten o'clock on that Tuesday morning when James led me into the whitewashed brick building on Main Street in Annapolis, Maryland, that housed The Law Offices of Daniel Harris & Associates.

James had assured me throughout the weekend that Daniel Harris was more than capable of jousting with Kyle Blanchette and Ken Ross—the scarily effective lawyers hired by Hardesty Software Corporation.

"I've worked with Daniel on several occasions," James had said. "He's a genuine legal eagle with claws of steel. I'd love to be a fly on the wall when Blanchette and Ross get a look at Daniel's name on the answer to their complaint. Their cursing will probably turn the air blue."

Over the course of the weekend, I'd built up a mental image of Daniel Harris that combined Sir Lancelot and the Terminator, with a sprinkle of Johnny Cochran to complete the recipe. Consequently, I didn't expect to be introduced to a trim man of perhaps sixty years who would never be mistaken for a superhero. He wore a well-cut navy blue blazer that set off his silver-fox hair. He had a narrow face, an aquiline nose, and a multitude of crows' feet that made me think he was tired—until I peered into his eyes. They gleamed with confidence and, thankfully, good humor.

Daniel extended a cool, bony hand and offered up a welcoming smile that seemed truly genuine. "Ah! The alleged malefactor!" he said, pronouncing "alleged" in three syllables: *all-edge-ged*. "I am delighted that you don't look like the kind of person who might do nefarious things to Hardesty Corporation. Juries are often tempted to make an incorrect assumption on the basis of mere appearance." His warm smile morphed to a sly leer. "Of course, if I have my way, this case will never get to a jury. And I *always* have my way."

I giggled, I burbled, I felt a load lift off my shoulders. His prideful words, silly as they were, made me feel much better.

My mood soared even higher when Daniel slapped James hard on the back, the way that men do when they know each other well. Perhaps all the glowing verbiage James had used to praise Daniel Harris was true.

We moved into Daniel's office, a richly appointed room with a lovely view of Annapolis. His desk and the various credenzas and tables were highly polished cherry wood; the two sofas and half dozen or so occasional chairs were upholstered in burgundy leather; the carpeting was plush beige wool; the draperies were patterned silk the color of dark chocolate. It took me a moment to comprehend that the various shades and tints were chosen to match the bindings of the hundreds of antique law books that filled the floor-to-ceiling bookshelves on the wall behind Daniel's desk.

The tide of concern that I'd wallowed in much of the weekend began to rise as I realized how much this room had cost to furnish. Daniel Harris must be an expensive—as well as a successful—attorney. James had mercifully not brought up the subject of money, but I—*we*— would have a hefty bill to pay even if Daniel vanquished Mitch Hardesty and Company. And what if Hunnechurch & Associates lost the case? Well, at least civilized nations had abandoned the notion of debtor's prison.

How on earth did you get yourself into such a mess?

James and I sat down on a sofa. Daniel pulled a chair close by, forming a cozy triangle of knees. His expression transformed once more— this time to the tender smile of a wise uncle.

"I enjoyed reading the summary of the facts you prepared," he said. "You tell your side of the story crisply and succinctly."

Daniel patted my hand. His smile had become softer, more empathetic. "My first piece of advice for you today is, *relax!* It's scary being sued, and justice moves slowly. In the unlikely event that we do go to trial, the date will be many, many months away. Don't let the legal wrangling get you down.

"My second piece of advice is: go with the flow. Fighting a lawsuit is rarely a logical process." His smile widened into an enthusiastic grin. "For example, I just told you that I intend to avoid a trial. Well, at the same time we're going to prepare thoroughly for one."

I suddenly grasped that Daniel Harris was blessed with the plastic countenance of a consummate actor. He had a repertoire of a thousand cheerful faces—an appropriate smile for every mood. No wonder he was a successful trial lawyer.

He switched to a let's-get-down-to-business smile.

"We'll begin by reviewing the complaint." He opened a leather-bound portfolio and handed James and me copies of the infernal complaint document. "If you turn to page five, you will see that Hardesty Software Corporation has charged your firm with a highly unusual form of malpractice."

I sighed. "An egregious violation of my fiduciary responsibilities."

Daniel nodded. "In plain English, Hardesty has called you an unprincipled cheat."

"Balderdash!"

"Hold that thought." Daniel reached into his folder again. "I have here a short clipping from the business page of the *Baltimore Sun*."

"I've seen the story."

"I'm sure you have—a brief news item about a leading software company bringing a malpractice lawsuit against a local human resources consultant. Unfortunately, the paper spelled your name right."

"Issuing a news release was a shoddy thing for Hardesty to do."

"I agree, but it's one more indication that Mitch Hardesty truly believes you committed malpractice."

"I did no such thing."

"Are Blanchette and Ross also wrong? They don't engage in frivolous lawsuits or spurious complaints. They seem to be confident that they can provide a jury with credible evidence that you are an unprincipled cheat."

"I repeat: balderdash!"

Daniel let the clipping flutter down into his folder. "The essence of Hardesty's accusation is that you intentionally misused the freedom of access you were given to senior people within the company."

"That's not true!"

James squeezed my hand. Daniel ignored me and kept talking.

"The particulars of the assertion are rather simple. While you were working in the bosom of Hardesty Software Corporation, you were given the opportunity to meet a speechwriter named Dennis Grant. You realized that Dennis had highly marketable skills, and you decided to betray Hardesty. You approached Dennis and brazenly encouraged him with your many wiles to abandon Hardesty and become your candidate. You subsequently found him a new position and earned yourself a significant fee." Daniel glanced at me. "By the way, how much did you earn by relocating Dennis Grant?"

"My standard recruiting fee is 30 percent of my candidate's first year's salary and estimated bonus."

"A princely sum! Ample temptation to betray one's client, especially . . ."

"I wasn't tempted."

Once again, Daniel ignored my interruption. "*Especially* since you had been disconnected from the Hardesty largess and told that no more work was forthcoming. That sounds like a good motive for betrayal."

"I have a dozen other clients."

"That many? Then you probably don't feel great loyalty to any one of them."

"Rubbish! I'm loyal to all my clients."

"Yet you helped a key employee find new employment." Daniel's smile became a predatory, almost malicious, smirk. "Even if Dennis came to you first, doesn't your decision to help him leave Hardesty represent *some* measure of disloyalty to a one-time client who trusted you fully?"

I started to answer but couldn't bring myself to say *no*.

"Gracious!" My heart sank as I eventually said, "If you put it that way, I do seem less than fully loyal to Hardesty Corporation."

A pained grimace replaced the nasty smirk. "Yet how could you ignore Dennis Grant's earnest plea for help?"

My head spun. "His what?"

"Did Dennis seem happy about working at Hardesty when you first met him?"

"He didn't say—although he did complain about being busy."

"Imagine that! A few minutes after making your acquaintance, he tells you how overworked he is."

"I assumed he wanted to keep our conversation short."

"You're much too modest." A beneficent smile exploded on Daniel's face. "When Dennis Grant met Pippa Hunnechurch, he saw the light at the end of a bleak tunnel—the answer to his unspoken prayer."

"He did?"

"Of course. He realized at once that you offered a ray of hope—an escape hatch from soul-destroying drudgery."

The penny dropped. Daniel had swapped sides and was zealously advocating my position. "Please go on," I said.

"Slavery has been abolished in the United States, but Dennis Grant lived in oratorical servitude. He understood that you possessed the power to free him from a grueling job he despised."

"Yea verily!"

"Did Dennis approach you immediately? Absolutely not! He waited patiently until Hardesty had severed forever its business relationship with Hunnechurch & Associates. Only then did he seek you out."

"Dennis is a wise man."

"Wise indeed. At that point in time, it no longer made any difference that he had met you in Hardesty's executive suite. He might as well have run into you at a party, or looked your name up in the telephone book, or found *www.pippahunnechurch.com* on the Internet." Daniel wagged a finger triumphantly. "Dennis Grant came to you for help. Your ethical responsibilities to provide that help clearly outweighed the debatable duty you owe to an ex-client who had not shown you an ounce of loyalty."

"Blimey!" I said. "You *are* good."

Daniel's smile melted away. "And yet—why would Dennis tell such a different story to Blanchette & Ross, attorneys at law? Why would he insist that you recruited him?" Daniel turned to another page in the complaint and read the same words that David Friendly had found: "It declares here that Mr. Grant was surreptitiously approached by Ms. Hunnechurch on three separate occasions: a Friday in mid-February, a Tuesday in late February, and a Wednesday in early March. The complaint further states that all your approaches took place in early morning in the Hardesty parking lot."

"Dennis showed up unbidden at my office," I said. "His story is a lie."

"Oh, it's far more than a lie. What we have here is a cleverly crafted assertion that will be difficult for us to disprove—unless you were out of town on those days."

I shook my head. "I didn't go anywhere in February and March. We were too busy getting ready for our wedding." James squeezed my hand again.

"Do you routinely approach people surreptitiously during the early a.m.?" Daniel asked.

"Why would I? Waylaying prospective clients is hardly a sensible marketing strategy, and potential candidates always come to my office."

Daniel leaned back in his chair and interlaced his fingers behind his head.

"That makes sense to me," he said. "Most candidates are excited at the prospect of a better job; they'll happily visit you. But what if you were trying to recruit a genius in his field? Let's say you had set your sights on the rarest of rare birds—a speechwriter so talented that you can count on one hand the number of comparable writers in the United States?"

"Dennis Grant hardly falls into that category."

"To the contrary. Should Kyle Blanchette ever get the opportunity to introduce Mr. Grant to a jury, its members will feel honored to be in the same room with him."

"If I find Dennis in the same room with me again," I said, glumly, "I will wring his miserable, lying neck."

Daniel's back-and-forth advocacy had finally hit home. It had taken awhile for me to "get it," but I now understood the dimensions of my problem:

One—the lawsuit turned on a single issue: Who made the first move—Dennis Grant or me?

Two—without solid evidence the case would come down to my word against his.

Three—most people, including most judges and jurors, would likely believe Dennis's story. After all, why would Dennis lie? He had no reason to pretend that he didn't come to me for help. Moreover, everyone knows that headhunters actively recruit good candidates. Executive recruiters recruit. It's that simple!

Daniel had grasped my predicament immediately. Now I understood—and from the glum look on James's face, so did he.

The three of us stared out at Annapolis until James broke the silence: "Even allowing that Grant has phenomenal credentials, I don't see the damage that's been done to Hardesty Software by helping him leave. Trade secrets have commercial value. Dennis merely ghostwrote speeches for Mitch Hardesty."

Daniel rocked forward in his chair. "I think you're right. The actual damages for luring Dennis away won't be enormous. But Hardesty will also ask for punitive damages—a vast additional sum of money to punish Pippa and discourage other greedy headhunters from taking advantage of their clients' openness and generosity."

"Oh, boy!" I said, with an unintended gulp.

"Asking is a long way from getting. Courts are generally reluctant to impose punitive damages."

"But it can happen?"

"Oh, yes. Punitive damages are awarded every day." He smiled a funereal smile. "But rarely if ever against *my* clients."

"Amen!" James said.

Daniel tapped the front of the complaint with a gaunt finger. "I don't know of another case like this one in Maryland—and precious few elsewhere. It would be great fun to argue it all the way up to the Maryland Court of Appeals."

"Not for me," I said.

Daniel laughed out loud. "Fear not—we may be able to bury your case with a procedural shovel."

"Pardon?"

"I intend to move for a dismissal. We'll ask the judge to throw Hardesty's case out of court."

"A dismissal on what grounds," James asked.

Daniel adopted an inscrutable smile. "I have an idea, but I need to do more legal research. If my brainchild pans out, I'll tell you about it next Monday before our motions hearing."

"Next Monday?" James's voice bubbled with surprise. "How did you arrange a hearing so quickly?"

"Consider it a minor miracle. The Anne Arundel County Circuit Court put an extra motions hearing day on the June calendar—and well, I have friends here and there in high places. Ken Ross will be lead attorney for the plaintiff. He agreed to expedite the hearing as long as we can both take advantage of it. Ken plans to make a motion for discovery of documents in Pippa's recruiting files."

"My files?" I blurted. "What does he expect to find in my files?"

"Evidence that you contacted Dennis Grant first."

"But Dennis contacted me first."

"Then there's no smoking gun for Ken to find." Daniel punctuated his reply with a toothy smile. "What about the other way around? Do you have *any* evidence that Dennis showed up on your doorstep uninvited?"

I hesitated. "Give me an example of what you mean."

"You might have logged his unexpected arrival in a visitors' book. Or maybe he sent you a follow-up e-mail thanking you for seeing him without an appointment. Or perhaps he explained the purpose of his visit to your receptionist."

I shrugged. "None of the above. I don't keep a visitors' log, we never communicated by e-mail, and Dennis arrived late on a Friday afternoon, after Gloria Spitz, my associate, had gone home."

Daniel chuckled. "Well, if this were an easy case, you wouldn't need me." He snapped his folder shut. "Go through your files. Send me a copy of every piece of paper you find that concerns Dennis Grant or Hardesty. Maybe we'll get lucky."

"We Brits don't like to rely on luck." I rose to my feet. "There has to be a reason Dennis Grant is lying, and I intend to find it."

It was Daniel's turn to look puzzled. "How?"

"By applying the research skills that Hunnechurch & Associates uses every day. A good headhunter is a good investigator."

"Stop right there, Pippa!" Daniel stood up to face me, his face abruptly solemn. "Search your files, but *don't* poke around in Dennis Grant's affairs. Stay completely away from him. Don't even think about him. There are a thousand ways you can damage your case by accident."

James also stood up. I could tell he was itching to chime in, but he didn't go beyond rolling his eyes at my suggestion.

Daniel went on: "Put your trust in me, Pippa. If any investigating needs to be done, we'll do it. Do we have a deal?"

There is a time to argue and a time to acquiesce.

"I yield to superior forces," I answered, ambiguously.

I suppose I looked sincere because Daniel reestablished his friendly smile, and James let out the breath he was holding.

"I wish all my clients were as reasonable as you," Daniel said.

Neither Daniel nor James noticed that I had my fingers crossed.

====

It was half past noon when James dropped me off at the corner of Ryde High Street and Chesapeake Avenue and sped away to an appointment in Baltimore. I watched the boxy Range Rover drive out of sight and wondered why James so enjoyed a vehicle obviously designed to survive a collision with a rhinoceros.

It has to be a guy thing.

I called Gloria on my cell phone. "Have you eaten lunch yet?"

"Nope. I've been waiting for you to get back. I'm dying to know what the lawyer said."

"Stay alive for ten minutes longer. I'll pick up lunch, but I give you fair warning: I'm in the mood for comfort food."

"Yum!"

I stopped at Hamburger Heaven and bought two Eternity Burgers with cheese and bacon, a large order of Angelic Fries, and two Strawberry Cherubim Shakes. I felt sufficiently guilty about the fat and calories to speed-walk the three blocks back to the old leather warehouse. I even climbed the stairs to the fourth floor rather than ride the elevator.

Gloria listened patiently while I talked, only occasionally with my mouth full. I ended with a simple admission: "Daniel didn't give me an option; I said what he and James wanted to hear."

"In other words, you fibbed to your husband and lawyer at the same time." She slurped her shake. "No wonder you craved an industrial strength hamburger."

"Daniel asked me to trust him, and I do, but we can't leave our future wholly in the hands of a lawyer. He simply doesn't understand our business the way we do." I ate the last morsel of my Eternity Burger. "Daniel didn't even mention Hunnechurch & Associates. He doesn't appreciate that our reputation is at stake, that we're certain to lose clients unless we prove our innocence. It's not enough that the court dismisses Hardesty's case against us; we must prove to the world that we've done nothing wrong."

"And so we're going to conduct an investigation."

"With one goal: to find out why Dennis Grant lied. Once we know why, perhaps we can find definitive evidence that he did."

"We have to investigate—ah, *surreptitiously*," Gloria said, with a laugh.

"Indeed! *Surreptitious* is our watchword for today." I switched gears, "What's on our calendar this month?"

"Lots of marketing work, which can be postponed. And two current searches that can run on autopilot for a while without harm." She slurped the last of her shake through her straw. "When do we begin?"

"After we fill Daniel Harris's order for any paperwork involving Hardesty. You search through our CD-ROMs; I'll browse our recent paper files."

We brought our clobber into the conference room; set the radio to WBJC, our local classical music station; and went to work. During the span of Brahms' Second Symphony and Offenbach's "Tales of Hoffman," we retrieved twenty-two pieces of paper—all related to the initial search I had done for Hardesty. Ralph Vaughn Williams's "Fantasy on Greensleeves" had just begun when a velvety voice reverberated from our reception room, "Is anyone home?"

"That sounds like Reverend Ed," Gloria said.

She whooshed outside and returned with Ed Clarke, pastor of Ryde Fellowship Church. James and I are members; so are Gloria and the Friendlys.

Ed, a lanky man in his early fifties, was seriously out of uniform. Instead of his usual liturgical robes or somber business suit, he wore a jaunty red polo shirt and walking shorts.

"You look surprised to see me," he said to me. "I was in the neighborhood, and I thought to myself, *If I visit Pippa, then Gloria will probably offer me a hot cuppa.*"

Gloria took the hint. "I'll make a fresh pot." She shut the conference room door as she left.

"Now you look suspicious," he said.

"No. I'm curious," I replied. "You've come a long way for a cup of tea."

"That's because I need a favor." He sat in the chair next to mine. "We have a vacancy on the committee that will nominate a new associate pastor. I'd like you to fill it."

Ed's request came as such a surprise that all I managed to say in reply was, "Why me?"

He beamed. "I came fully prepared to answer that question. To begin with, you are a successful executive recruiter. You bring specific skills the committee needs. Beyond that, you are personable, a team player, and a committed Christian: three traits that are essential to success on a pastor search committee. Most important of all, your integrity is unquestioned. You'll be a perfect addition to the committee. The church can rely on you to do a superb job."

Ed's paean of praise soaked in like summer rain on parched earth. I felt refreshed, renewed. How could I refuse his simple request?

"I shall be delighted to serve," I said, before I could stop myself.

"Wonderful! I'm sure that God will help you succeed. In fact, why don't we talk to him about it now? Will you pray with me, Pippa?"

Ed took my hand and closed his eyes.

I kept my eyes wide open—as realization of my blunder took root. Why had I agreed to do more church work? I had too much on my plate to take on a thankless chore. I already spent one evening a week at the church with my small group. I also seemed to serve on half of the *ad hoc* committees established at the church. I'd helped to plan the Lenten program, and helped to organize the ladies retreat, and helped to coordinate the last blood drive. Moreover—why me for this? I knew nothing about recruiting an associate pastor.

While Ed asked God to give me wisdom and discernment and help me keep my good humor, I silently prayed to be let off the hook.

A strange thing happened. I began to feel—*contented.* There's no other way to describe the delicious feeling I felt. My concerns seemed to fade in significance. My objections vanished. I knew, though I couldn't explain why, that I belonged on that committee.

Ed said, "Amen," and smiled at me; I managed to smile back.

Gloria arrived with tea. She gave Ed a sideways glance; he returned a slight nod.

You've been set up by the pair of them working together.

I didn't mind. The contentment that filled me that afternoon didn't allow room for irritation or annoyance.

Too bad the joyous feeling wouldn't last.

```
┌─────────────────────────────────────┐
│          Chapter  Four               │
└─────────────────────────────────────┘
```

WHY DID DENNIS GRANT LIE?

On Wednesday morning Gloria wrote those words with a marking pen on a four-foot-long strip of banner paper. She and I had stood on chairs and taped the banner high on the rear wall of our new conference room, directly opposite another banner on the front wall: *SAVE HUNNECHURCH & ASSOCIATES!*

"When you create a war room," Gloria said, "you need to concentrate your attention on what's genuinely important."

"I defer to your extensive military expertise." I added, "However, how sure are you that this double-sided tape won't do damage to our freshly painted walls?"

"Don't sweat the small stuff." She burnished the banner in place with her palm. "Neat walls won't matter if we can't figure out why Dennis lied."

"Point well taken."

But was there a simple answer? The more we thought about the question, the odder his decision to lie about it seemed. To convince a headhunter to represent you is no small thing; it shouts that one is well regarded and successful.

Head-hunting is typically a one-way endeavor; I seek out virtually all of the candidates I place. The reason of course is that employers give me my assignments. They ask me to find "pegs" to fit specific "holes" in their organizations. Once I have an assignment, the hunting of the head begins. Although I do place advertisements and use Internet job boards, the fundamental technique in my profession is networking. I call people, who guide me to other people, who send me to still other people. In time—perhaps many weeks—I may find myself talking to the perfect candidate. Chances are this person will tell me he or she is perfectly happy and has no interest in a new job. And so I keep looking.

It is difficult to work the process in reverse. There's little I can do with an uninvited résumé except stick it in my files in the flimsy hope that an appropriate assignment will come along. And so I rarely accept résumés from job seekers.

Dennis Grant was a spur-of-the-moment exception. A friend had mentioned in passing at a meeting of the Ryde Chamber of Commerce that Militet Aviation might soon need a new speechwriter. When Dennis showed up with his stellar résumé, I straightaway decided to take a gamble. Although I had no inkling when—or even if—Militet would start its search, I presented Dennis's paperwork to the vice president of human resources along with a brief note: "The grapevine tells me that Militet is contemplating the hiring of an executive speechwriter. Perhaps this highly skilled individual will be of interest to you?"

She was delighted, and so was Dennis Grant, who received a generous offer from Militet only two weeks after he paid me his unexpected visit. Gloria and I were equally ecstatic; we had earned a hefty fee by doing little more than sending Dennis's résumé across town.

"It's amazing!" Gloria had said. "You created a *win-win-win* situation by ignoring standard operating procedure. Everyone involved came out ahead."

So it had seemed at the time. But now the "win" for Hunnechurch &
Associates had vanished in a blast of unfathomable dishonesty. I might
lose everything—my reputation, my business, my livelihood. And the
whole blasted business seemed out of my control. I felt like an ant about
to be squished by a steamroller.

I looked up at the big banner and muttered, "I shall never do anyone a professional favor again."

"Stop brooding and start hunting!" Gloria punctuated her command with a gentle poke in my ribs. "We need ammunition to shoot
back at Dennis Grant."

"Yes sir, yes sir—three bags full."

"*What?*"

"Ignore me. I suffered a short-lived episode of feeling sorry for myself. I shall stiffen my upper lip and buckle down."

"Consider yourself ignored." Gloria handed me a shiny new key.

"What's this for?"

"The conference room door. It's good practice to keep a war room
locked when it's not being used."

"Goodness! Do we really have to be so—*military?*"

"Hoo-ah!" Gloria made the "hoo" sound like a grunt.

═══════════

A day later our conference/war room was polka-dotted with white
papers and yellow sticky notes affixed to the wall. We had four categories of data—each given its own wall—each topped with its own
handwritten header label:

1. Hardesty Stuff

2. Dennis Grant: Background and Biographical

3. Action Items—Things to Do

4. Brainstorming about Dennis Grant

The Hardesty Stuff wall supported copies of the twenty-two items we had dutifully forwarded to Daniel Harris. My dealings with Hardesty had generated a small collection of routine paperwork. An initial letter. A handful of e-mails. A contract. Three candidate dossiers. Three sets of interview notes. A few follow-up e-mails. An invoice. A thank-you letter. Routine items.

"Assume that everything you find will, in due course, be given to Blanchette and Ross," James had said to me at breakfast.

"But that hardly seems fair," I protested.

"The idea is to surface all the potential evidence before the case goes to trial. They see our paperwork, and we see theirs. Now you know why most lawsuits are settled without a trial."

"I'm certainly not going to send the opposition anything that will strengthen their case against me."

James hesitated, then said, "A *good-ole-boy* lawyer I knew in Georgia once told me, 'When you go looking for evidence, work hard not to find anything that doesn't help you make your case.'"

"Heavens! I'm not devious enough to destroy damaging evidence."

"Exactly! So don't worry about what will happen to what you turn up."

Gloria and I had gone to work with gusto. Our triumph was the Dennis Grant wall. We posted an impressive array of background information about Dennis—interesting details I'd extracted from his résumé, gleaned from the notes I'd taken when I interviewed him and spoke to his references, and that Gloria had found on the Internet.

Detail: Dennis rode his custom-made mountain bike to work every day and kept it chained against a steam pipe in the Hardesty Building's executive garage.

Detail: Dennis was a widely quoted advocate of banning automobile traffic in cities and forcing everyone to commute on a bicycle.

Detail: Dennis has changed jobs on average once every three years. I remember feeling a pang of gloom as I wrote the note. Kenneth Ross would certainly argue that Dennis had worked for Hardesty only a year and a half and consequently "wasn't ready" to make a move yet.

Detail: Dennis had coauthored a best-selling textbook on how to write executive speeches. Gloria groaned as she pressed the sticky note to the wall. "The last thing we need is *more* evidence of the man's know-how."

Detail: Dennis was a skilled cook of Indian food. The *Ryde Rebel,* our gossipy, irreverent, independent newspaper, had published a long article about Dennis the previous October, entitled "The Ghostwriter Who Curries Favor with His Curries."

"There's a title you don't hear much anymore," Gloria said when she finished printing the copy of the article she'd retrieved from the *Rebel's* Web site. "Ghostwriter" has gone the way of disco dancing.

"Corporate speechwriters are no longer required to be ghostly," I replied. "No one expects senior executives to write their own speeches."

"Why not?"

"I suppose because they are so busy."

"That makes me mad," Gloria said, with a frown. "An executive taking credit for words that another person wrote is like cheating in school. Students can't hire experts to do their work for them merely because they're busy."

"Stop brooding and keep searching," I said. "You are our lead ammunition gatherer."

"Foobah!" she said as she returned to her computer.

Gloria looked up a moment later. "You won't believe what I just found. Dennis was an Eagle Scout."

"Why does that surprise you?"

"Boy Scouts take an oath to be truthful, and Eagle Scouts are at the top of the scouting ladder. Maybe we can get him *de-merit-badged,* or whatever they do to scouts who misbehave."

"What's the point of bogging down in the ethics of scouting? Dennis is forty-five years old; he must have disconnected from the scouts more than a quarter century ago."

"Not really. He helped to launch a local Boy Scout troop last year. There's an article about him in the *Baltimore Sun*."

"*Another* article?"

Gloria picked up on the surprise in my voice. "Now that you mention it, I've retrieved a surprising amount of published material about Dennis Grant in the *Sun* and the *Ryde Reporter*. More than a dozen newspaper stories in the past twenty-four months—including a piece when he arrived at Hardesty and another when he started to work at Militet."

"The man must have his own publicist."

"Should I write that down and hang it up?"

"I was only joking. Press on with your Interneting. I'll try to add a few more 'Things to Do.'"

We had so far identified the paltry sum of three activities to perform when we finished Dennis's wall:

1. *Commission Collier Investigations to do background check on Dennis Grant.* As Gloria put it, "You never know what will fall out when you shake the tree."

2. *Pippa will contact Dennis's references again.* Perhaps one of them might be willing to offer an explanation for his shoddy behavior. This was a weak "perhaps" at best. I didn't hold out much hope that one of his former employers would know why Dennis lied—or would be willing to tell tales out of school.

3. *Find out if Dennis was recruited by a headhunter in the past.* We had no idea how we would go about doing it, but it would be useful to quantify his prior experiences, if any, with executive recruiters.

I stared at the mostly blank wall. There must be *something* productive we could do—something more energetic than merely gathering bits and pieces of disconnected information.

Think, Pippa! You pride yourself on your ingenuity.

I stared at the wall for five minutes, then gave up. Perhaps I could kick-start my creativity by switching to the Brainstorming about Dennis Grant wall.

We had made reasonable progress trying to suss out the workings of Dennis's deceitful mind. The first column of sticky notes was headed Why Dennis Might Want to Leave Hardesty. We invented seven possible explanations so far:

1. Too much work at Hardesty? Too many weekend hours?

2. Personality conflict with another person in the executive suite? Bad chemistry?

3. Not enough money? Not enough opportunities for personal growth?

4. Dangerous daily commute? Dennis pedals his bicycle across Ryde, along busy roads.

5. Ethical concerns? Maybe Dennis doesn't like Hardesty's products? Maybe he's been forced to lie in his speeches?

6. Boredom? Maybe Dennis is tired of writing dull speeches about computer software?

7. Wanderlust? Perhaps Dennis wants to work away from Ryde? (Militet has other locations around the world.)

I thought of an eighth explanation: Self-defense. Maybe Dennis had made a serious on-the-job mistake and wanted to bail out before he got fired. I began writing on a sticky note.

That makes no sense at all!

I crumpled the note. If Dennis was about to get the old heave-ho, why would Mitch Hardesty care if I saved him the trouble of doing the job?

I turned my attention to the other brainstorming column: Why Dennis Might Choose to Lie about Us. We had dreamed up four possibilities—all of them either feeble or improbable:

1. Saving face? He made a promise to stay with Hardesty and doesn't want to admit he broke it on his own.

2. Fear of conflict? Perhaps Dennis is a person who avoids conflict and feared to admit that he acted first?

3. No burned bridges? Maybe Dennis imagines that he'll return to Hardesty one day and didn't want to burn bridges.

4. Fear of reprisal? Hardesty wants to punish us. Maybe Dennis is afraid of Mitch Hardesty's wrath?

The sticky notes seemed to whirl as I stared at them.

"I have not a shred of creativity left in me this morning," I announced glumly.

"Your brain hasn't been fed recently," Gloria countered. "Why don't we eat lunch and brainstorm at the same time? I could go for Indian food."

We ordered a take-out lunch from The Punjab, a new Indian restaurant that had recently opened on Ryde High Street, around the corner from an Indian grocery shop called Bombay Spices & Rices. I often ate Indian food during my years in England, but I'd fallen out of the habit when I moved to Maryland—mostly because the closest Indian restaurants were in Baltimore.

I picked a shrimp curry, medium hot. Gloria opted for a fiery chicken vindaloo. We also ordered a vegetable rice pilaf to share and a selection of pickles and chutneys. Gloria brewed a fresh pot of strong Assam tea while we waited for lunch to arrive.

"I think our information walls are impressive," she said, after she poured us each a tall mug.

"True—although I wish we could identify a logical reason for Dennis's perfidy."

"Maybe he became annoyed with the tricky British words you spoke to him?"

"Very funny."

"*Perfidy* means lying—right?"

"With a helping of disloyalty thrown in." I blew across the surface of my tea to cool it, then took a slow sip. "As it happens, I had little face-to-face time with Dennis because we placed him so quickly. It's a pity I didn't tape-record the minutes he spent in my office. Then we might have something concrete—a recording of Dennis begging me to find him a job."

Gloria's face lit up. "Why didn't I think of that? It's not too late to catch Dennis saying the wrong thing. I have a cassette recorder that will fit under your clothing without being seen and a tiny wireless microphone that will hide behind your bra strap."

"Don't they call that 'wearing a wire'?"

"Technically, a wire is a radio transmitter, not a recorder, but the idea is the same. Your challenge is to stand close to Dennis and get him talking." Her smile abruptly faded. "Except that he'll never agree to see you. I'm sure that Blanchette and Ross told him not to talk to anyone about the case. Especially you."

I reached for the phone. "Perhaps Dennis is like me and doesn't take legal advice well."

I called Militet's main number and asked for Dennis Grant. He answered on the third ring.

"It's Pippa Hunnechurch," I said without giving him a chance to respond. "It's been almost two months since we last spoke. I would love to chat with you for a few minutes—perhaps over a cup of coffee or even lunch."

"What do you want to *chat* about?"

I ignored the irritation in his voice. "I always follow up on my successful placements. I like to revisit the whole process—find ways to do even better with the next candidate. It's my version of the well-known quality assurance process."

It was perfectly true. I do like to receive feedback from successful candidates.

I heard Dennis snicker. "Nice try, Pippa," he said, "but Kenneth Ross warned me that you'd probably call. He told me to hang up when you did."

"Hang up? That is completely uncalled for, considering . . ."

I heard a click and the line went dead. I finished my sentence anyway: ". . . considering the determined efforts I made to find you your new position."

I slammed my receiver down. "You ungrateful, ill-mannered wretch!" I glanced at Gloria. "Do *not* say I told you so."

"Me? *Never!*"

Our lunch was delivered shortly thereafter. We shared our meals; the anger I felt at Dennis Grant overwhelmed the heavy-duty spiciness of the chicken vindaloo. I took pleasure in every tongue-flaying bite.

"I need a short walk to clear my head," I said when we had finished, "accompanied by an antacid to repair my innards."

"Go to it. I'll hold down the fort."

"You don't mind?"

"*Uh-uh.*" She smiled prettily. "I'll get more work done without you moping around."

━━━━━━━

In spite of what occurred less than an hour later, I did not set out to visit James's new office in Ryde at the exact moment that his new furniture was being delivered. My simple intention was to stroll a few blocks along Ryde High Street, perhaps as far as the gourmet ice cream shop at the

corner of Severn Lane, then return with renewed vigor to think about
Dennis Grant. Lurking in the back of my mind was the idea that a small
scoop of amaretto gelato would be a salutary aid to my creativity.

But I soon began to stride rather than stroll down Ryde High Street,
zigging past office workers returning from lunch and zagging around
shoppers perusing the storefronts. Surprisingly, my anger at Dennis increased with each step. I decided that he was *worse* than impolite and
ungrateful; the blighter had all but attacked the hand that fed him.
I'd done him the favor of finding him a grand new job, and he'd repaid
my kindness by turning on me. His lies had turned on a drip, drip, drip
of anxiety in my mind that felt like a Chinese water torture. Would the
case go to trial? If so, would I prevail in court? If not, could
Hunnechurch & Associates survive?

Time—and distance—pass quickly when one is bubbling over with
annoyance and resentment. It seemed mere seconds later when I discovered that my "short walk" had taken me to the Riverview Towers, on
the corner of Ryde High Street and Mulberry Alley. I had covered more
than two and a half miles in only thirty-five minutes, without even
thinking about it.

Now Mulberry Alley had long been one of my favorite destinations in
Ryde: a narrow *cul de sac* near the bottom of Ryde High Street. The main
thoroughfare makes a sharp turn to the left on its run down to
the Magothy River. The alley is located at the tip of the "elbow," branch-
ing off to the right. Little more than a city block long, its precincts hold
a dozen boutiques and specialty shops that sell the kind of scrumptious
wares one finds on Rodeo Drive in Beverly Hills. I love to browse through
them even though the prices are invariably too rich for my purse.

Equally dear are the rents in the Riverview—a restored gem of an
office building built early in the twentieth century. A realtor had shown
me an elegant office suite back when I first launched Hunnechurch &
Associates. Exquisite digs—but the deposit alone would have consumed
most of my start-up cash. I chose two far less expensive rooms in the

utilitarian Calvert Building. I worked there happily for nearly two years until Gloria joined the firm and we moved into our present offices.

James, however, fell madly in love with the Riverview at first sight.

"I wouldn't have believed that a small city like Ryde would have an edifice this grand," he had said, his Southern drawl on full power. "The Riverview is the ideal new home for The Peachtree Consulting Group."

"Do you really require such a posh headquarters?" I asked. "As you explained to me, your office is merely your base of operations. You are largely a one-man band who travels far and wide to deliver your seminars and help companies fine-tune their international marketing efforts."

"That's too narrow a perspective," he said with a sniff. "An impressive office is an investment in business development. Clients feel more comfortable dealing with a consultant who looks successful." He sniffed again. "Upgrading your offices might attract a few new clients to Hunnechurch & Associates."

That imprudent comment had cost James two dozen roses.

He also ignored my misgivings and rented a pricy four-room suite on the ninth floor of the Riverview that did, indeed, offer a stunning view of the Magothy.

And so when I found myself in front of the building that Thursday afternoon, I faced a dilemma: Should I pay James an unannounced visit—foul mood and all? Or should I turn around and trot back to the leather warehouse?

Depart, Pippa! You're not fit company.

But then I spotted a large van parked next to Riverview's service entrance. The sign on its side proclaimed, "Linkletter Business Interiors."

Might the truck be delivering James's new furniture? I wondered.

There's only one way to find out.

I made for the Riverview's lobby—a symphony of marble floors, wood paneled walls, and eerie silence—stepped into the marble lined elevator, and pushed the button marked 9.

The front door to James's suite was locked—James had not yet hired a receptionist or an assistant—but I could hear activity somewhere inside. If furniture was being delivered, it must be via the back door. I tapped on the frosted glass until a shadowy figure appeared behind it and worked the lock.

"Pippa! I was about to call your office," James said.

"I'm not there."

He laughed, swung the door wide, and bent to kiss me.

"You must be a mind reader," he said. "My new furniture is here. I wanted you to be the first to sit on it. The ambience is *fabulous*. Even nicer than Daniel Harris's office. Come and see."

Two delivery men were busy hanging a massive cherry-wood framed mirror in James's conference room, but we worked our way around the various leather upholstered chairs and sofas, the solid cherry tables, the charming lithographs on the walls, and the imposing desk in James's office.

"Brilliant!" I said again and again. "Absolutely lovely. I'm certainly impressed." I tried to keep the annoyance out of my voice and kept telling myself *not* to estimate the total cost.

James knows what he's doing. He won't "ambience" us into the poor house.

We returned to James's reception room and sat down side by side on a graceful leather bench across from the receptionist's workstation.

"So what do you truly think?" he asked.

"*Truly?*"

"Give me both barrels."

"Well, you want to impress people, and so you shall."

"Good! We see eye to eye on the effect, if not the need."

I leaned over and kissed him.

"Now that my furniture has arrived," he said, "it's time to find a secretary-receptionist."

"Give me your specifications. I'll begin an immediate search."

James seemed lost in thought for several seconds. When he finally turned toward me, he was wearing his signature nice-guy grin, "I wouldn't dream of saddling you with such a trivial assignment."

"To the contrary! An uncomplicated search is just what I need to take my mind off the lawsuit."

James's grin didn't waver. "My mind is made up. I don't want to waste your time."

"I have plenty of extra time."

"I disagree. You have too much on your plate to fool around finding me a receptionist."

Straightaway my hackles began to rise. "Fool around? What do you mean by *that?*"

"I mean exactly what I said. You are an executive recruiter. Searching for a receptionist is fooling around." The grin was still there—barely.

"I must be getting thicker with age. You *don't* want me to headhunt for you."

"And you don't want me to consult for you." James crossed his arms. "Think back to the last time I gave you an itty-bitty suggestion about your business. We argued for the rest of the day. We wisely decided to operate our two firms independently."

"Thanks for your vote of confidence."

"Don't be silly, Pippa. I have every confidence in your skills, but we see the world of business from two different points of view. We'll both be happier if you do your thing and I do mine. Besides, I have a candidate coming in for an interview tomorrow. Her résumé is terrific."

I looked out the window behind me. There were three large sailboats on the Magothy River, propelled by colorful sails designed to capture the last bit of power from light summer breezes. As I watched them move toward the Chesapeake Bay, I felt tears form in my eyes.

Chapter Five

A GENTLE RUMBLE OF SNORING woke me ten minutes before our alarm clock was set to ring on Friday morning. I leaned over and kissed James's unshaven cheek then slid out from under our wedding-gift cotton sheets without disturbing him.

"Do not let the sun go down while you are still angry," Paul had advised the Ephesians. I hadn't been genuinely angry at James the day before—"somewhat irritated" is a much better description. I confess acting a tad cool toward James throughout dinner and later that evening. *Why,* I kept asking myself, *did James reject my kind offer to find a qualified receptionist for his precious consultancy?*

All my irritations vanished with the new day. One look at James, sleeping peacefully, his lips fluttering as he exhaled, recharged my matrimonial batteries with love and devotion. Determined to let him enjoy ten more minutes of noisy dreaming, I resisted the urge to kiss him again.

Do I snore also?

With that grim question churning in my mind, I slipped my feet into my bunny bedroom slippers—half of the matched his-and-hers set that Gloria had given us as a gag engagement gift. My slippers had the shorter ears, longer eyelashes, and larger powder-puff tails. I wore them every morning because their ample padding could prevent seriously stubbed toes as I inched my way around the overabundance of furniture in our tiny bedroom. The "last straw" had been the clunky Edwardian chest of drawers that now sat scarcely a foot away from the bottom of our bed. What else could we do? James needed a place to stow his shirts and knickers.

Directly across the hallway from our bedroom door was Hunnechurch Manor's sole bathroom. Before our wedding I often bathed in leisure, lingering in the tub while sipping my morning tea. Such simple pleasures were now impossible; James and I had become morning rivals for the use of the facilities.

I showered in haste, taking care to leave James his fair share of the hot water in our slow-heating water heater. Next I maneuvered my towel with balletlike grace, moving elbows and hips with precision in the tight confines between bathtub and sink, taking care to keep a safe distance from the toilet tank lid. This had been the only vacant flat surface in my prewedding bathroom; James commandeered it for his shaving cream, aftershaves, and deodorant.

The collection of precariously perched cans and bottles made me ponder whether a nineteenth-century townhouse was an ideal residence for two twenty-first-century people who had accumulated significant clobber. Perhaps it was a mistake to live in such tight quarters? Maybe we should find a bigger home with more room to spread out?

My doubts didn't linger long. The gentle voice in the back of my mind reminded me that Hunnechurch Manor was our home—a house I'd worked exceedingly hard to buy. I thought back to what Mum often said, "Because nothing we receive in this world is perfect, the good Lord gave people the ability to solve minor problems."

I immediately set myself a challenge: I would think of more efficient ways to organize our many possessions. After all, 735 Magothy Street had been built in 1867 to house a husband, his wife, and their five children. Certainly the two of us should be able to live comfortably within its cheerful walls.

I had begun to fold my towel into a narrow band—even our shared towel rack is small—when James let loose a great shriek: "*Nooooo!*"

My heart thumped. I dropped the towel and ran into the bedroom. "What's wrong?" I yelled.

"It's not there!" he yelled back. "It's gone! It was there when I went to bed. I distinctly recall checking, but now it's not there."

I couldn't imagine what had gone missing. I also couldn't help chuckling at the sight of James hopping on his left foot, frenetically trying to jam his right foot into a pair of sweatpants. He saw my amusement and glowered daggers at me.

"Calm down," I said. "Tell me what's not there."

"My *new* Range Rover!" He made "new" sound like an extraordinary quality.

"Your bloomin' car is missing?" My question equaled his pronouncement in volume. "You frightened me half to death because you mislaid your Range Rover?"

James flapped his arm at the wall. "It's not mislaid. I parked it last night on Magothy Street, under the streetlight. My car was there when I pulled down the shade, when we went to sleep. I lifted the window shade this morning, and it's gone!"

Lifted the window shade?

I suddenly remembered that I was in the altogether. I glanced over my naked shoulder and discovered that my bare backside was in full view of anyone who might be walking past Hunnechurch Manor. The only suitable garment in the vicinity was James's bathrobe—conveniently tossed on the bed. I hurled myself into it.

James skipped down the staircase three steps at a time, raced the length of our hallway, and flung open our front door. I followed after him at a reasonable pace but came to a quick stop when my toes trod our bristly doormat. I prefer not to walk barefoot on concrete sidewalks and asphalt pavement. I stepped back into our front doorway as James—shirtless, wearing his pair of bunny slippers—marched glumly across Magothy Street to an empty parking space some fifty feet from our house.

I wanted to ask, *Are you sure you parked it there last night?* I thought about reminding him, *It's so easy to forget where one parked his or her car.* Parking had become an increasingly difficult challenge in our neighborhood because most of the townhouses were owned by two-car—and occasionally three-car—families. There wasn't sufficient curb space on Magothy Street to accommodate so many vehicles.

It took every ounce of my self-control, but I managed to keep my mouth shut.

James turned toward me with the unhappiest expression I had ever seen on his face. "My new Range Rover . . ." he said, "it's been *stolen.*"

The despair he communicated pierced like a dagger. My common sense flew away, and in an attempt to help, I said absolutely the wrong thing. "James, are you sure? I can't imagine a thief nicking your big, boxy lorry."

James fixed me with his eyes. I could see flames of righteous indignation kindle and explode inside them.

"My Range Rover is not a *boxy lorry.* It is a highly desirable *sport-utility vehicle.*" When James is angry, he speaks slower, and his Southern drawl becomes more pronounced. He inserted several extra syllables within the phrase "sport-utility vehicle."

"James, I certainly didn't mean to disparage . . ."

"You may not see the many virtues of a Range Rover, but I—along with many other discerning people—do. What you call 'boxy,' we recognize as spacious. What you stigmatize as trucklike, we welcome as magnificently engineered robustness."

"You set her straight!" A masculine shout on my left was immediately countered by a feminine shout from my right: "Horsefeathers!"

Goodness! We've drawn a crowd.

Well, not quite a crowd. In reality, only two people—a man and a woman on their way to work—had stopped to watch the tall Southerner in sweatpants and bunny slippers converse in public with the still-damp Brit wrapped in an oversized bathrobe.

James began to talk to the bystanders.

"I don't know why," he said to the man, "but some women don't appreciate the virtues of a fine sport-utility vehicle."

"I'll tell you why," the woman shouted. "SUVs are big, clunky gas guzzlers."

"Lots of *other* women love their SUVs," the man shot back. "There must be ten sport-utes parked on Magothy Street. Who do you think drives them?"

I called to James again: "Please come inside, James."

He ignored me and spoke once more to the man: "I even acknowledge that I contributed to the loss of my Range Rover. I was foolish to leave it exposed and vulnerable on the streets of this miserable city."

The woman took umbrage at James's rash remark. "Hey! Wait a minute, buster! Ryde is a lovely city. Everyone parks on the street."

"Not *everyone!*" James inhaled deeply. "Shrewd people own garages. Those lucky citizens don't need to park their SUVs on Magothy Street."

"Hardly any of the townhouses on Magothy Street have garages."

"Exactly my point," James gestured wildly. "We deserve better than a crime-ridden neighborhood with inadequate on-the-street parking. We *deserve* a garage. We can certainly afford a garage."

The woman booed; the man cheered.

I ignored both my bare feet and flapping bathrobe and dashed to his side.

"James, I feel truly wretched about your car. However, neither of us is appropriately dressed to be standing in the roadway." I tugged on his arm, but he stood firm—peering first up and then down the street like some sort of human radar.

"Do you think a kid might have taken my Range Rover for a joy ride, then abandoned it nearby?" he asked.

"Why not? Anything is possible." I tried to sound optimistic as I tugged harder. "If your car has been abandoned, the coppers will find it quickly. Let's go inside and call them."

James nodded and took my hand. The crowd of two dispersed. I felt a guilty pleasure to see the man and the woman exchange nasty glances before they went their separate ways.

We made our way back to Hunnechurch Manor and were about to step inside when a familiar voice said, "Those are the most laid-back 'casual Friday' outfits I've ever seen."

David Friendly strode toward us, a wholly self-satisfied smirk on his face.

"I found a bunch of stuff about Dennis Grant in our central research archives and made you copies." He held up a thick manila envelope. "I decided to drop them off before you guys left for work. But I guess you have other plans for today—something that involves marching around Ryde in scanty clothing?"

Before James or I could answer, David spotted the empty parking space that had previously held the Range Rover. "Wouldn't you know it? There's a full-size parking space on Magothy Street directly across from your house." He made a face. "I parked two whole blocks away."

I peered at James and wondered how he would react to David's inadvertent gaffe. Fortunately, James had recovered his senses of proportion and humor. He started to laugh. Naturally I joined in. In seconds, the pair of us were gasping for breath and wiping away tears of merriment with the lapels of my bathrobe.

All the while David gaped at us as if we had lost our minds.

The spate of laughing had a marvelous effect on me. I felt joyous, utterly blissful, for the first time since Kelly the Shark handed me that blasted piece of paper.

═══════════

We told David about the vanished Range Rover. He immediately volunteered to cook breakfast while James showered and I got dressed. David shouted relevant tidbits of information up the staircase as he labored in our kitchen:

"Car theft is the fastest-growing major crime in Ryde. Last year more than three hundred cars and light trucks were stolen. A decade ago, back when I covered the police beat once in a while, the total was less than a hundred."

"Only a third of stolen vehicles are recovered intact."

"The cops think that many of the unrecovered cars—particularly the luxury models—are shipped to South America."

"The rest are probably stripped down for parts."

"More than half of the people who report stolen cars to the police don't know their own license plate numbers."

"A lot of people still leave their keys in the ignition or leave their cars unlocked. Not that it matters much—a good thief can get into a locked car in seconds."

When I finally joined David in the kitchen, I found him beating eggs.

"You make it sound hopeless," I said.

"'Fraid so. The Range Rover is gone for good. It was probably stolen to order." David poured the beaten eggs into a buttered frying pan, then rained down salt and pepper. "Did you call the police?"

"James did five minutes ago. They advised him to file an official report, then call our insurance agent."

"That's police-speak for *hasta la vista*, Rover!" David commenced to scramble the eggs with a whisk. "By the way, your tea should be fully brewed about now."

"Bless you!" I moved swiftly to the teapot on the table, poured myself a steaming cuppa, and said, "I wish we had *one* happy insight about car thievery to offer James. He was quite attached to that blessed SUV."

"You want happy? How about this: your new hubby has a fresh opportunity to go car shopping, which guys love to do. He even gets the chance to choose a more interesting color. I never did care for British racing green. A Range Rover looks much spiffier in dark blue."

While he's at it, maybe James will opt for a more sensible vehicle. Something smaller and less pretentious.

Did we really need a vehicle that was so big, so fancy, and so expensive—and such a choice target for car thieves? I hadn't tried especially hard to dissuade him a few months earlier. Perhaps I now had a fresh opportunity as well to encourage a change of heart.

James descended, his cheeks clean shaven, his shirt and tie coordinated, his countenance full of concern. "Can I use your car today?" he asked. "I have to drive to the Ryde police station, then to a late-morning meeting in Baltimore, and finally to an afternoon get-together in Columbia." He sighed gently. "Oh yeah, I guess I also have to arrange for a long-term rental car."

"The Beetle is yours," I said. "I'll ask Gloria to bring me home this afternoon."

"And I will be delighted to convey you to your office after breakfast," David said, with a wave of his whisk, "which, by the way, is ready."

James thanked God for our food; I helped David serve it. We ate quickly in relative silence—until I remembered why David had paid us a visit that morning.

"What did you dig up on Dennis Grant?" I said eagerly.

My enthusiasm surprised James; he gave me an odd look.

Rats! I had sounded just like a rebellious client who decided to conduct a clandestine investigation despite her lawyer's crystal-clear instructions to the contrary.

I tried to backpedal: "I mean, *why* did you search for stuff about Dennis Grant?"

David's face brightened. "Well, I've been kinda curious about your Mr. Grant ever since I read Hardesty's legal paperwork. I thought it strange that a man who switched companies would agree to support a lawsuit against you. I mean, what's in it for him?"

"That's a fascinating question, isn't it, James?"

The look on James's face didn't soften. I could almost see him thinking: *What is Pippa up to? And why?*

David went on: "I didn't expect to find much when I browsed through our electronic database, but I was wrong. We named Dennis Grant in six articles during the past two years. That surprised me, so I dug a little deeper. Dennis Grant was the subject of fifteen different news releases in our files—including nine releases that were issued by Hardesty Software. During the past year alone, we received more puffery about Grant, a backroom speechwriter, than about Mitch Hardesty, the chairman of the company. It makes you wonder if Dennis has a personal public relations advisor."

I bit my tongue; I'd had the same thought the day before.

David reached for the manila envelope he'd shown us earlier. "I made copies of the releases, just in case you might find them useful."

Regrettably, David slid the envelope directly in front of me. James instantly snatched it off the table. He might have been taking matches away from a child.

"Thank you, David," James said, "I'll give these documents to Pippa's lawyer this morning. He's taken complete charge of the investigation of Dennis Grant. Pippa and I have both promised not to poke around in the weeds because we don't want to accidentally damage the defense."

David shrugged. "Like I said, they're just a batch of recent news releases that say nice things about Dennis Grant. Do with them what you will."

A chirping sound from the living room made our heads turn in unison.

"It sounds like your parakeet has laryngitis," David said with a snicker.

"It's my cell phone, silly. Gloria is probably checking in." I stood up. "Pour me another cup of tea. I shall return."

But it wasn't Gloria. When I pushed the *Talk* button, a man on the other end said, without preamble, "Can you talk now? I have a proposition for you."

Dennis Grant!

I cupped my hand around the bottom of my cell phone and said softly, "What sort of proposition, Dennis?"

"You said that you wanted to chat with me. OK, I'll give you ten minutes, but there's a condition: I need you to return the speech drafts I sent you back in February." He took a breath, then added, "You still have them, don't you?"

My mind raced to connect the dots. In February Dennis had given me a handful of recent speeches as samples of his work. I'd forwarded copies to Militet along with his résumé. But now, months later, Dennis unexpectedly asked for them back. Why? Were the speeches somehow connected to the lawsuit? Would returning them to Dennis impact my case?

James was only twenty feet away. He might know the answers, but I couldn't ask for his advice: Without doubt he would grab the phone and hang up on Dennis. I tried to analyze the situation. If Dennis had called me a month earlier, I'd have returned his speeches immediately. What would I lose now by doing what Dennis asked?

Make a decision, Pippa. Say something.

I decided to begin at the beginning. "About a month ago we shredded the papers you brought to me."

"My drafts are gone?" I heard panic in Dennis's voice.

"No. We scanned the paper versions and made electronic files. I can print new paper copies for you."

"Fantastic! Copies of the drafts are fine. Let's meet as soon as possible. How about tomorrow?"

You want to meet him. You have to!

Playing coy seemed senseless. "Tomorrow it is," I said. "Do you have a location in mind? I'd prefer someplace inconspicuous."

"I go shopping every Saturday morning at Bombay Spices & Rices, the Indian food store on Hampton Lane."

"I know where it is."

"Good. We can have a chance meeting in the chutney aisle."

"When?"

"Ten-fifteen."

I hesitated. Why did I feel so uncomfortable agreeing to Dennis's request?

He pressed on: "You give me my speeches; I talk to you. Do we have a deal?"

I had no choice; I needed to find out why Dennis had lied to Mitch Hardesty.

"We have a deal. Bombay Spices & Rices. Tomorrow at ten-fifteen."

I switched off my cell phone and went back to the kitchen.

James stood waiting for me with a good-bye kiss. "I have a busy day planned," he said. "Expect me when you see me this evening."

I watched him leave, knowing all the while that I should run after him and tell the truth about Dennis Grant's phone call. I chose instead to remain in the kitchen and help David clear away the breakfast dishes. My excuse? None! I was merely irked to see James carry off David's packet of news releases.

"What's wrong?" David asked me as I stacked the last of the plates in the dishwasher.

"Why do you suppose anything is wrong?"

"I've been your friend long enough to know that look. Something's bothering you—and I don't think it's a stolen Range Rover."

It would have been easy to tell David a fib, but I'd done enough hedging and evading for one morning. A long moment passed while I pumped up the courage to be truthful. "I don't want to go to my office this morning. Take me to yours."

"To the *Ryde Reporter?* Why?"

"Two reasons. First, so that you can crank out another set of the news releases you so cleverly discovered. Second, so that I can browse in your archives for any other available crumbs of information about Dennis Grant."

David's brows drew downward into a fretful scowl. "*Tilt!* The last place I want to be is squashed between Pippa Hunnechurch and James Huston. My reportorial nose tells me that you are conducting the investigation your husband thinks you're not."

"I don't have a choice, David. Scratch that—*we* don't have a choice, because I really need your help."

"You do?"

I nodded. "I need a knight in shining armor who happens to work for a newspaper."

David smiled. "What else is new?"

I gave him a massive hug.

```
┌─────────────────────────────────┐
│          Chapter Six            │
└─────────────────────────────────┘
```

THE DETERMINED CLATTER OF HEAVY RAIN hitting our windows tempted me to cancel my meeting with Dennis Grant. I looked outside at a steady downpour that I knew would go on all morning. It was the perfect sort of soggy Saturday to curl up in an easy chair, sip tea, and read a mystery novel.

I didn't give in to temptation, more's the pity, and began the day by telling James another fib.

"Since you plan to spend the a.m. browsing for a new vehicle," I said, with a straight face, "I shall visit my office and tie up a few loose ends. You may have the Beetle again today if you drop me off at the start of your car trek."

"That's the best offer I've had all morning," James said as he folded the automotive section from the *Baltimore Sun* into a pocket-sized pamphlet. "I'll even pick you up when you're done toiling."

"Then we can go food shopping together. There's nothing in the fridge for dinner."

"Oooh! I love it when you talk domestic."

We left Hunnechurch Manor a few minutes before nine. James pulled into the bus stop in front of the restored leather warehouse. "Door-to-door service, Milady." He leaned over and kissed my cheek. I kissed him back, feeling exceedingly guilty, but also annoyed that James's self-righteous attitude made it necessary for me to skulk around behind his back. My investigation would be prudent and circumspect; the information that Gloria and I quietly gathered might help Daniel Harris build a better case for the defense.

Consider the intriguing fact I'd unearthed during my visit to the *Ryde Reporter* the day before. David had gone to the copying machine to duplicate the news releases about Dennis Grant; I sat in David's office using his desktop computer as a terminal to access the newspaper's electronic morgue. I quickly found the six articles that David had mentioned and verified that Gloria had retrieved them all during her search of media Web sites. And then I noticed another icon on the screen: *Noneditorial Search.* I shifted the cursor and clicked the mouse button.

The screen changed colors and I learned that *Dennis Grant, Algonquin House, Ryde, Maryland,* had purchased two "for sale by owner" ads in the real estate section. Once in November and again in early December of the previous year, he had offered his "lovely two-bedroom condominium apartment with spectacular river view."

My first thought: *Did Dennis have as nice a view of the Magothy as James?*

My second thought: *Hold on a minute! Why would a happily employed speechwriter want to sell his condo? Could it be that Dennis Grant had been preparing months earlier to move to another city?*

I tried to recall our initial encounter in February. Had we discussed the possibility of relocation? It would have been a natural topic of conversation. Most speechwriters are employed in the headquarters of major corporations—the kind based in New York City, Chicago, and Los Angeles. Finding Dennis a better job in Ryde had been an extraordinary piece of luck. The two ads didn't represent a "smoking gun" in

Dennis's hand, but they suggested that he had leaving on his mind long before I allegedly put it there.

Was it likely that Daniel Harris—who, according to James, had "taken complete charge of the investigation"—would have discovered the two ads? Not at all! This made it essential that my private investigation also move forward.

Gloria was waiting for me in our office. On the right side of her desk, neatly stacked, sat copies of the speeches I'd promised Dennis Grant. On the left side, in an untidy heap, were several items of miniature electronic equipment. She had a frown on her face.

"Is something amiss?" I asked.

"The weather. You're wearing a raincoat today. Tightly woven fabrics block sound. I can't decide which microphone will work best."

"I can leave my raincoat here."

She shook her head. "I don't know how Dennis thinks or if he's worried about you being wired for sound. But if I saw you coatless in the middle of a monsoon, my alarm bells would certainly go off."

She stared at the high-tech jumble for a while, then began to nod. "I've got a great idea. I'll pin a directional microphone inside your sleeve and run the leads to a microcassette recorder. It should do the job—as long as you keep your arm pointed in the general direction of his face." She held out her hand. "Give me your raincoat."

Having nothing more productive to accomplish while Gloria fed wires through my decades-old Burberry, I reread the speeches that Dennis had written.

The first two were presentations to Wall Street financial analysts. I thought them boring and overblown—full of platitudes, hyperbole, and fluffy self-praise that extolled the abundant virtues of Hardesty's software.

Speeches three and four were aimed at Hardesty's employees. They overflowed with sports clichés: "We need to keep our eye on the ball." "We must hold the line on spending." "We play in the major league of software companies." "Winning in the competitive marketplace isn't the important thing; it's the only thing!"

Please don't consider my reaction to these speeches as criticism of Dennis Grant's ability as a speechwriter. Dennis wrote to please Mitch Hardesty, an overblown exaggerator who liked to talk in clichés. One might say that Dennis used his skills to make the best of a bad situation.

I'd all but decided to ignore the fifth speech, the speech on the bottom of the stack, until the title caught my eye: Draft Remarks to the Hardesty Board of Directors about a Potential Acquisition. The date was January 16. Bold letters at the bottom of the first page proclaimed: **Hardesty Software Corporation Proprietary Information—Not for Public Release**

Blimey! Why do I have Hardesty company secrets in my files?

And then I remembered. Dennis had given me a copy of the speech along with a warning: "You asked to see samples of the different kinds of speeches I write. Well, a lot of my stuff includes proprietary data. I don't mind showing this draft to you, but please don't send it to another company"—he had laughed—"especially a competitor."

It was a two-page speech—perhaps six hundred words long—that reviewed Hardesty's dealings with a small, improbably named software company in West Virginia: the Mayberry Software Manufactory. I scanned the speech swiftly and stopped to read the last paragraph at the very bottom of the second page.

"In closing, let me review our actions. We looked at the ability of Mayberry's products to complement our product lines. . . . We investigated financing options. . . . And we performed a thorough due diligence examination of the Mayberry Software Manufactory with an eye towards acquiring the company. Our decision: go."

Hooray! No clichés, no puffery. A speech that actually might be worth listening to.

I put the five speeches into a rainproof yellow plastic file envelope.

"How are you coming?" I asked Gloria.

"I'm done routing the wires. The next step is to get you dressed."

Gloria helped me slip the Burberry on, first left sleeve, then right. "The microphone is attached to the seam of the sleeve, near the middle of your right forearm—feel it?" She pressed up on the sleeve. I could feel a small, cylindrical object touch the bottom of my forearm.

"Microphone. Check!" I said.

"The trick is to bend your right arm slightly. That will keep the bottom of the sleeve away from your arm. The microphone will do the rest; it's powerful enough to hear a fly buzz in Baltimore."

"Arm slightly bent. Check!"

"Move your right arm around." Gloria stood back to study her handiwork. "Good! I can't see the microphone at all."

"How do I work the recorder?"

"You don't have to do a thing. The recorder started operating as soon as I connected the microphone. It's recording right now. The mike will capture everything that happens around you for the next ninety minutes."

"Where is the recorder?"

"Deep inside your right pocket."

I began to reach into my right pocket; Gloria slapped my hand.

"Don't touch my recorder!"

"Hang on! How did you get the wires into the pocket?"

"Through a small hole in the fabric, naturally."

"You punched a hole in the lining of my vintage Burberry?"

"Suck it up, Pippa. It's almost ten o'clock."

━━━━━━━━━

We climbed into Gloria's tall four-wheel drive Dodge pickup truck and headed south on Ryde High Street. She let me out a block north of Hampton Lane. My plan was to look damp when I met Dennis. I had a vague idea that he would be more likely to talk frankly if I appeared faintly piteous.

"Happy hunting," she said, with a wave.

The damp look was easy to achieve. Windblown rain soared underneath my raised umbrella and found its way inside my raincoat and down my neck. By the time I'd reached The Punjab restaurant on the corner of High and Hampton, my hair was limp.

I hung a left turn into Hampton Lane and picked my way around the surprisingly deep puddles in the sidewalk. Many of the antique paving blocks had sunk into the ground; the unevenness that seemed charming in fair weather became a minefield of spatters on a day like this. I cheerfully admit that the wet clouds did have a silver lining: this normally busy corner of Ryde was all but deserted. No friends—and no lawyers—were present to see me arrive for my meeting with Dennis Grant.

I pulled open the front door of Bombay Spices & Rices and stepped into a festival of potent aromas that seemed even more pungent that day because of the heavy humidity in the air. The shop was only a few years old, but it had been modeled after a real grocery in New Delhi. I suspected that no expense had been spared to create a cramped, dark interior.

I let my eyes adjust to the dim lighting and looked around for Dennis. I didn't see him and for a brief moment wondered if he'd had a change of heart. Not meeting with me would be the sensible thing to do. Blanchette & Ross, Attorneys at Law, must have warned him to treat me like a first-century leper.

A voice behind me said, "I wasn't sure you would show up."

I spun around. There was Dennis Grant virtually glowing in a fluorescent orange rain suit. I realized that he must have bicycled to the shop in the rain.

"You're hard to miss," I said. "But in truth I didn't see you."

"I've been waiting for you in the back." He added, "Near the chutney."

"I thought you were joking about the chutney aisle."

Dennis was tall, fine featured, solidly built—the kind of man overly confident in his good looks. He studied me for several seconds, probably surprised by my obvious lack of adoration. His gaze eventually moved to the yellow plastic envelope tucked under my left arm. "Are those my speech drafts?"

"All five of them."

He reached for the envelope; I stepped backwards.

"Not so fast, Dennis," I said. "You'll get your speeches after I have my ten minutes of talk." I lifted my right arm slightly as Gloria had instructed. Dennis didn't seem to notice.

"Go for it," he said.

"Let me start, Dennis, by emphasizing that I am wholly bewildered by the *story*"—I stressed the word—"that you apparently told the lawyers who represent Hardesty Software. We both know that you came to see me first, yet you claim that I recruited you."

He made a disparaging gesture. "Who cares what I told those bozo lawyers? I tell one story; you tell another. We cancel each other out. This lawsuit is nothing but bluster and posturing. Mitch Hardesty knows he can't beat you. He's just pulling your chain."

Had the shop been well lit, Dennis would have seen my eyes flare in fury. For a split second I wanted to scream at him. But then, surprisingly, I recalled the verse from Proverbs we had studied in my last small group meeting: "A gentle answer turns away wrath, but a harsh word stirs up anger."

I forced myself to speak slowly and gently. "That may be the case, Dennis. If so, my chain is being pulled because of the story you told. Don't you understand that my lawyer will do his best to discredit your story? And that your lawyer will do his best to prove that I am a liar? We will both be ground up like sausages before this case is finished."

"I'm trembling with fear. *Not!*"

"That's where we're different. I am truly afraid of the damage this lawsuit might do to my consultancy. That's why I hope you will tell me *why* you claim that I recruited you away from Hardesty."

"I don't have to tell you anything. Give me my drafts, and we'll call it a day."

"Dennis, you came to me in February and asked for my help. I took you on as a candidate and found you an excellent job. I treated you honorably. I deserve the truth."

"The truth? What *is* the truth? Maybe you didn't beg for my résumé, but you sure took it fast enough when I showed up at your office."

I struggled to hide the burst of excitement I felt. Had the recorder captured his words? Did they represent a sufficient admission that he had lied?

Probably not, I decided. Dennis would insist that he brought the résumé to my office at my request. We needed a more definitive statement. But how could I encourage him to make one?

Dennis seemed amused by my silence; he began to chuckle. "I'll make you a promise. In a few days, Mitch Hardesty will forget all about suing Pippa Hunnechurch & Associates. He has much bigger problems than you to worry about."

"What happens in a few days?"

"I become his hero."

"How?"

"By showing what happens when you get sloppy with corporate speech drafts."

"I have no idea what you are talking about."

"Why would you? You're not as smart as me." He chuckled again. "For that matter, neither is Mitch Hardesty. But he'll thank me for pinpointing the treachery that threatens to tear apart his company. I'll bet that he offers me my old job back. Who knows? I may even accept." Dennis pointed to the yellow plastic file envelope. "I want my drafts— *now!*"

I should have slapped him across his face with the envelope, but once again I controlled my temper. I handed over the documents without a grumble.

"This is everything I gave you?" he asked.

I nodded. "Everything."

Dennis opened the envelope and paged through the speeches. He examined the last speech in the stack twice, then a third time.

"Yes! A widow strikes again!" He threw back his head and half shouted, "I love being right!"

The two other people in the shop—the chubby proprietor and a customer wearing a colorful sari—looked our way. Dennis seemed delighted with the attention. I felt self-conscious to be seen talking with such a loud-mouthed boor.

"I'm curious," I said. "Why do you need those copies? Surely you have the original speeches."

He replied with a withering scowl. "You really don't know squat about speechwriting, do you? You keep repeating the word 'speeches.' I keep correcting you. A speech occurs when a live person stands up and starts talking. I don't make speeches; I put words on paper. Get it? I write speech *drafts*. D-R-A-F-T-S."

I repeated: "You write drafts."

"Sometimes the speaker changes the words I write—usually for the worse. That's not my problem if he does. My job ends when I write the best possible draft. Is that simple enough for you to understand?"

I wasn't in a mood to be patronized. "I quite understand, Dennis." I could hear the edge in my own intonation. "A speech as spoken may be different from the speech draft as written."

"Hooray. The lady from England has learned how to use a new English word."

Dennis had finally pushed me to my breaking point.

"You arrogant clod!" I shouted. "You supercilious twit! How dare you mock me? I look forward to our day in court. I will enjoy watching my attorney eviscerate you in public."

"Give me a break! You came here hat in hand today because you're terrified of what could happen to you if the case went to trial. Ken Blanchette told me that your lawyer is a pussycat who will fold like a house of cards and settle the first chance he gets."

"Drivel! Twaddle!"

Dennis's response was a malevolent grin. "The real problem with consultants is that they don't know how to listen. Didn't I tell you earlier that there won't be a trial?" He slapped the plastic envelope full of drafts. "Don't worry your pretty little head. I'm going to make the nasty situation all better for you."

I needed to get outside; I needed to get away from Dennis Grant. I flung myself at the door, not even stopping to raise my umbrella.

I didn't see the first puddle. I stepped into it up to my ankle. I didn't care about the second or third. Gloria was waiting for me in a parking garage on Ryde High Street. I opted to take the most direct route—splashes or not.

How did that hateful ignoramus bamboozle you in February?

I pride myself on being a good judge of character. One has to be in my business because I vouch for my candidates. Somehow I had let Dennis Grant slip through my filter. I looked back over my shoulder at Dennis climbing on his bicycle. I muttered a string of curses—half directed at him, half at my own stupidity.

I heard an engine growl behind me. I'm not an expert, but I recognized it as the deep roar of a powerful engine. I remember thinking that the harsh noise was out of place because the falling rain was the predominant source of sound in Hampton Lane that morning. I also remember deciding that the roar wasn't interesting enough to make me look behind again.

A moment later I heard a deep thud. A clatter of metal. Breaking glass.

I turned in time to see a dark-colored vehicle in the distance make a sharp right turn. And then I noticed a fluorescent orange heap on the sidewalk perhaps two blocks away. My mind made sense of what I had heard and seen.

A hit-and-run accident.

Dennis Grant.

I began to jog down Hampton Lane. A woman screamed. Two men appeared next to the orange heap.

In seconds I was close enough to see that the jumper of Dennis's orange rain suit was sprinkled with red and that his head was bleeding.

More people came out onto Hampton Lane. No one seemed to care about the rain. A man covered Dennis with a poncho; I heard him place a 911 call on his cell phone. Another man put a folded jacket under Dennis's head.

"We better not do anything else," he said. "This guy is really badly injured."

I knelt down and shielded Dennis with my open umbrella. His eyes were closed; his face had lost all its color—except for the red streaks that trickled down his cheeks.

I looked around and took my bearings. We were in front of the Ryde Card and Party Store. Dennis's bicycle had smashed its front window and was lying—bent askew—atop a counter inside the shop.

I looked down at Dennis. He was motionless, lifeless, legs at odd angles. I wondered if he was dying. Or dead.

I didn't know that the ambulance had arrived until I felt my umbrella gently tugged aside. I saw three paramedics sloshing toward us, pushing a half-folded gurney that was laden with large red cases marked with white crosses. I stood up and moved out of their way.

I heard a woman say, "It's a good sign when they bring all their medical paraphernalia. They obviously think they can keep him alive." I heard a man say: "That woman in the tan raincoat was one of the first people I saw after the accident. Maybe she's a witness?"

Someone tapped my arm. I glanced around at an outrageously young police officer.

"Did you see what happened, ma'am?" he asked.

"A hit-and-run," I said. "I heard it more than I saw it."

A second copper appeared. "It's coming down in buckets," he said to his young colleague. "Why take witness statements on a wet street when Ryde Police Headquarters is less than a mile away? Let the detectives handle it."

The first copper nodded, then turned back to me. "You'll be more comfortable at headquarters, ma'am. My car is parked at the curb."

"A splendid idea—but let me make a cell phone call first."

I squeezed my umbrella's handle between my arm and my body so that I had two hands available to dial my cell phone. I called Gloria.

"Where are you?" she asked, snappishly. "I've been sitting in this damp garage for half an hour. You were supposed to have a ten-minute meeting with Dennis."

"There's no need for you to wait any longer. I'm off to Ryde Police Headquarters."

"You're *what?*"

I told Gloria about the hit-and-run. "Dennis is being placed in an ambulance, as we speak. I'm going to the *nick* to make a statement."

"I'll pray for him," she said, softly.

"A good idea that! And while you're at it, pray for me. I have no idea how I can explain my presence on Hampton Lane this morning."

Gloria replied with a curt, "I see."

"And I have an even more pressing problem. How will the coppers react if they discover that I'm wearing a 'wire' that managed to record an argument with the hit-and-run victim a minute or so before he was run down?"

"That's an easy problem to solve—ditch the recorder."

I didn't consider it noteworthy that Gloria hung up first—and rather abruptly.

Chapter Seven

I DON'T LIKE RIDING in police cars—not even in the front seat with an affable police officer who is determined to be sensitive and caring. I must have looked a sight to him: rain soaked, stunned by what I'd seen, and apprehensive to be on my way to Ryde Police Headquarters. He smiled benevolently and drove slowly while my mind ticked over at high speed.

The central nick is not a friendly place.

Three years earlier I'd spent several bothersome hours at the modern glass-and-steel structure—a combination constabulary and jail—that nestles behind Ryde's nineteenth-century town hall, first being fingerprinted and then interrogated by a hard-nosed detective—but that's another story.

You have no reason to fear the coppers today. You are merely a cooperative witness to a freak accident. However, since you don't plan to share the recording of Dennis Grant with them, you should definitely do something about the cassette recorder connected to a microphone inside your sleeve.

Slowly, discreetly, I slipped my hand into the right side pocket of my sodden Burberry and took hold of the miniature recorder. It felt like a candy bar with a wire attached to one end. I sensed minute vibrations of a motor turning deep inside. I slid my fingertips along the edge of the case until they reached the plug attached to the microphone cable. I tugged the plug loose from the recorder. The vibrations stopped.

I palmed the recorder and slowly, discreetly, brought my hand out of my pocket. I casually reached into a side compartment of my handbag and retrieved a packet of tissues. While there, I stealthily let the recorder fall into the bottom of my handbag—a vast black hole where all things disappear. I once spent five minutes finding car keys I accidentally dropped inside.

What about the microphone, Pippa?

The mike itself was out of sight, but the cable would certainly be visible if I chose to doff my damp mackintosh. Perhaps I could pull the whole contrivance loose? I reached back into my pocket and gently tugged on the plug end of the cable. Nothing moved—true to her word, Gloria had pinned the microphone and cable in place. I decided to leave well enough alone. Furthermore, it's hardly a crime to wire oneself for sound.

We arrived at the front entrance. "You seem happier," the young officer said as he pushed the button that unlocked my door.

"Indeed I am." I came up with a feeble smile. "Thank you for the ride. To whom do I report?"

"Ask for Detective King."

I recognized the aging desk copper sitting behind the Information window. His "bedside manner" hadn't improved during the three years since I'd last seen him. "Detective King is on the second floor," he said. He proffered a careless wave toward the staircase behind me. "Turn left at the top, then halfway down the corridor." He added, "If you want, you can use the coat rack and an umbrella stand in the lobby."

I declined his gracious invitation to stow my Burberry and brolly. Instead, I doubled the waterlogged raincoat over my right arm, keeping the microphone cable hidden in the folds, and hooked my umbrella over my wrist. I made for the staircase.

A man and a woman I'd seen on Hampton Lane were sitting on a wooden bench in the corridor. The woman—fiftyish, with brassy red hair—spotted the inquiring look on my face.

"You're in the right place, *hon*," she said with an unalloyed Baltimore accent, "but Detective King isn't here yet. That's her office." She pointed to a glass-paneled door. An engraved plastic sign read: Det. Cheryl King, Vehicular Crimes Unit.

The man—in his sixties, wearing an aqua-tinted Hawaiian shirt and tan shorts—slid closer to the woman to make room on the bench for me. Then he said to the woman, "I still say I saw a big, black sedan. Maybe a Cadillac limousine—or a hearse."

"We're not supposed to discuss the details," she said. "You heard the cop who drove us here. If we talk about what we saw, we'll lose our in-dividual recollections."

"Yeah—right! Like I'm gonna forget an accident that I watched hap-pen fifteen minutes ago."

"Well, you're wrong about what you think you saw. The vehicle in-volved was too tall to be a sedan. I think it was one of those large SUVs—and it may have been dark blue rather than black."

"No way! It was pure black. And there was something wrong with the muffler. That's why it was so noisy."

The woman leaned around the man and spoke to me. "What kind of vehicle do you think it was, *hon?*"

"I can't begin to guess," I said. "I merely caught a brief glimpse of the rear when it was two blocks away. I'm not very good at distin-guishing between types of American vehicles."

"You sound English."

"I am."

The man sniggered. "I bet there are tons of automobile accidents in England. You guys drive on the wrong side of the road."

❦

It was a statement made in jest, but it took my breath away. Ten years earlier a traffic accident in England had killed my then-husband Simon and my three-year-old daughter Peggy. A sun-blinded driver in a vintage Austin Mini had crossed to "the wrong side of the road" and struck our new Ford sedan head-on. I survived because Peggy wanted to be near her dad and I had agreed to ride in the back seat. My bodily injuries had healed completely, but my emotional wounds still remained vulnerable to innocent offhand gibes.

His smile faded; he seemed to realize that he had jolted me. But before he had the chance to ask me what was wrong, the woman knocked us both for a loop.

"What we witnessed wasn't an accident," she said in a commanding whisper. "Whoever hit that guy on the bicycle did it on purpose. I saw that big SUV peel out of Schooner Alley like it was on fire. It zoomed down Hampton Lane, picking up speed as it traveled. The driver didn't try to veer away—just hit the victim straight on. Didn't you see the remains of the bicycle inside the card shop? It got blasted through the window like a bullet."

"Do you really believe it was done on purpose?" the man asked, making no attempt to hide his surprise.

"Shhhh!" the woman hissed. "A cop's coming."

I glanced up. The young police officer who had been my chauffeur was walking toward us carrying three paper cups.

"Hot chocolate to help you dry out," he said. "Compliments of Detective King. She'll be up in a minute."

When he finished distributing the cups, I asked, "Do you have any news about the injured bicyclist?"

"Last I heard, his condition was critical. The docs were prepping him for surgery."

I grunted, not knowing what else to say.

The copper read my grunt as a sign of distress. "Yeah, I felt the same way when I saw the victim crumpled against the wall. It may take

awhile, but with your assistance we'll definitely nail the person responsible. Count on it!"

My mental alarm bell started ringing as the officer walked away.
Back at the scene he had used the word "accident." Now he spoke about
finding "the person responsible" in an unmistakably official tone.

I glanced at my bench mates. The Hawaiian-shirted man seemed
lost in thought; the redheaded woman had a full-of-herself smirk on
her face. My mind began to rev again:

You'll be much more involved than you first supposed.

Needless to say, I understood that hit-and-run is a felony in
Maryland—a serious crime under any circumstances. But I'd vaguely
assumed that the driver was a local soccer mom who panicked after an
unfortunate traffic accident. I supposed that the case would be wrapped
up in hours—with no help from me.

An intentional hit-and-run changes everything.

The attempted murder of a highly paid staffer at a major local corporation was sure to attract the media. There would be TV news cov-
erage. Police officers talking to reporters. Witnesses' names bandied
about in public.

James will find out you deceived him!

Daniel Harris will be furious!

Blanchette & Ross will figure out a way to use the meeting against you!

I slumped back against the bench feeling well and truly done for.

"Oops—watch your hot chocolate," the man said as I bobbled my
cup. I managed to straighten it before any hot chocolate spilled in
my lap.

The woman was still smirking. "Well, now we know where we
stand. The cops *need* our information."

"A pity I have so little to give them."

"Don't worry, *hon,*" she said, "I remember enough for the three of
us. I'm a wedding photographer; I have a terrific eye for detail." She
toasted me with her paper cup.

"Why me?" I murmured, wholly incensed at the unfairness of my situation. My goose was cooked even though I knew nothing that would assist the coppers with their inquiries.

Unless . . .

I perceived a glimmer of hope, a possible strategy. What if I were truthful but not obliging? I would share precisely what I heard and saw, but I would not volunteer any details of my meeting with Dennis Grant in Bombay Spices & Rices. After all, our noisy chat had absolutely no relevance to the *incident*. The coppers might see me as merely a routine pedestrian on Hampton Lane.

The man sitting next to me said, "Hey—this must be her."

A woman in a blue business suit, my height but more athletic, approached and said, "Good morning, I'm Detective Cheryl King."

The three of us stood up. I guessed that the detective was in her early thirties. She had the confident look of a fast-track professional destined for success.

"I'll try to do this as quickly as possible," she said, "but I prefer to interview eyewitnesses individually. Does anyone have an especially tight schedule today?"

I shrugged. What difference did it make when I got raked over the coals?

The redhead's reply endeared her to me forever. "You should talk to that woman first." She pointed at me. "She was way up the block when the victim was hit and didn't see much. There's no sense making her wait while I tell you my whole story."

Detective King looked at the man. He nodded his approval.

"Sounds like a plan," she said, and beckoned me to follow her.

Her small office featured the usual institutional green walls and black-and-white asphalt tile floor. She sat down behind a metal desk and pointed to the visitor's chair alongside. Her body language seemed friendly, aimed at putting me at ease. Good! I needed all the help in that realm I could get.

She asked for my name, address, age, occupation, and marital status, then jotted them down on a yellow pad. "The thing about an incident like this," she said, "is that you probably noticed lots more about the vehicle than your friend outside may think."

"Well, I know that I didn't see much. I was on the northern side of Hampton Lane about a block east of Ryde High Street. I heard the roar of an engine—then a thump. I turned around to see what happened. A vehicle was speeding away—and, oh yes, I saw the victim lying close to a building."

She scribbled several notes.

"Let's play a game," she said. "Close your eyes and try to visualize yourself on Ryde High Street. You're walking in the rain and you hear a thump. You turn. In the distance you see a vehicle racing off down the block. True or false."

"False. I saw the vehicle turn off Hampton Lane."

"A left turn or a right turn?"

"Definitely a right turn."

"Excellent! Visualize some more. The vehicle is making a right turn—giving you a great view of its right side. Is it a squat vehicle or a tall vehicle?"

"Tall."

"A long vehicle or a short vehicle?"

I thought about it. "Longer than a car."

"So it wasn't a car?"

I shifted in my chair. "Now that you mention it—it might have been a truck."

"Then we'll assume it was a truck. Did it have a license plate? You were too far away to read numbers, but knowing the color would be useful. Maryland license plates look white at a distance. Visualize the truck before it turned right. Was the plate white?"

I tried to remember. "I can't be sure, but the whole tail end of the vehicle seemed a solid color. Black, I think."

"Black it is! We'll assume that you saw a black truck. Some trucks don't have windows at the rear, some do. Did this truck have a back window?"

"Yes, I think it did."

"High or low?"

"High. Very high."

Detective King made more notes then peered at me. "So much for the long, tall, and black truck with the high rear window. Let's talk about the victim. You said that you spotted him lying close to a building? How is that possible? You were two blocks away at the time."

Yikes! A few simple questions and Bob's your uncle, she caught me in a discrepancy. How could I have known that the orange "lump" on the sidewalk was the victim?

Find an explanation other than you talked to a man in an orange suit two minutes earlier.

An essentially true answer popped into my head. "In fact, I didn't see the victim at first; I spotted a patch of bright orange on the sidewalk. A few seconds earlier I had glanced behind me—I don't recall why—and noticed a person in an orange rain suit climb aboard a bicycle. I put two and two together."

She nodded, then peered at me again—for what seemed an eternity. She finally said, "I won't need a formal statement from you at this time."

"You won't?" I heard myself squeak with blissful surprise.

"You've been helpful to me, but you're not a credible eyewitness. Defense attorneys usually take issue with the memory recall game we played. However,"—she gave me her business card—"please let me know if you remember anything else."

"I certainly will." I fought to keep a silly grin off my face. I could not have asked for a better outcome. I had been declared a nonwitness, a person of no interest to the police and no appeal to reporters.

"Do you need a ride home?" she asked.

"Thanks, but I think I'll walk."

"In the rain?"

I wagged my umbrella. "A little rain doesn't bother a Brit."

Especially a delighted Brit.

There's nothing like an unexpected reprieve to make one's spirits soar. I fled my inquisitor on wings of eagles.

Walking through the lashing rain lost its charm after navigating two puddle-dotted blocks. My shoes were soaked and my feet felt cold. Water squished around my toes with every soggy step I made. I took refuge in a gourmet coffee bar on Ryde High Street and used my cell phone to call Gloria. She didn't let me finish saying hello.

"Dennis Grant is the lead story on the radio news," she blurted. "He's in extremely grave condition, whatever that means, and the police have labeled the hit-and-run as a suspicious incident. They've asked for anyone who saw anything to contact them."

"I'm not surprised. The current crop of eyewitnesses leaves much to be desired." I described my bench mates at police headquarters and recounted my own interview with Detective King.

Gloria said nothing for several moments, then asked, rather crossly I thought, "Do you want me to pick you up?"

"No, it's gone past noon. I'll call James."

He answered on the fourth ring.

"I trust I didn't catch you in the midst of a test drive," I said.

"Nope, I'm in the Volkswagen, zipping along Romney Boulevard in the rain."

"Ah, my favorite therapeutic road." A thought struck me. "I've never seen any automobile dealerships in that corner of town."

Romney Boulevard is a charming two-lane road that curves and twists through some of the prettiest parts of Ryde. I've found that a drive the length of the Boulevard—convertible top down, speed somewhat above the limit—is a wholly reliable cure for a gloomy disposition.

James's voice became somber. "Did you hear about Dennis Grant?"

I gave James an ambiguous answer. "I just spoke to Gloria. She relayed the details as reported on the radio. A terrible tragedy—I have been praying for him."

"Where are you?" he asked.

"Sipping an overpriced cappuccino at the Ryde Coffee Café."

"I'll meet you outside in ten minutes. Buy me a double caffe latte to go." He added: "You know, I missed you this morning. Big time! I started to feel jealous of those 'loose ends' you needed to take care of."

I waited under the Café's canopy while a wave of guilt swept away the last of the jubilation I'd enjoyed with my coffee. In truth, I couldn't begin to catalog the many "ambiguous answers" I'd provided James in recent days. Deceiving my new husband was becoming easier with every telephone call.

What are you doing, Pippa? And where does it end?

Right on time, my blue Beetle convertible splashed to halt at the curb. I slid my folded umbrella behind the front seat, hopped in, and let James kiss my cheek.

The lies stop here! I told to myself. *Start with the truth about Dennis Grant.*

"Is everything OK?" he asked. "You look a little green around the gills?"

In for a penny, in for a pound.

"Undoubtedly, prison pallor—I spent much of the morning in the nick."

The Beetle's right front tire plowed through a puddle and sent a wall of water past my window.

"That's nice," James said.

"Pardon?"

"Sorry. The streets are tricky, and I was lost in thought. You were saying . . ."

My feeble joke had seemed a heaven-sent entrée to a *mea culpa*. But now I had lost my confessional momentum. Perhaps some small talk would get me back on track?

"What color is your new Range Rover?" I asked. "I've been told that blue is preferable to green."

He used his knees to steer the Beetle while he uncovered the sipping hole on his caffe latte. "I know you're going to laugh, but I'm having second thoughts about replacing the Rover. It's not the easiest car to park in my garage at the office."

"I won't laugh, but I reserve the right to say 'I told you so.'"

James let loose a surprisingly hearty guffaw. "I *love* your understated British humor."

That doesn't sound like the James Huston I married.

I glanced outside. We were still on Ryde High Street; James had driven past the right turn that leads to Hunnechurch Manor.

"It seems we're not going home," I said.

James took a deep breath. "I guess I have a confession to make." He took another breath. "I didn't go car shopping this morning."

"You didn't?"

A third breath. "I went house hunting."

"You looked at houses without telling me?"

"I didn't *look at* houses—I just drove past a few and got a little information about them. *Looking at* a house implies that I went inside. I figured that we'd go inside together."

"I am flabbergasted by your rhetorical hair-splitting!" The complaint had hardly left my lips when I realized that I was not the only creator of ambiguous answers in our household. If the gander can equivocate, why not the goose?

You have nothing to confess to James Lamar Huston.

James shrugged. "Well, I said what I did because I didn't want to upset you."

"*Well,* you did upset me."

"*Well*, we need a house big enough for the two of us."

"Our present home was designed for a family of seven."

"Architecture has advanced significantly in one hundred fifty years."

"Give me one good reason we need a bigger house." I wished that I could have withdrawn my reckless challenge the instant I hurled it at James.

He began his litany with a haughty, "My pleasure! I'll begin with the obvious: we need another bathroom for us and a downstairs loo for guests to use. We need a larger living room for entertaining. We need a full-size kitchen with a pantry and counter space for a few small appliances. I need a closet of my own and floor space for another chest of drawers. I'd love a home theater for our plasma TV screen and a practical location for our home exercise machine. We need a storage area to hold the furniture your mother sent. We need a guest bedroom. We need a place to put Winston. I need a proper home office—and so do you. And we need a garage for our cars. How many reasons is that?"

I stared silently out the side window for a while before my curiosity got the better of me. "Where did you *not* look at houses?"

"Founders' Woods."

"*Of course!* How silly of me to ask."

Founders' Woods was a posh gated community of oversized, overdecorated houses set on half-acre plots—a renowned locale for those who desired to live ostentatiously.

I closed my eyes until James urged me to open them by poking me in the ribs.

"Ouch!" I said.

"We're here!"

James steered the Beetle into a gatehouse complex that would have done any army base proud. He displayed a paper pass to a security guard who replied with a military salute and raised the traffic control barrier.

"Have you actually seen Founders' Woods?" James asked as we moved ahead along Admiral Hobart Strand.

"Indeed I have," I fibbed.

I yanked myself up in the seat. We were surrounded by enormous houses. To our left was "Tara." To our right "Mandalay." Farther down the road stood "Green Gables," then an old English manse that looked like "Penmarrick," and finally a castle, complete with a crenulated turret.

"This is ridiculous, James," I said. "We'd need *staff* if we were to buy one of these giants, which happily we could never afford to do."

He chuckled. "Not all the houses in Founders' Woods are mansions." He turned left on Sussex Lane. The houses became smaller and, though I was loath to admit it, more attractive.

James pulled up next to a nicely proportioned Cape Cod, painted Wedgewood blue, with a double garage. I could see a small greenhouse attached to the rear of the house and a swimming pool in the backyard. There were many large trees on the property and—*Rats!*—a discreet "For Sale" sign out front.

"This is my favorite," James said. "Four bedrooms, plus a library, plus a family room—at a price we can afford. A home like this is a fine investment."

"Hmm," I said. "It is a pretty house—even on a rainy day."

"If you have no objections, I'll call the realtor and schedule a visit."

I rubbed my brow. I had lots of objections. I hated the idea of abandoning Hunnechurch Manor. But, try as I might, I couldn't come up with a good reason not to look inside.

"Go ahead." I heaved a weighty sigh. "I promised to honor and obey."

Chapter Eight

YOU CAN BET THAT I felt sorry for myself when we arrived back home. I had been yelled at by Dennis Grant, interrogated by Cheryl King, blindsided by James Huston—and it was only a little past one p.m. The weather did nothing to cheer my glum mood: the hammering rain had given way to a dreary mist that made one feel damp to the core. Consequently, I was less than overjoyed to see Gloria's truck parked in front of Hunnechurch Manor and Gloria's face wearing a sour look.

What else can go wrong on one weekend day?

"We have to talk," she said. She glanced at James and added, "Alone!"

James fled inside as if he'd been poked by a high-voltage cattle prod.

"Shall I make us some coffee?" I asked hesitantly.

"Don't bother. I've got lots to do after I tell you off."

"You're mad at me?"

"Try *livid*."

"May one ask why?"

"A *human being* we both know, who also happens to be one of our firm's most successful candidates, was brutally attacked this morning. You were one of the first persons to become aware of it. Did you give his name to the prayer squad at church? Did you make an attempt to assist his family? Did you take serious action to lend *any* sort of helping hand?" Gloria wagged her head to punctuate her answers: "No! No! And no! And then, to cap off a really miserable performance, you seem proud of the fact that you are a rotten witness and can't help the police find the hit-and-run driver."

She stopped so that I could respond. When I didn't speak, Gloria attacked from a different angle. "I've spent the past two hours trying to understand why you acted this way. I've come up with only one explanation. Dennis's role in the lawsuit has made you so mad at him that you forgot about being a Christian." She gave me a painless poke in the solar plexus. "There! I've said my peace. Now you can fire me if you want."

She crossed her arms, set her jaw, and waited for me to respond.

Blimey! I thought. *Gloria is right. You have been a rotter through and through.*

I had been shocked to see Dennis injured, but I hadn't experienced much worry or anguish about him. I hadn't even included Dennis on my mental list of things that had spoiled my day. I tried to catalog my different emotions that morning. One of them—I had to admit—had been a sense of relief. If Dennis died, then surely the lawsuit would fade away—wouldn't it?

Gloria had hit the bull's-eye. I had let my reaction to what Dennis had done completely overwhelm my humanity—not to mention my Christianity. It shouldn't have made any difference in my thinking that the Dennis Grant I spoke to this morning was "less nice" than the Dennis I'd dealt with in February. But clearly it had.

You have no excuses for your shoddy behavior.

I said to Gloria, "I won't fire you if you give me a big hug. I feel abysmal."

She lifted me off my feet.

"It's tough to love one's enemies," I said.

"Hey, it's your decision, but you might try putting some trust in God. I've heard that he helps people get through tough situations when they ask him. If I remember right, it's called praying."

Prayer! The notion hadn't entered my mind.

"Point well-taken," I said.

As I watched her big white pickup drive away, I wondered, *What would I do differently if I numbered Dennis among my true friends?*

That's a no-brainer. You would try to visit him at the hospital.

I dug my cell phone out of my purse and rang James.

"Why the call?" he asked. "You're standing right outside our front door."

"Not for long. I'm off to Ryde General Hospital to . . ." I hesitated.

James finished my thought: "To visit Dennis Grant."

"Precisely!"

I waited for an argument. After all, our lawyer had told me to stay away from him.

"Do you want me to come along?" he asked.

Bravo James!

"Perhaps next time."

"What about lunch? I've made each of us a personal pizza."

"Keep mine warm. I shan't be long."

I drove to the hospital and parked in the adjacent visitors' garage.

The woman manning the visitors' desk in the lobby offered an efficient, "May I help you?"

"I've come to visit Mr. Dennis Grant," I said. "G-R-A-N-T. An ambulance conveyed him to the hospital this morning."

She typed on her keyboard, squinted at her monitor, then looked up at me. "Dennis Grant was admitted to our trauma unit. Are you a relative?"

"No, I am a—*ah*—business colleague."

"Only family visitors are allowed in the trauma center."

"I am a *close* business colleague."

"Sorry. No exceptions."

"What is his condition?"

"I can't tell you anything more." Her eyes narrowed suspiciously. "If you are a reporter, you can get an authorized statement at our public relations office."

The words rang with finality. I knew that arguing with her would be futile. Nonetheless, I was about to try when I heard a familiar voice call my name. "Pippa? Is that you?"

I spun around. Joyce Friendly, in her operating room garb, waved at me from across the lobby. I dashed to her side.

"Why is the queen of the night shift here during the day?" I asked.

"We swap shifts during vacation season. This week I am working days. What brings you to Ryde General?"

"A patient named Dennis Grant. He was struck by a vehicle on Hampton Lane."

"Oh, yeah—the head injury that came in about eleven-fifteen."

"Dennis is the speechwriter who brought so much excitement to my life."

Joyce gave me an astonished look. "The speechwriter in your lawsuit?"

"The very same. He is in the trauma center. I'd like to know how he's doing—perhaps even visit him. Your receptionist told me to get lost."

Joyce nodded sagely. "Only next of kin—or significant others—are allowed in the trauma center. However . . ."

"However?" I repeated hopefully.

"I'll take you down to the trauma center waiting room. Let's see what I can wangle."

I followed her along a corridor, past a bored security guard, to the newest wing of Ryde General. The wall colors were welcoming pastels.

The floors had home-style carpeting rather than officelike asphalt tiles. The telephones at the nurses' station warbled rather than rang. Our journey ended in a cheerful visitors' lounge. The place felt friendly and hospitable because potted plants, tall book cases, and the occasional divider screen carved the room into a series of cozy seating areas.

"Stay put," she said. "I'll find out what I can."

I chose a comfortable lounge chair near an antique travel poster of a bucolic French country scene. The grass and rolling countryside made me think about the pretty Cape Cod on Sussex Lane. I had no doubts it would prove a perfect house with more than enough space for the two of us. But it would never be *my* house—not in the same way that Hunnechurch Manor had become *my* American dream. Why couldn't James understand the way I felt? He had never really given the townhouse a chance. A few minor inconveniences had clouded his judgment.

I looked through a row of potted plants and saw a woman I recognized sitting in the adjacent alcove. I needed a moment to attach a name to the semifamiliar face. Of course! Carol Ericsson, Hardesty's vice president of corporate communications. She had given top-level approval—the final executive sign-off—for the marketing writer I'd recruited during my brief, one-shot headhunting assignment at Hardesty. I'd met with her once, for perhaps fifteen minutes, when the search began. Our chat had been friendly and good-humored. She impressed me as a thoroughly competent professional.

Carol, an attractive redhead of perhaps forty, was staring off into space, outwardly lost in thought. Her face had the puffy look of recent crying. Her clothing—sweatshirt and slacks—was rumpled and her hair was tousled. I guessed that she'd left for the hospital in a hurry. Why not? She had worked with Dennis Grant for a year and a half and probably grew to respect him. Both were communicators; both reported directly to Mitch Hardesty.

I thought about joining her, then changed my mind. She didn't appear in the mood for chitchat with a near stranger. There was a copy of *National Geographic* on the low glass-topped table in front of me. I sank back into my chair and read about plant life in Antarctica.

Joyce returned with an ominous expression on her face. "Dennis Grant is in a profound coma," she said as she sat down opposite me. "He's not expected to come out of it anytime soon."

"I knew that he'd hit his head. I didn't realize how badly."

"He has a fractured skull." She touched the top of her head, toward the left side. "We know there's internal swelling, but head injuries are dreadfully hard to diagnose. There may be serious damage that the doctors can't see."

Joyce brought her hands together as if she were gripping a ball between them. "There's not much extra room inside a human skull. The brain is protected by a cushion of cerebrospinal fluid, but a really severe blow forces the brain to smash against the surface of the skull. The impact disrupts nerve cells and tears blood vessels. That's what happened to Dennis."

"Will he wake up?"

"That's the first question I asked," she said, with a shrug, "but no one was willing to commit to a prognosis yet. The original plan was to transport Dennis to the University of Maryland's Shock Trauma Center in Baltimore. They are the regional gurus on head injuries. But our team decided the risk of moving him is too high, so we borrowed a neurologist from Shock Trauma. She's examining him now."

"Poor Dennis."

"There's also an orthopedic surgeon working to stabilize his right leg. He suffered several compound fractures to his femur and fibula." She touched my right thigh and right shin. "He'll need a year of physical therapy once he heals."

"Assuming the doctors manage to sort out the damage to his head."

"This is a place of answered prayer. I've seen more miracles than I can count."

"Well, now I understand the no-visitors rule."

Joyce nodded. "They might let a close family member sit with Dennis—but no one else. Not until he wakes from the coma."

My gaze drifted to Carol Ericsson. She hadn't moved. *How*, I wondered, *had she outwitted the hospital's bureaucratic barriers?* Maybe she also had a friend in high places.

Joyce pulled my attention back. "Incidentally, Pippa, you look unusually pale today. I'm surprised, because you've told me a zillion times that rain is responsible for that fabulous English complexion of yours. On a day as wet as this you should be as pink as a baby's bottom."

"My lack of color is a simple matter of distress overcoming humidity. I was walking on Hampton Lane when a truck hit Dennis. I heard the sickening thud."

"My goodness! You're an eyewitness."

"*Earwitness,*" I corrected. "Unhappily, I had almost nothing of value to tell the police."

"You've been to the police station too? Lord, I'd be white as a sheet of copy paper."

I let myself sigh. "And then there's the whole business of Founders' Woods. James wants to move there. He has fallen in love with a spiffy four-bedroom house."

Her eyes lit up. "Wow! That's—what's the Brit explicative you often use? Oh, yeah. That's *brilliant!*"

It took Joyce a moment of looking at my unsmiling visage to realize that she had misinterpreted my response.

"Uh-oh," she said. "I get it. *James* wants to move, but you don't."

I shook my head. "I love my townhouse on Magothy Street."

"I'm sure you do. But now it's time to find a home that both of you love." She grinned playfully. "They say that two can live as cheaply as one, but two definitely need more space. Not to mention three."

"I shall ignore the ludicrous implications embedded in your re-mark," I said with a feigned sniff. "The truth is, I like living in town, close to the High Street. Founders' Woods isn't *me*."

Joyce leaned close and said, "I refuse to feel sorry for someone who has the opportunity to live in Founders' Woods. David and I would move there instantly if we could afford it. Heavens, Pippa, it's a charming community."

"Harrumph! I would have expected more sympathy from a pur-portedly sympathetic medical professional."

"No sympathy here, but I tell you what," she patted my hand, "let's go to the cafeteria. I'll buy you a hot cuppa."

"That would be love-er-ly."

No sooner did we stand up than Carol Ericsson came charging out of her alcove to confront me. Her hands were clenched, her stance ag-gressive. She looked me square in the eyes.

"I remember *you*! You're the headhunter who created all the prob-lems." The pain in her voice seemed mixed with alarm. "Why are you here? Who did you come to visit?"

"I heard the awful news about Dennis Grant," I said, evenly. "I de-cided to visit him, but the hospital won't let me in to the trauma unit."

Carol challenged me with a determined glower.

"You have no right to visit Dennis at a time like this!" she said. "Only people close to him should be here. That doesn't include *you*. You aren't his friend."

Carol's blast of venom caught me by surprise. I blurted out, "To the contrary, I'm quite fond of Dennis."

I noticed Joyce wince. I tried to build context around my impul-sively spoken words. "What I meant to say is that I gained considerable respect for Dennis when we spent time together."

Her face became a mask of fury.

"What is it with you married women?" She made an angry gesture toward my wedding band. "Why don't you leave Dennis alone? If you're tired of your husband, find someone sleazy to fool around with."

Her words rendered me speechless. My patience had reached its limit. I could not deal with another accusation—especially one that scaled the heights of absurdity. I threw up my hands in surrender.

I backed away from Carol Ericsson and sped out of the waiting room. Joyce came after me.

"It's a common reaction, Pippa," Joyce said while jogging alongside. "She's mad at her inability to help Dennis, so she lashed out at the nearest available target. Normally, the nurses get yelled at."

"I declare this horrid Saturday over!" I said, without breaking stride. "I'm going home—where I shall soak in a hot bath, crawl into bed, and pretend that today never happened."

"What about your cup of tea?"

"Drink it on my behalf, Joyce. I am no longer fit company."

━━━━━━━━━━

I tried to take my mind off of me by praying for Dennis as I drove to Hunnechurch Manner. All I could manage were a few feeble phrases. "Help him, God. Keep him safe. Don't let him die."

The rain and wind had returned; the closest parking spot was a block away. Halfway home my umbrella blew inside out, and I abruptly remembered that James and I planned to make a trip to the supermarket to buy dinner.

I shall tell James that an occasional fast is good for the health.

With that improbable thought buzzing in my mind, I approached my front door. It swung wide before I could jam my key in the lock.

"Have a cup of tea," James said as he took my umbrella and pressed a mug between my hands. "Your bath is steaming as we speak."

"Ah, Joyce called."

"She gave me strict orders. I am to treat you like antique porcelain this afternoon. Nothing but tender loving care." He twisted my umbrella inside in and propped it outside the door. "Give me your coat. I'll hang it in the kitchen to drip."

I laughed. "I love that woman. However, I can't become a Coalport teacup quite yet. Unless you want to skip dinner, we have to make a food run."

"Dinner is a done deal. I called Maison Pierre and ordered two complete dinners to be delivered at six. Pierre Renauld himself suggested Caesar salad, fresh-baked rolls, Coquille Chesapeake, asparagus hollandaise, and Apple Tart Tartin for dessert." James bowed from the waist. "A meal befitting the lady of Hunnechurch Manor."

"I'm flabbergasted."

I heard a chirp from the second floor.

"You put Winston in our bedroom?" I asked.

"Just for a few hours. I've slightly rearranged our living room."

"You have?"

"All will be clear as the afternoon progresses. Your bath awaits, Milady." He bowed again. "And feel free to dress with unreserved informality. Our home shall be an island of privacy today."

James appeared to be having a good time—so would I. I twirled out of my damp Burberry, kicked off my wet shoes, and followed the heady aroma that rolled down our staircase. James had prepared my bath with a heavy dose of the lavender bath salts I'd brought home from England.

I let Winston out of his cage. He followed me into the bathroom and perched on the rim of the tub while I soaked.

"The problem, laddie," I said to him, "is that I still think of Dennis Grant as a *jerk*. I know it's a horrible thing to say about someone who is lying in hospital, hurt beyond words. But there it is. Does that make me a bad person?"

Winston chirped softly.

"I agree. It definitely seems the sort of predicament that one should give to God."

I heard the doorbell ring, then murmurings in the distance that sounded like Gloria talking to James. She neither came upstairs nor shouted up to me.

Winston chirped again.

"Another wise observation, laddie. Whatever they're doing, they're doing because they care about me. I will do my utmost to enjoy it."

I put on silk pajamas, a frilly dressing gown, and my bunny slippers.

"Can I come down now?" I called from the top of the stairs.

"Why certainly." James had intensified his Southern drawl. "Join me in the living room."

I tried to act nonchalant, which proved a truly Herculean feat. James had rearranged our tiny living room to create an intimate home theater. He had pushed our sofa to the center of the room directly in front of the plasma TV panel and surrounded the sofa with the system's many speakers. Our coffee table was laden with assorted goodies, including my uneaten personal pizza.

"The second part of Joyce's prescription," he said, "was to do nothing today except watch classic love stories. I asked Gloria to buy us a selection of DVDs to choose among. She bought five: *Casablanca, Gone with the Wind, Doctor Zhivago, An Affair to Remember,* and *Moonstruck.* According to the gal at the video store, all five are on the list of the top-twenty romantic chick flicks. Pick two. One before dinner. One after."

"I doubt there are enough hours in a single day to watch both *Gone with the Wind* and *Doctor Zhivago.* So let's do *Casablanca* before dinner and *Moonstruck* after." I sniffed the air. "Is that popcorn I smell?"

"Gloria also brought us microwave popcorn, sodas, a midnight snack, and the makings of breakfast tomorrow. We are a wholly self-sufficient island of privacy."

I cried at the end of *Casablanca* for the hundredth time, and James said "Here's looking at you, kid" to me at least once every fifteen minutes during dinner.

"We have to listen to Joyce more often," I said as I polished off what must have been a double portion of Apple Tart Tartin.

"She also urged us to communicate more effectively. She said—wait a minute, I took notes." James found a clump of small yellow stick-on notes. He had scribbled a few words on each. "First, we have to make time to talk more often. Second, we have to listen for what the other person means, not merely to what he or she says. Third, we have to learn, despite our years of living alone, that we both have to agree on important stuff—even though it seems only my business or your business." He peered at me. "What did you tell her about us?"

"Not much. I said that you wanted to move to Founders' Ridge but that I preferred to live in Ryde."

James looked at me sheepishly. "I suppose I raced down that particular road a tad quickly."

"And I suppose I set up roadblocks too quickly. We really don't have enough space in Hunnechurch Manor to swing the proverbial cat." I looked around our wee dining room. James had partially disassembled our home exercise machine to give us more elbow room for dinner.

"There are worse things in life than being cramped for space, Pippa. I have been overbearing and stubborn lately. Please forgive me."

"Well, when two people our ages get married, it's not easy to agree about everything."

"Like folks say," James said, "mature people like us are set in our ways."

"We're used to running our own lives."

"We find it difficult to compromise."

I giggled. "That should be enough pithy sayings to hold us for the rest of the evening."

"They may be old chestnuts, but they're mostly true. I've gone car shopping by myself for at least ten years. But now I have to acknowledge that you will often use the car that I buy. In other words, I have to give you the opportunity to disagree with my choice."

"We can still enjoy *some* individuality, Mr. Huston. You select your vehicle and I shall choose mine."

"If you feel that way, maybe I'll buy me a big pickup truck?" He slipped back into his thick drawl. "Every good ole Southern boy should own at least one."

"Don't you dare! I frequently ride in Gloria's pickup. Getting myself into the front seat is like climbing a tree."

"I rest my case!"

Those four little words sent a shiver through me.

The kind of cars we owned, even the size of our home, were minor concerns compared to the lawsuit that hovered over our life. I might have made a bad situation even worse by moving ahead with an investigation despite the warnings of our lawyer and my husband.

For the second time that day, I wanted to acknowledge my duplicity. The words of contrition were on my lips, but I couldn't seem to speak them. Why spoil a great meal with a confession?

And then James kissed me.

As it turned out, we never did watch *Moonstruck* that evening.

Chapter Nine

JAMES AND I ATTENDED the early contemporary worship service at Ryde Fellowship Church the next morning. I am a stalwart, eleven o'clock, traditional service churchgoer; but this Sunday posed an unusual circumstance. The chairman of the associate pastor search committee had scheduled an "everyone must be there" meeting at eleven. The only way I could resolve the scheduling conflict was to sing along with our praise band.

I freely admit that I favor a pipe organ to guitars during worship. I also prefer the grand old hymns to recently written devotional songs. James, however, seemed to enjoy the livelier music. He enthusiastically belted out the words projected on the sanctuary wall. Had we discovered another area where our preferences didn't mesh?

After the service James went off, as he put it, "to *actually* go car shopping."

"Have fun in moderation." I planted a sloppy kiss on his cheek. "And think sensibly."

I watched James drive away and decided that after-service fellowship was the perfect way to spend the fifteen minutes before my meeting began. I'd even get a cup of tea.

Gloria, a stalwart contemporary service fan, broke away from her circle of friends when she saw me.

"What did you think of the sermon today?" she asked.

"It had my name on it. That's exactly how I felt yesterday."

Reverend Clarke had spoken about a key verse in the fortieth psalm: "For troubles without number surround me; my sins have overtaken me, and I cannot see. They are more than the hairs of my head, and my heart fails within me."

The core of his message had been simple. At times like that don't even try to go it alone. Turn your troubles over to the Lord.

"By the way," I gave Gloria an inconspicuous hug, "thanks for providing the movies and snacks for our stay-at-home evening."

She pulled away, looking unhappy. "I'm feeling convicted about yelling at you in front of your house. It's not my call whether anyone is a good or bad Christian. Please forget everything judgmental I said."

"Don't sweat it. You did good!"

"Really?"

"Really."

Gloria looked around. "Where's the hunk?"

"*James* is visiting car dealers."

"How are you getting home?"

"I will call James later. I have a boring meeting to attend first. Thanks to your devious scheming with our minister. Which leads me to a question I've meant to ask for days. Why would you conspire with Reverend . . . ?"

Gloria deftly interrupted. "I'm sure you noticed that I put Dennis Grant on the 'Pray For' list in the bulletin. But you may not have seen this morning's *Baltimore Sun*. There was a long article about Dennis Grant that quoted the Ryde Police. They're calling the hit-and-run a 'criminal assault with a motor vehicle.' They think a black truck or SUV hit him, but they don't have evidence to identify a specific vehicle. Whom do you suppose tried to kill him?"

"I have no idea—or any interest in speculating. Back to my question: Why did you and Reverend Clarke conspire to put me on the search committee? Answer honestly. It won't do to tell lies inside a church building."

Gloria averted her eyes. "Remember the 'vacancy' that Ed mentioned?"

"Indeed."

"That was me. I served on the committee for two whole meetings."

"When did you become a member?"

"About a month ago."

"You never told me."

"I figured I wouldn't last." Her voice trailed off to a near whisper. "I was right."

"Oh dear! I definitely don't like the sound of that. Why are you no longer a member?"

Gloria mumbled something.

"Sorry, I didn't hear you."

"Monica DeVries."

"The chairperson of the committee?"

Gloria shrugged apologetically. "She and I don't often agree. We're like chalk and cheese—did I use the English idiom correctly?"

"Aha! Now I understand. *You* were first choice to provide those 'specific recruiting skills' that Ed Clarke said the committee needs."

"I've been a member of Ryde Fellowship longer than you. That's the *only* reason he chose me."

"What's wrong with Monica DeVries?"

Ed Clarke introduced me to Monica at the Lenten dinner last February, but I knew almost nothing about her. She always attended the early service, and our paths rarely crossed.

"Absolutely nothing," Gloria said. "She's intelligent, insightful, well-organized."

"Gloria!"

"I'm serious! Monica is OK—except she and I have an itty-bitty chemistry problem. We throw off sparks when we're together."

"I don't believe you. Gloria Spitz gets along with everyone. You're a paragon of even-temperedness."

She grimaced. "Monica can act like Attila the Hun but with twice as much ego. She likes to get her way no matter what."

"Give me an example of Monica at her worst."

"Well, our most recent fight began when I disagreed with Monica's decision to schedule a meeting this morning in competition with the traditional service. I waited until we were alone and told her what I thought. She said, 'Gloria'—Gloria shifted to a high-pitched voice—'while I value your opinion, I must point out that you are merely a junior member of this committee and have no right to challenge my administrative decisions.'"

"I can see the sparks flying."

Gloria smiled awkwardly. "Yeah. Just before she fired me, I told her what she could do with her administrative decisions."

"Bully for you!"

She tapped her watch. "Better get going. Monica doesn't like committee members to arrive late."

I made my way through crowds of worshipers arriving for the eleven o'clock service—stopping for several hellos—and found the small adult-Christian-education classroom that Monica had reserved for our meeting. The sexton had arranged the room's four tables in a square. Monica had chosen the power seat, at the corner opposite the door, where she could watch people come and go. I hadn't seen her standing up in four months, but I recalled that she was hardly more than five feet tall. I pegged her age at forty-five, give or take a year. She had yellow blonde hair, expensively dyed and styled. She wore a loose-fitting blouse that made her look more overweight than she actually was.

There were five other committee members seated around the square. I took a "weak seat"—my back to the door, near the center of my table—to ensure that I didn't signal any sort of challenge to Monica's authority.

"Now that we're all here—*at last,*" she said, with an obvious glance my way, "I shall open in prayer. 'Father, I ask your blessing on this team. Please be with us in our work. Guide our hearts and minds and hands as we call an associate pastor to our church. In Jesus' name.'"

We all said, "Amen."

Monica slowly surveyed her team. It seemed another way to announce her power and exert her control. After looking everyone in the eye, she beamed at me and said, "We are privileged to have a new member with us today. Pippa Huston operates an employment agency in Ryde. She recently married James Huston, a well-known business consultant. Pippa hails from England, but we won't hold that against her. She became a member of Ryde Fellowship Church about three years ago. Reverend Clarke assures me that even though she is still learning the ropes of being a new bride, she is willing to spend some time working for this committee. Well, we'll do our best not to overload Pippa with too much work."

Monica led the group in brief applause. I acknowledged everyone in turn and wondered if there was a heavy object within reach that I might throw at Monica. In the end I settled on jotting an angry note on the pad I'd brought with me:

Monica DeVries. Arrogant twit! Find a painful way to repay Gloria.

Monica continued: "Now I think we should introduce ourselves to Philippa. I'll go first. My name is Monica DeVries. I sell real estate. I am married to Jack DeVries, a professor at the University of Maryland." She tilted her head like a movie star in a glamour shot. "I'm sure you recognize my face. It's on the side of every Ryde Transit bus that runs along Ryde High Street."

I'd seen the blonde on the bus go by countless times. The big headline read "DeVries Realty Knows Ryde Real Estate." But the Monica sitting in front of me bore little resemblance to the Monica reproduced on cardboard. The heavily airbrushed mobile photograph depicted a woman thirty pounds lighter and ten years younger.

I made an addition to my notes: *Old photo plastered on bus. Does this violate truth-in-advertising laws?*

The other members introduced themselves in turn. I jotted down the details:

> *Don Henley. Pharmacist. Member of the church for eight years.*
> *Carrie Logan. High school student. Member all her short life.*
>   *Looks bored.*
> *Becky Smith. Elementary schoolteacher. Grew up at Ryde*
>   *Fellowship. Pretty.*
> *Harry Smith. Insurance agent. Married to Becky. Member for five*
>   *years.*
> *Rose Robinson. Employee communications manager, Militet*
>   *Aviation. Member for six years.*

I craned my neck to get a better look at Rose, then added an appendix to her entry: *Has managerial appearance and demeanor. Find out more about her—ask for her résumé. Potential candidate for senior corporate communications positions?*

"Excellent," Monica said. "Now that we're all friends, let's get to work."

"Point of order, Madam Chairperson," I said. "I need to set the record straight before we begin our meeting. Everyone—please call me Pippa Hunnechurch. I use my maiden name in Maryland."

Monica blinked.

I went on: "I am definitely *not* an employment agent. Hunnechurch &
Associates is an executive recruiting firm."

"Ah . . . well . . . yes . . . I see," Monica blithered, in quick
progression.

I kept talking: "I learned the ropes of marriage more than a decade
ago. James Huston is my second husband. Consequently, I am determined to be a fully participating member of this committee. I prepared
for this meeting by reading the Associate Pastor Requirements
Statement that our church council developed and also the advertise-
ment that this committee wrote. I understand that we have received
several résumés and that our purpose today is to listen to sermon
recordings provided by the most promising candidates."

Monica quickly reestablished her supremacy as chair of the committee. She eyed the members again, with one exception: she didn't include me in her scan of the room.

"*I* called this meeting," she said, with heavy emphasis on the *I*, "so
that you may have the same opportunity that I've enjoyed, to hear ex-
hilarating sermons from four dynamic ministers of word and sacra-
ment. Ryde Fellowship Church is *blessed* by the abundance of godly
men who have responded to our need for an associate pastor. I listened
to their sermons in awe. How, I asked myself, can I possibly select the
best from among such magnificent preaching?" She paused. "I expect
that you will have the same reaction I did."

When the other members merely nodded at Monica, I realized why
Ed Clarke was so insistent that I serve: Someone had to stand up to the
chair of the search committee, or else she would choose our next associate pastor all by herself.

Gloria must have been tempted to karate-kick her across the room.

Monica hoisted a portable boom box cassette player atop the table
and pressed the *Play* button. A friendly and confident voice began by
reading Mark 12, verses 41 through 44, the well-known story of Jesus
watching with admiration as a poor woman gave two small coins—

everything of value she owned—to God. The candidate used the tale of the widow's mite to build a compelling sermon about sacrificial giving.

James needs to hear this, I thought. *I doubt we're giving enough.*

Monica cued another tape. "The next sermon explains a verse from Proverbs, specifically Proverbs 30:32: 'If you have played the fool and exalted yourself, or if you have planned evil, clap your hand over your mouth!'"

A brilliant idea that, Lord! Someone should clap a hand over Monica's mouth. She has clearly played the fool by exalting herself.

I found this sermon much less convincing than the first—probably because the second candidate delivered a straightforward lecture that told us what the Scripture meant and how we should apply it. The first pastor had painted a word picture that transported me to the temple in Jerusalem. I had *seen* Jesus saying, "I tell you the truth, this poor widow has put more into the treasury than all the others. They all gave out of their wealth; but she, out of her poverty, put in everything—all she had to live on."

And then I had a curious thought: *We're listening to speeches!*

I don't know why the notion hadn't dawned on me before. A sermon is a special kind of speech. We would probably choose the candidate for associate pastor who was the best speechwriter of the bunch.

A gripping speech has the power to change hearts and minds.

I should have listened intently to the other sermons—one on the parable of the prodigal son, the other about the Samaritan woman at the well—but I spent the rest of the meeting musing about the influence of Dennis Grant, speechwriter. Among the questions I pondered:

Does Dennis have the skill to capture the imagination of listeners?

Do his speeches have the power to change the hearts of Hardesty employees?

When the fourth preacher said, "Amen!" Monica DeVries—still ignoring me—gave the committee its marching orders. "We will listen to these four inspiring men again at our next meeting. Coincidently, their second set of sermons address different verses from Paul's Epistle to the Romans. Because the church council expects us to evaluate the theological soundness of their preaching, I ask that each of you reread Romans before our next meeting on Wednesday evening."

The whole letter? I don't have time to do homework!

I gritted my teeth and held my tongue. What else could I do after my hasty declaration that I would be a full-fledged member?

I fled to the front entrance and called James, expecting a long wait. He surprised me by saying, "Five minutes, my love."

I could see a grin on James's face when the Beetle was still halfway down the street. Ryde Fellowship Church is located at the bottom of Romney Boulevard, a short walk from downtown Ryde. My first thought: *James had taken a restorative spin along the boulevard's distant reaches.* My second thought: *I know that smile! He's bought a new car.*

I had scarcely snapped my seat belt in place when James dropped an oversized brochure in my lap. The illustration on the cover showed a sleek gray sedan cruising through lighter gray fog.

"Instead of the Range Rover," he said, "I've ordered a BMW Series 5 Sedan. It has a 3.0 liter double-overhead cam engine, bi-xenon headlights—they look blue-tinted when you see them at night—and an electronic navigation system so we'll never get lost when we're driving. It has an automatic transmission and a gadget called dynamic steering control. The seats are leather and the stereo . . ." James frowned at me. "What are you smiling at?"

"I'd planned to talk to you about sacrificial giving, but now we may have to reduce our gift to the church."

"To the contrary." James emphasized every syllable. "The *Series 5* is significantly less expensive than the Range Rover. We'll be able to increase our gift."

James found an empty parking spot only three houses away from Hunnechurch Manor—a fortunate happenstance because a new rain cloud had settled above Ryde. We walked to our front door, arms entwined, ignoring the soft drizzle—a pair of carefree newlyweds.

But not for long.

═══════════

An irritated copper pounding on a front door makes a distinctive sound. One knows immediately that the person announcing his presence has not arrived for a congenial visit. We were in the living room, finally watching *Moonstruck*, when we heard four heavy thwacks that reverberated throughout our home.

"Are we expecting anyone?" James asked.

"Certainly no one who knocks like that."

There were three more thwacks.

James paused the DVD player, then scrambled to his feet. "I'll get rid of whomever."

I followed James into our hallway—vaguely concerned that "whomever" might not be easily chased away. The door swung open, and there stood Detective Stephen Reilly, my yellow plastic file envelope tucked under his arm.

When he saw me standing behind James, Reilly held up the file envelope. "Want to guess where we found this?"

"Howdy, Stephen," James said, clearly bewildered by Reilly's brusque tone.

"This isn't a social call, James. I'm here to arrest your wife or shoot her—I haven't decided which."

"In that case you'd better come in."

Tumblers in my mind clicked into place:

Observation: Reilly, a homicide detective, shows up with an item that I had given Dennis Grant.

Observation: Reilly is furious.

Deduction: Dennis Grant must be dead.

Deduction: The police know that I met Dennis at Bombay Spices & Rices.

Deduction: James will soon be furious too.

Reilly cleaned his wet shoes on our doormat in three angry shuffles. As he crossed our threshold, he produced an irate look, an exasperated head shake, and a put-upon groan—all directed at me. He shook James's hand and stomped into our living room.

I had known Stephen Reilly for three years. We had met profession-ally—*his* profession—which made it difficult to think of him as a friend. Nonetheless, we had built a cordial relationship because we both at-tended the monthly meetings of the Ryde Chamber of Commerce. I had held three different chamber posts: social chair, publicity chair, and pro-gram chair, my current job. Reilly served as the Ryde Police Department's ambassador to our business community. James met Reilly a few days after I did. They manage to get along famously.

"Dennis Grant died three hours ago," Reilly said. "We're treating his death as a homicide."

I'd guessed as much, but hearing my deductions confirmed made me shudder.

"I'm now in charge of the investigation." He fixed me with a solemn gaze. "You get one chance to answer my questions fully and truthfully. If I am unhappy with your responses, I will toss you in jail as a mate-rial witness. Understood?"

So much for our cordial relationship.

I nodded.

"Sit!" Reilly said.

I sat down on our sofa, which now occupied the center of our liv-ing room. Reilly moved in front of the plasma TV screen. James took up a position in the corner. His eyes were wide with surprise; he must have had a zillion misgivings, but—bless him!—he said nothing and didn't reveal the upset he surely felt.

"First question. What is your relationship to Dennis Grant?"

"I placed Dennis in a speechwriting job at Militet Aviation in February."

"Second question." Reilly held out the yellow file envelope. "Is this yours?"

"Yes. However . . ."

"Forget 'however,' the right answer is yes. We discovered your fingerprints all over the envelope and the contents. That was after we found 'Candidate Information Provided by Hunnechurch & Associates' neatly printed on the bottom of every page."

Bother! How careless of me. I am so used to seeing our tagline on materials we prepare for clients that I hadn't noticed it on the bottom of the copies we made for Dennis.

"Third question. Why did we find a pack of your documents tucked into Dennis Grant's rain suit?"

"Because, as I was about to explain, Dennis provided the sample speeches in that envelope. He asked me for a set of copies. I gave them to Dennis when we met at Bombay Spices & Rices on Hampton Lane."

James made a noise halfway between a gasp and a cough. I forced myself not to look at him.

"Fourth question. Why didn't you tell Detective King that you knew Dennis Grant, that you met with him *minutes* before he was killed?"

I was tempted to say that I considered the meeting of no relevance to the hit-and-run. Instead, I fessed up: "I hoped to keep the meeting a secret. My lawyer ordered me to keep away from Dennis."

"You're kidding? That's odd advice for a lawyer to give you."

"My firm is being sued by Hardesty Software. Dennis is—*was*—a key witness for Hardesty."

Reilly stared at me for a long moment. "What's your lawyer's name?"

"Daniel Harris."

"He's a civil litigator—supposed to be good at what he does. Does he know anything about criminal law?"

"Why would you ask that?" I corrected myself. "I meant to say, I don't know the answer."

"I'd find out if I were you. When I walked through the door, Pippa Hunnechurch was merely a material witness to a vehicular homicide. Now she's a suspect."

"Me? How?"

"You have a great motive for killing Dennis Grant. A dead man can't testify against you."

"Dennis was struck by a black truck. I was on foot."

"OK. You have a great motive for *having* him killed. Maybe you commissioned a hit-and-run driver to do the job?"

"You can't be serious! You *know* me."

I jumped up, but a gentle hand on my shoulder urged me back down. James had quietly joined me on the sofa. He spoke softly but with unmistakable authority.

"I suspect you're just pulling Pippa's leg, Detective Reilly. But if you do intend to travel any further down this road, I advise Pippa to stop answering your questions."

When this is over, Hunnechurch, give James a huge hug.

I held my breath, waiting for Reilly to respond.

He made a disparaging gesture, then looked directly into my eyes. "No, I don't think you killed Dennis Grant, but is there anything else I ought to know about your relationship with him? Is there anything exciting that you haven't told me?"

"You know everything I do," I said. "Honest."

It wasn't until after Reilly had left that I remembered the little tape recorder sitting deep inside my handbag. Honest.

```
╔══════════════════════════════╗
║        Chapter  Ten          ║
╚══════════════════════════════╝
```

MONDAY BEGAN WITH A BATTLE of facial gymnastics: Daniel Harris's tight-jawed lawyerly scowl versus my British stiff upper lip.

I'd spent the first fifteen minutes of our nine a.m. meeting recounting my meeting with Dennis Grant, my role as ear-witness, my interview with Detective King, and my visit from Detective Reilly. The only detail I held back was that I'd worn a wire to Bombay Spices & Rices. The tape recording of Dennis patronizing me would remain my little secret.

Daniel drummed his fingers on his desk occasionally while I spoke, but he didn't interrupt my narration. When I finished, he said, "Congratulations—you seem to have set a new freestyle record for client disregard of his or her attorney's legal advice."

He glared at me awhile, then said, "Let me recapitulate the imbroglio you created. *Recapitulate* means 'sum up,' and *imbroglio* is a highfalutin' word for *mess*. I might as well introduce a few fifty-cent words because you don't listen to simple English."

I tried to look suitably contrite.

Daniel kept talking. "In the entire state of Maryland, there was only one man you had to absolutely, positively stay away from—the primary witness against you in a lawsuit that will cost you a crushing amount of money should you lose.

"A week ago, you wanted to 'wring his miserable, lying neck,' but on Thursday you called Dennis Grant and requested a friendly chat, and on Saturday you did him a significant favor. You walked two blocks through a drenching rainstorm to hand-deliver a package of old—presumably valueless—speech drafts.

"You met with Dennis, you talked briefly, you even had the opportunity to ask why he perjured himself. Unfortunately, this epitome of deceit told you nothing of value. He didn't even thank you for sloshing through the rain. Instead, he made uncalled for comments about your lack of speechwriting know-how. You left your supposedly surreptitious tête-à-tête angrier at him than when you arrived.

"Coincidentally, another person, still unknown, decided to commit vehicular homicide in broad daylight in downtown Ryde. You heard a black truck lethally injure Dennis Grant mere minutes after you and he squabbled among the ethnic groceries.

"Faced with a police interview, you decide that the time is ripe for discretion. You give the police ambiguous answers to their questions because you worry that I—and your husband—won't understand how you could have been such a dimwit. Thanks to your deficient responses, the police now have reason to distrust Pippa Hunnechurch and consider her—I speak euphemistically here—a *person of interest*." Daniel pressed his lips into a sour grin. "Did I capture the high points?"

"With elegant sufficiency," I said.

"Assuming you wanted to do Dennis a favor, why didn't you just mail him his speeches?"

James, who had been magnificently understanding the evening before, gallantly came to my rescue. "The meeting at the Indian grocery store was Dennis Grant's idea. I think Pippa was right to find out what was on his mind."

"Nope. She was wrong because she didn't tell me that Dennis had called. At the very least I would have notified Blanchette and Ross. In the unlikely event that they had no objection to the meeting, I'd have sent one of my folks along with you to act as chaperone and witness of what he said."

"I guess I don't fully appreciate the . . . ah . . . *legal difficulties* that the meeting caused," James said.

Daniel responded as if I had asked the question. He looked straight at me.

"Your contact with Dennis has opened an ethical can of worms. Blanchette and Ross are sure to be concerned that Dennis revealed a key aspect of their legal strategy to you."

"Dennis didn't tell me anything."

"Let's hope he didn't know anything." Daniel drummed his desktop again. "Then there's the other side of the coin. Did you let slip anything of value to them?"

"I doubt it," I said, "but if I did, it died along with Dennis."

Daniel drummed a few more bars, then glanced at his watch. "That reminds me—I have a phone call to make. Contemplate your sins while I'm gone."

Dan's office was dark that morning. The closely drawn curtains admitted only a thin strip of sunlight that cast a narrow band of illumination on the wall behind us. Daniel had the lean, hungry look of Dracula. Maybe bright sunshine filling his office would dissolve him into a pile of pink foamy froth?

"Why the sudden smile?" James asked.

"I imagined Daniel as a vampire."

James chuckled. "I thought you pictured lawyers as sharks?"

"Two wholly appropriate figures of speech."

Daniel returned carrying a manila file folder and looking more dyspeptic than ever. "My call was to Ken Ross. He informed me that Hardesty is determined to press on despite Dennis Grant's death."

"Did he tell you why?" I asked.

Daniel shrugged as he dropped into his chair. "Who can guess Mitch Hardesty's motives? Maybe he genuinely feels aggrieved at you? Maybe he wants to frighten other consultants into line?"

"I had hoped the lawsuit might crumble without Dennis to testify," James said.

"Hardesty Software is the plaintiff. Dennis Grant was merely a witness to the perfidy they allege. Live testimony is always best, but because Dennis is dead, the depositions he gave Blanchette and Ross can be read aloud at the trial. At least the parts that get past my vigorous objections." Daniel scratched his ear. "Incidentally, I also told Ken that Dennis asked for copies of his speeches, which Pippa provided on Saturday and which are now in police custody."

"I suppose that opposing counsel has a right to know about the meeting and the speeches," James said to Dan.

Daniel nodded. "Correct. We might even score some points for being forthright. Besides," his eyes twinkled, "I wanted to hear Ken's reaction when I told him."

"I presume he reacted as you did?" I said.

"Oh, I'm far more tranquil than Ken Ross." Daniel paused to let us snicker. "He went ballistic—mostly at Dennis Grant. This is hardly the best time to criticize Dennis, but he must have been a nightmare witness. Ken didn't have much leverage to keep him in line."

"We had the same idea," I said. "We couldn't figure out how Dennis would benefit by cooperating with his ex-employer."

"Who's 'we'?" James asked.

"Gloria and me," I said quickly. This was hardly the right occasion to credit David Friendly for his astute observation.

Daniel went on. "Ken did make one interesting comment, though. He said, 'Thanks—I should have known about that meeting.'"

"I don't get it," I said.

"He probably hired an investigator to follow you around and rummage through your life."

Cor Blimey!

I must have looked bowled over because James patted my hand, and Daniel quickly added: "I wouldn't worry too much. It's one more sign that Blanchette and Ross don't have much to work with."

I thought back to Saturday morning. It had been pouring and the traffic on Ryde High Street had been heavy. An observer following two or three car lengths behind Gloria's tall pickup truck might easily have missed me slipping down out of the passenger seat at a traffic light.

Gloria will know what to do.

The thought immediately calmed me. Gloria often followed people around; she would know how to counter a "tail," if I had one.

Daniel opened the manila folder, uncovering a thin stack of legal papers. I wondered how thick the pile would grow before the suit was resolved.

"Let's shift gears and consider what's going to happen today in court," he said. "I've decided to try something novel—*if* Pippa is willing to participate."

"What do you have in mind?" I asked.

Daniel responded to my question with one of his own: "Do you know what takes place during a motions hearing?"

"Uh, *no!*"

Daniel held up the document on top of the stack. "This is a motion, a written request that asks the judge to do something. This morning the judge will grant—or deny—motions that Ken and I have filed with the court. Ken has asked for virtually unlimited access to your files. He expects me to argue that his request is nonsensical."

"Is it?" I asked.

"Well, John Cavanaugh is our judge today. He's a pretty sensible guy. I doubt that he'll give Ken the key to your office. The fact is, you haven't been uncooperative. You haven't had a chance to respond to the plaintiff's requests for information."

"All this happens in *what?* . . . a kind of mini-trial?"

"A motions hearing looks somewhat like a trial because the judge sits up front on a bench. But it's a much less formal proceeding. Plaintiffs and defendants rarely show up. The lawyers do all the work."

James spoke before I could ask why Daniel had asked us to accompany him.

"Your motion will ask for a dismissal of Hardesty's complaint—right?" he said.

Daniel made an "out of here" gesture with his thumb. "We want the case tossed out of court."

"Will the judge agree?" I asked.

"That's going to depend on you." Daniel grinned at me. "Our motion hearings will be considerably more interesting than most because I intend to put you on the witness stand and ask you three key questions about executive recruiting."

"Me? A witness? Today?"

"Don't sweat it! You'll enjoy being cross-examined by Ken Ross. He's fun to watch."

I remembered how David Friendly had described the man: *Ken Ross made his bones as a tough prosecutor in Baltimore.*

I peeked at James. He appeared as puzzled as I felt.

"What three questions?" he asked.

Daniel began to count on his fingers. "First, did Pippa need to fulfill specific educational requirements before she became a headhunter? Second, did Pippa take any kind of examination before she launched her business? Third, does the State of Maryland license, or otherwise administer, headhunters like Pippa?"

The answers gelled in my mind: *No, No,* and *No.*

How could three one-word answers benefit my case?

Daniel continued, "I'll also ask her the usual introductory questions and possibly a few follow-up questions—depending on the judge's reaction."

I remained puzzled, but James began to grin. "You plan to attack the theory behind their claim. Very clever, Counselor!"

"You got it!" Daniel brought his fingers together into a fist.

I hadn't a clue as to what they were talking about, but I'd acted humble enough for one morning. Instead of asking for an explanation, I pretended that I understood Daniel.

"Very clever, indeed. Would it be useful to practice a follow-up question or two?"

"Nope. I'd prefer all your answers to be spontaneous and unrehearsed."

That's what he wanted—and alas, that's precisely what he got.

═══════════

The home of the Circuit Court for Anne Arundel County, Maryland, is a misleadingly antique courthouse on Church Circle in Annapolis. From the street one sees a charming Georgian-style redbrick building, erected in 1824, with a stately cupola and a lovely arched entranceway. One soon discovers, however, that the historic building is the entrance to a large, modern courthouse complex built behind and below the original structure.

After we passed through security, Daniel Harris directed us to Hearing Room 3G. "I'll meet you there," he said. "I have to drop off some paperwork at the clerk's office."

As we approached 3G, I began to tremble.

"Calm down, Pippa." James led me to a corner and clasped my hands in his. "Pray with me."

I took a deep breath and let it out slowly.

"Father in heaven," James began, "we know that you are with us when we face trials and tribulations. Comfort Pippa today as she continues her good fight against perplexing enemies. Give Daniel Harris the skills to be an effective advocate for Pippa and grant Judge Cavanaugh the wisdom to make fair and just decisions. In Jesus' name. Amen."

"Amen, amen, and amen," I murmured.

Hearing Room 3G had windowless walls—cream colored and partially paneled in reddish-stained oak that matched the judge's bench—beige carpeting, and American and Maryland flags standing up front. At first I took it for a small courtroom, a miniature version of the sort one sees on TV. Once inside I realized that the room had been purpose-designed for relatively informal judge-and-lawyer hearings. The judge's bench was only slightly higher than a normal desk; there was no jury box and only three rows of seats to accommodate onlookers.

The handful of men and women sitting in the room—all lawyers, I supposed—were browsing through paperwork. No one seemed especially stressed. I decided that I could safely relax a tad.

Daniel Harris came into the room accompanied by a heavyset balding man, perhaps fifty, wearing a gray tweed sport coat. They sat down in the first row of seats.

"That must be Ken Ross," James whispered to me. "He doesn't look as tough as his reputation."

"Neither does Gloria Spitz."

"You'll do just fine." He squeezed my hand. "I have a feeling this lawsuit will be history in an hour."

Everyone stood when Judge Cavanaugh entered. Late forties, compact build, alert eyes, an easygoing air about him. Daniel had described him as "sensible." He did seem to broadcast sensibility—and also competence. I let myself relax another notch.

"Good morning, ladies and gentlemen." The judge took his place behind the bench. "Let's dive right in with Kensington versus Kensington."

I listened attentively as Judge Cavanaugh disposed of the two cases ahead of ours. Because the participants spoke plain English rather than legalese, I had no difficulty following the proceedings.

The first was a dispute involving a professional office building owned by a pair of doctors—Kensington the orthopedist, Kensington the obstetrician once married, now divorced. Cavanaugh made an aside about cutting the building in half, but neither lawyer seemed to appreciate the application of the biblical reference. After five minutes of lawyerly give-and-take, the judge ordered *She* to allow *He's* accountant to examine her financial records.

I found the second case—a heated dispute about a fence—more interesting. Two wealthy neighbors had apparently fought for more than two years about the placement of a fence between their adjacent properties. Because the trial was still months away, the owner of the fence wanted an injunction to prevent the other party from "destroying or otherwise harming the fence in the interim." Judge Cavanaugh refused the request. "We grant injunctions to prevent irreparable damage," he said. "A fence is easy to rebuild—should the plaintiff be foolish enough to move faster than the court." He consulted a piece of paper. "The next matter on the docket is Hardesty Software Corporation versus Hunnechurch & Associates."

Our turn. I joined Daniel at the plaintiff's table at the front of the hearing room.

The judge gave me a peculiar, *I-don't-recognize-you* look, then took a moment to scan two documents. I guessed they were the two motions up for his consideration.

"I was informed this morning," he began, "that the plaintiff's primary witness, in fact the subject of this proceeding, was killed on

Saturday. Nonetheless, plaintiff intends to move ahead." He glanced at Ken Ross. "Are those your intentions, counselor?"

"They are, Your Honor," Ross said.

"OK, let's tackle the plaintiff's motion for discovery." Judge Cavanaugh peered at Ken Ross over the top of his reading glasses. "Frankly, Mr. Ross, your request for a fishing license strikes me as premature. Why do you need the court's clout so early in the case?"

"We have a significant concern, Your Honor," Ross said. "Hunnechurch & Associates is a small firm that may not honor standard record-keeping practices. We want to make certain that material files are available to us—that they will not be discarded."

"Any comments, Mr. Harris?"

"Record-keeping does not pose a problem, Your Honor, because Hunnechurch & Associates owns a state-of-the-art digital records storage facility. I can assure the court that *relevant* documents"—Daniel spoke *relevant* slowly to emphasize the word—"will be provided to the plaintiff as part of routine pretrial discovery."

"Sounds good to me. Mr. Ross, try to work out a discovery arrangement with Mr. Harris. If you can't agree on a middle ground that makes you happy, come back with an appropriately bounded request for relief."

"Thank you, Your Honor," Ross said.

"The next item on our docket is defendant's motion to dismiss." The judge fixed his gaze on Daniel. "I must say, Mr. Harris, you've brought an intriguing trial balloon into court. Can you make it fly for me?"

"I'll do my best, Your Honor." Daniel paused, as if to collect his thoughts. Then he picked up the complaint as a prop. "The plaintiff's case presumes that Ms. Hunnechurch had an ethical obligation *not* to recruit Dennis Grant. Hardesty even asserts a breach of fiduciary responsibility on the part of Ms. Hunnechurch."

Daniel let the complaint slip from his fingers—an obvious sign of his disdain for its contents.

"The defense contends," Daniel went on, "that the alleged obligation does not exist. Further, we maintain that even if Ms. Hunnechurch had actively recruited Dennis Grant, she would not have breached any responsibility owed to Hardesty. For those reasons the complaint fails to state a cause of action and should be dismissed."

The judge turned to Ken Ross. "How do you feel about that, counselor?"

"In total disagreement," Ross said. "Ms. Hunnechurch is a business consultant, a member of what has been called an emerging profession. As such, her clients have a right to expect ethical behavior in exchange for the considerable fees she commands."

Daniel gestured toward me. "With your permission, Your Honor, Ms. Hunnechurch is ready to provide material testimony to the court."

Judge Cavanaugh's eyebrows arched in surprise. "Live testimony! My, my—this is getting really interesting. You understand, of course, that your client will be an equal opportunity witness. Mr. Ross will also get a chance to question her."

"Ms. Hunnechurch looks forward to testifying, Your Honor."

The judge spoke to his bailiff. "Swear her in, Joe."

I solemnly swore under the penalties of perjury that the responses I gave and statements I made would be the whole truth and nothing but the truth. I sat down in the witness chair.

Daniel approached me. "Please state your name and address."

"Philippa Hunnechurch Huston, 735 Magothy Street, Ryde, Maryland."

"Do you have an occupation, Ms. Hunnechurch?"

"Yes. I am an executive recruiter. My firm is Hunnechurch & Associates."

"Please tell us what an executive recruiter does."

"I identify and recruit suitable candidates for senior positions at client companies."

"Do you get paid for identifying suitable candidates?"

"Not quite. I get paid when one of my candidates is hired by a client company."

"In other words, you don't earn a fee for providing expertise to your clients—as say an attorney would."

"No. Not directly."

"How long have you been an executive recruiter?"

"Close to five years."

"What did you do before you started your company?"

"I was a junior recruiter in the human resources department at CentreBank in Baltimore."

"Did you have to meet any specific educational requirements before you became an executive recruiter?"

"No."

"Were you required to take any kind of examination before you hung out your shingle as an executive recruiter?"

"No."

"Were you required to get a license from the State of Maryland empowering you to be an executive recruiter?"

"No."

"So, one morning you simply announced to the world: Here we are—Philippa Hunnechurch & Associates, Executive Recruiters?"

I didn't care for the flippant tone of the question, but I nodded and said, "Indeed, that's more or less what happened."

"One last question: do you have a college degree?"

"Not a four-year degree," I said, "but I did earn my associate's degree at Anne Arundel Community College while I worked at CentreBank."

"Thank you, Ms. Hunnechurch." Dan turned toward Judge Cavanaugh. "As you can see, Your Honor, there is simply no basis in fact for asserting that Ms. Hunnechurch is a member of a so-called 'emerging profession'—whatever that might be. Executive recruiting has none of the hallmarks of a real profession: no body of knowledge, no necessary education, no license requirements—no *nothing.* Anyone can become a recruiter, instantly."

The judge frowned. "Are you suggesting that this purported lack of professional status frees Ms. Hunnechurch from the need to operate ethically?"

"Ms. Hunnechurch certainly has a duty to obey the law and honor her contractual obligations, Your Honor, but beyond the obvious there are no definitions of ethical behavior for a headhunter. Unlike law, medicine, accounting, and other true professions, executive recruiting does not have a recognized code of professional responsibility."

Daniel held up another piece of paper.

"Hardesty Software Corporation clearly understood these limitations when they hired Hunnechurch & Associates. The company required Ms. Hunnechurch to execute a nondisclosure agreement, a kind of contract, that ensured she would treat the corporate documents she saw as confidential. Had Hardesty similarly wanted Ms. Hunnechurch to avoid contact with its key employees, they could have easily appended an appropriate clause to the agreement."

Daniel seemed to grow taller as he spoke; his voice took on an almost hypnotic power that riveted my attention.

"Your Honor, there is absolutely no foundation for the claim that Philippa Hunnechurch Huston was ethically bound not to recruit Dennis Grant. To reemphasize what I said earlier, plaintiff's complaint fails to state a cause of action and must be dismissed."

I surveyed the hearing room. Judge Cavanaugh wore a smile of respect, James a smile of relief, Daniel a smile of achievement, and Ken Ross a thin-lipped smile that seemed rather sinister.

As for me, I felt too confused to generate any sort of smile. Had Daniel ridiculed my occupation? Was executive recruiting really a "know nothing" vocation? Could *anyone* become a headhunter merely by hanging up a shingle?

"Well done, Mr. Harris," the judge said. "Your balloon has definitely caught my attention. Let's see if Mr. Ross can shoot it down."

"Thank you, Your Honor," Ken Ross said. "I do have a few questions for Ms. Hunnechurch." He sauntered next to me. "Let me start by saying that I applaud your tenacity, Ms. Hunnechurch. I'm sure you've worked hard to build a business—even if we accept Mr. Harris's notion that there isn't any substance to what you do."

I nodded, not sure how else to respond.

"Ah, then you do consider yourself successful?"

"Moderately successful. We have about a dozen clients in Ryde."

"I recently came across a brochure. In fact," he reached into his breast pocket, "I have it with me today. Does this look familiar?"

I recognized the fold immediately. It was the brochure I had pressed into Kelly the Shark's sneaky hand.

"Yes. It's a copy of our marketing brochure."

"It's well written—who wrote the words?"

"As a matter of fact, I did."

"I congratulate you for your writing skills." He turned to the inside page. "You describe yourself as 'highly skilled' . . . with 'experience you can rely on' . . . a 'recruiter with an excellent track record of completing tough assignments successfully.'" He looked at the back cover. "And here's a fascinating claim: 'We are proven *professionals.*'"

Ross let the despicable *P* word hang in our minds for several seconds before he continued. "It also says in your brochure that you are a member of the Ryde Chamber of Commerce. Is that true?"

"Yes. I am a member."

"So am I." He paused then asked, "Has NAER approved your application yet?"

"Pardon?"

"Forgive me. I shouldn't use acronyms. Isn't it true that you recently applied for membership in the National Association of Executive Recruiters?"

Rats! How could he know that?

I had mailed the application scarcely a month earlier. I hadn't even mentioned NAER to Daniel Harris because it didn't seem to have anything to do with Hardesty. Who told Ken Ross?

The only conceivable explanation popped into my head: I had asked five local companies to act as my supporting references. One of them must have shared my request with Ross—or more likely with the investigator he'd commissioned to perform a comprehensive investigation of me.

"Yes. I have applied to NAER," I said.

"That doesn't surprise me. According to the association's Web site, NAER members 'set the standards for the industry' and have a goal 'to continually enhance quality and methods through education, interaction, and professional competence.'" He looked at me with faint amusement. "Do you think they'll let you join?"

"I would hope so."

"Well, let's ponder that for a moment. Are you aware that NAER promulgated a code of ethics for executive recruiters?"

"Yes. I am."

"How foolish of me!" He threw his hands up in mock distress. "Naturally, you've had to have seen the code of ethics. It fills the first third of NAER's membership application. Your counsel didn't know where to find definitions of ethical behavior for headhunters. Perhaps you should show him NAER's paperwork?"

Ken Ross had become more theatrical, his voice louder, his gestures broader.

Brace yourself. He's getting ready to pounce.

"Then you must know, Ms. Hunnechurch," he said, "that NAER's code of ethics calls for recruiters to refrain from soliciting candidates from client companies."

"I didn't solicit Dennis Grant. He came to me."

"We'll have ample opportunity to discuss that at the trial. Today I have one more question for you: Do you believe that you are a member of an emerging profession? Yes or no!"

"Well . . ." I hesitated.

"That sounds like an eloquent silence, Ms. Hunnechurch. I take it that your answer is *yes*?"

Judge Cavanaugh spoke up. "Let's not make assumptions, Mr. Ross. Give Ms. Hunnechurch a chance to answer the question."

"Certainly, Your Honor," Ross said. "Let me ask you again, Ms. Hunnechurch, do you view executive recruiting as an emerging profession?"

I knew that James wanted me to say *no* and that Daniel wanted me to say *no*. But my conscience refused to go along.

"Yes," I said softly. I could hear myself quiver.

Daniel Harris still had a smile on his face, but now it seemed resigned. I couldn't bring myself to look at James. He must be furious.

Ken Ross took a step backwards. "Thank you, Ms. Hunnechurch, for your candor. *Of course,* executive recruiting is an emerging profession." He turned to face the judge. "Give it time, and headhunting will acquire all the paraphernalia of the older professions—including a code of professional responsibility and state licenses."

Judge Cavanaugh took a noisy breath. "I'm sorry, Mr. Harris. Opposing counsel has muddied the waters sufficiently that I can't conclude as a matter of law that executive recruiting is not an emerging profession. Defendant's motion to dismiss is denied."

A shudder ran through me. This was what it was like to lose in a court of law. I didn't like the feeling.

Chapter Eleven

"I'M IN A MOOD TO PLAY HOOKY this afternoon," I said to James as we left the courthouse. "How about you."

"Sure. Why not?" He heaved a monumental sigh. "I definitely don't feel like working anymore today."

"Are you upset by our morning in court?"

"I'm fine."

"Truly?" I said. "You don't sound fine."

"Trust me. I'm fine."

"Then what shall we do?"

"You choose."

"It's delightful outside," I said. "Let's have a light lunch, then stroll around Annapolis."

"Whatever you say."

"Hang on then. I'll tell Gloria what we're doing." I called Gloria, announced that I'd be gone the rest of the day, and summarized what went on at the wretched hearing.

"Ouch!" she said. "I prayed for a dismissal."

"Me too."

"Do we keep investigating?"

"I don't know. Let me think about it."

I switched off my cell phone and buried it my purse. Ms. Hunnechurch was out of pocket until further notice.

It was a bright June day, not too warm, with a pleasant breeze. James put on his sunglasses and said grudgingly, "Annapolis is a pretty city."

"Indeed! The guidebooks insist that you will find more authentic colonial buildings in Annapolis than in any other historic U.S. city. Not surprising, since it dates back to 1649."

James grunted and looked around. "Where are we right now?"

"The streets of old Annapolis radiate like spokes from two wheels. The larger wheel is State Circle; its hub is the Maryland State House. The smaller wheel is Church Circle; it has St. Anne's Church at its center. The circles are a long block apart and are built on the two highest pieces of land in the city. State Circle is slightly higher than Church Circle. The Anne Arundel Circuit Court is on the rim of Church Circle."

"That's obviously St. Anne's Church." He tipped his head toward the charming nineteenth-century redbrick church, with its gray wooden steeple set atop a redbrick tower.

"You're looking at the third church on the site. It was built in 1858. The original St. Anne's was finished in 1704."

Another grunt. "So who was the 'Anne' that everything around here is named after?"

"Ah, that's a common misconception. There are actually *three* Annes. The city was named in honor of Princess Anne, King James II's youngest daughter, while Anne Arundel County was named after the wife of Lord Calvert. And St. Anne is the legendary mother of Mary, grandmother of Jesus."

"It's too blasted confusing," James said, with unwarranted anger. I didn't question his conclusion.

The top of Annapolis's short Main Street begins at Church Circle. We walked downhill toward the waterfront, window-shopping in the boutiques and specialty shops.

We stopped for lunch at Chick and Ruth's Delly and ordered two of their classic sandwiches: corned beef, coleslaw, and Russian dressing on rye bread. James insisted on having a vanilla milk shake; I chose a more appropriate beverage to accompany corned beef: a can of ginger ale.

We continued to the bottom of Main Street, then jogged left to Dock Street for a better view of the boats in Ego Alley. The Annapolis City Dock is inside a narrow, dead-end channel that's officially called Market Slip. Most locals use its unofficial name, earned because skippers are likely to show off their craft by parading slowly along the slip. Some captains experience great difficulty turning around in the restricted waterway, much to the amusement of onlookers.

On a whim we boarded an Annapolis water taxi and took a quick ride across Spa Creek to the Second Street dock in the Eastport neighborhood of Annapolis. From there we ambled back to downtown across the Spa Creek Bridge. James said nothing during most of our walk.

I finally asked, "What's wrong?"

"Nothing."

"That answer won't do. You are gloom personified, and you look a million miles away."

"I'm busy thinking about things," he said.

"What things?"

James shrugged. I let him be.

We drove home in silence. James had lost his tongue and acquired a frown.

When we turned on to Magothy Street, I could stand it no longer. "I have done nothing to deserve the silent treatment, James," I said. "Tell me what's on your mind—*now!*"

"OK, you asked. We're paying Daniel buckets of money to tell us what to do, and you ignored him this morning."

"I did no such thing."

"My mother had a favorite verse from Proverbs when I was young. *'Pride only breeds quarrels, but wisdom is found in those who take advice.'*"

"How dare you even suggest that I acted pridefully today! I sat in that witness chair like a sheep being sheared, while Daniel Harris destroyed any pride I might have felt in my *occupation*. Clearly I can no longer call executive recruiting a profession."

"I knew you'd react this way. I should have kept my mouth shut." He added one of his signature gloomy head-shakes. "Anyway, my opinion doesn't matter; we can't undo the damage you've done. Let's forget it and try to move on."

Because it was only two-thirty in the afternoon, James found a parking space for my Beetle in front of Hunnechurch Manor. He yanked the hand brake, slammed his door, and stormed into the house ten paces ahead of me. He made a right turn into the living room; I continued on to the kitchen to make a pot of tea.

The blighter is being terribly unfair—and wrong!

After the hearing, Daniel Harris had spent fifteen minutes giving us what he called a "debrief."

"We have to look at the big picture," he had said. "The judge rejected both motions, which means that absolutely nothing changed today. The fact is, very few motions to dismiss are granted. Even fewer when Blanchette and Ross act as plaintiff's counsel."

"I feel that I let the team down," I said. "You had the judge won over until I answered *yes* to that blasted question. I wish I'd said *no*."

"It wasn't your fault, Pippa. Opposing counsel asked for your truthful opinion about head-hunting. That's what you provided. I don't expect my clients to lie under oath." A guilty smile flickered on his face. "Besides, we were in trouble long before Ken Ross skewered you with a question you didn't want to answer. It's my fault that I never heard about the National Association of Executive Recruiters or its code of ethics. They are what really did the damage this morning. I should have asked you about trade associations last week." He patted my shoulder. "Don't sweat what happened today. This was merely round one. The good news is that we fought them to a tie."

I remember glancing at James, hoping to see him nod his agreement—possibly even say something encouraging. He mostly stared at the walls and occasionally stared at his watch.

As I filled the electric kettle, the title music from *The Guns of Navarone* reached a crescendo loud enough to rattle the cups and saucers on the cupboard. James must have cranked our home theater system to full volume.

Well, what better way for a man to sulk than to watch a quintessential guy movie, an improbable World War II adventure story full of machine guns and explosions? It was one of James's favorite flicks. He had ordered the DVD on the Internet. The two women in the cast, I recalled, had minor supporting roles. One of them was shot as a traitor to our side.

There's a notion that might cheer James up.

Even a closely watched kettle eventually boils. I brewed a pot of jasmine tea, the blend James liked best, assembled a suitable peace offering, and made for the living room.

"I brought three different kinds of cookies," I announced to James.

He all but ignored me.

Our furniture was back in appropriate positions, with the sofa against the wall. I set the tray on the coffee table and sat down next to him.

He edged away from me.

"Now you've done it!" I yelled above the din of a chattering machine gun. "I am properly cheesed off. I have done my best to make amends. I have tried to communicate with you for hours, but you are determined not to forgive me."

"I'm trying."

"Not very hard."

James pressed the *Pause* button on the DVD player's remote control. The guns on the screen fell silent, but James did not. He turned to me angrily. "You didn't have to play along with the opposition's lawyer, for crying out loud? If you had said no—or even 'I don't have an opinion'—the judge might have granted the motion. But your foolish pride got in the way."

"I prefer to believe my attorney. The odds were slight that the court would grant a motion to dismiss."

"From now on follow your attorney's lead. He had Judge Cavanaugh eating out of the palm of his hand. The judge wanted to toss the case out of court. And he would have if you . . . "

I interrupted James. "He *might* have if I had lied under oath. Sorry! I'm not prepared to perjure myself."

"That's hogwash! Admitting that head-hunting is not a profession is telling the truth."

"I beg your pardon!"

"Let's face facts. Daniel Harris had it right. You don't need special training to become a recruiter; you merely go to work."

"Ah—as opposed to being an international management consultant."

"Well, every consultant I know holds at least two university degrees, plus several years of relevant experience as a manager. Our clients expect us to have solid credentials. We work a lot like physicians. We diagnose corporate ailments."

"So that's why you need a fancy office and a fancy car. I'm surprised you don't want to build yourself a hospital."

"Very droll. Ha. Ha."

"Tell me, *Doctor* Huston—is that why you also need a fancy house in Founders' Woods?"

"Actually, as you well know, I want a *modest* house in Founders' Woods." He grabbed a cookie. "Of course, if Hardesty takes us to the cleaners in court, we're not going to be able to afford anything with a roof."

He didn't say "thanks to your foolish pride" out loud, but I imagined the thought echoing through the room.

James pressed the *Play* button. Gregory Peck and David Niven resumed shooting at villainous Germans. I stood up with all the dignity I could muster and returned to the kitchen—with my tray of goodies.

What in heaven's name had happened to us?

Before we married, James had often said that God had brought us together. We had been two lonely people. Me, a widow—still bitter about the loss of my husband and daughter, still blaming God for their senseless deaths. James, a confirmed bachelor—still guilty about the frequent trips away from home that alienated his first wife and led to their divorce.

We had found each other and fallen in love. We expected to live happily ever after, but scarcely two months after our marriage, we had begun to bicker routinely. It wasn't the idea of fighting that frightened me; most happily married couples have the occasional spat. But our arguments were about the building blocks of our life together. Where we should live, for example. And how to spend our money. And what we thought of each other's career. We dug our heels in over issues that went to the very heart of our marriage. Moreover, the frequent barrages of negativity in our relationship made it difficult to patch things up. It seemed to me that we remained angry longer after each squabble.

Was our love merely being tested? Or had we each chosen the wrong mate?

I found myself sniffling at the idea. James and I loved each other; we were best pals. We couldn't be fundamentally wrong for each other. No way!

I heard the sound of knuckles rapping on wooden molding. I looked behind me and saw James standing in the archway between our dining room and kitchen. He had a sheepish grin on his face—the sort I'd seen a lot of lately.

"Can I have another cookie?" he said.

"You may. Along with your cup of tea."

"One other thing—we can't fight anymore today."

"We can't?" I said.

"Nope. I'm scheduled to go on a business trip tomorrow."

"To Denver, if I remember?"

"Correct. But I can't leave town if you're mad at me." He took another cookie. "It's an iron-clad rule. Almost a commandment."

"It's an excellent rule," I said. "However, I'm not angry at you. I believe you are angry with me."

He shook his head. "I'm annoyed and disappointed with the outcome of the hearing. I wanted us to be out from under the cloud of the lawsuit. Until we are, both of us will have short tempers and even shorter fuses."

"I've noticed."

James went on: "My mother had another favorite proverb: 'A gentle answer turns away wrath, but a harsh word stirs up anger.'"

"I didn't show my surprise. Two days earlier, I had offered myself the very same wise advice. I merely nodded as James said, "I think we should agree to speak fewer harsh words and also to recognize that it's going to be tough to make sane decisions about houses, cars, furniture, offices, and the other normal stuff in our lives."

"I feel the same way," I said, as a torrent of relief swept through me. The James I knew and adored was back. We hadn't resolved our disagreements, but he had devised a face-saving way for both of us to reestablish a relaxed condition of domestic détente. It was a compromise we could live with without bickering. At least for the rest of the day.

"Tell you what," I said. "Rewind *The Guns of Navarone,* or whatever you do to restart a DVD. I'll watch it with you, then we can order out for Chinese food."

"OK, I guess."

"You guess?"

"It's such a pretty afternoon that I'd rather go for a spin with the Beetle's top down—maybe drive over to Oxford on the Eastern Shore. Later we can overdose on crab cakes at the Fisherman's Inn at Kent Island Narrows."

I grabbed James's arm. "I love it when you read my mind."

═══════════

I didn't fall asleep easily that night, perhaps anticipating that our fragile détente would give way to a new cycle of marital warfare. I was awakened—only minutes later, it seemed—by James, who was moving around our bedroom in the way that husbands do when they are attempting to be quiet and let their wives sleep.

He didn't succeed. His heavy tiptoeing, the squeaking floorboards as he walked back and forth, and the thump of opening and shutting drawers, merged together into a cacophony that made me think of a fight in a bird sanctuary.

My side of our bed is closest to the window. Daylight was beginning to creep past our blinds. I attempted to turn my back on the dawn by rolling toward James's side—and found my nose pressed against a large, solid object.

"Good heavens!" I said in a raspy voice. I willed my eyes to open.

"You're up!" James said. "I tried not to wake you while I packed."

"I know. Thank you." I cleared my throat. "Why is your suitcase in our bed?"

"Sorry about that, Pippa. But my half of the bed is the only flat surface on the second floor." He tugged the suitcase closer to the edge.

"What time is it?"

"About a quarter to six," he said. "You'd better think about getting ready. We have to leave for the airport in an hour."

Why do we have to leave for the airport?

My still-sluggish mind finally grasped the answer. With only one car in the family, I had promised to drive James to the airport.

I slipped out of bed, found my bunny slippers, and padded off to the bathroom. I showered quickly, then went downstairs to make tea, coffee, and a simple breakfast while James finished packing. Our toaster had just popped up two English muffins when I heard glass breaking upstairs, followed by a rather vivid word spoken loudly by James.

"Are you all right?" I called up the stairs.

"I'm fine," he shouted back, "but the bottle of aftershave you bought for me isn't. I knocked it into the bathtub by accident."

I winced. James had asked for the high-priced brand by name. The small bottle had cost more than sixty dollars—a princely sum for what now had become a few ounces of drain cleaner. Surely there had been a safer place to keep it than atop our toilet tank?

And where would that be, Pippa?

"Forget about proverbial cats," I murmured. "There's not enough room in our bathroom to swing a gerbil."

Is this really the ideal home for James and you?

I wasn't dense; I knew that our bedroom was too small and our bathroom absurd. Even our kitchen was barely livable. The narrow countertops were overwhelmed with our few appliances. My little dinette table and chairs were scrunched against a wall. And I had to move one chair out of the way when I wanted to open the door to the back garden.

Why are you so committed to Hunnechurch Manor?

James seemed in fine fettle when he arrived downstairs for our simple breakfast. "The whole second floor really smells great," he said. "I should be clumsy more often."

"I'm truly sorry about your aftershave. I'll replace it for you while you're gone."

"Why thank you, ma'am—but this time, you pick the scent. A designer fragrance is too elegant for a good ole boy from Georgia."

It dawned straightaway that James was trying—really trying—not to start a new argument.

You have to do the same, Hunnechurch.

I set out a jug of orange juice and a selection of preserves and marmalades to accompany our muffins. We ate without talking for a while. If there was any tension in the air, I couldn't feel it. And then I spoke: "When you get back, I want to tour the Cape Cod you found in Founders' Woods."

"You sound *serious.*"

"I am. My love affair with this townhouse is foolish. We need a home where we can live together comfortably."

James nodded. "OK. I'll call the realtor when I get back."

"Good. We need more space—as quickly as possible."

He peered at me cautiously.

"What?" I asked.

"Can I ask what changed your mind?"

"Certainly. *I* was happy in Hunnechurch Manor. *We* will never be."

The sun was beginning its climb into the pink-clouded sky when we left for Baltimore Washington International Airport. It would be another glorious day. James was positively chatty during the trip. He told me about the receptionist candidate he had interviewed the previous Friday. "She has great skills; I plan to phone her references when I'm in Denver." He suggested that we travel to New England in October to see the color of the autumn leaves. "You'll love driving the new BMW—or we could even take the Beetle and keep the top down." He even asked about the associate pastor search committee. "I wouldn't want the responsibility. Imagine the damage you'll do to the church if you guys make a mistake."

And then James broached a surprising subject. "Are you going to do any more investigating of Dennis Grant while I'm gone?"

"Goodness! It's such a lovely morning, I'd forgotten all about the lawsuit."

"It's still hovering over us—like the sword of Damocles."

I couldn't help sighing. "What do you think I should do? This time, I promise to heed your advice and counsel. There will be no more fibs or ambiguities between us."

"What do you want to do?"

"Well, I've been thinking about what Daniel Harris said yesterday. The only person I had to stay away from was Dennis Grant, and he's dead."

Out of the corner of my eye, I saw James nod. "True, Daniel didn't warn you off other folks."

I waited for James to continue. When he didn't, I said, "Do you think I should press forward with my investigation?"

"For the LORD gives wisdom, and from his mouth come knowledge and understanding."

"That's from Proverbs, isn't it?"

"Chapter 2, verse 6."

"Another of your mother's favorites?"

"It was her standard reply whenever I asked a really tough question that she couldn't answer for me."

"Oh boy! You want me to decide."

"Yep. I trust your judgment." He chuckled. "Besides, when you and Gloria get to galloping in a direction of your own choosing, it's best to get out of your way."

We arrived at the airport with ample time left for a proper good-bye. I steered the Beetle behind a van that was unloading a large family and turned off the engine. A state trooper glanced our way but didn't seem to mind that we sat in the car chatting.

"Call me the minute you land in Denver," I said. "I'll be in my office."

"I promise."

"And at home this evening too."

"Definitely," he agreed.

"And at least three times every day you're gone."

"Without fail."

"You can kiss me now," I touched my cheek with my finger. "Here will do fine."

James took my raised hand in his, then grasped the other. He pulled me to his side of the Beetle and gave me a more suitable kiss.

"Can I fly to Denver too?" I said, rather breathlessly. "I'll even carry your luggage."

James became stonyfaced. "I'm no good at being noble, Pippa, but it doesn't take much to see that the problems of two consultants often seem like a hill of beans. In a day or two, you'll understand what I mean." He began to whistle the "Marseillaise," the national anthem of France.

"Excuse me?"

It took me several seconds to grasp that James was doing a Humphrey Bogart impression and that he had paraphrased Rick's famous words from the airport scene of *Casablanca*.

James opened his door, flipped the seat-back latch, and yanked his suitcase out of the backseat in one fluid motion. He came around to the driver's side of the Volkswagen, clucked my chin through the open window, and said, "Here's looking at you, kid."

He waved at me and walked away. I watched him join the crowd and disappear inside the terminal.

I laughed and cried at the same time.

"Oh, James," I murmured as I drove along toward the airport exit ramp, "we have to make our marriage work. We have to!"

```
╔══════════════════════════════════════╗
║        Chapter  Twelve                ║
╚══════════════════════════════════════╝
```

MY SOLO DRIVE BACK to Ryde gave me both the time and the opportunity to brood about my unsettled future. In rapid progression I reflected on the three major sources of turmoil in my life:

1. The Hardesty lawsuit and its impact on Hunnechurch & Associates

2. The investigation that Gloria and I had begun

3. My impending move to Founders' Woods and my loss of Hunnechurch Manor

The last item, I decided, was hardly worth dwelling on. I might hate the idea of leaving Magothy Street, but James and I needed an adequate home. The joys of a proper bathroom would quickly overwhelm the hassles of moving—and even my initial reluctance. By Christmas my much adored townhouse would be one of my fond memories, stored away alongside Chichester, England.

End of discussion, Hunnechurch!

The lawsuit, though, seemed a different kettle of fish. It had become the focal point of my life—a looming presence that could not be ignored. James had chosen an apt figure of speech. Hardesty's legal action threatened Hunnechurch & Associates like a sword hanging by a thread. The trial was months away, but I knew that a verdict for the plaintiff would put us out of business and destroy everything I had worked so hard to create.

And we could easily lose the case. I'd had an unpleasant taste of courtroom reality during the motions hearing. Ken Ross had swiftly eviscerated my lawyer's strategy and made me look the goat. The same thing might come to pass at the actual trial—a possibility that didn't bear thinking about.

But even if the jury determined that I had told the truth, my trip through the Maryland courts—memorialized by a string of articles in the *Baltimore Sun*—would inevitably blacken my reputation. The taint of the lawsuit had already frightened off a handful of potential clients; our current clients might seek less notorious recruiting firms as the suit progressed.

Perhaps *all* of them would.

I lose no matter what happens in court.

I began to sniffle. I dug a fresh tissue out of my purse and imagined how my sister Chloe, that impeccable example of gritty British fortitude, would react if she saw me crying for the second time that morning. She would probably cluck her tongue and say in her crisp English accent, "Sniveling doesn't fix anything, Pippa. Once you wipe your face dry, the problem still remains—unless you gave your problem to God."

I felt myself smile. In this situation Chloe would be half right. My tears could not stop the lawsuit or find new clients for Hunnechurch & Associates during the months ahead. But as for giving my problem to God, well, the more I gave it away, the more he seemed to toss it back in my lap. After all, a few divine words whispered into Judge Cavanaugh's ear the day before would have guaranteed a dismissal.

The tears returned when I thought about our so-called investigation. Gloria and I had put our major marketing campaign on hold to learn why Dennis Grant had lied. What other choice did we have? It seemed foolish to go after new clients until we made certain that that *bloomin'* sword didn't slice Hunnechurch & Associates into tiny pieces. We needn't have bothered—our investigatory efforts had come to naught. We had discovered a few disconnected facts but nothing of real significance. We needed substantive proof that Dennis had lied under oath, the kind of evidence that would sway a judge and jury.

Who has it? Where can we look?

The only person who really knew why Dennis Grant chose to lie was Dennis Grant himself, and he was about to be . . .

I realized with a start that I didn't know where, when, or even if Dennis Grant would be buried. Once again I had managed to push the tragedy of his death to a back corner of my mind.

Dennis was your candidate. You have to attend his funeral.

I made a mental note to learn the arrangements and reached for another tissue.

I had used a full pocket pack of tissues by the time I reached the entrance to the underground garage beneath the refurbished leather warehouse. It was a cramped, single-level garage, with lots of thick columns that made parking even a small car like mine a daunting challenge. Although the morning felt half done, it was only ten past eight, and the garage was only a third full. My favorite space was still available: an easy-to-access spot midway between two columns. I centered the Beetle between the painted stripes on the first try.

I tipped down the sun visor and opened the mirror. My eyes were red from crying and my lipstick slightly lopsided from kissing James.

Nothing that can't wait until you're in the office.

I gathered my clobber, locked the Beetle, and made for the elevator. I didn't notice the woman standing in a shadow until she startled me by saying, "You're Pippa Hunnechurch, right?"

She moved toward me into the light: late twenties, slender, my height, with dark straight hair cut fairly short, prominent cheekbones, and features I thought striking rather than pretty. Her attentive eyes were large and the palest of blue. She wore a sleek slate-gray suit that seemed well tailored and expensive.

Before I could answer her question, she asked another: "You remember me, don't you, Ms. Hunnechurch?"

All at once, I did.

"We met in Hardesty Software's executive suite," I said. "You were Dennis Grant's administrative assistant." It took me another moment to recall her name—Rachel Wilson. "Good morning, Rachel. It's nice to see you again."

She extended her hand and smiled. "I've been waiting here since seven. I wanted to see you, but I didn't know what time you started work."

"Good heavens! Why didn't you call me?"

"This way is more private. Nobody at Hardesty Software is supposed to call you or visit you. The chief counsel sent an executive memo around yesterday. We're supposed to report any contact you make with a Hardesty employee."

"Do you know why I've been declared a corporate pariah?" I asked.

"Not really." The ends of her mouth turned down in a fetching move. Rachel projected a curious blend of sophistication and innocence I'd never before seen in an executive assistant. Quite endearing, I thought. She added, "No one tells me anything."

I saw no reason to be reticent with Rachel: "I am being sued by Hardesty because your chairman believes I recruited Dennis away from the company."

She frowned. "That doesn't sound right. I thought that Dennis contacted you—that he wanted to leave Hardesty."

I resisted the urge to run forward and hug her. Instead, I said, calmly, "That is precisely what did take place."

She replied with an *I-knew-it* grin.

I went on. "By any chance did Dennis discuss his intentions with you?"

At first she peered at the wall behind me. Then she twisted the wedding band on her ring finger. Finally she shook her head. "Gosh—the truth is I don't remember all the details. But I'm pretty sure that Dennis told me he wanted to look you up."

My heart sank. Ken Harris would cut her testimony to ribbons if we tried to call her as a witness. I tried another tack.

"How long did you work for Dennis, Mrs. Wilson?" I asked.

She began to giggle. "I'll tell you a secret. I'm really not married—although people at Hardesty think I am. That way I don't get hit on by guys in the building." She held up her left hand. "This ring saves a lot of 'I'm busy tonight' fibs."

"I shan't tell a soul," I said, surprised that Rachel would need to resort to an old ruse in this day and age. "Now—getting back to Dennis, how long did you work for him?"

"About a year. Dennis was already the chairman's speechwriter when I came to work for Hardesty."

"I expect that he often confided in you."

"Sometimes," she agreed.

"Is there anyone else Dennis might have shared his intentions with?"

"His intentions?"

"His desire to visit me or possibly his decision to leave Hardesty." I added. "He may even have written a new résumé or put together an application letter expressing his interest in a different speechwriting position."

As she thought, her countenance became unguarded, almost childlike. She gave a small sigh and said, "Well, I suppose it's possible he talked with Carol Ericsson, our vice president of corporate communications. They used to be . . ." she hesitated. "Dennis and Ms. Ericsson were really good friends, if you take my meaning."

Really good friends. Now I understood the grief on her face when I'd seen Carol Ericsson at Ryde General Hospital.

Rachel tapped my arm. "I hate to be pushy, but I don't want to be late for work."

"Silly me! You waited an hour for me to arrive, but I've done most of the talking. How can I help you?"

"Dennis called me on Thursday," she said softly. "He asked me to find some of his old speech drafts. I told him that the information technology staff had completely erased the hard disk in his computer two months ago. That's when he mentioned that he might call you." She looked down at the concrete floor. "I feel guilty now that Dennis is dead. *Horribly* guilty."

"Then the disk wasn't erased?"

Her eyes snapped up. "Quite the contrary! They wiped his hard disk the day after he left. However . . ." Another sigh. "Other people in the executive suite may have copies of his drafts. You know—in their computers or maybe paper copies in their files. I didn't feel like agreeing to a scavenger hunt when Dennis called last week. But I intend to look around today. I'll send what I find to his next of kin."

I felt touched—and amused—by her misplaced compassion. "Do you really think that's necessary?" I asked.

Rachel shrugged. "His mother lives out west. I don't know what she'll do with old Hardesty speeches, but I'm going to send them to her. I hope you'll do the same." Rachel pressed a Hardesty business card into my hand. The front read "Dennis Grant, Executive Speechwriter." On the back someone had written "Mrs. Harrison Grant" and an address in Portland, Oregon.

"You want me to send Dennis's mother speeches?" I said, fighting hard not to laugh out loud.

Rachel nodded. "You send copies of the drafts you gave Dennis." She looked at me hopefully. "You did give him some, right?"

"Yes. Shortly before he was killed."

"Good! If you can remember which drafts they are, I won't have to look for them inside Hardesty." Rachel reached into a handbag for a small notepad and a ballpoint pen. She looked so unassumingly earnest waiting to take down my words that I found myself wanting to help her.

"I perused the copies rather quickly," I said. "I remember a couple of speeches aimed at financial analysts, a pair intended for Hardesty employees, and one unusual talk to the board of directors about a planned acquisition. All rather dull, I'm afraid."

She giggled. "You sound like me. I never liked typing the final versions of his speeches. I could never understand what they were about." Her face grew serious. "I just realized—your descriptions don't give me much information about the speeches, do they?"

"Alas, no. I'm sorry." I had a thought. "I know how to resolve your dilemma. I shall mail you copies of the drafts. You can then forward them to Mrs. Grant along with whatever additional speeches you unearth at Hardesty."

"That's a wonderful idea, but I don't want to put you to unnecessary trouble."

"No trouble at all. You shall have the drafts by the end of the week."

"You're much nicer than the woman described in the memo," she said. "I can't imagine why we would want to sue you."

I thanked her—and meant it. Rachel's naive remark had left me feeling revived, almost buoyant.

━━━━━━━━━

I continued upstairs to my office suite and found Gloria singing as she worked at her computer. "A sunbeam, a sunbeam. Jesus wants me for a sunbeam. A sunbeam, a sunbeam . . ."

"Gracious! I haven't heard that song since I was seven years old."

She replied without looking up, "I helped out at Godly Play at church on Sunday. The tune is still stuck in my head." She added. "Do you want a laugh?"

"I desperately need one."

"You got a reminder postcard from the Ryde Chamber of Commerce about next Monday's meeting. It's sitting on top of the *In* basket—you might want to take a quick peek."

I groaned when I saw the postcard. "Hardesty Software Corporation Shares Its Secrets! Learn all about one of Ryde's superstar companies. Meet and greet Hardesty's friendly executives."

Months earlier I had booked Hardesty to give the Chamber's June presentation. Now I, in my program chair role, would have to sit through it politely, smiling all the while.

"One can hope," I said, "that Mitch Hardesty will be out of town."

"Speaking of out of town, did you get James safely to the airport?"

"More than an hour ago."

"An hour? Wow! Traffic must be unusually heavy today."

Gloria's workstation was an elegant cherry-veneer desk and credenza in our reception room. I peeked over her shoulder. She was composing an e-mail message to Ryde Accounting Services, one of our dormant clients. We sent the vice president of human resources a "tickler" every other month to keep Hunnechurch & Associates alive in her mind.

"I exceeded the speed limit all the way home," I said. "However, I was waylaid in the garage by Rachel Wilson. She used to be Dennis Grant's administrative assistant at Hardesty."

Gloria rotated her swivel chair to face me. "A Hardesty person talked to you this morning?"

"And provided three interesting tidbits of information. First, I am *persona non grata* at Hardesty. Second, Dennis had a serious relationship with Carol Ericsson, one of the Hardesty vice presidents. Third, Dennis may well have told Carol of his intention to leave Hardesty."

I sat down in Gloria's visitor's chair and related the details of my *ad hoc* meeting. When I finished, she nodded sagely. "The bottom line is that Carol Ericsson could be our smoking gun, and Rachel Wilson seems like a clueless flake."

"Your elegant summation has captured the essentials."

Gloria peered at me warily. "So what happens next?"

"You send Rachel the speech drafts, and I'll have a chat with Carol—if I can convince her to see me."

"That's *not* what I meant." Gloria gave an impatient toss of her pretty head. "Are we still trying to learn why Dennis lied?"

"Indeed we are. I would also like to find solid evidence that proves he did."

"Yeah! We're expanding our investigation."

"With James's blessing. We should be able to do anything we want provided that we remain unobtrusive, inconspicuous, and . . ."

Gloria interrupted, "And surreptitious. I know, I know." She spun her chair around in a full circle. As she passed by her computer, she touched the key that sent the e-mail message. "Detecting is tons more fun than marketing," she said cheerfully. "I do it a lot better—although I think I sold a small recruiting gig yesterday." She added, "To a new client."

"Splendid!" I truly meant it. We needed all the business we could get. "Tell me everything."

"There's a new tenant on the second floor of this building," she said. "Lotus Flower Foods is the east coast branch office of a Japanese company. I think they import frozen Oriental entrées from Japan, Taiwan, and Korea. Anyway, Mr. Fujinami called yesterday."

"*Konnichi wa Fujinami-san.*"

"Not quite. *Konnichi wa* is 'hello' when you meet someone in person. When you answer a phone call you say *moshi moshi.*"

"The things they teach you in the Maryland National Guard. Moving right along, what did Mr. Fujinami want?"

"A new associate sales manager."

"Someone who speaks Japanese, I presume."

"Hai!" Gloria said. "I began the search yesterday."

"How does one say 'Thank you very much' in Japanese?"

"Domo arigato gozaimasu."

I said, *"Domo arigato gozaimasu,* Gloria," punctuated with a crisp, Japanese-style head bob.

We brewed a fresh pot of strong Assam tea and spent the next two hours in my office brainstorming ways to enlarge the scope of our investigation. We kept avoiding the most obvious source of information, until Gloria finally said, "You and I can talk to people who knew Dennis 'til we're blue in the face, but the mother lode of his stuff is in his apartment. Writers take work home. They have home offices with computers, and date books, and sticky yellow notes tacked to the wall."

"We both know that Dennis's estate won't give us permission to browse through his apartment. Even if they were so inclined, Blanchette & Ross would veto our visit."

"Perfectly true."

"Remind me where Dennis lived."

"Algonquin House, the big condominium at the bottom of Ryde High Street, across from the Waterside Hotel."

"Right. He tried to sell his apartment earlier this year." I poured my third cup of tea. "Is there a way we can browse through Dennis's things *surreptitiously?*"

Gloria took a while to contemplate my question. Among her more exotic detecting skills are the know-how to silence burglar alarms and the how-to of picking locks. She uses them infrequently—after much deliberation.

"Let's find out," she said as she reached for her telephone.

Gloria dialed a local number and switched on the speaker. A man answered on the second ring: "Good morning, this is Terry Collier."

"Hi, Terry," Gloria said. "Got a couple of questions for you. I've got the speaker turned on. Pippa's here with me."

"Howdy, Pippa," he said.

"Hello, Terry," I replied.

"First question," Gloria said. "How goes the background check we ordered?"

"Almost finished, but don't get your hopes up. The most exciting aspects of your man's life are his hobbies. Bicycle riding, cooking, scouting, and ecotourism to endangered rain forests and the like. Otherwise, he's a rather boring fellow who lives a quiet life, saves most of his significant earnings, and toes the straight-and-narrow line."

"Next question. If someone wanted to take a closer look at our man's personal possessions, would that be feasible?"

I didn't understand Gloria's query at first, but then I realized that she had asked her question in a shrewd way that didn't even hint she might skirt the law. Neither she nor Terry had mentioned Dennis's name once during the conversation—or implied that he was dead.

I heard the rustle of paper and guessed that Terry had referred to his case notes. He made an ominous "hmmmm" then said, "I'd say it's a no-go. Too many bells and whistles."

"Gotcha! Thanks."

Gloria broke the connection.

"You heard Terry," she said. "The Algonquin House has too many advanced security features for an easy break-in." Gloria seemed annoyed. "So much for that idea."

"Where does that leave us?"

"Nowhere. We have to start thinking outside the box."

I've never fully understood that metaphor. Where is the box? What's inside it?

A call on our private line interrupted my musing. I lunged at the phone and half shouted, "James, you must be in Denver."

"At the rental car lot. I miss you already."

I felt tears sting my eyes. "Same here. You are the only man whose bunny slippers I want to find under my bed."

Gloria grimaced; she made a gagging gesture with her index finger toward her open mouth. "I'll be at my desk," I heard her say as she left. "If I don't throw up, I'll order us lunch."

I chatted with James for nearly ten minutes. He did most of the talking—about the charms of the Cape Cod house in Founders' Woods. He had been able to reach the realtor before he boarded his flight in Baltimore, and guess what?—the house was still available and even more affordable than James had first thought.

The sound of James's delighted voice made me feel joyous. I listened patiently to his gushing and spoke the appropriate "gosh" and "how nice" at the right times.

"Ooops. There's my car. Gotta run."

"Call me later."

"You bet." He hesitated, then asked quietly, "You really don't mind moving?"

"I really don't. Not anymore."

"I love you, Pippa." He rang off.

Before I had the chance to get utterly weepy again, Gloria charged into my office. "You won't believe who's on hold, waiting for you to get off your private line."

"Give me a clue."

"Her initials are Carol Ericsson."

No doubt about it—my official banishment from Hardesty Software had dramatically increased my popularity in the company's executive suite.

I snatched up the phone again.

"I want to begin with an apology," she said. "My behavior at the hospital was appalling. Please forgive me."

"Certainly. I hope you will accept my condolences for your loss."

Carol was silent for a long moment. "Well, I guess you can't keep secrets from a good headhunter."

I didn't have a clever response, so I said nothing.

Carol went on. "We should talk about Dennis face-to-face, but you've been declared off-limits. I need to be sure that no one from Hardesty will see us together. I have a place in mind."

"Where?"

"Have you ever been trapshooting?"

"What's that?"

"I guess the answer is no. The idea is to shoot at clay pigeons with a shotgun."

"Sounds unnecessary."

She actually laughed. "I suppose it is. However, I shoot trap at a public range in northern Anne Arundel County. I could meet you there at, say, two this afternoon."

"It's a date." I added. "By the way, what does one wear to shoot clay pigeons?"

"Comfortable shoes."

Our lunch arrived five minutes later—two pastrami on rye sandwiches from the delicatessen across the street. Ambrosia wrapped in aluminum foil. Thinking back, my sandwich might have tasted delectable because of my superlative mood. All manner of folks had developed an urge to talk about Dennis Grant, and I was feeling grand.

Chapter Thirteen

WE DOUBLE-CHECKED the driving directions that Carol Ericsson had given me using the mapping program inside Gloria's computer.

"It's 18.7 miles to the Anne Arundel Shotgun Sports Range," she said. "Thirty-eight minutes estimated travel time. You should leave Ryde at one-fifteen."

I looked down at my dress pumps with their two-inch heels. "That leaves me just enough time to zip home and change into my walking shoes."

"While you're at it, ditch the skirt, blouse, and linen jacket. A casual shirt and blue jeans are more appropriate on a trap range."

"I bow to your years of gunnery experience—although keep in mind, I intend to watch, not shoot."

"You'll love it. The smell of burned gunpowder on a warm afternoon is *rousing*."

At five minutes before two my Beetle bounced along a gravel road cut through a dense patch of trees. I had opened my sunroof and

I could hear the sound of gunfire—a shot every few seconds—growing increasingly louder.

The road ended next to a single-story log building with a painted sign over its front door that read "Club House." I parked the Beetle and saw Carol waiting for me on a path that led toward the back of the building. True to Gloria's prediction, she wore a plaid shirt and light blue jeans. Her dark red hair was tucked into a black baseball cap.

"Let's take care of safety first," she said as she handed me a pair of odd-looking earmuffs made of red plastic. "Electronic hearing protectors—the latest technology. The microphones on the outside pick up normal conversation but won't transmit a loud bang to your ears."

The gadgets worked as advertised. When I donned them, the ongoing barrage of gunshots sounded miles away.

She went on. "Next, it's important to me that you understand why I'm here. I've fired a thousand shotgun shells since Dennis died. Maybe I'm taking out my anger on defenseless clay pigeons. Maybe it's merely something to do. Possibly I'm a shallow person. I don't care why trapshooting helps. All I know is that demolishing targets helps me to get through the day. Does that make sense?"

I nodded. People find different ways to cope with grief. Who was I to deny the comforting properties of gunpowder?

We walked behind the building to a waist-high wooden rack that held two shotguns.

"I brought a gun for you, just in case. We can fool around while we talk about Dennis Grant—knock down a few birds for fun. Are you game?"

"I'd rather not," I said. "I know nothing of the sport."

She ignored the distress in my voice and showed me a palm-sized disk, painted fluorescent orange, which resembled a miniature flying saucer.

"This is a clay target—also called a 'clay pigeon' or a 'clay bird.' It flies through the air like a little Frisbee, thanks to a throwing machine inside the trap house." She pointed to a small shed half buried in the ground. Beyond its roof, a pie-shaped open area, roughly thirty yards deep, stretched to a stand of trees.

"When you're ready to shoot," she went on, "you shout 'Pull!' The *scorer*—the man sitting on the tall chair behind us—pushes a button, and the machine does its thing."

She grinned. "Here's the fun part. The throwing machine continuously swings from side to side. Sometimes it flings the bird left, sometimes straight ahead, and sometimes toward the right. You have a fraction of a second to figure out the trajectory."

"Quite a challenge," I said, "for those who take pleasure in shooting guns."

"There are five stations on a trap field," she said. "A round of trap consists of five shots from each station. Since this is your first lesson, I'll shoot from the center. It's the easiest."

I looked to our left. The club had four trap fields. Only one other field was in use. Three gunners blasted away at targets with enthusiasm.

"I've never fired a shotgun in my life." I left unspoken my determination not to start now.

"Happily, trapshooting is easier than it sounds because you point a shotgun rather than aim it. Moreover, you shoot a *cloud* of lead at the target." She handed me a shotgun shell—a red plastic cylinder with a brass base. It looked about the size of my thumb. "There are 350 tiny lead pellets inside. A single pellet is enough to break a fragile clay bird."

I put the shell back in her hand. "Thanks, but no thanks."

Don't blow it Hunnechurch, you're on the edge of being rude.

Carol didn't seem to mind my snippiness. Perhaps she'd pegged me as a captive audience—someone who would waste hours of time for a morsel of useful information about Dennis Grant.

She reached for a utilitarian looking shotgun—the barrel and other metal parts were blued steel; the stock and forearm were oiled walnut. "This is my pump-action," she said, "a great gun for a beginner. It holds five shotgun shells, but you load one at a time when you shoot trap."

She pointed the barrel downrange and loaded a shell through an opening on the left side. When she snapped the forearm forward, the gun made a soft metallic clank.

"This little doohickey under my thumb is the safety button," she said. "Slide it forward and the gun is ready to fire."

I retreated several paces away.

She lifted the shotgun to her shoulder.

"Pull!"

An orange flying saucer soared out of the trap house. Carol swung the barrel to follow its path. *Bang!* A cloud of orange bits floated to the ground like fairy dust.

I said the first words that came into my head. "That's incredibly cool!"

"Not what you expected—right?" She pumped her gun's forearm to eject the spent shell, then reloaded.

"Not at all."

"Pull!"

A second target catapulted toward the trees. *Bang!* The bird vanished in a fascinating orange puff.

"Bravo!" I said.

"Pull!"

Bang! Another target disintegrated.

"You are brilliant at this."

"I have a secret," she said. "I imagine that I'm shooting at a gal named Rachel Wilson." She glanced at me over her right shoulder. "Do you know who she is?"

I hid my surprise with a pensive stare. "I've met her. She worked for Dennis."

"She did a lot more than work for him. Pull!"

Bang! Hit.

"Rachel Wilson is the reason I asked you here today. Pull!"

Bang! Hit.

"She's responsible for the mess you're in at Hardesty. Pull!"

Bang! Hit.

"It's only fair that you know what really happened."

Carol kept her shotgun pointed at the ground while she spoke. "Dennis thought about living with me. He even put his condo up for sale late last year. But we decided that we had to keep our relationship a secret. After all, we both reported to Mitch Hardesty; we both often attended the same meetings; and we both knew that Mitch hates office romances. Our discretion would prevent unpleasant complications. At least, that's what Dennis kept telling me." *Clank!* Carol loaded another shell. "And then Rachel Wilson became more important in Dennis's life." Carol swung her shotgun back to her shoulder. "Pull."

Bang! Hit.

"What can I say about Rachel?" Carol said. "Young. Attractive. Young. Ambitious. Young. Untrustworthy as they come. *Young!*" She sighed. "It galls me to admit that Dennis swapped me for a younger woman. It's such a cliché. Pull!"

Bang! Hit.

"To make matters worse," she said as she reloaded, "Rachel is married. She turned my poor, weak Dennis into an adulterer. Pull!"

Bang! Hit.

"Want to hear something funny? A detective visited me yesterday. He asked for my whereabouts on Saturday morning and wondered if I owned a black truck. Pull!"

Bang! Hit.

"Lucky for me, I'd driven to a gun show in Crownsville, Maryland, in my Mercedes sedan, with three other people. Besides which—how could I ever kill Dennis? I still love the jerk. Pull!"

Bang! Her aim was off. The target glided to the ground and shattered.

"See! Everyone misses sooner or later. Why don't you have a go?"

I surprised myself by saying, "Why not?"

Carol gave me a pair of yellow-tinted safety glasses to wear, then showed me how to nestle the shotgun's rubber butt plate against my shoulder, how to gaze along the barrel, and how to squeeze the trigger gently. She clipped a leather pouch to my belt and dropped in a handful of shotgun shells.

I moved to the shooting station, loaded the gun, and lifted the barrel.

"Pull!" I yelled, louder than necessary.

The clay pigeon soared high to my right. I followed it diligently with the barrel but forgot to pull the trigger.

"Ha!" Carol said. "I do the same thing sometimes."

"Pull!" This time the target veered slightly to my left.

Bang! The shotgun kicked hard against my shoulder. I saw the undamaged bird fall to the ground.

"I missed." I said.

"It takes awhile to get the hang of trapshooting. The trick is to point in front of the moving target. That's called 'leading' the bird."

Two more shots, two more misses.

"You're still shooting behind the birds. Keep way ahead of the next target."

"Pull!"

The bird split apart into several pieces. No fairy dust this time, but at least I'd scored a hit.

"Good shot!" Carol said. "You nicked that one with a few pellets."

I completely missed the next two pigeons but pulverized the two after that.

My tally for twenty-five shots was six downed birds and an exceedingly sore shoulder. Nonetheless, I had thoroughly enjoyed the experience. Carol also appeared in a good mood; I decided to risk a direct question.

"Carol, did Dennis ever mention his intention to seek my help?"

"'Fraid not. He decided to quit long after we, uh, stopped discussing such matters. But I can tell you why Dennis abandoned the best job he ever had." Carol laid the pump shotgun against the rack. "Rachel Wilson engineered Dennis's leaving. She wanted him far away from me because I would have won him back.

"Rachel understood that Dennis would soon come to his senses. So she convinced him that he deserved more money, not to mention the honor of writing speeches for a more important boss than Mitch Hardesty. *She* encouraged Dennis to contact you." She broke into a wry smile. "We can both blame our recent misery on Mrs. Rachel Wilson."

"Perhaps we can," I said. "But why did Dennis lie to Mitch Hardesty?"

"I consider Dennis Grant the second most self-centered person I've known—the kind of man who expected to be wooed by a headhunter. My guess is that his ego couldn't admit that he did the wooing." Another wry smile. "Dennis saw himself as the center of the universe. I'm sure he never supposed that his little fib would cause Mitch to go bananas and file a lawsuit against you."

I probed my sore shoulder and felt a bruise forming. "*Bananas* is the perfect word to describe Mitch Hardesty's overreaction."

"Mitch is the most self-centered person I know. No one leaves the company—unless *he* fires them. Dennis's departure made him furious. So he sued you." She laughed. "Overreaction is a way of life in our executive suite. Last year we had an admin on the floor who referred to Mitch as a 'blowhard' in an e-mail. He found out and fired her. He then sent an e-mail to the entire staff saying, 'I'm the best at what I do. Call me *blowhardest,* if you are so inclined—anything else is demeaning.'"

"I love it! *Blowhardest* is a perfect moniker for Mr. Hardesty."

"Yeah. But now *Blowhardest* has a tiger by the tail. He's too proud to admit that lawsuit against you is hurting us too. Did you know that Nailor & McHale stopped working for Hardesty Software when they learned why we filed suit?"

"*Really?*"

"Oscar McHale delivered the news personally, said he won't risk a future lawsuit against Nailor & McHale based on spurious ethical claims. Mitch threw him out of our building." She poured a box of shotgun shells into the leather pouch clipped to her belt. "The truth is, we could use a good headhunter right now. Mitch needs a full-time speechwriter who understands him the way Dennis did. You could find the right person in days."

"Except for one minor detail—Mitch Hardesty hopes that the Maryland Circuit Court will put me out of business."

"That could change in a flash if Mitch learns the truth about Dennis." Her eyes began to gleam. "Go after Rachel Wilson. She has *all* the facts. Get your lawyer to depose her. Make her sweat. She'll crack like a clay pigeon hitting a brick wall."

"I shall mention the idea to my attorney." I quickly changed the subject. "Carol, what arrangements have been made for Dennis's funeral?"

"Saturday at ten a.m." Then she added. "In Portland, Oregon."

"Oh my."

Carol laughed out loud. "Send flowers. It's more than Dennis would do for you."

She reached for the second shotgun. It looked much more expensive than the pump action. Flawlessly polished metal. Gold inlays on the side. Wood that might have graced an elegant piece of furniture.

"This is my target gun," she said. "The one I shoot in competitions."

I watched her shoot down ten birds in quick succession. Each made a pretty yellow puff in the sky.

My mind filled with unanswered questions as I drove back to Ryde for the second time that day.

Why would two women, both "good friends" of Dennis Grant, choose the same day to rebel against a company edict and share secrets with me?

Could Carol Ericsson be right about Dennis's pride? Had Dennis put my future at risk merely because he felt reluctant to admit that he'd called a headhunter first?

Why did Rachel admit to being unmarried but not mention her relationship with Dennis Grant? And what was Rachel's real agenda? The more I replayed our conversation in the garage, the crazier it sounded to send speech drafts to Oregon.

One question seemed easy to answer: Why did Carol tell me her tale of woe?

Three hundred years ago a British playwright named William Congreve first observed that hell has no fury like a woman scorned. Anyone could see that Carol Ericsson wanted to punish Rachel Wilson. What simpler way than by using me and my attorney to crack her former rival and probably get her fired, to boot?

Much of Carol's story rang true. I could imagine Dennis falling away from her and toward the younger Rachel. But the idea that Rachel encouraged Dennis's departure because she feared Carol . . . *pure wishful thinking.*

I had to swim against a current of people when I arrived at my building at four-forty-five. Everyone else in the lobby was leaving for the day.

Surprisingly, the front door to our office suite was locked. When I turned my key, I found David Friendly sitting at Gloria's workstation, using her Web browser to check his e-mail.

"Your associate has left the premises," he said. "And no, I don't have any idea where she went. It looked like a spur-of-the-moment trip."

"When did all this happen?"

"I dropped by about four. She asked me to hold down the fort 'til you got back." He held up a mug. "She brewed a fresh pot of tea before she left. Great stuff! She called it 'Russian Caravan' blend."

"My favorite afternoon tea. I shall join you in a cuppa."

As I poured, I said, "You usually tell us when you plan to visit."

"Like Gloria, I took a spur-of-the-moment trip too."

"Curious behavior from a man as well organized as you are."

"Yeah, well, I'm not that sure that I want to go ahead with what I'm here to do."

"I won't even try to understand what you just said." I sat in Gloria's visitor's chair.

David took a deep breath. He peered at me over his mug with somber eyes. "The other day you asked for my help. I may need your help in return."

"It goes without saying that I shall . . ."

"Stop!" he interrupted. "Don't agree until you hear me out." He hesitated. "I plan to write an article for the *Ryde Reporter* that could propel me to a new level of fame and fortune—an article that might win a Pulitzer Prize—an article about deceit, treachery, disloyalty, and revenge at Hardesty Software Corporation."

A sip of tea went down the wrong way. I began to cough but managed to say, "You rotter! You plan to write a *bloomin'* exposé about me."

"Not necessarily."

"What does *that* mean?"

"I don't think you're directly involved," he said.

"Cripes! Thank you for that."

"Although you might be." He frowned. "Trouble is, I can't tell you anything with certainty."

"David, I command you to stop this piffle immediately. Speak English and start at the beginning."

"The beginning?" He smiled. "That would be the moment you called me your knight in shining armor."

"David . . ."

"I'm serious. I felt touched. I decided to look beyond our archives for details on Hardesty Software. I called two of my contacts in the financial community to find out what the smart money thinks about the company."

Our front door opened. Gloria came in carrying a canvas zip-top tote bag. I smiled a greeting at her, then gave my attention back to David. "Keep talking."

"Hardesty has a new nickname on Wall Street: 'Hard Luck' Software."

"Catchy."

"Naturally, I was intrigued. So I dug a little deeper, asked a few more financial types why institutional investors are down on Hardesty."

"And?"

"There are two reasons. First, Hardesty is in the midst of a genuine financial crisis. The company quietly laid off ninety-three full-time employees last month. Second, the company can't seem to do anything right in the marketplace. Hardesty hasn't won a new government software contract since last September—almost ten months ago. The company's been outbid in ten recent acquisitions."

"Yikes!"

"With a capital Y."

"Sounds like a case of raging bad management," I said.

"Maybe. But I'm betting on another possibility." David rocked his swivel chair forward and set his mug down. "I have a friend," he said softly, "who has a friend who specializes in industrial security. It's a close-knit fraternity, and the guys sometimes compare notes among themselves. Anyway, my friend reports there's a rumor going around that Mitch Hardesty personally commissioned background checks on the company's senior executives. He's especially interested in anyone who's had an unexplainable increase in wealth."

Gloria, who had quietly perched on the edge of her workstation, whistled softly. "Sounds like Hard Luck Software has a corporate spy."

David nodded at Gloria. "That was my interpretation of the rumors too. Mitch Hardesty thinks that competitors have been able to out-maneuver the company because one of his key people is selling confidential information."

"Do you know which firm is doing the background checks?" she asked.

"I don't *know* anything. My conjecture of industrial espionage at Hardesty rests on a foundation of gossip, innuendo, and speculation. I intended to scrap the notion until someone killed Dennis Grant." David paused to let his words sink in. "What if the murder of a former Hardesty executive wasn't a coincidence? What if Dennis is somehow connected to the mess at Hardesty?"

I felt a frisson of excitement race down the small of my back. I said, "What if David Friendly can weave the threads together into a tale of deceit, treachery, disloyalty, and revenge?"

"That's the biggest what-if." He raised his hands in a gesture of frustration. "Don't get me wrong—I'm not being modest. I have the skills to write a blockbuster article. What I don't have is enough solid information about Hardesty Software Corporation."

"I know that feeling well."

"Both our investigations might be more productive if we join forces, work together, and share what we learn."

"Three cheers for a grand idea."

Once again David interrupted me. "It's a *risky* idea. Working together means that you'll be poking around in a murder. That can be dangerous. And there's an annoying problem. I can't disclose my confidential sources to you. I won't go back on the promises I made to keep their identities secret. Worst of all, my final story could make you look bad. I don't know if you've played an accidental role, either for good or evil. But whatever we discover, I plan to tell the unvarnished truth in my article."

"I repeat. Three cheers for a grand idea."

David pulled me to my feet and applied a massive hug.

"Our first challenge," he said, "is to patch the biggest hole in our operations. How do we get information from *inside* Hardesty?"

Gloria cleared her throat. "All taken care of," she said.

"Pardon?" I said.

"How?" David said, simultaneously.

"Remember those ninety-three employees Hardesty let go?" Gloria said. "The company has begun to use temporary personnel to do their work. I saw an opening for a part-time administrative assistant posted on the *Jobs in Ryde* Web site—right next to our ad for a Japanese-speaking sales manager. I applied for the job. The temp agency wants me to start at Hardesty tomorrow. I'll do miscellaneous clerical work in the executive suite."

"Are you mad?" I said. "Gloria Spitz can't work for Hardesty Software. You would be recognized immediately. Blanchette & Ross will do nasty legal things to us—help me, David."

"Some sort of injunction, I suppose," he said, "if the judge thought you pulled a fast one."

"Precisely!" I squeaked. "Not to mention that Daniel Harris would undoubtedly send me packing. We—*I*—simply can't take the risk."

"Can you think of another way to nose around Hardesty's executive suite?" She gave me a chance to respond. All I could do was shrug. "Me neither," she continued. "And please give me some credit. I've been trained as a private investigator; I know what it takes to do a successful undercover investigation." She held up the canvas tote. "I wore a disguise at the interview. I'll wear it at Hardesty."

"One might as well try to camouflage the queen of England."

"I shall return," she said. She went into my office and shut the door.

David shook his head. "I agree with you—it can't be done. *Nothing* will hide that gal's great looks."

"Men are *so* predictable." I emphasized my criticism with a high-powered raspberry, blown with verve and precision. Then I poured myself another mug of tea.

The door opened and *another* woman emerged. Gloria had put on a mousy-brown wig, some sort of makeup that made her complexion look pasty, and tortoiseshell eyeglasses that drew attention away from her eyes. She'd donned a man-style shirt that was one size too large and a pair of baggy khaki pants.

It was a simple but effective disguise. I had to admit that Gloria looked frumpy.

"Hi," she said. "Call me Helen Nelson."

"Even if you could succeed, *Helen,* I reject any scheme to deceive Hardesty. We are fighting against a charge of unethical behavior. Sneaking you into the executive suite is unlikely to improve our reputation."

"I admit that I used a false name and told a small little fib to get the job. I claimed that I worked as a secretary at Collier Investigations for the past two years. Terry Collier will back me up when they check my references. But the rest of my résumé is the truth." She lifted the wig off her head. "I'll do a good job at Hardesty."

"I don't like it. Actually, I hate the suggestion."

"It's a *temporary* assignment." Gloria moved her hands close together to portray the brevity of "temporary." "Three little days—tomorrow, Thursday, and Friday. I plan to act ethically at all times. I won't lie, I won't steal, I won't interrogate other staff members. I'll do exactly the menial chores I'm told to do." She folded her eyeglasses. Gloria Spitz had returned. "Plus, I'll listen. I'm bound to hear something interesting during the next three days."

"What if I forbid you to do it? And threaten to fire you?"

"It won't work." She laughed. "If you fire me, I'll have a new job to go to."

I glanced at David. The silly grin on his face told me that he was thinking delicious thoughts of the priceless intelligence Gloria would provide. Or maybe he had imagined a good place to hang his Pulitzer.

Inevitably, perhaps, I felt myself succumbing. Like it or not, I needed the information that Gloria might gather. Necessity is the mother of invention—and also of rotten decisions.

Chapter Fourteen

I AWOKE EARLY on Wednesday morning with a severe case of the I-don't-have-anything-useful-to-do-today blues. I thought of James consulting in Denver, David Friendly researching his article, Gloria playing undercover agent at Hardesty Software—but I had nothing fruitful planned for the day. The only appointment on my calendar was the seven-thirty p.m. meeting of the associate pastor search committee; the sole high priority item on my to-do list was my instruction to myself to reread Paul's Epistle to the Romans. The thought of spending my evening with Monica DeVries made me groan—and so did, I confess, the prospect of plowing through the most theologically challenging book in the New Testament.

Face it, Hunnechurch, Gloria and David have taken charge of the investigation.

I wanted to contribute, but I didn't know how. Trying to interview more denizens of Hardesty's executive suite seemed out of the question. Even if they violated their corporate edict against meeting with me, what good would talking to them do? My chats with Rachel Wilson and

Carol Ericsson had generated more questions than answers—questions that pointed rather far afield of what we needed to know.

"Who cares why Rachel admitted that she wasn't married?" I said to myself in the mirror as I brushed my teeth.

Gloria had done something magical with our phone system so that all incoming calls at Hunnechurch & Associates automatically transferred to my cell phone. The upshot was, I had no particular reason to rush to the office that morning.

In fact, nothing is stopping you from working at home for the rest of the day.

I donned my oldest, softest jogging suit; brewed a pot of tea; toasted an English muffin; and brought my study Bible to the kitchen table. I also toted Winston's cage in from the living room. "We're on our own today, laddie. We need to keep each other company."

I had finished two muffins and the fourth chapter of Romans when my cell phone rang.

"Hunnechurch & Associates," I said.

"*Hmmm*—that strikes me as a mighty formal way to greet your husband," James said. "I had hoped for darling or honey."

"Goodness, James, I hardly supposed you would call so early—it's only six-fifteen in Denver."

"My alarm rang seconds ago. Naturally the first thing on my mind this morning is you."

"Really?"

"Truly."

The remainder of my British reserve melted away. "Oh, James. When you're not at home, I think about my years of being single. I wonder how I ever managed by myself."

"Same here. You mean everything to me, Pippa."

"And don't you ever forget that," I said emphatically.

"I'll sure try not to, ma'am," James drawled. Then he asked, "Is anything exciting going on in Ryde that I should know about?"

His obvious question caught me off guard. Should I tell him that Gloria had placed herself inside Hardesty as a part-time private eye?

Of course, you should! You promised yourself an end to fibbing and ambiguous answers.

"Our investigation has taken an unforeseen turn, my love," I said. "Gloria has gone undercover at Hardesty Software. On her own initiative, and against my urging, she accepted a temporary assignment in the Hardesty executive suite."

I waited for the explosion, but none came. "Well, if it was anyone other than Gloria doing the snooping," he said calmly, "I'd be upset bigtime. Mitch Hardesty has a burr under his saddle about industrial spies. His security people will skin her alive if they catch her, but Gloria's probably good enough to stay uncaught."

"Gloria has given her word to detect rather than spy. She will keep her ears open while she performs menial chores in the hope that she'll come across something useful. But it's odd that you should mention industrial espionage. David Friendly believes that a genuine industrial spy recently toiled inside Hardesty Software. He has joined forces with us."

"Who told David that?" James interrupted me, his tone abruptly harsh.

"I don't know. He mentioned a friend who has a friend—but it's all rather hush-hush."

James said nothing in reply. I heard his steady breathing over the line.

"Is anything wrong?" I finally asked.

"Of course not. What could be wrong?" He added, "I wouldn't have expected David to waste his time chasing silly rumors."

I forget what we chitchatted about for several more minutes. I was in the mood to talk, but James seemed to have other things on his mind. He finally said, "Sorry, love, I have to say good-bye and get ready." I pressed the *End Call* button and peered guiltily at my Bible.

No! You can't stop reading Romans yet. It's fourteen pages long, and you're only three pages in.

I pressed on, as Paul himself recommended, and soon came across, "And we know that in all things God works for the good of those who love him."

This familiar verse perpetually amazes me. I know—*sort of*—that it's Romans 8:28. Yet it always seems brand-new when I read it. I began to ponder the thorny patch in our marriage that James and I had just come through. Had God used the stress of the lawsuit and our differing opinions about Hunnechurch Manor to strengthen our relationship?

Ask James—later! Meanwhile, keep reading!

By ten o'clock, I'd finished my pot of tea and the ninth chapter of Romans—well past the halfway mark. I gave in to bleary-eyed temptation and decided that I'd reviewed enough of Paul's letter to appreciate a good sermon on the subject if, and when, I heard it.

"Paul won't mind if you slack off some," I told myself. "It had been Monica's overzealous idea to read the whole letter."

I zipped my Bible into its carrying case and opened my attaché. Gloria's success attracting a new client inspired me to try a bit of marketing. I began making cold calls to companies in and around Ryde. By eleven-thirty I felt talked out. However, I'd located three executives who were willing to learn more about Hunnechurch & Associates. I fired up my laptop computer, logged on to the Internet, and sent myself an e-mail reminder to prepare three information packets—complete with copies of our new brochure.

One of the three prospects, the vice president of human resources at a computer security consultancy that recently relocated to Ryde, had been unusually enthusiastic. "Recruiting key people," he had said, "is one of those specialties that's best left to specialists."

"A wise attitude," I'd replied.

"It's the secret of my success." He laughed. "When an expert who can help me do a better job is a phone call away, I reach for the phone."

"Ah, then I expect to hear from you soon."

I puttered around the kitchen and brewed a fresh pot of tea while his amiable words—"an expert who can help me do a better job"—percolated in my mind.

Cripes! What a dolt you are.

I had completely forgotten about two experts who could help *me* do a better job. My sister was married to a clergyman, yet I hadn't asked Chloe or Stuart for their advice about serving on the associate pastor search committee. I reached for the phone and dialed England.

"Pippa!" cried Chloe. "How wonderful to hear your voice. Why just this morning Stuart and I lamented the fact that you and your charming new husband live three thousand miles from home. We miss the two of you dreadfully."

"Maryland is our home, Chloe."

"How brave of you to feel that way."

"Yes, well, we miss you too." I said. "Is Stuart there?"

"Of course. Where else would he be?"

I silently counted to five. "Chloe, please call Stuart to the telephone. I want his counsel."

"About what?"

"Pastoral matters. Specifically, what one needs to be a successful pastor."

I heard her gasp. "Good heavens, Pippa! I hope you haven't felt what you believe to be a call to the ministry."

"Chloe, please ask Stuart to the telephone."

"I speak with complete candor, Pippa. The pulpit is not for you."

"Get Stuart now!"

"I am sure you mean well, but you are far too *flighty* to be a sound shepherd of a flock."

"Flighty? Rubbish! I am an ideal person to take holy orders."

"You can't be serious."

"Why not? I would look positively fetching in a cassock."

"Pippa! That's *blasphemous!*"

I let her sputter a long moment before I said, "Relax, Chloe, I am pulling your leg. The pulpit is in no danger from me. I enjoy being a headhunter."

"I should hope so." She sniffed. "Give me a moment. I shall find Stuart."

I heard murmuring and the occasional "Oh dear" before Stuart came on the line. I wasn't surprised when he dove right in: "Chloe tells me you are in fine fettle and particularly irksome today."

"She deserved to be irked," I said.

Chloe fought back. "I merely tried to fathom your puzzling interest in the pastorate."

"Simple," I said. "Last week I became a member of our church's associate pastor search committee. I need practical advice. How does one identify an effective pastor?"

"Prayerfully," Stuart said.

"Naturally we pray," I said quickly. "That goes without saying. What I need to understand are the characteristics of a successful candidate. Is it more important to have a strong theological underpinning? The skill to deliver exciting sermons? The ability to be wise counselor? Physical stamina? A sound marriage? A stable private life? A good sense of humor? A strong moral compass? The know-how to delegate responsibilities?" I caught my breath. "Choosing a pastor is so confusing."

"Yes, I'm sure it can be. Fortunately, the choice of pastoral leadership will ultimately be made by a higher authority than your committee."

"Not so, Stuart. Ryde Fellowship Church is not part of a hierarchy. We don't report to a bishop."

"I have a significantly *higher* authority in mind."

"Pardon?"

"One assumes that your committee has been reading candidate histories and listening to taped sermons," Stuart said.

"Indeed we have," I agreed.

"Well and good—as long as you remember that your chief responsibility is to identify the pastor who best fits God's purposes for your congregation. In other words, you have been brought together to pool your collective wisdom and discern the will of God."

My smugness evaporated; I abruptly understood what Stuart meant. "Blimey! Our client in this search is God."

"Precisely," Stuart said. "He is the reason your church exists."

"Oh, dear! I've put the cart before the horse."

"A common human failing—but easily corrected."

"I wish I had spoken to you before I agreed to serve on the blasted committee. My wisdom is stretched rather thin these days."

"You won't face the challenge alone, Pippa. The Holy Spirit will be with you at every step of your deliberations." He added, "We'll pray for you."

"Please do—and thank you."

"On that, I shall leave you in the competent hands of your sister. I must get back to my sermonizing."

Chloe is an expert interrogator; I expect her to ask a string of astute questions whenever we chat. But her sheer perspicacity that day amazed me.

"Now that we're alone, I have a question for you. Has James experienced any difficulties settling in?"

"Difficulties?"

"Don't be coy. Four months ago James Huston was a happy bachelor in Atlanta, Georgia; today he's a married man in Ryde, Maryland. Marrying you has forced the dear man to cope with a major change in geography, a cross-ocean wedding, the tribulations of married life, your many idiosyncrasies, and the indignities of taking up residence in a miniscule townhouse barely large enough for a single woman. One would expect James to suffer the odd difficulty of adjustment."

I hesitated a moment too long.

"I thought so! Tell me all—sister to sister."

I sighed as heavily as I could to signal that I was answering under duress. "If you must know, we're having—*had*—a bit of bother over Hunnechurch Manor."

"Go on."

"We plan to move to a larger home."

"A wise decision. Your home is impossibly small."

I couldn't help springing to the defensive—not after thirty-five years of arguing with Chloe.

"My townhouse was home to a family of *seven*."

"Ah yes. The famed Welsh rope merchant you so often talk about. What was his name?"

"Llewellan."

"I'm sure Mr. Llewellan and his kin were happy as bugs in a rug, but he undoubtedly owned far fewer possessions than James and had much more modest expectations. As I recall, James lived in a rather large house in Georgia."

"Chloe—the bother is no more. I have agreed to move. End of story." The line fell silent for a while. "Chloe?"

"Curious," she said. "I expected the major difficulties in your new marriage to center on Hunnechurch & Associates and the Peachtree Consulting Group."

Chloe's declaration knocked me for six. "You *expected* us to fight?"

"Certainly. It can be remarkably difficult for two people such as you and James to properly express love for each other at first."

"I beg your pardon!"

"First Corinthians 13:4."

"Blast you, Chloe. I've spent the past two hours with my nose in the Bible. I don't intend to open it again merely to understand your non-sensical comments."

"One suspects you know the verse. 'Love is patient, love is kind. It does not envy, it does not boast, it is not proud.'"

"And your point is?"

"Think on it, Pippa. Think on it."

━━━━━━━━━━━

I forgot all about First Corinthians because I had other, more pressing, things to think on that afternoon. James took a backseat to my concerns about Gloria's undercover detecting and the upcoming evening meeting of the associate pastor search committee. They flipped back and forth in my mind like adjacent channels on a telly.

Click. I imagined Gloria running through the executive suite, trying to escape a burly security guard.

Click. There stood Monica DeVries, lecturing me like a schoolgirl for failing to complete my homework assignment.

Click. Over to Gloria, being led away in manacles. Is that why she hadn't called and assured me that all was well?

Click. Back to Monica—finger pointing, head shaking, face a mask of dismay as I told her I had no intention of reading the second half of Romans. Ever!

I actually felt cheerful when the time came to leave Magothy Street. Driving across town to Ryde Fellowship Church would put my brain to productive use, if only for fifteen minutes.

A note hanging on the front door announced that our meeting had been moved to the sanctuary. I wasn't surprised. Monica DeVries had mentioned the previous Sunday that she wanted us to hear the candidate tapes "in a more realistic setting," as she put it. Perhaps it would help. Or perhaps Monica craved to chair the committee from the pulpit.

Don't be unkind, Hunnechurch. Monica probably doesn't mean to be difficult.

The lights in the sanctuary were dimmed except for a powerful spotlight that shone on the empty pulpit. Monica was sitting behind the table that Reverend Clarke uses to celebrate the Lord's Supper. She smiled at me when I walked down the aisle. I chose a seat in the third row of pews on the left side—where James and I usually sit on Sundays.

Monica called the committee to order promptly at seven. "Heavenly Father," she said, "once again we ask you to guide our hearts and thoughts. Bless our meeting this evening by giving us perception and good judgment as we move ahead in the process to find a new associate pastor. In Jesus' name. Amen."

Monica scanned the room. "Do we have any prayer requests before we get started?"

There were two requests. The first was a prayer for healing for Don Henley's mother, who had heart trouble; the second was a prayer for safety for Rose Robinson's brother, an army helicopter pilot on duty in Korea. I thought about praying for resolution for my lawsuit, but my problem seemed so minor in comparison to the health and welfare of living people.

Monica switched to meeting mode. "As you know," she said, "I am committed to authenticity. I think it essential that we hear our candidate pastors in an authentic locale that mimics an actual Sunday worship service," she said. "I have asked Randy Donner, our sexton, to operate the sanctuary sound system." She waved toward a glass-windowed booth in the rear of the sanctuary; the gray haired man inside waved back. "Randy has placed a loudspeaker behind the pulpit so we will hear the sermons delivered authentically."

I looked to my right in time to see Carrie Logan, our high school student, roll her eyes. I bit back a grin; a loudspeaker behind the pulpit seemed a tad overdone—even by Monica's standards.

She gave a "play tape" signal by pointing her finger. The friendly and confident candidate I'd liked on Sunday began to speak. His voice, amplified by a real sound system, sounded much crisper and clearer than the distorted output of the boom box. I could even detect a slight Bostonian accent.

Kudos to Monica. This is a better way to review the sermon tapes.

I settled back in the pew and let myself listen. Candidate A—we still hadn't been told his name—had crafted a fascinating sermon by combining two verses that I had never before heard linked together:

Romans 10:9–10: "That if you confess with your mouth, 'Jesus is Lord,' and believe in your heart that God raised him from the dead, you will be saved. For it is with your heart that you believe and are justified, and it is with your mouth that you confess and are saved."

Psalm 141:3: "Set a guard over my mouth, O LORD; keep watch over the door of my lips."

Candidate A had set up a classic dilemma. On the one hand, the proper use of the spoken word saves us. On the other hand, the wrong use of the spoken word—gossip, or slander, or revealing secrets, for example—can lead to disaster.

The wrong use of the spoken word for revealing secrets . . .

I wish I could remember the whole sequence of mental steps that built the idea in my mind, but I wasn't really paying attention. That's the odd part—my mind was wandering when I suddenly thought, *the wrong use of written words intended to be spoken can also reveal secrets.*

A speech draft can be chock-full of confidential information. Consider the speech Dennis Grant had given me as a sample of his work—a speech meant only for the ears of Hardesty's board of directors. Those "written words intended to be spoken" might do significant damage to Hardesty in the hands of a competitor.

I sat up straight. What had Dennis Grant said to me in Bombay Spices & Rices? It had been a twofold rant. First, he would show Mitch Hardesty "what happens when you get sloppy with corporate speech drafts." Then Mitch would thank him "for pinpointing the treachery that threatens to tear apart his company."

I slid out of the pew and half walked, half ran to the narthex. I used my cell phone to call David.

"I've had an extraordinary idea," I said. "We should talk. Tonight."

David recognized my imperative tone immediately. He didn't waste time with spurious questions. "Where?" he asked.

"At my office. The paperwork I need to show you is there."

"When?"

"I'm at the church, at a meeting that should be over by eight-thirty. Round up Gloria. I'll meet you at the office at nine."

I quietly returned to my pew, working hard to ignore Monica's critical stare. We listened to three more tapes, but to be perfectly honest, I didn't hear a thing. My mind was racing, contemplating a flood of related questions.

When—and how—did Dennis discover that his speech drafts were spreading Hardesty's secrets outside the corporation?

Had his discovery triggered his decision to leave Hardesty? Or to ask for my help?

How did the espionage scheme work?

Was Dennis involved in the scheme?

If not, who was responsible?

How many confidential speeches did Dennis write? What were they about?

Why did he need a copy of one of the speeches he gave me?

Was Dennis murdered because of what he discovered?

A voice caught my attention. "Mrs. Huston, can we have your attention, *please!*"

I looked up. Monica stood at attention, rapping her knuckles on the communion table, glowering at me.

"Sorry, Monica," I said. "It's late and I went wandering." I decided not to correct the "Mrs. Huston." She knew perfectly well that I preferred Pippa Hunnechurch in Ryde. Moreover, I've dealt with enough arrogant professionals over the years to know that arguing is a waste of effort.

"Well, now that you're with us again," she said, "I ask you to pay attention. I feel that every member of our committee has an important role to play—even newcomers."

I nodded, kept silent, and reminded myself that deep down inside Monica is an insecure individual.

Her abrasive behavior is really about her—not about you.

Monica began to smile—or perhaps "simper" is a more accurate description.

"Excellent! Now that your mind is where it belongs, I can give you your assignment for the next meeting."

Assignment? I'm sure my jaw dropped in surprise.

Monica continued. "Because of your broad experience as a human resources professional, I'd like you to listen again to the tapes we heard this evening and evaluate the presentation skills of the four candidates. Please be prepared to give us a brief report at our next meeting on Sunday."

Everything I'd learned about handling difficult people—starting with *Rule 1: Stay calm!*—vanished from my mind. I could feel my anger bubbling over.

I jumped to my feet. "I think not, Monica. I will not allow you to punish me like a daydreaming child in school."

"Punish you? I don't understand what you mean." Her smile hadn't wavered. She looked eerily serene.

"Then let me spell it out in words of one syllable," I said. "I won't do it. No take-home work."

"Really? You told us you wanted to be a fully participating member of this committee. Several other members have taken on additional assignments."

I glanced around at the other members. They seemed bewildered, almost embarrassed by the unexpected squabble.

An icy feeling tore through me. *Mortification.* I managed to squeak out, "In that case, I shall of course complete the evaluations."

I sat down, wishing I could erase and replay the last five minutes.

Hardly your finest hour, Hunnechurch.

Chapter Fifteen

My EXCITEMENT BUILT as I drove north on Ryde High Street. The blend of speeches and spying made a heady, exotic mixture to contemplate—even though I couldn't see how a tale of purloined drafts might help in my defense against Mitch Hardesty's lawsuit.

"Three heads are better than one," I muttered. Perhaps the three of us thinking together could identify the elusive "smoking gun" that would get Hunnechurch & Associates off the hook.

The security guard in the lobby of the restored leather warehouse—a jovial man nearly as old as the building—sat inside an information kiosk made of aged red bricks that matched the warehouse's exterior. He winked at me when I signed in.

"You guys having a party up there?" He gestured toward the box of doughnuts I'd bought at the Krispy Kreme drive-through that is across Romney Boulevard from the church.

"I doubt it," I replied. "However, should we start to enjoy ourselves, I'll give you a call." I lifted the lid. "Have a doughnut." I felt tempted myself but decided to wait until I had a hot cuppa in my other hand.

Gloria and David were both standing inside Gloria's workstation, watching our small ink-jet printer toil away mightily. The housing jittered as the print carriage whizzed back and forth. I joined them and peeked at the document in the printer's output tray: an eight-by-ten-inch color photograph of Mitch Hardesty.

"May one ask what you are doing?" I said.

"Well, as long as I'm *here* tonight," Gloria emphasized the "here" strongly, "I might as well print out the photos I gathered of the key players in Hardesty's executive suite."

"Ah, you had something else planned for this evening."

"I was watching the baseball game on TV. Some of us"—she glanced meaningfully at David—"are Baltimore Oriole fans."

"I won't complain about missing the game," he said to me, "as long as you hand over the box of doughnuts."

"Done!"

I lifted the edge of Mitch's photograph. Beneath it was an elegant portrait of Carol Ericsson. "These are excellent pictures. Where did you get them?"

"Most of them are official public relations photos. I downloaded them from Hardesty's internal network on this." She showed me a black plastic widget that I could have mistaken for a small key fob. "It's a *dongle*—a memory device that plugs into any computer and works like a miniature hard drive. This one holds a gigabyte of data. Of course, not everyone on the eighth floor has a PR photo. The other shots are candids I took with my new digital camera." Gloria held up a little silver cylinder perhaps five inches tall and a half-inch across.

"That stick is a camera?" I said, with genuine surprise.

"Disguised to look like a fancy fountain pen." She laughed. "You can't tell a book by its cover—or a clever undercover detective by her clothing."

Gloria donned her eyeglasses, put her hands on her hips, and twirled in place like a fashion model. "This is what 'Helen Nelson' wore to work today."

Her nondescript, roomy brown dress concealed her curves. Her sensible shoes had almost flat heels, subtracting an inch from her usual height. Her makeup and eyeglasses did a good job of changing the shape of her mouth and eyes. And there was something else. *Why, I wondered, did Gloria's disguise look much more natural than it had the day before?* I realized, with a jolt, that she had dyed her celebrated blonde hair mousy brown.

Gloria saw me staring at her locks. "It had to be done," she said. "Wigs are for more mature females of . . ."

"Don't say of my age!" I warned.

"I was thinking of Monica DeVries." She added, "Which reminds me—how goes the search committee?"

"Don't ask."

"Uh-oh! What happened?"

I let myself grimace. "If you must know, I became a thoroughly whiney prat and made an absolute fool of myself."

"In other words, you lost your cool."

"Completely."

"Monica is great at making people overreact. It's a talent—she knows just how to push your buttons."

"Yes, well, I have no desire to dwell on the maddening Ms. DeVries anymore this evening." I turned to David. "I need a doughnut to help me forget."

"Along with a big mug of strong tea?" Gloria said.

"The biggest!"

"I'll take care of the goodies. You guys get comfortable in the war room."

David hefted a large cardboard box. "My research notes," he explained, before I could ask. "Now seems an appropriate time to combine them with yours."

I unlocked our conference room and switched on the lights.

"Amen!" David said when he saw our SAVE HUNNECHURCH & ASSOCIATES! banner. He made a quick tour of the room, scanning the sticky notes and pieces of paper we'd taped to the walls. "I'm impressed," he finally said.

"Darn right!" Gloria said. "We do good work." She had arrived with a tray laden with our teapot, a carafe of coffee, the doughnuts, and a box of English biscuits. "Let's get this meeting on the road."

David and Gloria took seats at the conference table. I strode to the wall labeled Dennis Grant: Background and Biographical and slapped my palm against five documents that Gloria had hung at shoulder level with double-sided tape.

"Here they are," I said. "The speech drafts that Dennis Grant submitted to us as samples of his writing skill. Mitch Hardesty delivered two of them to outside audiences, two more to employees, and the fifth, the special draft, to the corporation's board of directors."

"Dennis Grant gave you a copy of a speech to the board?" David sounded incredulous.

"He trusted Hunnechurch & Associates." I smiled demurely and unstuck the draft from the wall. "Dennis asked me to hold the information confidential. He relied on our prudence and discretion."

"That's . . . ," David struggled to find the right word, "outrageous! The document you're holding contains proprietary information. It should never have left Hardesty's executive suite."

"Dennis would certainly agree with you in principle. He made an exception with this speech because I had asked him for representative samples of his work. He told me that many of the speeches he wrote dealt with proprietary topics."

"As a matter of fact, that's probably true." David rummaged in his cardboard box and retrieved a clamped-together sheaf of papers. He flipped pages to find a specific sheet. "When I interviewed Mitch Hardesty last year, he told me, and I quote, 'I steer the company using speeches I present to the board of directors. Preparing a board speech forces me to make strategic business decisions. After all, I need something to tell my speechwriter. It also forces my staff to read about my decisions because I circulate each draft throughout the executive suite and ask for their comments and suggestions. I try to produce at least one strategic speech each week.'"

I sat next to David and set the draft down in front of him. "What if a member of the staff decided to circulate Mitch's strategic speeches *outside* the company?"

He stared at the draft for a while and then began to nod. "That would explain why Hardesty Software can't do anything right in the marketplace. A steady leak of the company's strategic plans would be disastrous. Competitors would know what Mitch intended to do. They could beat Hardesty Software to the punch in proposals to government, in new product introductions, in pricing—in everything that matters."

"You are a man who likes what-ifs. Here are three more: What if Dennis Grant discovered the link between his drafts and leaked Hardesty information? What if he found compelling evidence of corporate espionage? What if he planned to present his conclusions to Mitch Hardesty?"

"Is that why he wanted his speechwriting samples returned?"

"This particular draft most of all." I tapped the two-page document with my index finger. "Dennis exploded with excitement when I gave him the copy. He talked about being a hero. He even expected Mitch to offer him his old job back. There must be something inside that proves the connection between spying and speeches."

"When did you figure all this out?"

"At tonight's meeting of the associate pastor search committee."

David let out a laugh. "Imagine that—something useful happened during a church committee meeting." He rocked back in his chair. "I love your theory. It fits the facts we have perfectly. Pippa Hunnechurch is probably the smartest Brit since Isaac Newton."

"Why thank you, kind sir." I added, "I only wish that were true."

David looked askance at me. "When did you start arguing with my compliments?"

"Hunnechurch & Associates still has a nasty lawsuit hanging over our heads. My alleged smarts can't find a solution to that predicament."

Gloria joined in. "Maybe Dennis left Hardesty because he realized someone was committing espionage with his speeches? Maybe he didn't want to work in a den of thieves?"

"The timing is all wrong," I said. "Dennis must have made his discovery long after he left Hardesty, or else he wouldn't have asked me for copies of the drafts."

"I stand by my effusive praise," David said. "You've neatly described how the spying was done at Hardesty. We can also conclude that Dennis was hot on the trail of the spy."

"That's true!" Gloria said. "Dennis must have been close to identifying a specific person—or else why murder him?"

David swiveled his chair to face Gloria. "Right! Which has to mean that the corporate spy, and doubtless the person who murdered Dennis Grant, is one of the Hardesty executives who read speech drafts."

"I agree," she concurred. "We have a narrow field of suspects."

"Do we know who they are?" David asked.

"Absolutely!" Gloria said. "Mitch circulated a speech today. One of my chores was to distribute the copies. I delivered five—to four vice presidents and a director."

"I don't know any of them," David said unhappily. "I interviewed Mitch Hardesty at his home. I didn't get to meet any of his senior staff."

I tried to get back in the conversation. "I met most of the Hardesty execs four months ago, but I barely recall their faces."

David acknowledged me with a grunt and Gloria with a nod.

"Why don't I give you a virtual tour of Hardesty's executive suite?" Gloria said to David. "I can use the photographs to introduce you to the key people who read speech drafts."

"Great idea!" David said.

"I'll get the pictures from the reception room—and a roll of double-sided tape."

I didn't see any point in arguing with Gloria as she flew past me. She and David appeared determined to play the private detective game. I chose a doughnut and began to munch.

"What a gal!" David said. "She has endless enthusiasm."

"Endless," I agreed, my mouth full.

Gloria returned in a flash and took up a position near a patch of empty space on the Hardesty Stuff wall.

"Let me start out with some geography," she said. Hardesty Software Corporation has a new five-story building in Ryde Business Park—really two buildings side by side connected by a covered walkway. The building on the left, the administration building, houses the usual corporate activities—accounting, human resources, purchasing, and the rest. The building on the right, the operational wing, is where programmers develop software. Hardesty does work for the federal government that requires programmers to have secret, and even top secret, security clearances. The operational wing meets government security requirements. It has revolving door gates, surveillance cameras all over the place, and special locked, soundproofed working areas that people call "skifs."

David interrupted. "S-C-I-F—pronounced *skif*—is short for Sensitive Compartmentalized Information Facility."

"I didn't know that," Gloria cooed.

"No reason you should. It is a rather arcane term."

"Moving right along," I said, "Hardesty's executive suite is on the top floor of the administration wing."

Gloria didn't skip a beat. "It's fairly modest as executive suites go," she said for David's benefit. "Nice but not overly luxurious."

She spread her stash of photographs on the conference table.

"This is a great week to meet Hardesty executives and find out what they are doing," she said, a trifle smugly I thought. "They're all in town getting ready for the board meeting next week. Today I worked for Frank Robinson, the vice president in charge of support services." Gloria held up a photo of a smiling, round-faced man with a shaved head. "Frank is about forty-five, a man who never sits still. He oversees the telephones, the computer networks, the help desk, the printing shop, the mail room, the library, the security staff—the list goes on and on. I spent most of the afternoon stuffing loose-leaf binders with paper copies of the slides the executives will present to the board of directors."

She tore off two lengths of tape and affixed Frank's photo to the wall.

I glanced at David. He had rocked his chair backward into a relaxed posture and appeared wholly satisfied with Gloria's thumbnail description. *Should I mention,* I asked myself, *that Frank had once been a business reporter like David?* That bit of trivia had been part of the small talk we'd exchanged four months earlier, at lunch.

Let Gloria do her thing without interruption. She's having such a good time.

"Next we have Ed Block," Gloria said, "Hardesty's chief financial officer. He looks much friendlier in person than in his picture."

I squinted to see Ed's photo. Both in life and on paper, he had the pinch-faced look of a natural-born bean counter. Unfortunately, the photographer had made him look even more funereal.

Gloria continued: "Ed is about forty. As I understand his role, he's responsible for keeping the company on an even financial keel. Mitch Hardesty is the visionary who conceives new products and serves as the outward face of the company, while Ed works out of sight, in the back room. He has a reputation as an exceedingly tough financial manager. He personally supervised the recent round of layoffs."

The next picture made me chuckle: Ben McDonald, vice president of human resources, with a vacant stare on his face.

"I used my digital camera," she said. "Ben had no idea he was being photographed." She stuck Ben's picture on the wall. "His corporate biography gives his age as fifty-two. He strikes me as a nice guy—easy to get along with, soft-spoken, caring."

I found myself nodding in agreement. I had met with Ben on five separate occasions. He came across as a gentleman of the old school.

"Ben's presentation to the board will discuss the long-term impact of the layoffs on the company's ability to recruit new people." She shrugged. "I don't think he likes using temp employees to replace full-timers."

Gloria's third photograph presented a man I'd never seen before. "Broderick McGee is Hardesty's chief counsel," she said. "He's about fifty and also a vice president. Everyone calls him Rod. Another nice guy."

"I hate him already," I muttered.

To my surprise, David heard me—and responded. "Don't! He's probably on your side. I'll bet Mitch Hardesty had to order him to move ahead. After all, you're not worth suing."

"Is that another compliment?" I asked.

"You know what I mean. The cost of prosecuting the lawsuit is more than they can ever squeeze out of you."

"Thank you for that charming thought."

"You *know* what I mean."

Gloria took charge again. "Rod isn't supervising Hardesty vs. Hunnechurch," she said. "His presentation to the board includes the case names for current lawsuits. We're not on his list."

I tugged my chair closer to Gloria. Perhaps "Helen Nelson" had learned a useful thing or two. "Who do you suppose is giving direction to Blanchette and Ross?" I asked.

"It has to be Mitch Hardesty," she answered confidently.

If so, the man is a nutter. Imagine the chairman of a growing corporation investing his priceless time to beleaguer me.

"The last of the vice presidents who read speech drafts is Carol Ericsson," Gloria said, "the *tsarina* of corporate communications. She's considered a workaholic—a real company person. I shook her hand but never got the opportunity for a chat. Maybe I'll have better luck tomorrow."

Carol looked vivacious in her photograph—less weary, less battered, less fortyish than the woman I'd watched shoot clay birds the day before. I could easily imagine Dennis Grant falling in love with her.

Gloria displayed unusual fussiness when she posted the fifth photograph. She applied the double-sided tape with finicky exactitude; she carefully squared the picture, eliminating any tilt to the right or left.

"Here," she finally said, "is the cutest guy in the Hardesty executive suite. Stan Young, director of corporate planning."

"He looks kind of ordinary to me," David said.

"Stan is thirty years old, holds a Ph.D. from Duke, and was a member of America's Olympic swim team," Gloria said, dreamily. "To top it all off, he's single."

"Yeah, but what has he done lately?"

Gloria took David's flippant comment seriously. "I think he's planning a new line of software for the Department of Defense."

David pitched his chair forward with a metallic twang. "A new product line? Are you sure?"

"Pretty sure. The title of his presentation to the board was 'Progress Report—Next Generation Products for DoD.'"

"Rumors about new products have floated around outside Hardesty for several months, but no details have ever shown up." David looked at me. "When did Dennis Grant leave Hardesty?"

"The last Friday in March."

"Almost three months ago," David said softly. "More evidence that your spying-through-speeches theory is correct. When Dennis left, the flow of confidential information about the company dried up."

I thought about it. Why would a corporate spy stop operating? Even if Mitch Hardesty didn't have a full-time speechwriter, surely there were other sources of valuable information within the company.

I might have discussed the point with David, but Gloria turned a pirouette and asked, "How did I do?"

"You are a virtual virtuosity," David said. "However . . ."

"Why is there always a however?" she asked with a sham frown of upset.

"*However,*" he went on, "you've introduced us to a dream team of hard-working, loyal employees. We've assumed that one of the five is a corporate spy and a murderer. Which one is the rogue executive?"

"It's too early to tell. Give me a few more days in the executive suite, and I'll have a better idea."

I stared at the Hardesty wall and tried to conceal the annoyance I felt. Gloria had gone undercover to gather evidence that Dennis Grant lied—not to hunt for spies and/or killers. She was on my payroll, not David's. We needed to talk about her improper priorities—soon.

When I looked up at Gloria again, she had moved across the room to our Dennis Grant: Background and Biographical wall. She seemed to be preparing yet another photograph for display.

"More pictures?" David asked.

"Just one," she replied. "I found a great shot of Dennis Grant in the archives. He looks like a male model."

Indeed he did. A skilled portrait photographer must have taken the elaborately lit close-up of Dennis's face. The image was head and shoulders in quality above the other corporate photos. Why would Hardesty Software spend big bucks to produce a portrait of a man who worked behind the scenes?

I answered my own question: "Hardesty didn't. Carol Ericsson did."

"Did what?" David asked.

"I understand now why you received so many news releases about Dennis Grant. Carol Ericsson wrote and distributed them. She took on the role as Dennis's personal publicist."

"Because . . ."

"Because she loved Dennis and wanted to advance his career." I went on, "He repaid her devotion by finding a younger woman."

"Rachel Wilson," Gloria said offhandedly.

I wheeled around. "How did you know that? I never had the chance to tell you what Carol told me."

"Well, the romantic triangle in question is not exactly public knowledge at Hardesty, but it's hardly a deep dark secret either," Gloria said. "Remember those binders I stuffed today? I worked alongside an administrative assistant named Candice Connelly. She usually supports Carol Ericsson."

"And naturally you got to chatting about her boss's love life."

Gloria reddened. "I admit that I promised not to ask pointed questions, but it was an opportunity I couldn't resist—two women alone in a conference room doing mindless work. We were hip deep in slide presentations, so I steered the conversation to speechwriting."

"And . . ."

"I heard an earful about Dennis Grant. Apparently only three people on the eighth floor liked Dennis—Mitch Hardesty, Carol Ericsson, and Rachel Wilson. Candice called him a tiresome jerk, arrogant and abrasive, a real pain to work with. She hated his guts."

No surprise there. I thought him a jerk too.

David chuckled. "I guess some people make it difficult to honor the ancient Roman proscription not to talk ill of the dead."

I immediately felt guilty for my musings, and so apparently did Gloria. She began fussing with the photographs that remained on the table. I changed the subject. "It really amazes me how much Gloria, essentially an outsider to the organization, was able to learn in only one day. Corporate espionage seems a remarkably easy endeavor."

David shrugged. "Corporations are forced to trust the people who work for them, or else they'd never get any work done. Trouble is—people often let you down." He reached for the speech draft I'd given him earlier. "Here's a perfect example. There's a huge notice on the front page: 'Hardesty Software Corporation Proprietary Information.' Nonetheless, Dennis Grant gave you a copy." David scanned the pages quickly. "I wish we knew why he considered this document evidence of spying. It's a pity he didn't tell you."

"Actually, he may have told me—amidst the insults and accusations. I didn't pay attention to all that he said."

Gloria spoke up. "It's a shame we don't have the recording of Dennis talking to you when you gave him the drafts."

"I forgot about the recording! We do have it!" I leaped out of my chair with sufficient vigor to knock it over. "I didn't throw your little recorder away. It's in the bottom of my bottomless handbag, which I left sitting on your workstation."

Gloria took less than a minute to retrieve the cassette and set up a player. We quickly identified the segment that might be significant:

Pippa: What happens in a few days?
Dennis: I become his hero.
Pippa: How?
Dennis: By showing what happens when you get sloppy with corporate speech drafts.
Pippa: I have no idea what you are talking about.
Dennis: Why would you? You're not as smart as me. For that matter, neither is Mitch Hardesty. But he'll thank me for

pinpointing the treachery that threatens to tear apart his company. I'll bet you he offers me my old job back. Who knows? I may even accept. I want my drafts—now! (PAUSE) This is everything I gave you?
Pippa: Everything.
Dennis: Yes! A widow strikes again! I love being right!

"I don't get it," Gloria said. "The only widow I know of in Hardesty's executive suite is Nancy Hitchcock, the chairman's executive assistant."

"It is a rather cryptic comment," I said. "'A widow strikes again.' What can one make of it?"

"Lots—if *one* is a writer," David said. "Hand me that speech draft." He turned to the second page and looked at the bottom. A moment later I watched his mouth curl into a merry grin. "Seek and ye shall find. The makings of a widow."

"May one ask *what* are you talking about?"

David chortled as he explained. "Typesetters invented the word centuries ago. A *widow* is the last line of a paragraph printed all by itself at the top of the next page. Read the last paragraph of the speech draft:

> *In closing, let me review our actions. We looked at the ability of Mayberry's products to complement our product lines. . . . We investigated financing options, . . . and we performed a thorough due-diligence examination of the Mayberry Software Manufactory with an eye towards acquiring the company. Our decision: go*

"See?" David continued, even more delightedly. "There's no period at the end of the sentence. The draft must have ended with a widow on the third page—a widow that somehow got separated from the rest of the document."

"How could that happen?" Gloria asked.

"Easily. A one-word widow creates a mostly blank third page. The page probably got left behind in the output tray of someone's laser printer."

I took a closer look. "When I read the draft, I assumed that Hardesty planned to acquire Mayberry. But what if the complete final sentence was 'Our decision: go *slowly*.'"

"Yes! Yes! Yes!" David, a wild look in his eye, upended his cardboard box, spilling reams of papers, brochures, and booklets on the conference table. "I will personally hug the first person who finds a report from a consulting firm called The Madison Group. Look for a thin document, ten pages at most, with a date of late April or early May."

Gloria earned the hug.

"Who is The Madison Group?" I asked.

"A Washington, DC-based competitive intelligence firm. Very expensive. And very good. I borrowed this report from a company that paid several thousand dollars for it." David nearly tore the document apart turning pages.

"Got it!" he shouted, and began to read aloud. "After significant research into the matter, The Madison Group is convinced that Hardesty's widely rumored acquisition of Mayberry is just that—an unsubstantiated rumor." David nearly broke into song. "The spy slipped up! The spy slipped up. The spy slipped up. He circulated the speech draft without the widow—which eventually triggered a wrong rumor."

I contributed to the revelry. "The bloomin' widow was responsible for the erroneous rumor."

Gloria chimed in. "A widow strikes again."

"We need a group hug," David shouted. "What a team! *What a team*."

Chapter Sixteen

WE CALLED IT A NIGHT at one on Thursday morning. Perhaps I'd consumed too much strong tea at the office, or maybe I had grown used to not sleeping alone. For whatever reason, I slept badly. I tossed and turned in my bed, brooding about the "accomplishments" of our impromptu get-together.

Gloria had climbed grinning into her pickup truck, overjoyed with her first-day successes as an undercover detective in Hardesty's executive suite.

David Friendly departed in equally high spirits, bubbling enthusiastically about "an exciting new stream of evidence" for his blasted article.

I went home in a sour mood, convinced that my one and only associate had left me high and dry.

Gloria loves playing private eye. Your little lawsuit can't compete for her attention.

The idea filled me with gloom. The irresistible charms of corporate spying and murder had obviously seduced Gloria Spitz. She had become so wrapped up in David's investigation that her sole contribu-tion to helping Hunnechurch & Associates survive had been a pair of half-baked suggestions: "Maybe Dennis left Hardesty because he real-ized someone was committing espionage with his speeches? Maybe he didn't want to work in a den of thieves?"

I finally drifted off at three, but my eyes popped open at six-thirty. I lay still for a while, debating whether to fall back asleep. When I even-tually decided I should, I felt too awake to manage. Furthermore, I was ravenously hungry. All I had eaten during the past sixteen hours were a lite TV dinner and two Krispy Kreme jelly doughnuts.

An extended hot shower partially unclogged my foggy head but did nothing to put me in the mood to cook for myself. I threw on my trusty, though now-rumpled, jogging suit and walked three blocks south along Magothy Street to the Blue Spot Café. I chose a sunlit table near the large front window and ordered the traditional English breakfast.

"Are you sure, hon?" the waitress asked, evidently fooled by the ath-letic look of my outfit. "It's high fat, high carbs, and high calories. Our big breakfast ain't on nobody's diet."

"I'm quite sure." I exaggerated my British accent. "I've been enjoy-ing fry-ups since childhood. My arteries are well acclimated."

"Whatever." She scribbled on her order pad. "Tea or coffee."

"Coffee," I said eagerly. "An endless supply."

The Blue Spot's chef deserved a gold star for audacity. He or she abandoned all pretense of healthful cooking and prepared a proper English fry-up: Two thick rashers of bacon. Two plump sausages. Two fried eggs cooked to perfection, with runny yolks and solid whites, slightly browned at the edges. A fried tomato. Several fried mushrooms. A helping of baked beans. And a thick slice of fried sourdough bread accompanied by a large dollop of orange marmalade.

By eight o'clock my plate was empty, the waitress had refilled my coffee cup four times, and I had grown weary of feeling sorry for my-self because of Gloria's apparent defection. A curious thing happened as

I sipped my fifth cup of coffee. I wondered if I had been too quick to dismiss Gloria's questions out of hand.

My unease began as a minor niggle: What, after all, was my evidence that Dennis had not linked spying and speeches until after he left Hardesty Software?

My niggle quickly blossomed into full-blown doubt. I had made an inference based on a single fact: Dennis had asked me for copies of his speech drafts. But what did that really prove?

My doubt escalated into the urge to immediately validate what Dennis knew—or didn't know. Imagine my lawyer's delight if I could prove that Dennis's conscience had driven him out of Hardesty.

I dug my cell phone out of my handbag. Hardesty staffers are known for starting work before eight. I could probably reach Rachel Wilson and Carol Ericsson.

Then what? What will you ask them?

I couldn't pose the obvious question: Did Dennis say anything to you about corporate espionage before he left the company? David would never forgive me if my indiscriminate use of the *E* word on the eighth floor accidentally short-circuited his precious article. I needed an innocent question that would probe the state of Dennis's knowledge.

A few more sips of coffee and I invented one. I could find out if Dennis had access to The Madison Group's report while he still worked at Hardesty. I dialed Hardesty's main number and asked for Rachel Wilson.

"Oh, hi, Pippa," she said after I identified myself. "I meant to thank you. I received the copies of the speech drafts."

"You're most welcome, Rachel. I called today because I have a question for you. Does Hardesty subscribe to reports published by The Madison Group?"

Rachel fell silent. I could imagine the gears in her head turning ever so slowly. "The Madison Group?" she eventually echoed.

"Yes. It's a Washington-based consulting firm that sells competitive intelligence to large companies like yours."

"I don't remember hearing or seeing the name."

"Then you never heard Dennis talk about the firm."

"No. Never."

"Do you have any of his correspondence? He might have mentioned The Madison Group in a memo."

"I don't have anything belonging to Dennis." I heard annoyance enter her voice. "He took what he wanted when he left. We destroyed his other files and correspondence."

"It's important to me. Would you check? Perhaps some of his papers survived."

"I'm sorry. I don't have the time to fool around. I'm supporting a major board meeting next week. Please don't bother me with nonsense again."

Click.

Nice work, Hunnechurch. You lost one of your few friends in the enemy camp. Why did you push Rachel so hard?

My only excuse was my still-muzzy mind. I shouldn't have even troubled Rachel with a call—a humble administrative assistant would have little to do with the rarified realm of competitive intelligence. No, my best bet was Carol Ericsson, a Hardesty vice president.

I dialed her direct number. She picked up on the third ring.

"Ericsson."

"Good morning, Carol, this is Pippa Hunnechurch."

"Hey! Want to go trapshooting again?"

"I'll consider it—once the livid bruise on my shoulder disappears." I changed tack. "You sound chipper this morning."

"I've been at my desk since six-thirty. Getting ready for our board meeting next week."

"I presume they happen once each month?"

"Yeah, but not like this one. Our June meeting is a midyear performance review and corporate health check. Every department head gives a presentation to the board describing challenges and solutions.

My job is to summarize our marketing communications campaigns and public relations strategies."

"Since you are busy, I will get right to the point. Does Hardesty receive competitive intelligence reports prepared by The Madison Group?"

"Now there's a coincidence. About a week before Dennis died, he asked me the same question."

"A week?"

"Don't act so surprised. We occasionally met for lunch. I enjoyed seeing him—even on his terms." She sighed. "When it came to Dennis Grant, I abandoned all my pride."

I pondered for the umpteenth time why so many successful, intelligent women fall in love with clearly unsuitable men. The phenomenon has long confused me, probably because my mother and sister have different explanations. Mum favors the straightforward, "Love is blind." Chloe insists, "An amazing number of women are 'miswired' to believe that it is better to have loved a clod than never to have loved at all."

Carol went on, "You must have a crystal ball. How did you know that Dennis bugged me about The Madison Group?"

Rats! I hadn't expected her to respond to my question with one of her own. I had no choice but to offer a small fib as my reply.

"No prognostication gizmos of any sort, Carol. Dennis mentioned The Madison Group's reports to me several months ago. He believed they might help Hunnechurch & Associates identify potential clients and candidates. If Hardesty subscribes, I'd love to peek at a recent report. We are always in the market for useful business development tools."

Carol laughed. "Do you have twenty thousand extra dollars lying around?"

"Pardon?"

"That's the annual cost to subscribe to their monthly reports."

"Ouch."

"I had the same reaction." Carol took a breath. "According to Dennis, Militet strategic planners dearly love The Madison Group. He suggested that I find out whether Hardesty gets their reports. I had no idea, so I checked with Stan Young, our director of corporate planning. He told me the price. He also told me that Mitch Hardesty personally rejected his request that we subscribe."

We said our good-byes. As I rang off, my gloom returned because I now had no doubt that Dennis Grant had twigged to the link between speeches and spying long after he had quit his post at Hardesty Software. I could even guess why he had invited Carol to lunch. Dennis wanted to verify that no one on the eighth floor received The Madison Group's reports. He had succeeded; Dennis knew that his revelations would come as a complete surprise to Mitch Hardesty.

I paid my bill and speed-walked back to Hunnechurch Manor, hoping that a brisk pace would burn off a few forkfuls of the vast breakfast I'd eaten. Once home I decided to devote the rest of the morning to the homework I'd been given by Monica DeVries.

Your most logical course of action, I reasoned with myself, *is to get the candidate evaluations out of the way. Then you won't have the harebrained assignment looming large for the rest of the week.*

I had no idea why Monica assumed that I possessed the know-how to compare the presentation skills of four young pastors. But, having agreed to deliver an evaluation, I now felt a responsibility to do a proper job.

I recalled several good presenters I've listened to over the years and identified four key qualities one can detect while hearing but not seeing a speech: enthusiasm, confidence, sincerity, and *listenability.* The last was my made-up label for a catchall category that encompassed such vocal attributes as tone, accent, speaking pace, and modulation.

James had assured me that his home theater system included a cassette player. Winston offered an occasional chirp of advice from his corner of the living room as I took ages to find the tape deck behind a plastic panel near the bottom edge of the wooden cube, switch the blasted thing on, then figure out how to load my first cassette.

I curled up on my sofa with my notepad and pencil on my lap. I closed my eyes—the better to evaluate Candidate A's presentation skills. Alas, I fell thoroughly asleep before he'd finished reciting his passage from Romans.

━━━━━━━━━━

My ringing cell phone roused me. I glanced at the display as I pushed the *Send* key. The time: eleven-thirty a.m. The caller: Gloria Spitz.

"Where are you?" she asked in a loud whisper. "I rang the office first—you aren't there."

"I am at home. Where are you?"

"In the ladies' room on the eighth floor. It's the only place I can use my cell phone to make a private call."

I heard a flush in the background. Gloria waited for the noise to subside before she continued. "We have to talk. Do you know an out-of-the-way spot we can meet during lunch hour?"

"I have a better idea. You come here. I'll make you a sandwich." I added, "What do we have to talk about?"

"Gotta run," she said. "I'll see you at twelve-fifteen."

Her abrupt severing of our connection should have made me suspicious, but my groggy brain ignored the warning signals and began to plan. Gloria would arrive in forty-five minutes—which gave me enough time to brew a pot of strong tea, put a ready-to-bake French baguette into the oven, replay Candidate A's stirring words, and build Gloria's sandwich.

I had enjoyed the sermon the first time I heard it; it lost nothing the second time around. The message itself struck me as excellent, but my task was to go beyond the actual substance of the sermon. I gave Candidate A good marks for enthusiasm and equally high grades for sincerity and confidence. All three qualities poured forth as he spoke.

I was less generous with listenability. I thought his voice friendly enough but also a trifle monotone and droning.

Surprisingly, I found myself looking forward to hearing the three other candidates again. I even anticipated, with growing excitement, presenting my analyses at the next associate pastor search committee meeting.

Your homework may actually help the other members reach a better decision. More kudos to Monica.

Two conflicting images of Monica DeVries took shape in my mind. The first Monica was the effective committee chair who knew the right way to choose a new pastor. The second Monica was the mean-spirited, arrogant twit who made enemies every step of the way.

Does her competence excuse her arrogance? Do I have to abide her unpleasantness for the sake of her skills?

"Two good questions, laddie!" I said to Winston in passing as I strode from living room to kitchen.

I considered various replies as I mixed a bowl of curried tuna salad. Although I wanted to answer "Absolutely Not!" my sensible side kept insisting that we lived in a world where many unpleasant people enjoyed the luxury of behaving badly because they brought valuable talents to their occupations and professions. Dennis Grant and Mitch Hardesty would certainly count among their number.

A sharp thump on my back door stopped my philosophizing—and startled me. I looked up at Gloria's smiling mug.

"Why the skulduggery?" I asked as I let her in.

"It would blow my cover if someone saw me marching through your front door."

"Silly me for not thinking."

"What?"

"Never mind. What would you like on your curried tuna salad sandwich? I recommend Major Gray's chutney and sliced Vidalia onions."

"Yum!"

I searched for my bread knife; Gloria sat at my kitchen table and commenced talking.

"I helped rearrange the boardroom this morning," she said, "which gave me a chance to meet more junior staff. The scuttlebutt is that Hardesty Software has serious money troubles. People think there'll be a second round of layoffs after next Friday's board meeting." She added proudly, "I bet David doesn't know that yet."

"Quite possibly." I lopped off the ends of the loaf with two swift chops.

Gloria kept talking. "I surprised myself these past two days. I have a real knack for deep cover work. Helen Nelson fits right in. People trust me; they open up and tell me their secrets. I also like being an undercover detective—a real private eye on a real case. It's much more fun than being a bodyguard or trailing people around."

"Is that a fact?" I hacked the loaf in half. *Chop!*

She went on. "I had two lucky breaks this morning. First, I looked around the storeroom on the eighth floor and found Dennis Grant's laptop computer. The disk drive had been 'wiped,' to obliterate the files. Kind of unusual inside a corporation."

"I'd have expected an executive storeroom to be locked."

"It was. But Nancy Hitchcock keeps the key in the top drawer of her desk. I borrowed it for a while."

"I see." I slashed the two pieces of bread lengthwise.

"My second lucky break was the chance to be alone in Ben McDonald's office long enough to examine the locks in his desk and credenza. I should be able to pick the locks in any of the executive offices. All except Mitch Hardesty's office; it's protected by a dozen different silent alarms. Of course I spotted them right away."

"I don't see!" I threw my bread knife into the kitchen sink.

"What's wrong?" Gloria asked.

"You are!" I barely kept my irritation in check. "You talked me into supporting this inane deception of yours by promising not to lie, not to steal, not to act unethically. One would assume that rifling through locked filing cabinets falls under one of these categories."

"Well . . ."

"Precisely! Do you have any idea of the disaster that might befall Hunnechurch & Associates should Helen Nelson be unmasked?"

"Well . . ."

"Obviously, you don't—not to mention the high probability that you will be arrested and charged with a crime."

Gloria replied with a long-suffering smile. "Don't you understand? I'm invisible—a temporary administrative assistant. The lowest of the low. When I walk around the eighth floor carrying a stack of binders, no one even notices that I'm there. The execs treat me like part of the furniture. That's the beauty of being Helen Nelson: there isn't any risk."

I hesitated. Gloria's calm, logical response had taken the wind out of my righteous indignation.

Her smile became conspiratorial. "I've really learned a lot during the past two days," she went on. "For example, I'm not so sure that we can jump to the conclusion that Dennis Grant was murdered by a corporate spy. We have to keep an open mind at this stage in my investigation. At least two people on the eighth floor disliked—even hated— Dennis. One of them may have heard about his interest to return to Hardesty and decided to prevent him from coming back." Her eyes began to gleam. "Nancy Hitchcock, the chairman's administrative assistant, is a possible suspect. She loathed Dennis Grant because he mistreated the support staff. They had several noisy fights before he left Hardesty. I also need to take a long, hard look at Frank Robinson, the vice president of support services. Dennis reduced him to tears at a management meeting by poking holes in a reorganization plan that Frank had worked on for nearly a year. You shame someone like that, you're gonna have an enemy for life."

"What does any of this piffle have to do with our lawsuit?"

"Piffle?" Gloria's smile gave way to a puzzled frown.

"You've confirmed that Dennis Grant could be a miserable human being. Who cares? I knew that before you became Helen Nelson. Where is the information that will save Hunnechurch & Associates? Where is the 'smoking gun' you promised to find?"

"I'm still looking for it. Good investigations take time."

"Happily you will soon exhaust that precious commodity. Your three-day temporary assignment ends tomorrow afternoon. I shall be delighted when you shake the dust off your feet as you leave Hardesty Software."

Gloria looked down at her hands. "That's what I came here to talk about. The folks at Hardesty like my performance so much that they want me to commit for another week. The big board meeting is next Friday; they need lots of help to get ready for it. I said OK."

I finally lost my temper.

"I'll not allow it!" I bellowed. "You work for me. You will leave Hardesty tomorrow, as planned."

Gloria stood up and looked me straight in the eye. "I'll leave Hardesty when I'm good and ready, Pippa. It's dumb to yank a successful operative on a whim."

"You are not an operative. You are Gloria Spitz, *associate* executive recruiter. Let me emphasize the word *associate*; it means that you do what you are told."

"What happens if I don't?"

I foolishly shouted the first thing that came into my mind. "Leave Hardesty or you no longer work for Hunnechurch & Associates."

"Fine with me. I quit!"

She slammed my back door as she left. I watched the glass panes quiver and felt a gust of pure despair pass through my body.

Gloria Spitz was no longer my associate—or my friend.

```
┌──────────────────────────────────────┐
│  Chapter  Seventeen                   │
└──────────────────────────────────────┘
```

AWAKING WITH A STIFF BACK is an unpleasant way to start one's day. That was my condition on Friday morning because I slept the whole of Thursday night curled up on the sofa in my living room. That came to pass because I spent Thursday evening watching *Gone with the Wind* in one sitting on James's home theater while nibbling slightly stale curried tuna sandwiches. That followed an afternoon full of busywork—from vacuuming Hunnechurch Manor to completing my evaluations of the three other candidate pastors—all of it intended to keep my mind sufficiently occupied that it would not replay my disastrous lunchtime fight with Gloria Spitz.

I couldn't bear to contemplate the possibility that we might never talk to each other again.

Gloria and I had fought before, but this fight felt different. The intensity of our hostility frightened me. Our prideful anger had generated more than enough heat to burn through the bonds of friendship and love that held us together.

Don't let that happen, Lord.

I hobbled to the kitchen, filled the kettle, and thought about play-ing hooky from my office for a third day. After all, did I have a good reason to get dressed and leave home?

Yes, Hunnechurch, you have a splendid reason! You have wasted too much time moping around. This is the first day of the rest of your career.

The offices of Hunnechurch & Associates seemed unusually vacant when I unlocked the front door. Gloria had straightened her desk and removed the plants and photographs she kept on her workstation. She had even emptied her wastebasket and tidied the pencil jar.

"You seem to be a solo practitioner once again," I murmured un-happily as I looked around our suddenly bleak reception room.

Four years ago I followed the lead of many one-woman businesses and tacked on "& Associates" to my name. Back then the word had conjured up images of unrestrained growth—a building full of head-hunters. Today it brought tears to my eyes.

I sat down in Gloria's chair and opened the accumulated mail. Along with the usual bills, we had received two candidate résumés for the associate sales manager post at Lotus Flower Foods—the search that Gloria had launched.

Stop making yourself miserable! Call her!

I reached for her telephone. I could smell Gloria's favorite cologne, "Escape," on the handset. I dialed the number for Gloria's cell phone.

A delay, an odd sounding ring, then a mechanical voice speaking the system message: "The subscriber you are calling is currently not on the network. To leave a voice mail for the subscriber, press *one* now."

Gloria must have turned her cell phone off. I pushed one, waited for the beep, then said, "Gloria, I feel abysmal about our fight. Please call me at the office. We need to talk."

I thought about calling "Helen Nelson" at Hardesty but quickly changed my mind. A temporary employee wouldn't have an assigned telephone; the process of finding "Helen" in the executive suite would call undue attention to Gloria—exactly the consequence I wanted to avoid. No, Gloria would have to return my call.

But will she?

The morning crept by. I paid six routine bills, made five unpromising marketing calls, caught up on my e-mail correspondence, and assessed the pair of candidate résumés. Both managers struck me as capable of doing the job. Hardly the most significant work I've done, but real work nonetheless.

My telephone didn't ring once. I called Gloria's cell phone again and listened to the same recorded message. I left a second voice mail: "Please call, Gloria. I know you are upset at me, but let's talk about it."

At noon I decided to take a brisk walk before lunch, which proved to be a foolish idea. The season's first sustained mass of steamy southern air had rolled into the Chesapeake region overnight. The midday sun, the ferocious heat, and the oppressive humidity conspired to make my blouse cling to my back before I'd walked two blocks. I made a U-turn on the sidewalk, took refuge in our neighborhood delicatessen, and ordered my usual: pastrami on rye bread. I stood under an air-conditioner duct as I waited for my lunch and enjoyed the strong blast of frigid air.

Blimey! You forgot about James. He'll expect chilly rooms when he gets home tonight.

The previous owner of my row house had spent a pretty penny to install central air-conditioning in the nineteenth-century structure. The costliest challenge was adding ductwork that didn't ruin the antique look of the interior. Before I married, I rarely used the system—preferring a bit of heat to a whopping electric bill. I enjoyed spending hot summer evenings in my garden and discovered that a fan in my bedroom was often sufficient to keep me comfortable.

James, though, liked the fully air-conditioned life—a year-round temperature of seventy degrees in every room in the house. Central air-conditioning was as essential to him as running water. I had meant to flip the switch as I left for work, but in my haste to depart I'd walked right past the thermostat.

I pictured the sun pouring heat into my roof, turning the upstairs into a veritable oven. On a day like this, it would take hours to cool both stories of Hunnechurch Manor—if my air conditioner could even overcome outside temperatures that approached one hundred degrees. I changed my sandwich order "to go," made a quick detour to the office to lock up for the weekend, and aimed the Beetle toward Magothy Street.

I had done enough Hunnechurch & Associates work during the morning not to feel guilty about returning home. Even so, I set up a proper home office when I arrived: laptop computer on the ladies writing desk in my living room, a real telephone at my fingertips, a high-speed Internet connection, and Venetian blinds shut to reduce distractions from outside my house. I cranked the air conditioner to maximum and phoned the sales manager candidates to set up initial interviews at my office. Remarkably, I reached both on the first try. Conveniently, both requested interviews on the upcoming Tuesday morning. I scheduled one at nine o'clock and one at eleven.

I called Gloria's cell phone twice more. Still off the network. It seemed pointless to leave more messages.

At three I opened my Web browser and accessed a travel site that shows the current position of aircraft flying over the United States. I watched, fascinated, as James's—Frontier Airlines, nonstop from DEN to BWI—flight made its way across the midwest. When the blip on the map reached West Virginia, I turned off my computer and set out for Baltimore Washington International Airport.

Alas, this particular Friday afternoon combined the usual rush-hour traffic *plus* masses of people leaving town for a weekend at the beach. It took ages to get beyond Ryde, and I seemed to crawl along Route 301-50. I made up some time on Interstate 97 North and

managed to find a spot in the hourly-parking garage a few minutes before the scheduled landing time of James's flight.

I jogged through the elevated walkway that connected the garage to
the terminal building and checked the first flight status board I found.

Blast! James's plane had landed ten minutes early.

No problem! I would switch to Plan B: namely, call James and
arrange a convenient place to meet.

I reached into my handbag. To my surprise, my cell phone was off.
Moreover, it wouldn't turn on because I had allowed my battery to fully
discharge.

Another thing you forgot to do today, Hunnechurch.

I instituted Plan C—my only remaining option—and headed for
the Frontier Airlines baggage claim area on the lower level.

The place overflowed with people. A river of road warriors arriving
home from business trips joined a river of bargain hunters returning
from vacations. I let myself be swept along toward the baggage carousel
that served Frontier Airlines.

James can be impatient in crowds. I looked for him where the
carousel snakes through the wall—the point where arriving bags first
enter the terminal. Sure enough, there he stood.

I pushed toward him.

"James."

He turned and smiled—the same high-voltage smile that had made
my knees weak the first time I'd met James. He greeted me with a kiss
and held me tight for a long moment.

"I wish they'd made a sequel to *Casablanca*," he said. "Then I'd
know the right words to say."

"If the truth be told, I've never been a Humphrey Bogart fan."

"You mean I've wasted four showers perfecting my impression of
him? I could have been singing instead." He finished with an extra-
vagant pretend sigh.

"OK, you can do *one* Bogart line."

"In that case," James put his arm in mine and said, in his best Bogie voice, "Pippa, I think this is the beginning of a beautiful weekend."

I laughed. "Oh, I hope so. I have made a complete dog's breakfast of nearly everything I touched this week."

James spotted his suitcase and grabbed it. We made our way upstairs and—still arm in arm—crossed back to the non-air-conditioned parking garage.

"Wow, it's hot." James halted for an instant. "Tell me that you turned on the air conditioner at home."

"Our abode is spot on the way you like it. A notch below glacial."

"*Ah* am much relieved," he said with a put-on Southern drawl.

We found the Beetle. James lobbed his bag into the narrow rear seat. I tossed the keys to him and said, "You drive."

"Sure. And you can tell me what went wrong this week."

True to his implied promise, James listened without comment—except for the occasional *um* and *uh-huh*—while I recounted the events of my checkered week.

We reached the outskirts of Ryde before he spoke. "As I see it," he said, "your week has been a mixture of bad and good. The single worst event is Gloria's quitting. However, I'm confident that she will soon be back. It's not physically possible to separate the two of you permanently."

"Amen!"

"Also on the bad side, you haven't found your so-called smoking gun. That's certainly worrisome, given how hard you've looked."

I sighed for real. "There may not be a smoking gun, James. We may never be able to prove that Dennis Grant lied, which means that Mitch Hardesty might win. Oh, how I wish that I hadn't spoiled Daniel Harris's strategy. I should have happily acknowledged my ineptitude."

James, bless his heart, understood that I had exaggerated a tad. He simply patted my knee and went on. "The least bad item is your spat with Monica DeVries. Is there any reason I can't accompany you to the next meeting—as an observer?"

"I can't think of any."

"Good. I'll show you a useful technique or two that I use for coping with individuals of Monica's type."

"And for the second time the people said, 'Amen!'"

"Now for the good side," he said. "Thanks to your outstanding perceptiveness—there is such a word, isn't there?"

"Indeed, there is."

"Well, thanks to your perceptiveness, your stalwart band of investigators has uncovered a nasty industrial espionage scheme that baffled many other people."

I started to say, "I suppose," but changed my mind. "What other people do you mean?"

"Ah, no one specific. I used a figure of speech that includes all those folks on Wall Street who are trying to understand why Hardesty Software has performed so badly of late. The three of you have done an invaluable service for Mitch Hardesty."

"I thought you were trying to cheer me up."

James laughed. "Another good by-product of your perceptiveness will be the bliss you bring to Monica DeVries. I expect her to take credit for the fine evaluations you did."

I began to snigger.

"But the *goodest* part of your week . . ."

I interrupted. "*Goodest* is not a word."

James ignored me. "The *goodest* part of your week is about to happen—now that I'm back from Denver."

I squeezed his arm. "Home, James. As fast as you can."

━━━━━━

Saturday morning began brilliantly with a hot cuppa brought to my bedside by James, along with a wake-up kiss.

"Goodness!" I said. "You're dressed."

"I have a full day planned. After I serve you an elegant breakfast, I need to run several errands."

"What sort of errands?"

"Never you mind."

I forced myself to smile. Another "surprise for Pippa" seemed on offer.

Ah, well. It's all part of the James you love.

He continued in a stuffy British accent. "And what does Milady fancy this morning to break her fast?"

"What are my choices?"

"You may have anything you desire—as long as it's a ham and cheese omelet accompanied by rye toast."

"Make it so, James."

"Certainly, Milady. Breakfast is served in ten minutes."

James bowed and backed out of our bedroom, while whistling "Rule Britannia."

Scarcely five minutes later, dressed in my bathrobe and bunny slippers, I trotted downstairs.

"First things first, James. I need another cup of . . ."

I gasped. Gloria was sitting at our kitchen table.

I glanced at James. He shrugged and said nothing.

"I'm sorry I crashed your breakfast," Gloria said. "There's something I have to show you—then I'll be on my way."

I heard hesitancy in her voice as she offered to leave. I took a chance.

"Gloria, please don't go. I truly meant what I said to you yesterday."

She looked puzzled. "You didn't speak to me yesterday."

"Not directly. I left a message on your cell phone—because it seemed to be switched off all day."

"Of course I switched it off. I returned the cell phone to your office. It's sitting in the bottom drawer of my former workstation. Hunnechurch & Associates owns the phone—not me."

"Then you didn't hear me say how abysmal I feel about our fight or that I wanted to talk to you."

"I really doubt you want to talk to me."

"But why?"

"You didn't answer your cell phone all day. I tried to call you three times."

I'm sure I gawked at her. "I couldn't answer my phone. The battery was dead."

She gawked back. "It was?"

James chimed in. "Should I set a third place for breakfast? We have more than enough omelet."

"Yes!" I peered at Gloria hopefully. "Please stay."

She smiled at me and nodded slowly.

We hugged. We apologized for our ill-chosen words. We hugged again. We cried and sniffed. We hugged once more.

James poured a cup of coffee for Gloria while I served the omelets. He said a prayer and we tucked in. I took time to murmur my own prayer of thanks for the privilege of enjoying breakfast with James and Gloria—two people I loved beyond measure.

Gloria ate quickly. She moved her plate to the sink and cleared an area on the kitchen table in front of her. I wondered why she suddenly seemed determined—and excited. And then I remembered; she had come to Hunnechurch Manor for a purpose that morning.

"Yesterday I found something weird and important at Hardesty," she said. "It's not quite our smoking gun, *but,* well, you tell me what you think it is."

She carefully placed a scrap of paper on the table in front of her. It looked like the top half of a page torn from a small notebook—the kind that has a spiral binding along the top edge. It was covered with handwriting.

When I reached for it, Gloria stopped my hand.

"Don't touch the surface," she said. "If we're lucky, there may be useful fingerprints to lift. If you have to pick it up, grab the edges."

Gloria carefully turned the scrap of paper toward me. The handwriting was neat, precise, and easy to read:

> *Darling, I'm in danger! Someone figured out the real reason I left Hardesty Software Corporation. A black truck almost ran me down last night, and I think I'm being followed. If anything should happen to me before I see you again, tell the police to read my old speech drafts carefully. Pippa Hunnechurch has copies.*

"It's obviously a note from Dennis Grant," Gloria said when I'd finished reading. "It must have been written last week, not long before he was killed."

"Where did you find it?" I asked.

"In one of the burn baskets in the executive suite."

"What's a 'burn basket'?"

"Imagine a big plastic garbage can with its lid padlocked shut and a slot on top that accepts sheets of paper. It's a safe place to discard any proprietary documents you want to get rid of."

"I get it. The contents are burned to destroy them."

"These days they shred and recycle the discarded paper, but the original name stuck." Gloria made an impatient gesture. "Anyway, the burn basket in question was standing inside Dennis Grant's old office. Rachel Wilson told me it had been there since he left Hardesty. She used it to dispose of his old speech notes."

"But Dennis quit three months ago."

"That's the thing about a burn basket. It doesn't get emptied every night like a wastebasket. The contents aren't shredded until the basket is chock-full. I figured it was worth looking inside, just in case any of Dennis's files were still there."

"You said it was padlocked."

Gloria grinned. "With a light duty, four-tumbler padlock that took me fifteen seconds flat to pick." Her grin faded. "Unfortunately, I didn't find any other relevant documents. The basket was half full of old financial spreadsheets. This note was lying on top of the pile."

James had moved next to me and read the note over my shoulder. "Are you sure that Dennis wrote those words?" he asked.

"Completely sure," she said, proudly. "Rachel gave me a sample of Dennis's handwriting."

"How on earth did you manage that?" I asked.

Gloria's grin returned. "With extreme investigatory cleverness. I told her that my hobby was handwriting analysis. I said that I'd heard a lot about Dennis and would love to do a posthumous evaluation of his personality."

"Rachel doesn't sound very bright," James said.

"She's a good person," Gloria said, "but naïve for her years. She lent me a soppy love letter that Dennis sent her—a letter she had unfolded and refolded a hundred times. Naturally I told her that Dennis was a great guy deep down inside, that his handwriting indicated superior intelligence and sensitivity."

"I take it that the letter and the note matched up," I said.

"The handwriting on the letter was identical—right down to the fancy loop in the capital *I*. The person who wrote the love letter also wrote the note that I found."

I stared at the scrap of paper awhile.

"Did 'Darling' toss the note away," I finally said, "or did someone else intercept it?"

"I asked myself the same thing," Gloria said. "Let's assume that Dennis mailed the note to 'Darling.' Everyone in the executive suite has a personal 'In' basket. It would be possible to intercept an incoming envelope but also very risky. Besides, how would the thief know the envelope contained a note from Dennis? The only sensible answer is that 'Darling' decided to obliterate the note by tossing it in a convenient burn basket."

"OK, that brings us to a most significant question," I said. "Who is 'Darling'?"

Gloria took a moment to compose her reply. "There are two possibilities: Carol Ericsson and Rachel Wilson. My money is on Carol. Rachel never would have thrown the note away."

I nodded. "I have to admit—I lean that way too. But if Carol is 'Darling,' she has been lying to me all week. She knows the real reason that Dennis left Hardesty. She has our smoking gun in her head."

Gloria's face became grim. "It's worse than that. I think 'Darling' is Hardesty's corporate spy. Carol Ericsson probably murdered Dennis Grant."

Chapter Eighteen

I DIDN'T RELISH another wearisome session with Monica DeVries—not after spending a low-stress Saturday with James. He had returned from his mysterious errands late in the morning, about the same time an approaching cool front triggered an afternoon of heavy rain. We stayed indoors reading, listening to music, and catching up on each other. I managed to clear my mind of Mitch Hardesty, lawsuits, murder, corporate espionage, associate pastor candidates—the whole caboodle of challenges on my plate.

When Sunday morning rolled around, Monica was still in the back of my mind. Because we slept a trifle too late, it took a flurry of last-minute activity to get us to church on time for the nine-forty-five contemporary worship service. We took seats near the rear of the sanctuary. James usually preferred to be in the center of the congregation; today he chose a pew on the far left of the sanctuary, near an exit door.

Halfway through the service, though, not even the joyous spirit of the praise songs could hold back the images of Monica that flooded my mind's eye. I remembered her smug simper, her excessive formality, her withering glare—the way she had embarrassed me at our previous meeting.

Toward the end of the offering, James nudged my arm and whispered in my ear. "Let's leave now."

"The service won't be over for ten minutes," I whispered back.

"I know."

James slipped quietly out of the pew; I followed him a few seconds later. We met in the narthex, then found an out-of-the-way corner in the hallway that led to the adult Christian education classrooms.

"What are we doing?" I asked.

"Lurking invisibly. I want to see your friend Monica arrive."

We hadn't long to wait. Monica, her brassy blonde hair glinting in the overhead lights, swept into our assigned classroom.

James glanced at his watch. "She turned up a full fifteen minutes early," he said. "That's impressive."

"It's obvious why Monica is overpunctual," I said. "She wants to establish the classroom as her turf. She also wants to communicate to the rest of us that she is the hardest working member of the committee."

"Well done! You understand power signals too."

"Shall we join her?"

"Not yet. Wait 'til a few other people get here. I'd like to have an audience in the room when I walk in."

We waited ten minutes, during which Rose Robinson, Carrie Logan, and Don Henley ambled into the room. None of the three seemed especially eager to be there.

"Let's roll," James said. "You take your usual seat. I'll follow you in thirty seconds and introduce myself to Monica." He added, "Don't laugh when you hear what I say."

I walked through the door. Monica smiled at me—the smile of a woman who felt in complete control. I found it difficult to look her straight in the eye. I sat down and began to fiddle with the evaluation reports I'd brought and the four sermon tapes she had given me.

The door swung open. James entered the room with a shuffling walk. He held his body in a way that made him appear three inches shorter. He approached Monica timidly, almost deferentially. He produced a superstrength smile and said, softly, "Good morning, Mrs. DeVries, my name is James Huston."

Monica gaped at James's handsome face for several seconds, then extended her hand. "Ah, Mr. Huston, how nice to meet you at last."

"Pippa has told me so much about the fine work being done by your search committee"—he emphasized the "your"—"that, well, I wanted to see the group in action. Would it be possible for me to sit in the back of the room and watch the proceedings? I promise to be quiet as a mouse; I won't say a word."

Monica seemed to glow. "Certainly, Mr. Huston! You are most welcome to visit our little meeting. But *please* take a seat at the table. I've heard wonderful things about the Peachtree Consulting Group. Don't hesitate to share your expertise with us."

James sat down next to me and folded his hands together like an obedient kindergarten child. Monica beamed at him. I stared at my notepad and began to doodle large question marks.

James had warned me against laughing. In fact, I felt bewildered by his fawning performance. What had been the point of feeding Monica's insatiable pride?

Becky and Harry Smith entered the room a few moments later and received a nasty frown from Monica for being the last members to arrive—even though the time was a full minute shy of eleven o'clock.

Our chairperson cleared her throat and, with a great show of piety, delivered the opening prayer. I guessed what would happen next.

"We have an honored guest with us today," Monica said. "Mr. James Huston is sitting in, to watch us at work." She smiled at James. "I always ask newcomers to say a few words about themselves."

"An excellent idea," James said; "very wise of you to suggest it." He paused, as if to gather his thoughts. "My accent tells you that I am from

the South. Atlanta, Georgia, to be specific. I am a management consultant. My clients include several leaders of the local business community"—he tipped his head toward Monica—"I'm sure that Mrs.
DeVries knows them all."

I glanced at Monica out of the corner of my eye. She looked ready
to swoon.

James went on. "As a brand-new member of the church, I've been
fascinated by the sheer courage involved in serving on this committee.
Just the other day, in fact, I told Pippa that I wouldn't want the awesome responsibility you have accepted. The pastor you select will serve
the church for many years. I pray that you identify the pastor that God
has selected for us."

"Well said, Mr. Huston!" Monica gushed. "With our awesome responsibility in mind, let us move to the first item on our agenda. I have
asked Mrs. Huston," she simpered at me, "to report on the presentation
skills of our four pastoral candidates."

I felt James poke my knee under the table. I looked down. He had
scribbled a note on a yellow pad:

1. Thank *her* for your assignment. You *loved* the work.

2. Ask *her* which candidate she wants to hear first?

My bewilderment soared. What was James thinking? I shuffled
papers while I considered what to do. In the end I decided to
follow James's advice on the theory that I had willingly accepted his
help.

"Thank you, Mrs. DeVries," I said. "I must tell you—and the committee—that I thoroughly enjoyed the opportunity you gave me to evaluate the candidates."

I paused. Monica smiled and nodded regally.

"Before I begin to review the candidates," I went on, "I have a question for you. Do you have a preference as to which candidate I review
first?"

"That's an excellent question," she said, doing her best to appear thoughtful. "You know, I think you should choose, Pippa. After all, you performed the evaluations and clearly know best."

Blimey! Monica sounded almost human. Moreover, she had stopped calling me Mrs. Huston. James's object lesson was brilliant; one could push Monica anywhere simply by praising her first.

The other members of the committee also took notice. Rose Robinson winked at me, clearly amused by James's strategy. The Smiths seemed to be fighting back smiles.

I opted to evaluate the candidates in alphabetical order, beginning with Candidate A—the order in which we had listened to the sermon tapes. I described my four evaluation categories—enthusiasm, confidence, sincerity, and listenability—and launched into my reports.

I'd almost finished when I noticed James about to pass me another note. This time I anticipated what he wanted me to say.

"Thank you again, Monica, for the opportunity to evaluate these fine candidates. As you recognized, my expertise is limited to executive recruiting. I know little about theology or pastoral skills. Although I have concluded that Candidate A has the best presentation skills, that is only one aspect of the qualifications we want our next associate pastor to have."

"Well done, Pippa! A superb evaluation." Monica began to clap; the other members joined in. James squeezed my hand. I amazed myself by blushing.

Monica waited for the noise to die down. "Let's move on to our next report. Mr. Henley has evaluated the accuracy of our candidates' scriptural references."

Don Henley took a deep breath and began, "Why thank you, Mrs. DeVries. I can't tell you how much pleasure I have received delving into Scripture this past week."

I bit my tongue to stop from laughing out loud.

====

"Let's go for a drive in the Beetle with the top down," James suggested.

I peered at the sky. No sun, mostly overcast, with occasional patches of blue. The temperature was in the high sixties. In short, a typical summer afternoon in England.

"Sure," I said. "But drive slowly. We can't talk when the wind noise is roaring around us. And I have several thousand questions to ask you."

We left the church and toodled along Romney Boulevard. We soon reached the twisty bits. James had fun maneuvering the Volkswagen through the curves; I leaned back and savored whizzing below the canopy of trees.

"Where did you learn so much about pride and arrogance?" I eventually said.

"Mostly by watching myself. I happen to be one of the world's greatest experts on pride." He smiled at me in the rearview mirror.

I laughed. "Very funny, indeed!"

"I'm serious. Back in Atlanta I taught three Sunday school classes on the subject. You know the old adage, 'Set a thief to catch a thief.' It shouldn't come as a surprise to you—I can have problems with pride."

"In truth, I have noticed a symptom or two."

"My office, for example. I know that you've asked yourself, 'Does James really need a splendiferous view of the Magothy River to make his business a success?'"

"Well, I have wondered about your swish workplace."

"I won't deny that I enjoy my plush surroundings, but they really, truly serve a functional purpose. As I tried to explain the other day, my office is a kind of stage set. Remember, I have to impress the likes of Mitch Hardesty."

"Yes, but is that merely a convenient excuse for excessive opulence? One can use the same argument to justify an office that replicates the hanging gardens of Babylon."

"Good. You've identified a serious problem. Pretend you're one of my old students in Atlanta. Tell me how to recognize when my actions are driven by pride rather than need."

I thought about it. "It seems to me that pride becomes a problem whenever you set out to glorify yourself."

"Exactly! If I do that, I end up deceiving myself. We take the full credit for our talents, our gifts, our accomplishments. We end up believing we are superior to the people around us. C. S. Lewis got it right when he wrote, 'Pride leads to every other vice: it is the complete anti-God state of mind.' Ultimately our pride drives God out of our lives." James negotiated an especially sharp curve; our tires squealed. "That's what makes pride such a powerful enemy."

I laughed. "Or a powerful weapon. You played Monica DeVries like a well-tuned violin."

"That's another reason not to be prideful; your pride can be turned against you."

"Poor Monica. I felt sorry for her by the end of our meeting."

"I've met many people like Monica DeVries. Take away her excessive pride, and you find a competent person underneath."

"I had that very discussion with Winston the other morning. Should Monica's talents excuse her bad behavior?"

"No, but sometimes it's worth the effort to prevent the bad behavior. That's one of the keys to being a successful manager."

We came to the end of Romney Boulevard. "Where to now?" James asked.

"My favorite scenic overlook would be nice."

"You got it!"

James made a U-turn. "You haven't posed the question that someone in my class invariably asked: Is there such a thing as good pride?"

"Pride goes before destruction," I said, in ponderous tones, "and 'a haughty spirit before a fall.'"

James laughed. "Proverbs 16:18. The classic warning against pride. And don't forget what Jesus said: 'For everyone who exalts himself will be humbled, and he who humbles himself will be exalted.' That's from Luke, chapter 14. However," James paused for effect, "Jesus also said, 'Let your light shine before men, that they may see your good deeds and praise your Father in heaven.' That's from Matthew, chapter 5."

"And your point is?"

"I think we all need a helping of self-esteem to make it through the day. It's OK to commend a colleague for doing a good job, or to take satisfaction in the good work we do, or to enjoy the fruits of our accomplishments. It's also OK to have deep affection for something we treasure."

"As long as the self-esteem, or enjoyment, or affection doesn't blossom into destructive pride," I said.

"You took the words out of my mouth."

"Is that what I did with Hunnechurch Manor?"

James reached over and patted my hand. "It's easy to understand why you love our townhouse so much. Hunnechurch Manor is a symbol of your success—visible proof that your hard work paid off."

"Indeed. But then I allowed the symbol to overwhelm my common sense." I heaved a sigh. "Not to worry; we'll soon put things right and have a proper house we can both enjoy."

"Truer words were never spoken."

"Pardon?"

"We're here."

James drove along the gravel road that ended on a bluff overlooking the Magothy River. A light breeze was blowing off the bay. The sun seemed determined to burn through the rest of the overcast. We would have a beautiful afternoon and evening. I watched three sailboats tacking toward the mouth of the Magothy and recalled what Chloe had said when she reminded me that love isn't proud. "Think on it, Pippa. Think on it."

Good advice, that.

Chapter Nineteen

PEOPLE SAY THAT good things happen in threes. That was certainly my experience on Monday morning.

Good Thing Number One was my joyful discovery of untapped executive recruiting business to be had in Ryde. The new *Directory of Ryde Businesses,* published by the Ryde Chamber of Commerce, came in the morning mail. Several recent additions seemed just the sort of companies that might benefit from our services.

Good Thing Number Two was that, contrary to what I'd begun to believe, not every businessperson in Ryde knew I had been sued by Hardesty Software for consulting malpractice. Human resources managers at the new arrivals were perfectly willing to chat. In scarcely an hour, I'd made appointments to visit three executive offices the following week. I cheerfully entered the times and places in my computer calendar.

Good Thing Number Three was a telephone call from Gloria. "You know where I am and why I can't talk for long," she announced in a raspy whisper barely louder than the sound of running water that

I heard in the background. Gloria had reclaimed her Hunnechurch & Associates' cell phone from her desk drawer and was once again "broadcasting" from the ladies loo in Hardesty's executive suite.

"You know all the shopping I've been doing lately?" she said. "Well, I've had some good luck. You should see my purchase as soon as possible."

"Shopping?"

"Yes. *Shopping.*" She repeated the word slowly and precisely.

The penny dropped. Gloria was talking in a simple code.

"I understand," I said. "You found something interesting at Hardesty."

"Superinteresting. In just the right color for the occasion we have in mind—smoky gray."

I felt my heart skip. "You found our smoking gun?"

"What I found fits great," she said. "But it's only one part of the whole outfit. I'll need to do lots more shopping. However, I definitely want you to see what I bought today."

"When?"

"I plan to take a late lunch—from one to two."

"Where?"

"Where else? My usual stomping grounds."

"Here in the office, you mean?"

"I can't think of a better place to meet."

"I'll buy us lunch."

Click.

I could have had Hamburger Heaven deliver our order, but the day was glorious and I felt too keyed up merely to sit and wait. I left the office at twelve-fifteen and completed the round trip of six blocks in less than a half hour. At one o'clock I was sitting next to Gloria's workstation, our Eternity Burgers, Angelic Fries, and Cherubim Shakes neatly lined up on her desk, anxiously watching the clock creep ahead, wondering if Gloria had found a weapon that would defeat Mitch Hardesty in court.

"It's only one part of the *whole* outfit," she had said.

"Well, half a loaf is better than none," I murmured. At least it might provide a booster shot of hope.

I expected to see Gloria come through the front door and was surprised once more when "Helen Nelson" arrived and quickly shut the door behind her.

My face must have given me away. Gloria smiled and said, "I don't like wearing this shapeless dress any more than you like looking at it— although, there is a guy in accounting who's asked for my phone number three different times."

"We can reminisce about your love life after you show me your discovery. I am beside myself with curiosity."

Gloria gave me a single sheet of paper, folded in half. "I found this in Dennis Grant's old office. It must have fallen behind his credenza."

It was a neatly word-processed document divided into two columns. On the left side of the page: a list of headhunters, including Hunnechurch & Associates. On the right side of the page: a list of local companies and the addresses of their career opportunity Web pages. On the bottom of the page, in the "footer": *CE for DG by RW—January 17.*

"While you think about it," Gloria said, "I'm going to eat lunch." She peeled the wrapping off her hamburger, then flattened the foil with her hand. "Want a fry?" She offered me the bag.

I took a French fry and began to nibble.

"This is exactly the sort of list that a job hunter would make for himself," I said.

Gloria nodded. She had taken a big bite of her burger, rendering more elaborate communications impossible.

I continued. "The initials on the bottom suggest that RW—Rachel Wilson—typed a document that CE—Carol Ericsson—prepared for DG—Dennis Grant."

"Happens every day," Gloria managed to say. She paused to use a napkin. "Hardesty executives are mostly of the old school. They hate to do their own typing. They write stuff on yellow legal pads, then give it to the administrative assistants for word processing. They even have dictating machines in the executive suite."

Gloria said "dictating machine" with the same disdain as one might dismiss a Stone Age axe.

"The date on the bottom," I continued, "suggests that Dennis contemplated leaving Hardesty long before he contacted me."

Gloria, who had taken another bite, grunted her assent.

"Bless you, Gloria," I said. "You've made a remarkable find."

"Smoky, but not quite a smoking gun," she reminded me. "By itself, the list doesn't prove anything. I could have counterfeited that page this morning." She chomped down on her burger again. I let the sheet fall on Gloria's desktop and waited patiently for her to swallow. "But now we know for sure that we're on the right track. There may be a word-processing data file in Rachel's or Carol's computer that has an official date stamp on it. If I can find that, we're talking *real* evidence. And I have a feeling there are other lists and memos floating around Hardesty. I intend to search for them and anything else that can help us prove that Dennis was actively hunting for a job."

Had we, I wondered, *crossed a moral line in the sand?* When Gloria "searched for" things, she picked locks, downloaded private files, went places she didn't belong. I was condoning, even abetting, her conduct. But what choice did I have? For Hunnechurch & Associates to survive, we needed to go beyond "smoky" and undercover the "real evidence" lurking in the executive suite.

I offered a feeble protest. "Won't people mind you searching their offices?"

Gloria gave me an exasperated look and slurped a sip of shake. "I'll do my looking in the evenings. Nobody will think twice if I decide to stay late and finish some work."

"I hate the idea of you alone after hours. Dennis Grant was murdered."

"I'll keep my eye peeled for black vehicles in the executive suite."

"Gloria, I am serious. At least I should be there with you. I could stand guard at the door; watch your back while you search."

She shook her head. "It won't work, Pippa. You can't get upstairs after hours because you don't have one of these." She flicked the plastic identity badge that hung around her neck on a lanyard. "Besides, I'll do a better job of taking care of myself if I don't have to worry about you."

Gloria wolfed down the rest of her Eternity Burger. "Oh, and one more thing"—she crumpled the foil wrapper into a tidy ball—"tonight will be the safest evening of the week to browse around the executive suite. Most of the big hitters are going to be at the Ryde Chamber of Commerce meeting. With *you*."

Rats! Once again I had let the monthly meeting slip from my mind. The thought of spending an evening with people who considered me *persona non grata* didn't generate much eager anticipation, but as the chamber's program chair I had to attend—even if the atmosphere promised to become a tad strained.

"However," Gloria added, "your wish came true."

"What wish?"

"Mitch Hardesty will not attend. He flew to New York for a meeting with security analysts."

"Please stay far away from his office. Even though you are confident you can deal with the alarms, I don't want you taking the risk of . . ."

Gloria had stopped listening. "Gotta run!"

"Helen Nelson" departed, leaving me Dennis Grant's job-hunting list and also a minor problem to solve. James, still without a car of his own, planned to use my Volkswagen to drive to a consultant's association dinner and shindig in Annapolis. I had to arrange transportation to and from the chamber meeting.

I called David Friendly.

"Are you covering the chamber of commerce meeting tonight?" I asked.

"Wouldn't miss it for the world. I intend to do mini-interviews with as many Hardesty Software execs as I can. I especially want to chat with 'Darling.' It's about time I met Carol Ericsson. She's going to be one of the stars of my article, even though she doesn't know it yet."

I realized that Gloria had briefed David about the scrap of paper she'd found in the burn basket. He, in turn, had obviously agreed with her conclusion that Carol Ericsson was the guilty party. I supposed that Gloria would also tell David about Dennis's job-searcher list she had just unearthed and any other discoveries she made. In theory, the three of us had joined forces and were working together as a single team; still, I felt odd about Gloria detecting for David and me at the same time.

Get used to it, Hunnechurch. That horse escaped from the paddock ages ago.

"How goes the article?" I asked him, with all the enthusiasm I could generate.

"Fabulously. I've just received fresh confirmation that Dennis Grant's speeches were the source of the leaks. According to one of my friends of a friend, the quality of information about Hardesty Software declined significantly at the beginning of April."

"Dennis left Hardesty at the end of March."

"Bingo."

"Well done, David. Now—to the reason I called. I need a lift to Mariners' Hall this evening."

"My pleasure. I'll pick you up on Magothy Street at seven."

━━━━━━━━━━━

The monthly meetings of the Ryde Chamber of Commerce begin promptly at seven-thirty, which encourages most of the attendees to come directly from their offices, wearing their daytime business clothing. As a result, our meetings have maintained their formality in our age of increased casualness. Even David had put on a sport coat and tie.

"Undeniably natty," I said as he reached over and opened his Volvo's passenger-side door for me. "Nary an editorlike rumple or ink stain in sight."

He stuck his tongue out at me, then said, "I'm going to let you out a half block away from Mariners' Hall. It won't do for the Hardesty folks to see us march in together. Tonight I'll be wearing my award-winning reportorial hat."

"Your head is growing bigger so quickly that I worry about your reportorial hat. If it gets any tighter, it may cut off oxygen to your brain."

David laughed, worked the Volvo's gearshift, and let out the clutch.

In fact, he was right. My proximity might well discourage Hardesty people from talking to him—or at least put them on guard.

"Feel free to avoid me like the infamous plague," I said. "I shall return the favor and keep my distance."

Mariners' Hall, situated near the bottom end of Ryde High Street, is a lovely old building that dates to the early nineteenth century. The Commodore's Ballroom, large enough to seat three hundred people, has an impressive chandelier overhead and a small raised wooden stage on one end. Monthly chamber meetings typically attract seventy-five members and guests. Ten rows of chairs accommodate everyone and leave a large, open area in the back of the room for before-meeting socializing, networking, and refreshments.

I signed in at seven-fifteen, found my name tag, and poured myself a glass of ginger ale. I estimated that fifty other participants had arrived before me. I made the rounds—greeting those members who might still consider me an ethical businessperson. When I finished, I scanned the room for Hardesty executives.

On the stage: Stan Young, director of corporate planning, fussing with an electronic projector, doubtless getting ready to give tonight's presentation.

Against the far wall: Broderick McGee, chief counsel, talking with Ken Ross and Kelly the Shark—probably about me. I ignored the shiver I felt.

Near the front of the room: Ed Block, chief executive office, chatting with John Tyler, the chamber's longtime president. Tyler owned Ryde's largest commercial real estate firm. Perhaps he had helped Hardesty acquire its headquarters building.

In the tenth row of chairs: Rachel Wilson, sitting by herself, head down, reading a piece of chamber literature she must have taken from the rack near the refreshment table.

In the eighth row of chairs: Carol Ericsson sitting alongside David Friendly, talking earnestly. He had landed his quarry without difficulty.

I tried not to stare at Carol but couldn't stop looking.

Is she "Darling"? Am I watching a corporate spy and a murderer?

From where I stood, the lines on her face seemed deeper than when I'd seen her at the trap range, but then I might be merely observing the different modeling effect of indoor lighting compared to daylight. Or perhaps she was simply tired. Although her outside appearance said little about the inner Carol Ericsson, she didn't look like a killer to me. More's the point, I fancy myself a good judge of dishonesty. I had peered into Carol's eyes. I truly believed that she had loved Dennis Grant.

Dennis! I suddenly remembered—his funeral had taken place on Saturday in Portland, Oregon. I had meant to send flowers but had forgotten.

Another in a long list of gaffes you've made this month.

I glanced back at Carol. Of course she looked tired; she had spent the weekend in airports and on airplanes.

Someone tapped my arm. I spun around.

"Good evening, Pippa," Rose Robinson said.

"Well, well! You must be representing Militet Aviation."

She nodded—then smiled. "By any chance is that remarkable husband of yours going to be here tonight?"

"Alas, he is in Annapolis."

"Well, the next time you see him, give him my congratulations for wrapping Monica DeVries around his little finger."

"I shall." I tipped my head closer to Rose. "I have a question for you—on a rather unhappy topic: Dennis Grant."

Her smile faded. "We've been told not to talk about Dennis Grant, Pippa."

"Are you aware that I placed Dennis at Militet?"

She nodded again, slowly. "Kind of, now that you mention it."

"My question is simple, Rose: Was Dennis happy at Militet? You decide whether you can give me an answer."

She sipped her drink. After a long moment she shrugged. "I can't see the harm in giving you my opinion. I worked with Dennis on two projects. I think he preferred Hardesty to Militet because he liked being the only speechwriter on the staff. We have three. Dennis once told me that he wanted more 'face time' with our president."

The lamps in the chandelier blinked off and on. John Tyler's voice boomed through the loudspeakers: "If members and guests will please take their seats, our program is about to begin."

I thought about Dennis as I watched Rose walk away. I recalled how he bragged about becoming a hero to Mitch Hardesty. "I'll bet he offers me my old job back. Who knows? I may even accept."

Perhaps Dennis did regret leaving Hardesty? Perhaps he really wanted his old job back? Two uncertainties that might never be resolved.

David appeared at my side and whispered. "How about we sneak out? It's going to be a boring presentation—all the usual corporate platitudes and self-praise. Hardesty e-mailed me a copy of the PowerPoint slides this afternoon."

"An excellent plan."

I nonchalantly followed David through the crush of people moving toward the rows of seats. We slipped through the back door just as John Tyler invited Rabbi Sid Adler, the spiritual leader of Ryde Temple, to give the benediction.

"Did you learn anything new?" I asked David as we left Mariners' Hall.

"Mostly I learned that Carol Ericsson is a piece of work. She's icy as an Alaskan glacier and just as slippery—all the skills required to be a world-class corporate spy."

"Is she a murderer also?"

"I wouldn't be a bit surprised," David said, in a tone that proclaimed his utter confidence in Carol's guilt.

Why, I asked myself, *did the little voice in the back of my mind disagree with everything David had just said?*

Chapter Twenty

"MIGHT WE HAVE LEAPED to judgment too quickly?"

I hesitated in front of David's Volvo. He had unlocked the passenger door for me, then moved around to the driver's side.

"I haven't leaped anywhere," he said. "After due consideration I believe that we have identified Hardesty's corporate spy and quite probably the person who murdered Dennis Grant." He took a moment to peer at me over the roof of the car. "However, I can tell by the sour look on your face that you have a different take on Carol Ericsson."

When I didn't respond with anything more than a quick nod, David said, "OK, tell me what's bothering you."

"Sure. But you probably won't like it. Our central assumption doesn't feel right to me. The simple truth is that Carol Ericsson doesn't strike me as the clandestine agent sort. She certainly wouldn't be in it for the money. Vice presidents of growing companies don't lack for the occasional bob or two."

I slid into my seat and tugged the seat belt tight.

"I agree with you," he said as he pulled his door shut. "Based on appearances, Carol is about as spylike as, *say*, Gloria Spitz."

I laughed. "Touché! One shouldn't judge a book by its cover."

David started the engine and shifted into gear. "But when you probe below the surface, like I did this evening, you find there's a lot more to Carol Ericsson than meets the eye. For starters, she knows far too much about Hardesty's inner workings than a humble corporate *flack*."

"A what?"

"*Flack* is a mildly derogatory term for a press agent, the shady ancestor of today's public relations professionals." David backed out of our parking spot. "My point is that Carol understands more than she should about Hardesty Software's corporate strategy. The other corporate communicators I know, and I deal with dozens every day, are good at getting information and passing it on. That's their primary role. Carol talks like she's a working member of Mitch Hardesty's brain trust."

"Are you accusing her of being too smart or too knowledgeable?"

"Not really. I gave her the opportunity to show off, and she did. I told her I wanted to do a story about Mitch Hardesty's ability to manage a young company in a time of corporate adversity. She went on and on about Mitch's accomplishments—and also her analysis of the causes of the adversity. She rattled off details and reasons like a professor at Harvard Business School."

"I still don't buy it. I don't see Carol Ericsson as a secret agent."

"A dinner at *Maison Pierre* says I'm right."

"Coquille Chesapeake?"

"What else?"

"You're on!"

We exited the parking garage across from Mariners' Hall and turned right on Ryde High Street. David glanced at me. "Do you mind if I open the sunroof."

"A brilliant idea."

An electric motor in the roof churned. Because this was one of the longest days of the year, with sunset more than an hour away, the evening sky was still bright. I enjoyed the breezes that swirled around my head as David tootled along well below the speed limit. Traffic had dwindled to a few cars here and there. David didn't seem to be in a hurry.

"How about you?" he eventually asked. "Did you learn anything new tonight?"

"I confirmed my suspicion that Dennis was less than happy at Militet. I think he wanted to return to Hardesty as Mitch Hardesty's speechwriter."

"Why did he decide to leave in the first place?"

"Well, he gave me the usual reasons for moving on. He wanted a higher salary and the chance to work for a larger company. Militet offered both."

"But then our hero discovered he had made an awful mistake," David said, mockingly. "Something in his life at Hardesty Software proved more alluring in the long run."

"Apparently so. I think writing speeches for Mitch Hardesty made Dennis feel important."

We turned right on Magothy Street. I gazed out of my window; Hunnechurch Manor was only three short blocks away. I could almost taste the hot cuppa I planned to brew. Did I fancy Darjeeling? Or Russian Caravan? Or perhaps a flavored tea like Earl Gray?

A glint of motion in the Volvo's side mirror caught my attention. I bent forward to get a better view. A tall, black vehicle—some sort of truck with a huge bumper—had moved directly behind us.

I heard a loud *bang*.

The Volvo's rear window shattered above my head, flinging rounded fragments of safety glass throughout the interior.

A second *bang*—followed immediately by a loud metallic *clang*. I couldn't resist looking behind me. The driver's side corner of the Volvo's backseat was shredded.

"Someone's shooting at us!" I shouted.

"I know," David shouted back. "Keep your head down."

Another *bang*. The passenger window on the driver's side exploded in a new shower of glass fragments. David let out a sharp, "Ouch!"

"Are you hurt?" I screamed.

"I think I cut my hand on something. I'll be OK."

I scrunched down in my seat as best I could and struggled to keep my head below the edge of the window. It was the only protection in sight. David gunned the engine; I felt the Volvo accelerate. He flung the car from side to side to thwart the shooter's aim—not an easy chore on a narrow, eighteenth-century street, with cars lining both curbs.

Two more *bangs*—and *clangs*—in quick succession. My side window vanished in a puff of broken bits that rained down on me. I glanced up at cracks in the windshield and a nasty gouge in the dashboard.

Our tires squealed as David turned left, then left again. I poked my head up high enough to see we that were back on Ryde High Street.

"Hallelujah!" David said. "There's a cop car up ahead, across the street." David crossed to the wrong side of Ryde High Street and began to blow the horn.

I glanced at the side mirror. Shattered—but with still enough pieces of mirror in place to see that the black truck was no longer behind us.

"Thank you, God!" I murmured.

David, honking all the while, stopped the Volvo in front of the police car.

I began to shake. I had been the shooter's intended target; there seemed no other possible explanation of what had just happened.

But why? Why had someone tried so hard to kill me?

The answer came to me almost without thinking. The hit-and-run driver had seen me meet Dennis at Bombay Spices & Rices, had watched us bicker, had observed me give Dennis a plastic folder full of documents. The driver had right away guessed the contents: the speech drafts that Dennis had given me—including the draft that contained the typographical widow.

My connection to Dennis, the speech drafts in my possession, made me a dangerous loose end. The killer had silenced Dennis; I would be next. Because of a widow on paper, James nearly became a widower—and poor Joyce Friendly an authentic widow.

"Are you injured, ma'am?" A loud voice severed my chain of thought. I looked through my missing window at the same young copper who had driven me to the police station ten days earlier.

"Oh, it's you," he said.

"And bloomin' happy to be here too," I replied.

Another policeman had moved behind the Volvo. "Hey, Mark—take a look at the mess back here. You won't believe it. It's amazing anyone in the car survived."

Officer Mark—I knew his name at last—loyally remained at my window. "Do you need medical assistance, ma'am?" he asked.

"No. I'm not hurt."

"How about you, sir?" Mark leaned through the window to get a better look at David.

David's face was pale. He held the bottom of his left hand tightly with his right. Blood seeped through his fingers and along his wrist.

"You know," he said, "I think I got shot."

"Shot!" I shouted loud enough to make Mark flinch.

David smiled at me. "Relax. It's nothing but a big scratch in the fleshy part of my left hand."

"I'll call for an ambulance," Mark said. He stepped away from the Volvo, reached for the microphone attached to his lapel, and spoke a stream of alphanumerical police jargon that I didn't understand.

David, however, did. "Imagine that," he said. "I'm being called in as a 901S."

"Please translate."

"Ambulance required. Shooting victim."

Blimey! All I could think of to say was, "Does it hurt?"

"Not especially."

"Good!"

When Mark joined his buddy behind the car, David tilted his head close to mine. "We have two minutes to talk before this place is swarming with cops and emergency medical technicians. We have to decide what are we going to tell them."

"I plan to tell the coppers everything that happened."

"Fine—as long as you don't say anything about Hardesty Software, or Dennis Grant, or Carol Ericsson."

"I'll never get away with obfuscation, David. The police know that Dennis Grant was killed by a big, black truck. We will have to report that we were shot at from a big, black truck. The coppers are bound to make the connection. They will grasp that the driver wanted to kill me—and will certainly want to know why."

"I don't care about the conclusions they draw. What's important is that neither of us reveal the details of our investigation. If we give the police any substantive facts, we'll scoop my story and blow Gloria's cover. Promise me that you won't do either."

I nodded. "I shall try my best to keep silent."

David took a deep breath. "That reminds me—get a hold of Gloria. Tell her what happened."

"At once."

"One more thing . . ."

"Yes?"

"What are you going to tell James?"

"The whole truth and nothing but the truth—the very moment he gets home at ten. I suggest you do the same with Joyce."

David looked at his hand. "She'll be furious."

"At me, perhaps. The only thing you did wrong this evening was agree to chauffer me to and from Mariners' Hall."

All manner of flashing lights appeared outside. Red. Blue. White strobes. I slipped out of the car as a medical technician opened David's door. Officer Mark and his colleague were standing behind the Volvo. I joined them.

"Oh my!" I muttered when I saw the back of the car. The trunk lid, the rear fenders, the tail-lamp clusters were peppered with ugly holes.

"Buckshot," Officer Mark said. "Probably from a twelve-gauge shotgun. Each round contains nine lead balls, each the size of a thirty-two-caliber bullet. Judging from the number of holes in the back and the sides, the shooter struck the car at least four times."

"Five," I said.

"The balls can ricochet like crazy inside a car. One of them probably wounded the driver. You were lucky."

I felt the blood drain from my face. David and I had come within inches of being killed. God's providence—or dumb luck—had helped us get through virtually unscathed.

"Lucky indeed," I agreed.

"*Very* lucky, indeed," said a familiar voice behind me.

I turned and found myself face-to-face with Detective Stephen Reilly, his ID card hanging from a lanyard around his neck, a long-suffering smile on his face. Bad news traveled faster than I'd assumed within the Ryde police community.

"We received four 911 calls about the driver of a black truck shooting at a silver Volvo sedan on Magothy Street," he said. "I should be surprised that you were riding inside the Volvo—but you know, I'm really not." He turned to Officer Mark. "Have you identified the wounded driver?"

"Not yet. Although we ran the plates. The car is owned by David Friendly, of Ryde."

"*Who?*" Reilly raced to the front of the car.

"David and the detective have been friends for years," I told Mark.

Reilly called, over his shoulder. "Put Ms. Hunnechurch in my car. If she gives you any trouble, handcuff her to the seat."

"I shall go quietly," I said to Officer Mark.

He guided me toward an unmarked Ford sedan that had the un-mistakable look of a police vehicle. I settled into the somewhat seedy front seat and immediately regretted the promise I had made to David. Being questioned by the police is low on my list of favorite things to do. Lying to the police is even lower. Reilly wanted information of sub-stance, but I would have to play dumb—and make it convincing.

Child's play, Hunnechurch. You've done little that's brilliant as of late.

Sitting in Reilly's car gave me an excellent vantage point for viewing the comings and goings of official vehicles on Ryde High Street. I watched David walk to the ambulance, his hand bandaged. I watched the ambulance drive away. I watched a flatbed tow truck pull in front of David's Volvo. I watched the tow truck carry the battered sedan away. Last, I watched Mark's police cruiser leave the scene.

At twenty past eight, amidst all the watching, I tried to call Gloria's cell phone. No answer—although the network acknowledged that her phone was turned on. I imagined her still busy breaking and entering, and I recalled what David had said about "blowing" Gloria's cover.

You also have to protect "Helen Nelson's" identity.

The streetlights came on a moment before Reilly returned to the car. His pulled his door shut and said, "Tell me what happened on Magothy Street?"

"A truck appeared behind us," I said. "Five shots were fired. David brilliantly maneuvered the car to safety. The whole thing was over in the blink of an eye."

"Admirably succinct. Now tell me *why* the shooter took a monu-mental risk to attempt murder on a residential street on a quiet summer evening."

"I don't know."

"Funny thing—David didn't have an answer either. He's acting as closemouthed as you are."

I shrugged. "I have no idea why we were attacked."

"View halloo!" Reilly switched to the annoyingly good English accent he adopts when he wants to be sarcastic. "Can it be that Pippa Hunnechurch just spoke the *W* word? I think she did. In fact, I'm sure she did. Pippa said 'we.'"

I glowered at him.

The sun had set, but the streetlights provided ample illumination inside for Reilly to see my angry face. He countered with a smirk, then continued his harangue in his normal voice. "Twenty minutes ago I figured that David Friendly was your typical innocent bystander—a man in the wrong place at the wrong time. I figured that the buckshot was meant for you. Now I'm not so sure. Maybe the shooter wants both of you dead?"

I tried not to show my surprise—or that my mind was racing.

David represents a bigger threat to the corporate spy than you do.

An exposé revealing corporate espionage—even one published in the *Ryde Reporter*—would shine a dazzling spotlight on Hardesty's executive suite and simultaneously illuminate the murder of Dennis Grant. There would be no place to hide once David made public the link between spying and speeches.

What if the killer knew about David's investigation—guessed that you shared information with David?

He had come to my home, spent hours at my office—every visit made without any attempt at concealment. He had interviewed Hardesty executives and asked questions that might have aroused suspicion. And he had tapped his network of "confidential sources"—friends of friends who might easily work both sides of the street. Perhaps a dubious friend had warned the killer that a nosy local reporter was asking questions about leaked Hardesty secrets.

Reilly poked my arm. "I hope you're going to share your thoughts with me, Hunnechurch," he said.

"I have nothing to share, Detective."

He held up a small plastic envelope. "See this misshapen lead pellet? We dug it out of the back of the passenger's seat. If the shooter had taken better aim, we'd have removed it from you."

"I am wholly aware of my recent peril."

"Really? In that case you probably realize that without your help we don't stand a chance of finding your shooter—who almost certainly is the same person who murdered Dennis Grant."

Reilly didn't expect me to reply. He kept talking. "All we have now are a handful of conflicting descriptions of the truck. Big. Black. Probably a pickup with a bed cap. There couldn't be more than a hundred thousand black pickup trucks in Maryland. Naturally, no one spotted the license plate."

"I'm sorry. I've told you everything I can."

Reilly shook his head. "I've said it before, and I'll say it again. You are a rotten liar." He made a vague gesture. "I've got people walking Magothy Street. If we're lucky, we'll recover a fired shotgun shell. If we're extra lucky, we'll find a partial fingerprint. And the next time you and David get shot at, we can compare shot shells—match up the firing pin indentations and the extractor scratches."

"I am sure you are doing everything you can."

"I advised David to leave town for a while. If I were you, I'd go back to England—maybe for a decade or two."

"You've made your point, Detective."

"Since you don't intend to help me, Hunnechurch, get out of here." He reached over and opened my door. I stepped out of the car and slammed the door a trifle harder than necessary. He started his engine and drove away. Chivalry is dead in the upper echelons of the Ryde Police Department.

I was scarcely five blocks from Hunnechurch Manor, but I had no intention of walking home along dark streets. Not that night.

I called Ryde Cab. The cab arrived one minute later; our trip took even less time. I gave the driver a fat tip and told him to stay put until he saw me step safely inside.

I remember thinking, *There's nothing like a shotgun blast to sap one's courage.*

Chapter Twenty-one

JAMES DUBBED IT our "Come to Jesus" meeting. We gathered at eleven on Monday night in our dining room at Hunnechurch Manor to review our options and decide what to do next. The five participants were:

James—stern faced, resolute, acting more like a leader than I'd ever seen him before.

Gloria Spitz—still in her Helen Nelson garb but with an unhappy expression that hinted at the anger that simmered inside.

David Friendly—with his left hand in a large bandage, looking somewhat groggy from the medications he'd been given at Ryde General Hospital.

Joyce Friendly—continually glancing at David, looking worried, occasionally glancing toward the living room, where seven-year-old Peter Friendly lay sleeping on our sofa.

And me—my courage restored, once again surrounded by the people I loved best.

By midnight David, Gloria, and I had presented all that we discovered, all of our theories, and all of our conclusions. Gloria also offered an item of new information relevant to the attack on David's Volvo.

"Most of the big shooters at Hardesty," Gloria had begun but quickly realized her *faux pas.* "Sorry about that," she said, with a tip of her head toward David. "Four senior executives went to the chamber of commerce meeting to make an appearance. But only two stayed for the presentation—Ed Block and Stan Young. The other two, Broderick McGee and Carol Ericsson, left right after the reception. They were back in the executive suite by eight, so they could do more preparation work for the upcoming board meeting. They scared the stuffing out of me when the elevator door opened. I didn't expect anyone to interrupt my searching."

David responded excitedly. "You're saying that Carol Ericsson had plenty of time to trail us out of the meeting, follow my Volvo with her truck, blast away at us, then return to Hardesty Software."

Gloria nodded. "More than enough time."

David continued. "When we last talked about it, Pippa doubted that Carol was our corporate spy." He glanced at me. "Do you feel that way now?"

I shrugged. "In truth, I'm still unconvinced that Carol is responsible. I've met with her, looked her in the eye. The idea that she is a murderer just doesn't feel right to me."

"Maybe I can help change your mind," Gloria said. "Since I heard about the latest attack, I've been playing with that technique you taught me. I put together a job description for the person who leaked Hardesty secrets, killed Dennis Grant, and tried to kill you. I came up with a list of six essential requirements:

"One—access to Dennis Grant's speeches.

"Two—the ability to manipulate Dennis Grant, including getting him to leave a job he loved at Hardesty.

"Three—the financial resources to buy a big truck.

"Four—extreme coolness under pressure. Consider that the person killed Dennis and attacked you during daylight in public places. That takes courage and maturity.

"Five—experience with shotguns. It's not easy to shoot high-power buckshot loads; the shotgun kicks like a mule.

"Six—high intelligence coupled with great strategic thinking skills. This scheme took lots of planning.

"Only one person I've met at Hardesty Software meets all six of these requirements: Carol Ericsson."

"Assuming you are right," I said, "how do you get around Carol's alibi for the morning when Dennis was killed? She claims she was in Crownsville, Maryland, at a gun show."

"Nobody's tested her alibi. What if she'd stashed the truck at the gun show before she drove there with her friends? Crownsville is fifteen minutes away. She could have made a quick trip to Ryde, killed Dennis, and gone back to the show before anyone missed her."

David spoke up. "I've always like the notion that Carol has an accomplice—that she leaves the dirty work of murder to someone else."

"It's possible but not likely," Gloria said. "Remember when the attacks took place. One on a Saturday morning, the other on a Monday evening. She scheduled them outside of normal working hours, when she would be available."

Everyone at the table looked at me. My only reaction was to shrug again. "Perhaps it's wishful thinking on my part, but I can't envision Carol as a murderer."

James, who had taken on the role of acting chairperson, said, "Whether Carol Ericsson is the perpetrator or not, our most important chore tonight is to find a way to deter future attacks on Pippa and David. Any suggestions?"

Gloria lifted the bottom edge of her blouse and turned around, revealing a compact pistol in a small holster tucked into the small of her back. "From now on, I don't go anywhere without my Walther PPK."

James nodded grimly. "My H&K nine-millimeter automatic is up-stairs in my bed table."

David added, "I'm armed, too, at home. And our house is protected by an effective alarm system."

Joyce chimed in. "All this talk about guns makes me cringe. We've seen too much shooting already. I think there may be a less violent deterrent. It seems to me that Pippa and David are in danger for only one reason: the shooter wants to suppress information that Pippa, David, and Gloria have gathered. Am I right?"

We all nodded.

Joyce went on. "Well, that motive for murder goes away as soon as David makes the information public. I make a motion that David publish his article as soon as possible."

We were silent for a moment, then James said, "I second the motion! Once the truth is out—it's too late to kill anyone."

"Wow!" Gloria said. "It's so simple."

"Simple and brilliant," I agreed.

David hugged Joyce. "I'll finish my article on Wednesday and get it in Friday's edition of the *Ryde Reporter.*"

"Pippa and Gloria can lie low for a few days," James said, "until the article is published." He added, with a smile, "I know a perfect spot in northwest Georgia."

Gloria raised her hand. "Sorry," she said, "but lying low is not such a great idea. I'm on the verge of getting the evidence we need to win the lawsuit against Pippa. I need one more evening in Hardesty's executive suite."

"You've located our smoking gun?" I asked.

"Almost," she said. "I now know exactly where to look for the genuine smoking guns—inside Carol Ericsson's office. Possibly in her computer, maybe in a desk drawer. I brought the 'almost smoking guns' with me tonight."

Gloria and I both looked toward James. He hesitated a moment then said, "Show us."

Gloria had brought her laptop computer to the meeting. She set it on the table and lifted the lid. The rest of us gathered behind Gloria to observe the brightly glowing screen.

"I started my search this evening in Rachel Wilson's computer," Gloria said. "I was hoping to locate the document file for the job-seekers list I found in Dennis's office. At first I had trouble figuring out her log-on password. Fortunately, she'd written it down on a piece of paper stuffed in the back of her desk drawer."

Gloria poked at the keyboard and launched the word-processing program.

She continued explaining. "Once I had access to her hard drive, I ran into another problem. Rachel had set up hundreds of different directory folders—you know: folders inside folders, inside folders. I had to browse through each hierarchy. I finally reached a folder labeled 'Private Items.' I found three suspicious documents inside and copied them into my laptop."

Gloria pointed to a list of files.

"The third file is named 'M_Hardesty_Notes.' I can't open it because it's password protected. But the other two are plain old document files. Both are copies of documents that were originally prepared by Carol Ericsson."

James asked the question I wanted to. "How do you know that?"

Gloria looked back over her shoulder and grinned. "Simple. I clicked on the 'Document Properties' function. Both files were authored by 'C_Ericsson.'"

"Carry on," James said.

"The first document is Dennis Grant's most recent résumé. I'm pretty sure it's identical to the one he gave Pippa in February. We have a copy hanging on the wall in our conference room at the Hunnechurch & Associates office. The second document is a cover letter—the kind you submit with your résumé when you apply for a new job. Both files were created by Carol Ericsson on January 20 of this year. That's a full three weeks *before* the morning that Pippa supposedly accosted Dennis in Hardesty's parking lot."

"Carol clearly hoodwinked me," I said, with a sigh. "She—not Rachel Wilson—helped Dennis to leave Hardesty."

"We need to know the names and locations of the original date-stamped files," Gloria said. "Once we do, Pippa's lawyer can go after them."

"You do good work," James said to Gloria as he moved back to the head of the table. "And you're right—we need to know that those originals exist. Once we have names and locations, Daniel Harris can file a specific request for discovery."

"What's to stop Mitch Hardesty from simply erasing the files?" Joyce asked.

"I can answer that," David said. "Basically, the fear of going to jail. When my story hits the street, anything that Carol Ericsson did or touched—her computer, her diskettes, her backup files—will become potential evidence in her criminal trial. Mitch is smart enough to know that."

"OK, folks," James said. "How do we do what needs to be done?"

Gloria spoke without hesitation. "Helen Nelson needs to work one more day at Hardesty Software. She stays late again tomorrow night."

James frowned. "What happens if the executives decide to return to work tomorrow evening like they did tonight?"

"They won't. Mitch Hardesty invited his direct reports to the Baltimore Oriole's baseball game. They'll have dinner in the Hardesty corporate skybox at Camden Yards ballpark, then watch the game."

"Someone may not like baseball. We'll still have to find a way to guard your back."

"All figured out," Gloria said, proudly. "There are two routes into the executive suite. The ordinary path is via the building's lobby; you walk in and take the elevator to the eighth floor. The second route is just for Hardesty executives. They have a private, express elevator that connects the executive parking garage in the basement directly to the executive suite. We need two sets of eyes to watch for arriving executives. One person who can see the lobby, another person in the executive suite, sitting in the receptionist's workstation. There's a monitor in the work-station that's connected to a TV camera in the private garage."

"I volunteer to come along with you," David said.

Gloria shook her head. "You're not shapely enough. It has to be Pippa."

"Pardon?" I said

Gloria dug into her purse. "We can use this ID card to get Pippa into the executive suite with me."

She dropped a laminated plastic identification card on the table. The name on the card: Clarissa Mulray. The photograph: a woman of my age with roughly similar facial features.

"Until this afternoon," Gloria said, "Clarissa was a temporary em-ployee, just like me. I found her badge on her desk; she obviously for-got to turn it in. I'll do it for her on Wednesday morning, when I turn in my own."

"She's not as pretty as Pippa," James said.

Bless you, James.

"True," Gloria said, "but Pippa is the same height and build as Clarissa. Nobody will look closely at Pippa's badge, as long as she is wearing one. From a distance the most significant difference is hair color. Pippa will need to wear a brunette wig." She turned to me. "I have a wig you can use in my disguise kit. We'll style it tomorrow to give you Clarissa's do."

I smiled. "How can I say no?" I said. "I've always wanted to be a brunette for a day."

"I guess that means I loiter in the lobby," David said.

"Make that *we*," James said, forcefully.

"Nobody has to stand around," Gloria said. "There's a restaurant in the building—The Olde Ryde Saloon and Grill—with big windows that overlook the lobby. Anyone sitting at the table close to the windows has an unobstructed view of the elevators. You guys make like a pair of businessmen having dinner. Eat slowly, linger over dessert, and watch the lobby. Give Pippa a call on her cell phone if you see a Hardesty executive arrive. We'll leave via the parking elevator before he or she can get upstairs."

I completed Gloria's explanation, "And if I see an executive on the TV monitor I'm watching, we skedaddle downstairs via the main elevator."

"Piece of cake!" Gloria said.

I suppose that's what everyone thought at the time.

Our meeting broke up at one a.m. We ended by holding hands and praying for wisdom and safety. David, Joyce, and a sleepy Peter Friendly drove off in Joyce's Subaru wagon. James went upstairs to get ready for bed. Gloria lifted her laptop's lid again. .

"Before I go," she said, "let's take another shot at the password-protected document."

"What is it?"

"I don't know. It could be something Rachel Wilson typed for Mitch and then hung on to."

"I thought Mitch Hardesty has his own executive assistant?"

"He does. Nancy Hitchcock. But maybe Nancy was out of town when Rachel prepared the document."

"It probably has nothing do with our investigation. I feel awkward reading Mitch's private mail."

"I don't." Gloria started the word processor again and clicked on M_Hardesty_Notes.

A small window opened: Enter Document Password.

I tried every password I could think of. *Hardesty. Password. Barney,* the name of Mitch's dog. *Sandra,* Mitch's wife. Several different birthdays. And various combinations of *Admiral Hobart Strand,* the street Mitch lives on.

"Good Lord. Does Mitch live in Founders' Woods?"

"Yep. Supposedly his house looks like a castle."

"I've seen it. We will soon be neighbors."

Gloria and I brainstormed possible passwords for nearly ten minutes. No joy.

"I know when I'm licked," she said glumly. "One of these days I have to learn the proper techniques for hacking into a protected document."

She reached for the laptop's lid to swing it shut. All at once, I had an idea.

"Have some fun," I said. "Try *blowhard* and *blowhardest.*"

Blowhardest worked like a charm.

With Gloria peering over my shoulder, I scrolled through the contents. "This looks like a diary," I said, "although Mitch probably wouldn't call it that. In fact, our Mr. Hardesty has created a brag sheet in which to list his daily accomplishments."

"It sounds kind of kinky to me."

"To be fair to Mitch, this is exactly the sort of information one would need to write his biography. Perhaps the great man is thinking ahead."

"I'm sorry I wasted your time. I'll let you get to bed."

I pressed the *Page Down* key and idly scanned the page.

"Cripes!" I shouted. "Double cripes!"

All poor Gloria could say was, "Huh?"

I swung the computer sideways so that she had a clearer view of the screen. "Take a look. Tell me that my eyes have made a horrid mistake."

I heard her gasp. "I don't believe it! Mitch can't be right."

"My thoughts exactly, but I have a feeling that Mitch is utterly right."

"What are you going to do?"

"I am going to send you home. Then I am going to express my feelings appropriately."

Gloria folded her laptop computer. "Remember the Lord's Prayer. You are forgiven to the extent you forgive others."

"We shall see."

=========

I flew up the stairs toward the sound of water running in our bathroom. I threw the door open. James stood in front of the sink, a toothbrush in his mouth, a bewildered look on his face.

"*Yeth?*" he said.

"You bounder," I shouted. "You cad! You . . . *you* . . . dissembler! I trusted you completely, but you betrayed my trust."

He spit a mouthful of toothpaste into the sink. "What are you talking about?"

"You are working for Hardesty Software. Mitch Hardesty personally hired you to consult with him in the area of corporate information leaks, yet you told me nothing about it. You have gone over to the enemy!"

He rinsed his mouth and attempted one of the smiles I like so much.

"Forget it!" I hissed. "A smile won't work with me tonight. Neither will denying your deceitful employment."

"I wouldn't dream of denying my assignment at Hardesty. Mitch did hire me. No big deal—I'm a marketing consultant. Sometimes my work involves competitive counterintelligence. I'm good at it."

"How could you not tell me?"

"That's part of my deal with Hardesty. I say nothing to anyone about the work I'm doing for the company."

"Poppycock! I am your wife. You don't keep secrets from me."

"You're right!" James said. "James Huston, your loving husband, has no secrets from you. Not a one! But Peachtree Consulting Group—my company—has dozens of secrets that you will never learn."

"Now you are splitting hairs."

James took my hand. I pulled it away. "How many times have you told me that you're proud of your reputation as an ethical headhunter?" he asked.

"Countless!"

"Guess what, Pippa. I'm equally proud of my reputation as an ethical management consultant. We're both in businesses where people rely on our professional discretion and confidentiality. That means that we can't press one another for the details of our business relationships. Your clients and my clients must be confident that their business secrets are safe. Anything less and we might as well shut down our two firms."

I remembered Chloe's words to me a few days earlier. "Curious," she had said. "I expected the major difficulties in your new marriage to center on Hunnechurch & Associates and the Peachtree Consulting Group." Had she anticipated the challenge of keeping business secrets from each other?

Why not? Chloe figures out everything else in my life.

"How long have you worked for Hardesty?" I asked.

"Since January. Mitch was my first major client in Ryde."

"I also began to work for Hardesty in January. Didn't you worry that we might accidentally meet in the executive suite?"

"Not really. I usually meet with Mitch at his home."

"The castle?"

"Yeah. How did you know?"

"Never mind."

"See! You keep professional secrets too."

James took my hand again. This time I didn't object.

"Blimey!"

"What?"

"I just realized why Rachel Wilson told me she wasn't married." I squinted at James. "You *know* Rachel and Rachel knows you."

James smiled sheepishly. "A good looking admin on the eighth floor? Dark hair? Late twenties?"

"Exactly!"

"She tried to cozy up to me in January. Of course, I wasn't wearing a wedding ring back then."

"Naturally, she told you the truth—that she was single. And of course, when we got married, she worried that you might reveal her marital status to me. So she fessed up to me. Which was wholly unnecessary because you do such a fine job of keeping business secrets from your spouse."

"That I do. And I hope you do the same. We agreed to keep our business identities separate."

"I know we did. But isn't Mitch Hardesty . . . *different?*"

James sighed. "Yeah, I've been feeling funny about not telling you. In fact, I'm relieved you found out." He gave me a quizzical look. "How did you find out?"

"Wives find out everything," I said sagely. "Keep that in mind the next time you try to prevaricate."

Chapter Twenty-two

IT'S HARD TO REMAIN ASLEEP when one's gastric juices begin to flow. Early on Tuesday morning an indescribable aroma somehow incorporated itself into my dream. I imagined myself watching a cooking show on our home theater that James had just equipped with the latest futuristic accessory: Smell-o-vision. I marveled at the accurate smells of flaky pastry, savory spices, and sizzling beef.

My eyes blinked open and I reached for James, only to find an empty indentation in the bedclothes. I glanced at the clock: a quarter after seven. I had enjoyed a mere five hours of slumber.

Much too little, Hunnechurch. Go back to sleep.

I abruptly realized that the aroma beyond words was real. The extraordinary smell wafted through our little bedroom, compelling me to get out of bed and find an explanation. I threw back our summer duvet, found my bunny slippers and robe, and let my nose guide me downstairs.

James, fully dressed in slacks and shirt, stood smiling in the kitchen. He had set our kitchen table for breakfast and brewed a pot of tea. He handed me a hot cuppa.

"How long have you been up?" I asked as I took my first sip.

"Since five-thirty."

"My goodness! Why?"

"To surprise you."

"Well, you certainly have managed that. What is the source of that glorious smell?"

"Humble pie," he said.

"Humble pie?" I echoed mindlessly.

"From one of Mother Huston's favorite recipes. I figure it's time that you and I both had big helpings."

"James! Stop this nonsense immediately, or I will . . . I will . . ." My sleep-deprived brain couldn't invent a suitable threat to finish my ultimatum. I took several more sips of tea, then added: "Humble pie is fictitious. A figure of speech. There is no such thing as humble pie."

"You don't say?" James sniffed the air exaggeratedly. "My humble pie smells mighty real. Besides," James shook his head in mock disappointment, "you, of all people, should know better. Humble Pie began as a tasty dish in merry, old England, many centuries ago."

I took a step toward the stove. James moved in front of me. "You can't open the oven. The humble pie isn't done yet."

"This is intolerable, James. What are you cooking?"

He laughed and said, "Have a seat. All will be clear."

I muttered, "Blast you! James Huston, you are a morning person; I am not." Nonetheless, I took my usual place at our table.

James struck a professorial pose next to our stove. Face stern. Hands clasped together. "In precisely three minutes and thirty seconds," he said, "our oven timer will loudly proclaim that our humble pie is ready to consume. That gives me just enough time to explain its origins in excruciating detail."

I glared at James. "You are having entirely too much fun—most of it at my expense."

"You don't know the half of it," he said merrily. "This will be a morning to remember."

"A morning that will live in infamy," I mumbled.

"No. A morning of realized hopes and answered dreams. A day-break filled with surprises."

"Whatever! I believe you were pontificating on the subject of humble pie."

"Ah, yes." James made a throat-clearing sound. "As we all know, in current usage, the phrase 'to eat humble pie' refers to a change in one's circumstance, usually involving an admission of error and/or the making of an apology. If I apologize humbly, I can be said to have eaten humble pie. Do you agree?"

"Yes, yes, yes! Get on with it." I looked in my empty cup. "I need another cup of tea."

"Curiously, the modern meaning of 'to eat humble pie' represents significant change from the original concept of the phrase." James put his fingertips to his temples. "Let us depart on a journey of the imagination. Our destination is a bucolic forest in sixteenth-century England. Are you with me, Pippa?"

"When will this lunacy end?"

James took no notice of my rhetorical question. "The forest is lush, green, bursting with wildlife. A huntsman arrives. He spots a deer. He raises his bow and arrow. *Whoosh.* The deer is dead. That evening the nobleman who owned the forest dined on roasted venison. But the poor huntsman went home carrying the deer's less valuable parts—its heart, liver, and miscellaneous innards." James brought the teapot over and refilled my cup. "Understand so far?"

"Completely."

James lectured on. "In those simpler days, deer innards were called *umbles.* Mrs. Huntsman would take Mr. Huntsman's umbles and bake them into a pie, along with apples, currants, sugar, and aromatic spices. In short, umble pie. A modest dish suitable for a poor man. To eat umble pie meant that you acknowledged your place in the social pecking order. The rest is history. A few hops, skips, and jumps of the English language brought about the modern name and the present connotation. You and I will soon breakfast on genuine humble pie."

As if on cue, the oven timer *dinged.*

"Please assure me, James, that you did not bake a pie shell full of deer guts in my oven."

"Although I searched far and wide for fresh deer umbles, there were none to be had in Ryde—other than from the occasional road-killed deer."

"Yuck!"

"Happily, my mother's recipe calls for small cubes of steak instead."

James donned a pair of oven mitts and opened the oven door.

"Well, I admit that it looks yummy and smells out of this world," I said.

James carried the steaming pie—its crust a perfect golden brown—to the table and set it atop an insulated trivet.

"Humble pie was a tradition in the Huston household. We, of course, adopted the modern definition. We dined on humble pie whenever it was necessary for one of us to admit a major mistake. All the Hustons agreed that a dish of humble pie is much tastier than eating crow."

I laughed. "Is this your roundabout way of apologizing for something?"

"Yes." He sighed deeply. "I ran roughshod over your well-deserved enjoyment of the fruits of your accomplishments. For that I apologize. I also have found a way to make amends."

I tried not to look as bewildered as I felt. "I must be dense as a brick this morning, James. You will have to be more specific."

"All at the proper time. First, have a bowlful of humble pie."

James wielded a pie knife and serving spoon. Under its crust, humble pie à la Huston seemed a cross between beef potpie and a mince pie. He served it up in a pair of chili bowls.

"Delicious!" I crooned. "You should be inordinately proud of your humble pie." I ignored the fact that the pie was almost too hot to eat and wolfed down my first helping. I held my bowl out Oliver Twist fashion: "More, please."

Two bowls later I had almost forgotten that our unusual breakfast had been prefaced by an incomprehensible apology. James deepened the mystery by placing a shiny brass key on the table.

"Pick it up," he said. "You'll need it."

I looked first at the key, then at James's mischievous expression, and then begin to sip my fourth cup of English breakfast tea.

"What does it unlock?" I asked.

"My latest surprise for you." He chuckled. "Acquired yesterday evening."

"You were in Annapolis, at a consultant's meeting."

"An outrageous fib. I spent the whole evening in Ryde, signing papers, writing checks, walking around my new piece of property."

I nearly dropped the teacup in my lap. "*What* new piece of property?"

"James Huston is now a member of the landed gentry in this fine community."

"You bought the pretty Cape Cod in Founders' Woods?"

James grinned at me like a schoolboy for what seemed an eternity. "Absolutely wrong!"

"Then what did you buy?"

"The key in your hand unlocks the front door of 737 Magothy Street. I believe you know the house."

I recall that my mouth sagged open. "Seven-thirty-seven is . . . *is* . . . you must be joking! It's the bloomin' townhouse next door."

"Right on the other side of that wall." He gestured with his thumb over his shoulder. "I've temporarily named it Huston Manor."

My voice jumped an octave or two. "We own *two* townhouses?"

"Not for long. We will have a wedding as soon as possible, with a building contractor performing the ceremony. We'll create a perfect union by knocking down a few interior walls and adding several doors."

"We'll have a bigger house?" It was more of a question than a statement.

"Huston Manor is twice the size of Hunnechurch Manor. Our combined townhouse will have three times the space. We'll have a master bedroom big enough for two, a home office for each of us, a proper guest room, a comfortable home theater, and a kitchen big enough to cook in. Feel free to swing as many cats as you like."

"What about bathrooms?"

"Two full bathrooms upstairs."

"A miracle!"

"You can have the larger one."

"I'm in heaven."

"Plus a loo for guests downstairs."

"Glory be!"

"And of course a bigger backyard. We'll knock down the side wall. You'll have space for a real English garden."

"With a water feature!"

"A what?"

"A fishpond."

"Why would we want fish in our backyard?" he asked.

"We'll talk about it later. Tell me about our new living room."

"Roughly the same size as today."

"The same size?" I said. "Why not larger?"

"Because I plan to equip the new, improved Hunnechurch Manor with a one-car garage for my new car."

"Brilliant! I acknowledge that your new BMW sedan deserves to live indoors with us."

"Ah. I meant to tell you—I changed my mind again. I ordered a Mini coupe."

"A Mini? As in *little?*"

"Supercharged engine, six-speed transmission, high-performance tuning kit, leather upholstery. All in all, an ideal vehicle for parking in downtown Ryde, negotiating the hairpin turns of Romney Boulevard, and coping with the eighteenth-century width of Magothy Street."

I peered at James. "You've gone mad. Delightfully, wonderfully bonkers."

"Maybe. But give me credit for the method in my madness. You love this house. I love you. We need more space. With the stroke of a pen, I kept both of us happy."

"That's the virtue Paul left out of his list in 1 Corinthians. 'Love is patient, love is kind. It does not envy, it does not boast, it is not proud.' Love finds clever solutions to problems."

"Get dressed," James said. "I'll give you a tour."

I pulled my bathrobe tight, retied the belt, pocketed my new key, and strode toward my front door.

"Who needs clothes to walk around our new digs?"

———————————

I became Clarissa Mulray in Gloria Spitz's apartment. I did not enjoy my metamorphosis. Gloria had trimmed and styled a synthetic brunette wig to match the hairdo in Clarissa's ID photograph. The wig was hot and made my scalp itch. It felt as if I had dropped a helmet on my head.

Clarissa wore lots of makeup—including the sort of eyeliner and eye shadow that I never used. Gloria needed bright lights and a half hour to duplicate the right look—which my sister Chloe would have described as "veddy, veddy tarty." As Gloria worked, I thought about the delightful day I had spent with James—safe, secure, and blissfully happy in Hunnechurch Manor, sitting side by side as we used a computer drawing program to sketch possible floor plans of our expanded townhouse. At five-thirty, James drove me to Gloria's apartment, then continued on to meet David Friendly.

Clarissa's clothing, at least, was simple and comfortable: a pair of old blue jeans, running shoes, and a knit Hardesty polo shirt. "We're doing menial work after hours," Gloria explained. "The security guard will expect us to dress accordingly."

Gloria gave my cheeks a final swipe with her blush brush, then stood back and surveyed her handiwork. "The spitting image of Clarissa, if I say so myself."

"I'm not so sure," I said as I studied my new ugly self in a mirror. "Clarissa has a shorter nose than me. And her eyes are closer together."

"True. But you fill out the polo shirt better. I don't think the security guard will spend much time looking at your nose."

At six-thirty we prepared to leave. Gloria reached for her Walther PPK; she worked the slide, fed a round into the chamber, and activated the safety.

"Ready for bear," she said. She slipped the pistol into its holster in the small of her back.

We drove to the Ryde Business Park in Gloria's white pickup truck and found a parking spot almost directly in front of Hardesty Software's administration building.

"From this moment on, you are Clarissa Mulray and I am Helen Nelson. Don't forget!"

"No problem, hon."

"One more thing. Swing those hips—Clarissa is a bit of a flirt."

There was nothing old—or quaint—about the Olde Ryde Saloon & Grill. It was five years old—the same age as Hardesty's headquarters— and featured the faux wood furniture and plastic trimmings one finds in so many American restaurants.

The Saloon had acquired considerable fame across Ryde as a singles "pickup spot" on Friday evenings; further it had become popular with younger patrons because it offered great burgers and two drinks for the price of one during the five to six p.m. "happy hour." On that Tuesday evening, at a quarter to seven, the dining room was sparsely occupied. We immediately spotted James and David sitting at a table that provided a splendid view of the building's lobby.

David whistled when I approached their table; James merely stared.

I batted my made-up eyes at James and twisted a synthetic curl around my finger. "So big boy, do you have any plans for after the stakeout?"

"*Ah* do declare, ma'am," he drawled. "Has anybody ever told you that you are as good-looking as a hound dog on a hunt?"

"Thank you—I think."

David laughed. "I'm impressed. What did you do with Pippa Hunnechurch?"

"She's under here somewhere," I said.

A waitress appeared. "Can I get you gals anything to drink?" She dropped little cardboard coasters in front of us. I ordered an iced tea; Gloria, a ginger ale.

"Let's do a quick review," James said. "Where are your cell phones?"

"Hanging on my belt," I said, "so it's easy to reach."

"Mine's in my handbag," Gloria said.

James nodded. "Good. Tell me your timetable."

"We leave the executive suite no later than nine o'clock," Gloria said, "even if I don't find anything."

Another nod from James. "And if you hear a cell phone ring."

"We head for the garage elevator immediately. You will meet us downstairs, outside the entrance to the garage."

I jumped in. "If I see an executive arrive in the private garage, we'll immediately take the main elevator downstairs."

The waitress brought our drinks. "Would you like to see the dinner menu?" she asked.

"No thanks," Gloria replied. "I'm not hungry."

At that very moment my stomach rumbled loud enough for everyone in the vicinity to hear.

"I'm not hungry either," I lied. In fact, I had little reason to be hungry. I had eaten two more helpings of humble pie for lunch.

The waitress shrugged and went off to find richer pickings.

"We'll eat later," Gloria said. "Food tastes much better after you get back from a mission."

"Perhaps, but I intend to pocket a handful of mints when we leave the restaurant."

At seven on the dot, "Helen" stretched, stood up, and said in a voice that carried throughout the dining room, "No rest for the weary, Clarissa. We'd better go upstairs and get to work."

James held my hand for a long moment and gave it a squeeze.

I hung Clarissa's ID card around my neck and followed "Helen" out the side door of the Olde Ryde Saloon & Grill—the door that opened directly into the building's lobby. "Just do exactly what I do," she said. "You'll be fine."

We walked across the lobby, toward the receptionist's kiosk in front of the elevators. At this time of evening, the kiosk was manned by a uniformed security guard—a heavy-set man of about fifty who looked up with interest as we approached.

"Good evening, ladies," he said. "Working late tonight?"

"On the eighth floor," "Helen" said.

"Really? I thought that *executiveland* was empty tonight. Everyone's at the Oriole's game."

"Except for us. We're working on board meeting stuff."

"Fine with me. I ain't going to the ballgame either." He pushed a visitors' log toward us. "You have to sign in."

Gloria printed "Helen Nelson" on the next available line and added a signature in the appropriate space. She handed me the pen. I started to print a "P" but managed to convert it to a cockamamie "C" with a slightly flattened left side.

I held my breath as the guard looked at our ID cards and jotted down our card numbers on the visitors' log. My Clarissa Mulray camouflage did its job perfectly. He gave a quick glance to Clarissa's photo, then a brief gaze at me.

"Don't work too hard, ladies," he said.

"We won't," Gloria said. "A couple of hours and we're history."

We moved on to the elevators. Gloria pressed the call button. I looked back toward the restaurant's glass windows across the lobby. I knew that James could see me, but the subdued lighting inside the Olde Ryde Saloon & Grill prevented me from seeing James.

Somewhere above us, I heard an elevator start to move. I watched the lit numbers change above the door. *Eight, seven, six, five, four, three, two, one. Ding.*

The doors slid open. Gloria and I stepped inside.

"See what I mean?" She said. "It's going to be a piece of cake. From here on it's all downhill."

Gloria was as wrong as she could be.

Chapter Twenty-three

THE ELEVATOR ROSE quickly. So did my heart rate. Something was bothering me; something didn't seem right. But I couldn't sort out my concerns.

Stop whining, Hunnechurch. You are merely nervous.

I glanced at "Helen Nelson." She had a satisfied smile on her face, a look of enjoyment at the challenges of an undercover operation. She clearly did not share the increasing sense of dread that I felt.

The elevator doors swooshed open on the eighth floor. We stepped into the elevator lobby. Marble floors. Plants too perfect to be real. Complete silence except for the gentle whoosh of air from the air-conditioning vents.

Ahead of us, across the lobby, was a frosted glass door decorated with the Hardesty Software Corporation logo. "They keep the door unlocked during the day," Gloria said. "At night you need to use an ID card as an electronic key."

Gloria placed her ID card against a scanner. I heard a gentle *click*.
Gloria pushed open the door to Hardesty's inner sanctum. I followed
close behind.

I knew from my earlier visits in February that the only windows in
the executive suite were in the executive offices. The windowless central core was dimly lit that evening. Gloria flipped a switch and the
overhead lights blinked on.

"Let there be light," she said.

"And there was light," I added. "And it was good."

A few days earlier Gloria had described Hardesty's executive suite as
"fairly modest—nice but not overly luxurious." Maybe so, but the look
and feel were much more elegant than the plain-Jane, worker-bee
offices I usually visited. Plush carpet, thick and springy, the color of *café
au lait*. Walls covered with off-white fabric, made warmer by photographs of customers using Hardesty software. Substantial furniture
made of oak, clearly the product of a custom shop.

The first piece of furniture we came to was the eighth-floor receptionist station, a large high-walled cube that sat away from the wall.

"There's the TV monitor for the private garage," Gloria said. She
pointed to a small screen embedded at an angle within the workstation's desk. The image: a garage empty except for a single car.

"Wow. That's a Porsche Boxster convertible," Gloria said. "I'd love
one of those—in silver gray. It's fast as all get-out."

"Whose is it?" I asked.

"Obviously, it belongs to one of the execs."

"Actually, it's mine," said a woman's voice behind us.

We spun around.

There was Rachel Wilson, standing ten feet away, wearing black
slacks and a Hardesty polo shirt like mine, smiling her fetching-little-
girl smile. She cradled a pump-action shotgun in her arms. It was much
like the weapon I had fired at the trap range, except Rachel's gun
seemed a lot scarier: she had replaced its wooden shoulder stock with

a pistol grip that rested in her right hand. I could see her right index finger squarely on the trigger.

Rachel pumped the shotgun's forearm. It made an ugly *snick-snack* sound. She lowered the gun to waist level and pointed the barrel directly at me.

"I love your Clarissa Mulray disguise," she said. "Your hair looks perfect, and I applaud your great makeup job. The resemblance is uncanny."

I reached for my wig. It made no sense to keep the hot, itchy monstrosity on my head.

"Whoa, Pippa!" Rachel said. "Don't move a muscle. Don't even twitch. My gun is loaded with 'double-o' buckshot. Nine miniature cannonballs in each round. I can barely hold the barrel steady when I shoot. But you'll have a bigger problem. On the receiving end it's like getting hit with a nine-shot burst from a light machine gun."

I glanced at Gloria. Her gaze was fixed on the shotgun aimed at me. The grim look on her face told me that she took Rachel's weapon seriously.

My knees felt weak. I gripped the top of the workstation for support.

Rachel gestured at me with her shotgun. "We're going into the boardroom," she said. "The double doors on the other side of the suite. Walk slowly. Move one slow step at a time until you reach the doors. Then stop."

I did as I was told.

Gloria followed behind me.

Rachel waited until we had reached the door before she moved. She took up a new position alongside me, her shotgun level with my stomach.

"Open the door on your right, Pippa," she said. "Turn the doorknob, then push the door all the way open."

I obeyed.

"Now walk!"

I moved into the dark boardroom. I could sense Gloria behind me and Rachel behind her. I heard a light switch click. Three banks of overhead lights illuminated the biggest conference table I had ever seen. It was pear shaped and perhaps thirty feet long. The largest, most comfortable looking chair was at the narrow end of the table. I guessed that was where Mitch Hardesty sat.

"Keep walking!" Rachel barked. "Move to the head of the table and turn around. Stand away from the furniture. I want to see all of you at all times."

Again I followed her instructions to the letter.

She held the shotgun in her right hand by the pistol grip like an enormous handgun—still keeping it aimed at my midriff—and swung the door shut with her left hand. It closed with a solid thud.

"Welcome to Hardesty's boardroom, Ms. Hunnechurch." She smiled again, her expression not an iota girlish. The timid administrative assistant had been replaced by a hard-as-nails killer. "A lovely place to die, don't you agree?"

Rachel perched on the edge of the conference table.

I reached for a chair.

"No! No! No!" Rachel said. "You keep standing. I want your hands in plain view."

The initial shock began to wear off; my mind began to function again. In a flash I realized the horrible mistake that David, Gloria, and I had made.

Rachel Wilson had been visible everywhere we looked. But we had completely discounted her as a potential spy and murderer. Why? Mostly because she was a lowly administrative assistant. At the same time we had invented reasons to condemn Carol Ericsson because we had foolishly assumed that the corporate spy must be an executive.

I recalled the list of "job requirements" for successful corporate espionage that Gloria had presented the night before. In hindsight, Rachel met every one of them:

Rachel had total access to Dennis Grant's speeches. She typed them, for goodness sake!

Rachel clearly had the skills to manipulate Dennis and encourage him to leave the job he loved at Hardesty. She had proved that by maneuvering to displace Carol Ericsson and become Dennis's new girlfriend.

Rachel's earnings as a corporate espionage agent would give her the financial resources to buy a dozen pickup trucks—along with the pricey Porsche Boxster that was currently parked in the executive garage.

Rachel's icy demeanor as she held us captive amply confirmed her coolness under pressure.

Rachel had demonstrated her knowledge of shotguns. Why did we assume that someone like Rachel couldn't shoot straight?

Rachel, not Carol, would raise eyebrows if she left during regular working hours.

And lastly, there were Rachel's intelligence and strategic thinking skills. She had certainly snookered the lot of us with a "cookie crumb trail" of almost-smoking guns. Rachel had undoubtedly created the collection of documents and files that Gloria hoped would prove the innocence of Hunnechurch & Associates. Rachel had cleverly strung us along with invented paperwork that made it seem as if Dennis had planned all along to leave Hardesty. The documents had never existed, except in Rachel's computer—where Gloria had found them.

The "Darling" note that Gloria had found in the burn basket was certainly a fake too. Gloria had "proved" Dennis had written the note by comparing its handwriting with a letter supposedly written to Rachel. Clearly Rachel had written both items in her own hand.

And Rachel's attempts to deceive us didn't stop with phony evidence: Rachel had even made it easy for Gloria to find Clarissa's ID card. Most of all, she had done a magnificent job of setting up Carol Ericsson as the killer. Once Gloria and I were dead, the world would assume that Carol—a jilted lover—had first killed Dennis and then had finished us off using one of her many shotguns.

I had another flash of insight. After we were dead, Rachel would make Carol disappear—permanently. That would take the spotlight completely off Rachel's relationship with Dennis Grant. The police would find the "evidence" that we had amassed; they would conclude that Carol had been both spy and murderer—and had made a clean getaway.

Rachel would be free to launch her espionage scheme all over again at another company.

I glanced again at Gloria. Her expression seemed even more pensive. No surprise there—she had lots to think about. Gloria must have tumbled to our mutual miscalculation about Rachel. Gloria was doubtless also thinking about the pistol tucked in the small of her back. I hoped that her ruminations would lead her to realize that Rachel would be able to shoot me faster than Gloria could ever retrieve, aim, and fire her Walther PPK.

Rachel shifted the shotgun in her arms. "You know, Pippa," she said, "you must be the luckiest woman in Ryde. I shot five rounds at you yesterday, and you walked away without a scratch. That won't happen again."

She stood on both feet. She pointed the shotgun at the ceiling over my head and fired. The staggering *bang* made me flinch. I dropped to the floor, my ears ringing. Bits of ceiling tile and part of a fluorescent tube crashed next to me. My first thought was a silly one: I was about to be filled full of buckshot while wearing too much makeup and a ridiculous wig. How humiliating!

I looked around; Gloria had dropped to the floor also and curled into a ball, her demeanor appearing surprisingly timid. She almost seemed to be making herself invisible—definitely not like the Gloria I knew.

Rachel began to laugh—although I had difficulty hearing the sound at first. The din in my ears slowly faded. She gestured again with her shotgun and said, "Stand up."

I climbed to my feet and glanced up at the gaping hole in the ceiling tile.

"Don't worry about the damage, Pippa," Rachel said. "I hardly caused any. This room is encased from top to bottom in concrete and steel. It's utterly soundproof and fully shielded. In case you're wondering, the cell phone on your belt won't work—so don't even think of calling for help. We're alone up here—completely alone."

I realized that Rachel was right. I thought about James and David downstairs in the Old Ryde Saloon & Grill. They hadn't seen Rachel arrive because she had parked her Porsche Boxster in the executive garage and used the private elevator to ride upstairs. They would assume all was well on the eighth floor. The cavalry was not coming to our rescue.

"Hey, Helen," Rachel said. "You stand up too. Or would you prefer I call you Gloria Spitz?" Rachel sneered smugly at me. "Don't look so surprised, Pippa. It took me no time at all to figure out what you and David Friendly were up to. You didn't even try to conceal the fact that you were working together." She added, "But I thought it was really tacky of you to send your bleached blonde secretary to do your dirty work inside Hardesty."

Synapses deep in my brain suddenly fired.

Cor blimey! Rachel doesn't have a clue about Gloria's other skills and talents.

I looked away to hide the glee I felt. Rachel Wilson had made the same mistake we had. She had discounted the capabilities of a support person. She assumed that Gloria had merely followed orders given by David and myself.

Gloria had understood Rachel's blunder before I did. That explained her apparent timidity. She wanted Rachel to consider her harmless in every respect.

I knew what I had to do. I needed to make Rachel focus her attention fully on me—to ignore Gloria completely.

I tried to seem clueless. "Why would Hardesty need a boardroom like this? Why does a company build a room surrounded in concrete?"

Rachel frowned. "Boy, you are dumb. Hardesty Software develops software for the Defense Department. Obviously the senior executives occasionally look at top-secret information. This room is a Sensitive Compartmentalized Information Facility."

She's proud of what she knows. Keep her talking.

"Can I ask you another question? Please?"

"You can ask. That doesn't mean I'll answer it."

"Well, did you encourage Dennis Grant to visit me in February?"

She nodded proudly. "Of course I did."

"Wow! Everyone told me that Dennis loved Hardesty. He must really have respected your opinion."

The little girl smiled at me again. "Dennis was a pussycat. He did everything I told him to do."

"Boy! I wish my husband would listen to me like that."

"James Huston is a special kind of guy—much too intelligent for someone as gullible as you. He needs someone like me." Her eyes sparkled. "Maybe I'll try to comfort the grieving widower after you're dead. James and I would be great together. I could really help his career—maybe work with him. Do you know that I have a bachelor's degree in psychology and a master's degree in management?"

Don't lose it, Hunnechurch. Keep her talking—no matter what she says.

Rachel continued, "By the way, did you ever manage to open the Mitch Hardesty file that I left for Gloria to find?"

I shook my head. "No. I couldn't figure out the password."

"You can't do anything right, can you, Pippa?" Her smile blossomed. "No matter. I will be sure to pass the contents on to James. Mitch Hardesty really said some nice things about your new hubby."

"How could he? Mitch doesn't know James."

"That's what you think."

Rachel took a few steps forward. She slid the shotgun along the table. The barrel still pointed at me, but Rachel now held the gun by its forearm. Her hand was no longer near the trigger.

"I guess James never told you about working for Hardesty Software as a consultant," she said. "Or about getting to know me during his visits to the company?" She finished with a coy wink.

I tried to look suitably demoralized. Rachel seemed satisfied with my efforts.

"Please answer another question for me," I said. "What did Dennis do wrong? Why did you have to kill him?"

Rachel answered in a singsong voice. "For the very same reason I'm going to kill you. Dennis possessed a piece of evidence that might point to me. You have it in your office too."

"I do? What kind of evidence?"

Rachel took several more steps forward. "You are a genuine blockhead." She rapped my head with her knuckle. "I came to see you, remember? I asked you to send me something—and you did."

"Do you mean Dennis's speech drafts?"

She clapped both hands. "Well done. It took you long enough, but you finally understood."

I scrunched up my face. "Understood what? How can a few old speeches threaten you?"

"What a pity!" Rachel shook her head. "For a while there, you showed real promise."

I pressed on. "David Friendly says Dennis was murdered because of corporate spying at Hardesty Software. Is that true?"

Rachel pointed a finger at me. "Now you are getting warmer. David clearly has the smarts on your team. I'll have to finish him off next. Hit-and-run accidents are really becoming a problem in this town."

"Are you the spy?"

That silly question earned me another rap on the head. I began to rub the spot with my right hand.

"Not for much longer," Rachel said. "Hardesty Software is tapped out. I've got all the new information that's supposed to be presented on Friday." She chortled. "Of course, they'll need another boardroom. This one will take time to clean up."

Rachel rubbed both hands together. "It's time for me to move on. With my references, finding another job will be a snap. A company on the West Coast might be nice. I thought about Maryland, but I find the summers awfully humid. Don't you?"

I yanked off my wig and threw it hard at Rachel. She batted it away from her face, but the brief distraction was all that Gloria needed.

She leaped at Rachel.

I leaped for the shotgun.

I heard Gloria shout, "I am not a bleached blonde, you witch!" Out of the corner of my eye, I saw Rachel fly through the air. An instant later I heard her head smack the edge of the conference table. She collapsed in a heap on the floor.

Our work at Hardesty Software Corporation was done.

Epilogue

I STILL BELIEVE that Kelly the Shark looks as gentle as a lamb. A week after Rachel Wilson was arrested, Kelly poked her curly head into our reception room and delivered the good news that Mitch Hardesty had dropped the lawsuit against Hunnechurch & Associates. "The judge will do his thing in a day or two and make the dismissal official," she said. "I thought you'd want to know as soon as we sent the paperwork to the court and to your lawyer."

"Indeed, and thank you."

Her lawyerly scowl became a warm marketing smile. Kelly placed her card in my hand and purred, "Please think of *us* the next time you need effective legal representation."

I looked at the card and read her full name: Kelly Louise Lyons.

I shall always think of Ms. Lyons as Kelly the Shark. I shall also keep her card on file. Blanchette and Ross are awesome attorneys.

Kelly, however, was not the bearer of unexpected news. A day earlier Mitch Hardesty had looked me in the eye and agreed to drop the lawsuit. I visited him at his ersatz castle in Founders' Woods and made him an offer he couldn't refuse. I found him in his garden, driving golf balls into a net strung between two trees.

"Here's the thing, Mitch," I said. "David Friendly's article in the *Ryde Reporter* blew the corporate espionage story at Hardesty Software wide open. Everyone now knows that Dennis Grant was thoroughly stage-managed by Rachel Wilson—that she encouraged him to leave Hardesty after she had been deceived by the infamous widow. By getting Dennis out of the way, she hoped to keep the link between speeches and spying her secret. Your lawsuit against Hunnechurch & Associates is doomed to failure."

Mitch, tall and gaunt, with a reddish goatee, took a mighty swing. A ball struck the net with a loud thwack.

"Maybe so," he said. "But you helped Dennis to leave my employ. I deserve my day in court."

I realized that Carol Ericsson had been right about Mitch, that his lawsuit had largely been driven by pride.

"Oh, I see your point, Mitch. In fact, I want to make amends. If you end your lawsuit, I will find you a new full-time speechwriter for free. Of course, you will also have to forgive Gloria Spitz her trespass in your executive suite."

He leaned on his golf club and began to smile. "I think we may be able to settle out of court, as long as you can agree to my terms."

"Which are?"

"I have a new rule. All consultants work for me in secret. No news releases. No announcements to the chamber of commerce. No using me as a reference." He took another swing. "Don't even discuss your work with your husband."

I thought about arguing—but not for long. James had been right. As business owners, each of us had to maintain our own reputation for confidentiality. And more to the point, why would we want to waste our pillow talk discussing Mitch Hardesty?

The only person in Ryde totally opposed to the idea of maintaining confidentiality was Detective Stephen Reilly. When Reilly arrived at Hardesty Software's executive suite that fateful evening, he found the four of us—Gloria, James, David, and myself—still milling around the boardroom. Rachel had been taken away by an ambulance and was under guard at Ryde General Hospital, the crack on her head apparently not life threatening.

Reilly had been furious when we told him all that we had done at Hardesty. "You can't bypass the police and conduct your own investigation," he screamed. "You can't break a dozen laws, no matter how noble your purpose." He sighed heavily. "Hunnechurch and Spitz are lost causes, but I had assumed that we were friends, Mr. Friendly." He turned to James. "And I expected better of you, Mr. Huston." His face grew even more dour. "Frankly, I hope that Mr. Hardesty brings lawsuits against the lot of you."

"You are utterly right," I said, my hands raised in capitulation. "We admit acting foolishly, but we didn't have sufficient proof about spying, speeches, and murder to bring to you, and we didn't want to waste your valuable time."

"You've got to be kidding me, Hunnechurch. I hear baloney like that every day of the week. I'm immune to sweet talk."

Ah well. It was worth a try.

David suddenly grabbed my arm. "That's it! The perfect title for my article. *Spying, Speeches, and Murder.*"

More about David's article . . .

As he expected, "Spying, Speeches, and Murder" caused a major stir and prompted investigations by both Maryland and federal authorities. David's story was widely quoted in the *Wall Street Journal,* the *New York Times, Business Week, Time,* and other publications. And David was the "talking head" in a Public Broadcasting System documentary about the mounting threat of corporate espionage in America. There has been talk of a Pulitzer Prize, a New York publisher has asked David to write a book about goings-on at Hardesty, and a Hollywood producer (who loved the title) asked David to consult on a movie based on the article.

"I will obviously be played by George Clooney," David said. "Who would you like to play you?"

I thought about it. I am still thinking. I am open to suggestions.

David and I decided that the juiciest role in any movie to be made about Hardesty Software would be Carol Ericsson's. She was the misunderstood, maligned character who was wrongly accused of committing espionage and murder by the intrepid reporter and valiant undercover detective. Happily, justice triumphed at the end when the prideful chairman recognized her superior abilities and loyalty with a hefty raise. She also went on to win the Maryland State Trapshooting Competition.

Carol invited me for another afternoon of trapshooting. I plan to accept.

David and I had our far-ranging discussion about movie-making at Maison Pierre while I devoured a large helping of Coquille Chesapeake, my winnings in our wager as to Carol Ericsson's guilt or innocence. David was so delighted with the buzz his article generated that he invited James, Joyce, Gloria, *and* Stephen Reilly to join us for dinner. I am delighted to report that David and Stephen are fast friends once again.

Hunnechurch & Associates has also created a buzz—ours in the Ryde business community. We are bursting at the seams with new clients. Two of the human resources people I telephoned during my days working at home have given us assignments. And Gloria's successful search for an associate sales manager for Lotus Flower Foods led to two other recruiting gigs. Gloria and I are seriously considering adding a second associate. Of course, we would need larger digs to accommodate a third staffer.

"We can move to a fancy building too," Gloria said. "Just like James."

"I think not. We don't have to impress anyone."

My goal is to impress clients with the quality of our work. Case in point: I am presently conducting two searches for Peachtree Consulting Group. It seems that the new receptionist James hired on his own was an unmitigated disaster.

"How could that be?" I had asked.

He looked sheepish. "I guess I didn't do as thorough a check of her references as you would have."

"A beginner's mistake," I said with a prideful sniff. "I shall set things right." I added, "Now that you've wisely chosen Hunnechurch & Associates as your executive recruiting firm, how else may we assist you?"

"Actually, I need a conference planner, someone who'll organize my seminars."

"Consider the person found."

"My new planner should also be a good cook," he said.

"Whatever for?"

"To keep you amply supplied with humble pies. You clearly need another generous helping about now."

═══════

To avoid unnecessary pillow talk, I turned both of James's recruiting assignments over to Gloria Spitz, who has become a true associate recruiter. I am happy to report that the temporary hair dye she applied did in fact fade away after five washes, as the label promised. Gloria

telephoned the guy she had met at Hardesty and amazed him by agreeing to go out on a date. Oh, to be a fly on the wall when Gloria Spitz
opens the door instead of Helen Nelson.

———

Gloria and I have rescheduled our "How to Work Successfully with an
Executive Recruiter" seminar. A new set of invitations has gone out.
I made personal visits to our original invitees to give them copies of
David's article. Three of them agreed to give us a second chance. The
other two informed me of their intentions to hire Nailor & McHale.

"A wonderful decision," I said, meaning it. "You have chosen a competent, ethical search firm."

I have begun to think of Nailor & McHale more as colleagues than
competitors. I thanked Oscar McHale for his behind-the-scenes support of Hunnechurch & Associates. He agreed to provide an additional
endorsement to my application to the National Association of Executive
Recruiters.

We are now proud members.

———

I am equally proud of my membership on the associate pastor search
committee at Ryde Fellowship Church. I had always considered the job
a huge responsibility; now I have begun to have real fun doing it.
Monica DeVries told me that my new feelings prove beyond doubt that
I was called to the committee by God.

I believe she is right.

Incidentally, Monica and I are getting along surprisingly well—
much to the amusement of Reverend Ed Clarke and Gloria Spitz.
Monica no longer calls me Mrs. Huston, and I rarely need to employ
James's pride-busting techniques on her. We seem to have come to a
comfortable understanding: While we may never be close friends, we
can do God's work together as faithful servants.

The search committee narrowed down the search for a new associate pastor to two candidates. My favorite is the preacher with the friendly and confident voice, the sermonizer who could also tell a great story. Monica prefers the candidate who delivers what she calls "brilliant expository sermons" that are full of theological insights.

We will vote on it next week. I can't wait to see whom God chooses.

━━━━━━━━

I also can't wait to move back into the new, improved Hunnechurch Manor. Our planning for the second "wedding" of the year is going well. We chose a contractor in Ryde who specializes in restoring historic homes. He promptly came up with a plan for "marrying" our two townhouses without changing the exterior appearance of either—except for a discreet garage door in the front of the new addition. James still seems elated with his purchase; he hasn't complained once that the total cost of our new home will be somewhat higher than the price of the pretty Cape Cod in Founders' Woods.

James plans to photograph everything so he can make another CD to present in our new home theater. He recently ordered six comfy recliners as theater seating.

Until the work is complete (we expect to be living larger by Labor Day), we are enjoying the hospitality of our local Embassy Suites. Winston is bunking with Gloria. "Maybe she'll toughen him up," James said, "and get him to start talking."

━━━━━━━━

James picked up his new Mini Cooper. It is red with a white racing stripe across the roof and bonnet—sorry, the hood. Soon after, Chloe announced that Stuart also purchased a Mini. It seems that Reverend Parker-Hunnechurch had secretly coveted the original Austin Mini that zoomed around England when he was a lad. Our telephone bill has increased significantly. I have occasionally overheard the pair of them arguing about cam shafts, transmissions, and the virtues of leather upholstery. Chloe and Stuart are planning a visit at Thanksgiving. Chloe can't wait to see our new house; Stuart is eager to drive James's Mini.

═══════════════

The police never did locate James's stolen Range Rover; it is probably cruising the streets of Rio de Janeiro. However, they did find a big, black Ford pickup truck with a fiberglass bed cap: the vehicle that killed Dennis Grant. Once the police began to build a case against Rachel Wilson, they soon found that she owned a home in York, Pennsylvania, about seventy miles north of Ryde. The truck was parked inside Rachel's garage. There were traces of Dennis's blood and scrapes of paint from his bicycle on the large front brush guard.

The police discovered several other interesting facts about Rachel. Besides her house in York, she owned a three-bedroom ski chalet in New Hampshire and a condominium on St. John, in the U.S. Virgin Islands. She lived midweek in a modest rented apartment in Ryde that fit her salary at Hardesty Software.

The police believe that Hardesty was the third company Rachel had spied on. "Her kind of money takes time to accumulate," Reilly had told David in a recent interview for the *Ryde Reporter*. "Hence the whopping nest egg we found."

Corporate spying seems to be an exceptionally profitable endeavor. Her bank account contained more than four hundred thousand dollars. Her investment portfolio included nearly a million dollars worth of stocks, bonds, and mutual funds. Curiously, Rachel once owned a significant amount of Hardesty stock; she apparently sold it at a profit before her spying caused a serious decline in price. When Mitch Hardesty learned about her deep pockets, he launched a lawsuit against her claiming fraud and deceit.

Go Blanchette & Ross.

Speaking of lawyers. There is a rumor in Ryde that Rachel plans to hire Daniel Harris's law firm to represent her. It is a wise move, if true. Rachel will need a good attorney because Maryland courts still can impose the death penalty.

The police seem confident that Rachel will be convicted and—at the very least—take up lengthy residence in the Women's Correctional Facility in Jessup, Maryland, which is not far from Ryde. Ed Clarke spoke to me the other day and suggested that I consider witnessing to Rachel as part of our church's prison ministry. Gloria has encouraged me to say *yes,* but I haven't reached a decision.

In truth, I haven't yet forgiven Rachel for all the pain she caused. But I have taken to heart Peter's advice to "be compassionate and humble," to not "repay evil with evil or insult with insult." I know that if I do visit Rachel, I will bring her one of James's rapidly becoming legendary humble pies.

===================

Go back to the beginning of Pippa Hunnechurch's chronicles with these other titles!

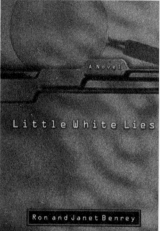

Little White Lies
A Novel
by Ron and Janet Benrey
0-8054-2371-0, $12.99
Pippa Hunnechurch's joy turns to confusion when Marsha drowns in what everyone assumes is a freak accident. After another death—this one clearly not an accident—Pippa is in a terrible dilemma in this contemporary mystery examining the high-stakes world of corporate recruiting.

The Second Mile
A Novel
by Ron and Janet Benrey
0-8054-2558-6, $12.99
Journey through this mystery with the beloved Pippa Hunnechurch again as she gains a new understanding of herself, God, and the power of going the extra mile.

www.broadmanholman.com